P9-CQV-926

Praise for Linda Warren

"Linda Warren's writing talent is showcased in *Texas Heir* as she engages her readers to the point of the rest of the world fading to the background. A must read from a must have author."
—*CataRomance.com*

"In *Texas Bluff*, Linda Warren portrays perfectly the relationship between a couple learning to trust all over again. The tension is real, as is the characters' uncertainty. This is an excellent story."
—*RT Book Reviews*

Praise for Debra Salonen

"Debra Salonen captures readers' attention with multifaceted characters, layered conflict and fast pacing."
—*RT Book Reviews*

"A wonderfully written love story with loveable characters. The plot is engaging and certainly keeps the reader riveted throughout the story. *His Daddy's Eyes* is just the sort of book to curl up with to while away some lazy afternoon hours."
—*HeartRate Reviews*

LINDA WARREN

An award-winning author, has written twenty-six books for the Harlequin Superromance and Harlequin American Romance lines. She grew up in the farming and ranching community of Smetana, Texas, the only girl in a family of boys. She loves to write about Texas, and from time to time scenes and characters from her childhood show up in her books. Linda lives in College Station, Texas, not far from her birthplace, with her husband, Billy, and a menagerie of wild animals, from Canada geese to bobcats. Visit her website at www.lindawarren.net.

DEBRA SALONEN

attributes her love of reading to her late parents, Daisy and Reuben Robson, who kept Deb's childhood home stocked with more magazines than anyone could read, everything from *Popular Mechanics* to *Time* and *Newsweek* to *TV Guide*. The fabulous photos in *Life*, *Look* and *National Geographic* offered a glimpse into worlds far beyond the rolling plains of South Dakota. The wonderful art in *The Saturday Evening Post* and poignant stories in *Redbook* and *Reader's Digest* spoke to the budding artist in her soul. It seems fitting that Deb's first freelance sale was an article entitled "The Bulls That Fell from the Sky," which appeared in *Country* magazine.

LINDA WARREN

Cowboy at the Crossroads

DEBRA SALONEN

That Cowboy's Kids

TORONTO NEW YORK LONDON
AMSTERDAM PARIS SYDNEY HAMBURG
STOCKHOLM ATHENS TOKYO MILAN MADRID
PRAGUE WARSAW BUDAPEST AUCKLAND

If you purchased this book without a cover you should be aware that this book is stolen property. It was reported as "unsold and destroyed" to the publisher, and neither the author nor the publisher has received any payment for this "stripped book."

Recycling programs
for this product may
not exist in your area.

ISBN-13: 978-0-373-68828-9

COWBOY AT THE CROSSROADS & THAT COWBOY'S KIDS

Copyright © 2011 by Harlequin Books S.A.

The publisher acknowledges the copyright holders of the individual works as follows:

COWBOY AT THE CROSSROADS
Copyright © 2002 by Linda Warren

THAT COWBOY'S KIDS
Copyright © 2000 by Debra K. Salonen

All rights reserved. Except for use in any review, the reproduction or utilization of this work in whole or in part in any form by any electronic, mechanical or other means, now known or hereafter invented, including xerography, photocopying and recording, or in any information storage or retrieval system, is forbidden without the written permission of the publisher, Harlequin Enterprises Limited, 225 Duncan Mill Road, Don Mills, Ontario, Canada, M3B 3K9.

This is a work of fiction. Names, characters, places and incidents are either the product of the author's imagination or are used fictitiously, and any resemblance to actual persons, living or dead, business establishments, events or locales is entirely coincidental.

This edition published by arrangement with Harlequin Books S.A.

For questions and comments about the quality of this book please contact us at Customer_eCare@Harlequin.ca.

® and TM are trademarks of the publisher. Trademarks indicated with ® are registered in the United States Patent and Trademark Office, the Canadian Trade Marks Office and in other countries.

www.Harlequin.com

Printed in U.S.A.

CONTENTS

To my sisters-in-law, Sondra Siegert,
LaVal Siegert, Melinda Siegert, Sandra Lenz
and Betty Patranella, who have supported me
wholeheartedly from the start. Thanks, ladies.

And thanks to Dr. Mark Fuller, DVM,
and Randy Rychlik, paramedic,
who shared their expert knowledge.

Any errors are strictly mine.

COWBOY AT THE CROSSROADS

Linda Warren

PROLOGUE

WHAT SHOULD SHE SAY TO HIM?

Rebecca Talbert knew she had to say *something,* but when she looked at Cordell Prescott words eluded her. He sat on the sofa in a dark suit with his elbows on his knees and his hands clutching a glass of punch. That expression of loss and sadness twisted her stomach into a hard knot.

She hated funerals, especially when the person was so young and had died so needlessly. Anette Prescott's death from alcohol poisoning had left not only a grieving widower, but a motherless four-year-old girl. Becca had never met Anette; in fact, this was the first time she'd actually met Cord. She knew Clay and Colton, his brothers; they were business associates of her father. Her parents were in Europe and she'd attended the funeral in their place. But she would have come, anyway, because she and Colton were close friends. There'd been a time she'd thought their relationship would develop into more, but the passion just wasn't there. And she wanted that passion, the kind of deep, lasting love her parents shared. Based on her relationships to date, she had a feeling she was going to grow old looking for it.

Becca took a sip of her punch and glanced around. They were in the large family room of the Prescott ranch house, a room that was attractively rustic with wood beams on the ceiling, a stone fireplace and hardwood floors. Colton had told her the ranch-style two-story house had been built by his great-grandfather in the 1800s and there'd been Prescotts here ever since. Cord was the rancher in the family; he'd continued to run Triple Creek, while his brothers had opted for another way of life in the city.

As the grandfather clock chimed, Becca realized she had to leave, and soon. She was on duty at the hospital in an hour, and it was a thirty-minute drive back to Houston. She set her glass on a table. It was now or never. She had to offer her condolences to Cord, then make her way out to where the cars were parked. A few family and friends had returned to the ranch after the funeral, and Colton had insisted she come, although Becca felt a bit out of place.

She took a deep breath and walked over to the sofa. When she sat beside Cord, he didn't move or acknowledge her presence.

"I'm so sorry about your wife," she said. It sounded lame even to her own ears. He'd probably heard those words a hundred times today.

He still hadn't responded, so she started to get up. She didn't want to cause him any more stress than necessary.

Then his voice came. "I just wish I understood. Why? Why did this happen? Anette never drank that much. I just don't understand it. And Nicki…" As he said his daughter's name, his voice cracked.

Becca did what she would have done with anyone who was in that much pain. She put her arms around him. He murmured something she didn't hear, and to her surprise, his arms locked tightly around her. She knew he had had a drink and she didn't know what he'd done with it. Nor did she care. She only wanted to comfort him.

As his arms tightened, she became aware of his strength and the tangy masculine scent that filled her nostrils. He was different from his brothers—in appearance, in manner, in aspiration. Clay and Colton had blond curly hair and blue eyes. Cord's hair was a darker blond with a slight curl and his eyes were brown. He also had a stylish mustache. Colton said that Cord took after their father with his love of the land. His brothers were businessmen and had never returned to the ranch after leaving for college, whereas Cord didn't want any other life. His manner, too, revealed a directness, a simple honesty that was quite removed from his brothers' more polished charm.

Becca didn't know how long they sat there with Cord holding on to her like a lifeline. She didn't mind. He needed to hold someone and he probably wasn't even aware of who she was. How could Anette Prescott do this to him? she found herself wondering. Cord seemed so family-oriented, and he obviously worshiped his little girl. From what Colton had told her, she knew Anette had been in a state of depression. She'd always wanted a child and had gone through several fertility procedures before she conceived Nicki. But once the baby was born, she sank into postpartum depression. Since it had continued for at least four years, it had obviously turned into a psychiatric disorder, maybe hormonal in cause, maybe not. She apparently functioned reasonably well, so it wasn't clinical, but she should have had some form of therapy. She could've gotten treatment, done something besides drink herself to death. Becca knew her opinion was tempered because of her medical training and because of the man trembling in her arms. But like Cord, she didn't understand.

"Mr. Prescott." A woman's voice interrupted them. "I can't find Nicki. I've looked everywhere."

Cord drew away and got to his feet. He stood at least six foot two, much taller than his brothers. "Don't worry, I'll find her," he said in a tired voice. "She's been hiding a lot since her mother…" He stopped, unable to finish the sentence.

Becca also stood, her heart aching for this man. "I'm sure she'll feel better when she sees you," she said softly.

He blinked distractedly at her. "Thank you, Becca," he murmured, walking away.

He knows who I am. It was silly, but she couldn't shake the warm feeling that gave her.

She hurried over to Colton. "I've got to get back to Houston," she told him.

"I know, and I appreciate your coming." Frowning, Colton ran one hand through his blond hair; until recently he'd worn it shoulder-length and she guessed he wasn't used to this newly short style. "I saw you talking to Cord. Did he say anything?"

"Just that he doesn't understand why this happened."

"Yeah, none of us do." He shrugged. "Cord keeps everything inside. Doesn't let his feelings out. We're worried about him."

"Cord will be fine." Blanche, Colton's mother, spoke up. Becca had never met Blanche before today. She'd heard Colton talk about her for years, and it was quite an experience meeting her in the flesh. In her sixties, she dressed as if she were much younger. She wore a tight-fitting black dress that ended four inches above her knees. The plunging neckline showed off her ample breasts and the diamonds around her neck. Her bleached blond hair was styled in a stiff pageboy, but no amount of artifice could hide the aging on her face.

"Anette was never right for him, anyway," Blanche was saying. "She hated the ranch and the cows and horses. I never figured she'd take the easy way out, though. I wonder who she thought was gonna take care of that kid upstairs. It certainly isn't gonna be me."

As Blanche walked off, hips swaying, Colton remarked with raised eyebrows, "Charming, isn't she?"

Becca didn't say anything. She could only stare after the woman in stunned silence. Blanche was crude and unbelievably hard-hearted. Still, Becca didn't know why she was surprised; she knew the story of Blanche Duffy and Claybourne Prescott. Blanche had married Claybourne when she was eighteen. He'd been sixty. It wasn't a love match—she'd wanted security and he'd wanted a son. His first wife and eldest daughter had died in a car accident. His second daughter, Edith, was still alive and in her seventies. She lived on the ranch, and Colton had mentioned that the relationship between Blanche and Edith was strained. Having met both ladies, Becca had no problem imagining the situation. Edith was a quiet, demure person, and Becca was sure that Blanche made her life a living hell. The Prescott family was an eccentric group, to say the least.

She kissed Colton's cheek. "Talk to you later."

"I'll call when I get back to Houston," he said.

Becca wished again that there was a spark between them. But they were just friends. Not for the first time, she wondered how Colton felt about her—whether he hoped for more than the easy companionship they now shared. They never discussed their relationship, but since Colton had opened a branch office of his computer company in Houston, they spent a lot of evenings and weekends together. Colton was almost forty, and if he harbored feelings for her, they had to talk about it. Why was she thinking about this today? she asked herself as she went into the foyer to get her purse. She and Colton had a good friendship and they were both adult enough to accept that. She glanced at her watch—three-ten. She'd better get moving.

Before she could reach the front door, she saw a small bare foot sticking out of a partially opened closet. It had to be Nicki. Becca opened the door and found a little blond girl sitting on the floor. Her curls were everywhere and her pink nightgown was wrinkled. She clung to a doll that was as big as she was.

"Hi," Becca said.

Nicki didn't answer. She buried her face in the doll's hair.

"Your daddy's looking for you."

At the mention of her father, Nicki raised her head. Her eyes were brown and filled with the same sadness Becca had seen in Cord's.

"I can't find my mommy," Nicki said in a tiny voice. "Daddy said she went to heaven, but I can't find her."

Becca's heart crumbled inside her, and she dropped to the floor and gathered the child into her arms, just as she'd done with her father. Nicki nestled against her.

"My mommy tells me a story," Nicki whimpered. "I can't sleep until Mommy tells me a story."

"I can tell you a story," Becca murmured, gently brushing blond curls away from Nicki's face. "I have a brother who's seven and I tell him stories. He likes the ones about monsters and dragons."

Nicki shook her head. "I don't like monsters. They 'care me."

"What kind of stories do you like?"

"The princess one" was her quick answer. "The princess with the fairy godmother."

Why did every little girl love that story? *Just wait, little princess, life will change your mind. There are no fairy godmothers in this world. And as for princes, forget it. They're all frogs.* God, was that cynical or what? She didn't actually feel that way, did she?

She searched her mind, trying to remember the story. "Once upon a time there was a girl named Cinderella. She lived with her wicked stepmom and mean stepsisters. They made her scrub the floors and do the laundry, and they were very unkind to her."

"That was bad," Nicki said.

"Very bad," Becca agreed. "Then one day her fairy godmother changed Cinderella's rags into a beautiful dress, and a handsome prince came and saved her from the wicked stepmother. They rode off into the sunset on his big horse and lived happily ever after." That was a drastically shortened version, but it seemed to satisfy Nicki.

Nicki stared at her with wide eyes. "My daddy rides a horse. Is he the prince?"

Before Becca could form a response, Cord appeared in the doorway. "Nicki, baby, I've been looking all over for you." He reached down and drew Nicki out of Becca's arms. As he did, his hand brushed against her breast, and a current of warmth shot through her whole body. This was crazy! His touch was innocent and unintentional and didn't mean a thing. Her emotions were just highly charged.

Nicki hid her face against Cord's shoulder, still clutching the doll. Cord stretched out his hand to Becca. She placed her hand in his and he pulled her to her feet. As soon as he released her, she straightened her black dress with as much dignity as she could and picked up her purse.

"I can't find Mommy," Nicki whimpered.

Cord winced, and Becca could see that he was trying to maintain his own composure. "I know, baby, I know," he whispered, dropping a kiss on Nicki's head.

Becca had a hard time controlling her own emotions.

"Thanks, Becca," Cord said. "I've got to get this one to bed." He kissed Nicki's cheek and headed for the staircase.

Becca stared after him with one thought on her mind. *Yes, Cordell Prescott is a prince.*

CHAPTER ONE

One year later

"I WANT BABIES AND A HUSBAND, and preferably not in that order," Rebecca said as she took a swallow of champagne.

"You've had too much to drink," her friend Ginger replied, studying the bubbles in her own glass. "Or maybe not enough," she added reaching for the bottle on the coffee table. They were in Becca's apartment after a big night of celebrating.

"Why aren't I happy, Gin?" Becca asked woefully. "I just finished my residency in pediatrics. I should be happy, ecstatic. All the hard work's behind me and now I can treat children like I've always planned. I don't understand why I'm not happier."

"Maybe you didn't do it for yourself," Ginger muttered. "Go to medical school, I mean."

Becca's head jerked up. "What are you talking about?"

"Maybe you did it for Emily and Jackson. Ever since you found out they're your real parents, you've been trying to be the perfect daughter—doing everything to be the daughter they wanted. But hell, Bec, no one's perfect. Not even you."

"You're drunk," Becca said, refusing to believe a word Gin was saying. At seventeen, she'd found out that Emily, the sister she adored, was really her mother and that Rose, her grandmother and the woman she'd believed to be her mother, was not. It had been a traumatic time, but she'd adjusted.

"Maybe." Gin hiccuped. "But the truth is a hard pill to swallow."

"I've wanted to be a doctor ever since I can remember," Becca said defiantly. "Finding out about my birth had nothing to do with it."

"Yeah, you started saying that in first grade. *I want to be a doctor like my sister.* Then *bam,* you find out your sister's really your mother and you *have* to be a doctor. There wasn't any other choice for you."

Becca stared at Gin with a mutinous expression. They'd been best friends since kindergarten and they knew each other better than anyone. Gin always spoke her mind, and that sometimes got on Becca's nerves—as it did now. She hadn't gone to medical school to please her parents. Or had she? God, she needed more champagne. She grabbed the bottle and refilled her glass.

"You're wrong, Gin," she murmured under her breath.

"Let me ask you a question," Gin said as she twisted her glass. "You have a month off before you join Dr. Arnold's practice in July. What do you plan to do with that time?"

Becca's eyes darkened, but Ginger didn't give her a chance to speak. She answered her own question. "I'll tell you exactly what you're going to do. You'll spend that month with your parents and Scotty, like you always do. You want babies? Well, doctor or not, you don't seem to realize you need a man to accomplish that. And you haven't had much of a social life in the past ten years, except for Colton who's always hanging around—like a little puppy waiting for your attention."

"Colton and I are friends," Becca said in a cool tone.

"I bet you haven't even slept with him."

"We don't have that kind of relationship."

"The man is forty years old, Becca. If he doesn't want that kind of relationship, there's something wrong with him."

"Shut up! You're making me angry."

Ginger took a long swig of champagne and set the glass on the table. "Damn, that was good. Your dad doesn't spare the bucks when he buys the bubbly."

Becca knew what Gin was doing—changing the subject—but Becca wasn't letting her get away with that. They had started this and they were going to finish it.

"My relationship with Colton is my business," she snapped.

Ginger lifted an eyebrow. "Did I say it wasn't?"

"You're making snide remarks and I don't like it."

"Okay, I'll keep my mouth shut."

Becca sighed. "I don't want to argue with you."

"Me, neither," Ginger agreed, and stretched out on the sofa. "All I'm saying is if you want those babies, you have to do something about it. You have to have a life of your own."

Becca settled back in her chair and didn't say anything. She hoped she wouldn't remember any of this in the morning, but she couldn't shake the discontent inside her. She should be so happy. She'd finally graduated from medical school with a specialty in pediatrics, and her parents had thrown a big party to celebrate her achievement. They were proud of her and had invited all her friends and family—including Colton. When she'd first met him, she had disliked him on sight. He was intelligent, good-looking and far too sure of himself. But as she got to know him, her opinion changed, and she found that he had a softer, more vulnerable side. It was an appealing quality in such a driven businessman.

Because of Colton's connection to her father, he spent a lot of time with her family. Did Colton think their relationship was more than friendship? Surely not. But after talking with Gin, she realized it was time to clear things up with Colton. She'd been saying that for over a year now and still hadn't done anything about it. They'd both been so busy and…

Damn, what was wrong with her? Why was she finding fault with everything in her life? She glanced at Gin, who was now snoring into a cushion. Becca smiled. She treasured her bond with Gin and was glad they hadn't lost touch after high school. Becca had come to Houston to live with Emily and Jackson after she'd found out they were her real parents, while Ginger had gone to secretarial school and had become a secretary to the CEO of an insurance company in Houston. They talked often, and Becca valued her opinion. That was why Gin's words weighed so heavily.

Maybe Gin was right. She'd spent the past ten years being Emily and Jackson's little girl. Even though she now had a medical degree, she still felt like that little girl. She had to find the woman inside, and maybe that meant leaving Houston... and her family.

How did she do that? She loved her family. As she yawned and stretched, she knew it would be one of the hardest things she'd ever have to do. But she also knew it was the only way to release this restlessness inside her—to find true happiness and all that crap. God, she'd had too much champagne. There was nothing wrong with her life. Oh, yes, there was. She wanted babies—babies with big brown eyes and...

IT TOOK BECCA TWO DAYS to recover from the hangover. She'd never drunk that much in her life, but she and Gin had really tied one on that night. It was a kind of release, she supposed. She'd worked so hard for so many years; she was exhausted, physically and mentally. A long rest and she'd be as good as new.

Gin was right about one thing, though. For a twenty-eight-year-old woman, soon to be twenty-nine, she spent too much time with her family. But she'd needed those years with Emily and Jackson and Scotty. They had connected as a family, and that was important to her. Leaving seventeen years behind hadn't been easy, and in retrospect she realized she hadn't. She had merged the two parts of her life, and she was happy with her relationship with Rose and Owen, her grandparents, the people who had raised her, as well as her relationship with Emily and Jackson. Then why...?

No, she wouldn't do this. It was Monday morning and she didn't have to go to work. It was her time off and she could do anything she wanted. Anything at all. Analyzing her life wasn't on that list. Carrying her coffee cup, she went into the living room and sat down in her favorite chair. She started to call Gin, but realized she'd be getting ready for work. Becca would call her later.

Try as she might, she couldn't keep her thoughts from drifting to her mother and the twists and turns in their lives. At seventeen, Emily Cooper had fallen in love with Jackson Talbert. Jackson and his father had come to Rockport, Texas, for a fishing trip. Rose and Owen, Emily's parents, rented cottages to tourists. Since it was November, the cottages were closed for the winter months, so Owen rented them the spare room. At the time, Rose, who was forty, had just found out she was pregnant. Emily was very upset by the news. She was in high school and embarrassed by the whole situation. That was why she'd done things with Jackson she wouldn't normally do. She'd wanted to get back at her parents. Well, that wasn't the whole situation, of course. She'd fallen for Jackson, and fallen hard.

Soon after the Talberts left, Emily found out she was pregnant. It was devastating news, and Rose had berated Emily for her stupidity. After several attempts to reach the Talbert family without success, Rose insisted Emily give up the baby for adoption. Emily fought it, resisted, to no avail. Rose and Owen had their own child on the way and couldn't help her.

Besides, all her life Emily had planned to be a doctor, and Rose wasn't letting anything interfere with that. In the end, Emily did what her parents wanted. After graduation, Owen took Emily to San Antonio, where the adoption had been arranged.

At the same time, Rose gave birth to a baby girl, who died after a few weeks. In a depressed and disturbed state of mind, Rose cancelled Emily's adoption, and when Emily's baby was born, Rose took her home and raised Rebecca as her own. Emily never knew. She went to college, then to medical school, never knowing the truth. Everyone thought Becca was Rose's—even Emily.

For years, Emily had nightmares about giving her baby away, and when Jackson came back into her life, she told him about the pregnancy. He was angry at first, and then they set out to find their daughter—neither of them dreaming that she was so close.

Becca took a sip of coffee as she relived the heartache of that time. She'd felt so angry when she found out what Rose had done. She'd been furious with everyone, including Emily. Especially Emily. The mother who'd let her go. But eventually they had gotten through all the pain, and Emily and Jackson were more deeply in love than ever. Now they had Scotty, too. Rose and Owen still lived in Rockport, and Becca saw them as often as she could.

Forgiving was easy, but forgetting was sometimes hard.

Someone had once asked her what you do when you discover you're not really who you thought you were. The answer was that you fall apart, then you pick yourself up and get on with your life. Now Becca was wondering if she should be making bigger changes in that orderly life of hers and—

The ringing of the phone stopped her thoughts. She put her cup down and picked up the receiver. "Hello."

"Dr. Becca Talbert?"

Becca recognized that voice. For the past year and at the oddest times she'd seen his face and the sadness in his eyes.

"Yes," she answered readily.

"This is Cord Prescott."

Becca already knew that. But why was he calling her after a whole year without a word? Why was he calling when they were practically strangers?

"You may not remember me," he said, "but I'm Colton's brother."

"Yes, I remember you, Cord, and your little girl. How are you?" Over the past year, she'd often asked Colton about Cord and his daughter. He always said they were "trying to adjust."

"Not good," he answered. "Colton said you're a pediatrician and I thought you might be able to help me."

"With Nicki, you mean?"

"Yes," he replied. "I know you're busy, but I'm not sure what to do anymore."

Becca curled her feet beneath her, settling more comfortably into the chair. "Tell me about Nicki."

"I've taken her to several doctors, even a child psychologist, but she won't talk to them. She just clings to me, and if I leave the room she screams and cries."

"Then she hasn't adjusted to her mother's death?"

"Not at all," he said. "She insists on staying in her room and she's hardly eating. She's lost so much weight I can hardly stand it. She used to love the outdoors, but she won't even ride her horse. She won't talk about her mother, and I'm at my wits' end. I think she's making herself physically ill with grief. I'd really like to get your professional opinion."

"Of course. I'd be glad to help any way I can," Becca said instantly, her heart heavy at the thought of what Cord was going through.

"Thanks, Becca. I'd appreciate it."

"But I'm not seeing patients until July."

"Oh."

There was a long pause. "Nicki doesn't do well in an office environment. I was hoping I could persuade you to come out to the ranch and see her."

This time Becca was the one who was startled, but it didn't take her long to decide. "I can do that. As a matter of fact, I have the afternoon free. Why don't I drive out there today."

"Thank you so much," he said earnestly. "Do you remember where we are?"

"Yes. But Cord…you have to understand that I treat the body. Nicki may need a psychologist. I've had courses, but it's not my specialty."

"Just see her, that's all I ask. Colton says you're a very good doctor—and I trust his judgment."

"Fine. I'll be there around four o'clock."

As Becca hung up the phone, she wondered what else Colton had told him about her. She shook her head. What did that matter? Nicki Prescott needed help, and she had to do everything she could.

CORD REPLACED THE RECEIVER with a long sigh. He remembered how comforting Becca had been the day of the funeral. He'd been so overwhelmed by anger, disillusionment and pain that he didn't remember much, but he remembered Becca. And she would help his baby. She had to.

He hurried down the hall to the kitchen. Della, the housekeeper, was sitting on a stool, peeling potatoes. At sixty-five, Della was a high-strung woman who never seemed to tire or lose energy. She'd been with the Prescott family since Cord was a young boy. Her hair was now gray and her blue eyes not as sharp, but in other ways she was unchanged.

"What are we having for supper?" he asked.

"Roast. Why?" She didn't look up, just kept on peeling potatoes.

"Because Dr. Talbert's coming to see Nicki, and I'm going to invite her to eat with us."

"Dr. Talbert?" Della raised her head, frowning. "Isn't that Colton's…friend? Becca, right?"

"Yes."

"Does Colton know she's coming?"

"No, and what difference does it make?" There was a note of exasperation in his voice that he couldn't hide. He hadn't called Colton because he didn't want a lot of people around. He wanted to keep this as private as possible, for Nicki's sake.

"None whatsoever," Della replied, returning to her potatoes.

"Becca will be here to see Nicki, that's all."

"It's time someone helped that child. She can't go on like this much longer."

"I know. That's why I want this evening to be special—calm and quiet—so Becca can interact with Nicki."

"Does the queen of the house know you're having a guest for supper?"

"I don't give a damn what Blanche thinks."

"Your mother doesn't like it when things are done without her knowledge."

"You can tell Blanche—" He stopped and took a breath. "Never mind, I'll handle Blanche. Just prepare an extra-special meal."

Della glanced at him. "You're very excited about this."

"I am. My daughter's life depends on it."

AS BECCA WAS TRYING TO DECIDE what to wear, she thought about Nicki. The child should have adjusted to her mother's death by now, but it was hard to judge with children. Trauma affected them differently. Becca could still hear her saying in that pitiful little voice, *"I can't find my mommy."* Death was so hard to explain to children, and Becca wasn't convinced she could help Nicki. However, she'd certainly try.

She dressed in a tan pantsuit and brown blouse, then brushed her long brown hair and let it hang loose down her back. Working or at school, she always wore it pinned up or clipped at the nape of her neck. As a teenager, her hair was much longer, an unruly mane that used to drive Emily crazy. But these days Emily never complained about Becca's hair. Considering everything that had happened in their lives, they got along exceptionally well.

Becca stared at her brown eyes and olive complexion in the mirror. Everyone said she was looking more and more like her mother. Becca had always thought Emily was beautiful, but she didn't feel *she* was. Emily had a grace and sophistication that Becca felt she lacked. Becca was more down-to-earth in both temperament and appearance. She had far less patience than Emily and often lost her temper. Emily never did, and Becca envied that about her. Becca envied everything about her wonderful mother; maybe that was her problem.

She applied lipstick and forced herself to stop thinking. All this free time, all this soul-searching, was making her feel confused. And she *wasn't* confused—she just needed to get her life and goals in perspective and then everything else would fall into place. Like her social life. Gin said she didn't have one, but Gin was wrong. She'd dated several interns, and each occasion had proved to be an exercise in restraint. They thought sex was the normal conclusion to a date. She didn't. She wanted love and passion—not just sex. Emily had told her when she was a teenager that sex without love was just an act and she would know when the time was right. So far, that time hadn't happened for her. In high school, her boyfriend Tommy had pressed her continually for sex, but she'd never taken that step. Not with him or with any other man.

When she'd found out about her birth, her world had been turned upside down and she rebelled, dating guys Rose and Emily disapproved of. Still, she couldn't degrade herself by sleeping with boys she didn't care about merely to punish her family. Later she was so busy with her studies that love eluded her, and she refused to have sex without it. Her feelings on the matter had to do with her upbringing and with Emily's influence. Now she was older and knew more about sex and life, but her standards hadn't changed. She was waiting for the right man…and love. Any nice guys left out there? One came to mind and she quickly grabbed her purse. She didn't want to keep a nice guy waiting.

BECCA HEADED FOR INTERSTATE 10 and drove out of Houston toward Beaumont. The city gave way to farmland and ranchland. Soon she saw the stone and wrought-iron entrance. The sign—Triple Creek. Prescott Ranch—appeared on a high arc above the cattle guard. She drove through, between wood rail fences, watching the grass sway gently in the breeze and the cows and horses grazing. The land was mostly flat with creeks and valleys; here and there she noticed some beautiful old oak trees.

The white stone ranch house came into view. Sprawling and roomy, it had a long front veranda with stone pillars and a wrought-iron fence that enclosed the backyard. She parked in front, grabbed her medical bag and walked to the door. She rang the bell, which she heard resounding throughout the house.

Cord opened the door, and for a moment Becca was speechless. He had on worn boots and jeans with a blue cotton shirt, the sleeves rolled up. His dark blond hair was combed neatly and curled onto his collar. His mustache and honed masculine features told Becca that here was a true Texas cowboy. That wasn't an idle impression. She knew from what Colton had said that Cord's appearance was a true reflection of his personality and his calling.

His mustache moved slightly as he said, "Come in, please. Sit down."

Becca walked past him through the large foyer and into the den. She took a seat on a leather sofa.

Cord watched her for a second, then sat opposite her in a matching leather chair. A saying he'd heard many times from Gus, his ranch foreman and Della's husband, came to mind. *That gal's been spit and polished until she shines.* Cord never paid much attention to Gus's sayings, but looking at Becca, he knew what it meant. Becca with her bright smile and sophisticated manner caught his eye like a shining star. No wonder Colton was so enamored of her.

"Thank you for coming. I'm really grateful," he said before he got completely sidetracked.

"You're welcome," Becca answered, glancing around. "Where's Nicki?"

"Upstairs in her room. As always."

"She's been in her room all day?"

"Yes. The only time she comes out is when I force her, and it's getting increasingly hard to do that since she cries most of the time."

"That's not good, Cord," she said in a solemn voice.

"I know—and I'm hoping you can figure out what to do," he replied.

She saw a familiar sadness in his brown eyes, but it was

much more intense than the last time, and something in her reacted strongly to that—just as before.

"Can I see her?" she asked with a catch in her voice. "I'd like to examine her."

"Sure." He got up and led the way toward the stairs. At the bottom, he stepped aside to let her go first. She wore medium heels and felt dwarfed by his height. But it wasn't only that. She was very aware of Cord Prescott—as a man. Maybe it was the cowboy thing. That persona intrigued her, as it did most women. Or maybe she just empathized with him because of what he was suffering, because of his grief and his fear for his daughter.

"Second door on the left," Cord said as they reached the landing. There were hardwood floors throughout the house and beautiful area rugs. A lot of the furniture was antique, probably dating from when the house was first built. Portraits of Prescott men were displayed on the wall of the staircase. Becca remembered Colton telling her that all the Prescott men's names began with the letter *C;* it was a tradition kept alive from generation to generation. She wondered why there were no pictures of Prescott women or wives. They could be in another area of the house, she supposed, and she would definitely ask Colton about it.

Cord opened the door and they went inside. Nicki sat in a children's rocker clutching the same doll she had a year ago. Becca was dismayed by what she saw. The child's blond curly hair was neatly combed and in pigtails, and she wore pink shorts, a matching top and sandals—but her cheeks were hollow and her little arms and legs were so thin. She reminded Becca of anorexic teenagers she'd seen. What had happened to this child?

Cord squatted beside her. "Baby, we have company. Do you remember Becca?"

Nicki hid her face in the doll's hair. Just as she had a year ago.

Becca knelt on the floor. "It was a long time ago, but I told you the story about Cinderella and the prince. The prince who rode a horse like your daddy. Do you remember?"

Nicki shook her head and didn't look at her.

"Would you like me to tell you another story?"

Nicki shook her head again, but Becca wasn't giving up.

"I know lots of stories," Becca said. "Of course, most of them are about monsters or scary stuff that my brother, Scotty, likes. But we're girls and we don't care for that kind of nonsense, do we."

Nicki still didn't answer and seemed to burrow into the chair.

"Baby, Becca asked you a question," Cord said softly. Nicki still didn't respond. "Look at me, baby," Cord added in that same soft tone.

Nicki slowly raised her head and stared at Cord. "I'm tired, Daddy. Make her go 'way."

Becca's heart sank, although she didn't know why, since she hadn't expected any miracles. It was just so painful seeing the child in this condition.

"I'm a doctor, Nicki," she told her. "I'm going to check your vital signs. Is that okay?"

Nicki didn't answer, but Cord nodded. Becca opened her bag and took out her stethoscope. Nicki's signs were weak, and Becca knew she was in a danger zone. Her first reaction was to get her to a hospital immediately, but something held her back. The hospital would only frighten Nicki, and she wanted to try a different approach first.

"Daddy, make her go 'way," Nicki whimpered, when Becca had finished her exam.

"Okay, baby," Cord said, smoothing Nicki's hair. Becca noticed that his hand shook slightly. "Della made some chocolate chip cookies. Why don't I get you one."

"Not hungry."

"Please eat something, baby." The ache in Cord's voice squeezed Becca's heart until she had trouble breathing.

"I'm not hungry, Daddy."

"Okay, baby," Cord said, and kissed her cheek. He got up, and they walked back down the stairs and into the den.

Cord started to pace; she could see he was terribly upset. "I can't take much more of this. I can't stand to see her in this state."

"Yes, she has deteriorated. Her body's starved for nourishment, she's dehydrated and her heart is weak."

"I don't know what else to do!"

Becca knew it was time for some hard truths, and Cord wasn't going to like what she had to say. But in the few minutes she'd been with them, she could see what part of the problem was.

"Are you familiar with the term *enabler?*"

He stopped pacing and stared at her. "What?"

"An enabler, Cord. That's what you are. You're enabling Nicki to stay in that room. You're enabling her not to eat. You're enabling her to do whatever she wants."

His eyes darkened. "What the *hell* are you talking about?"

"If Nicki doesn't want to eat, you don't make her. If she wants to stay in her room, you let her. You're giving in to her every whim—and it has to stop."

His eyes became blacker, if that was possible. "My God, you want me to force her to eat and to drag her out of her room?"

"I'm afraid so," Becca admitted.

"After what my daughter's been through, I would *never* do that to her."

Becca swallowed the constriction in her throat. "It's called tough love, and you have to do something, or Nicki will not survive this. Can't you see that?"

Cord swung away in anger, then swung back. “I think you should leave,” he said in the coldest voice she’d ever heard. “You’re not the doctor or the woman I thought you were.”

CHAPTER TWO

"NO," BECCA SAID without blinking.

"Excuse me?" Cord said, and she was chilled by his scorn.

"You asked me to help Nicki, and I'm not leaving until I get that chance."

"I've changed my mind."

She watched the stubborn look on his face and knew he was struggling with his own emotions. He didn't want anyone to hurt Nicki—ever again. He wanted what was best for his child, but he was blinded by love.

"Sorry, it doesn't work that way," she told him. "I'm here and I'm staying. You can clearly see that Nicki needs help. That's why you called me. At her age, her muscles and bones are developing, but without nourishment, that growth is being hindered. You may not like my methods, but for Nicki's sake, you *have* to give me a chance."

"I won't allow her to be upset."

His voice wasn't as angry or cold as before, and Becca felt a glimmer of hope. "Is being upset worse than the almost catatonic state she's in now?"

He didn't answer, just stared at her with brooding eyes.

Becca kept on. "She's going to get upset, Cord. You might as well resign yourself to that. She'll be reacting to external stimuli, and that's what she needs instead of this inert passivity."

He ran both hands through his hair in a weary gesture and sank into a chair. "I just can't take it when she cries."

At the pain in his voice, she took a deep breath. "Why don't you go outside and let me spend some time with her," she suggested, knowing she would get nowhere with Nicki if Cord was around.

His eyes met hers. "I don't know if I can do that."

"You have to," she said, her eyes not wavering from his. "I have to reach Nicki on some level, and I can't do that with you present."

He didn't say anything and Becca added, "At this point she needs to be in a hospital unless I can do something with her right now. You can either let me try, or call for an ambulance. It's your choice."

His face turned white and he drew in a long, shuddering breath. "Fine, you have until eight o'clock. Just be very careful, Becca. There is just so much I'll allow."

"I will not do anything that will harm her physically or mentally."

"That's all I need to know," he said as he moved past her.

"Cord," she said, and he turned back. "If you hear Nicki crying, please don't come inside."

There was a moment of indecision in his eyes, then he walked out the door.

Becca removed her jacket as she went into the kitchen. She had a plan in mind and it started with dinner. A gray-haired woman was putting meringue on a pie.

"Hi." Becca smiled. "I'm Becca Talbert and I'm hoping you're the housekeeper."

The woman glanced up. "That's me. My name is Della. What can I do for you?"

"What time does Nicki usually have dinner?"

"Dinnertime is six o'clock, but with the way that child eats, it's anybody's guess."

"I'm not trying to be nosy, but could you tell me how many people will be here for dinner?"

"Edie eats in her room and Blanche is out, as usual, so there'll be you and Cord."

"I see," Becca murmured. "Do you mind if I ask what you're preparing?"

Della lifted an eyebrow. "That's a popular question today, but we're having roast, new potatoes, carrots and fresh green beans." She pointed to a pan of rolls. "Homemade rolls are rising, and I just finished making a chocolate pie."

"Does Nicki like any of these things?"

Della shrugged. "When Anette was alive, Nicki ate almost anything. She loved chocolate pie. Used to stick her finger in the chocolate and lick it off and Anette would get mad. She wanted Nicki to be a proper lady and act like a grown-up." Della shook her head. "The woman was very peculiar."

"Sounds as if you didn't like her."

"Like?" Della seemed to study the word for a moment. "Can't really say. All I know is she got on my nerves. Too damn picky. All the food for Nicki had to be cooked at a certain temperature and it couldn't stay out too long and she wanted everything made from scratch. She also insisted that Nicki eat at certain times, never mind the rest of the household. In that case, I told her, she needed to cook the food herself, but she never did. I don't think she knew how to cook. She was a city girl with city ways and she hated this ranch."

"But she loved Cord and Nicki?" Becca knew she was gossiping but she couldn't resist. Besides, she told herself, she might learn some valuable piece of information, some fact that might help her.

"Oh yeah, that's why she stayed." Della put the meringue bowl in the sink. "I never knew she was drinking so much and neither did Cord. She hid it well. Such a tragedy." Della shook her head again. "Cord locked up her room and nothing in there's been touched since."

It *was* a tragedy, Becca thought, and now it was time to heal—for the whole Prescott family. "Colton mentioned that she'd been on antidepressants, too."

"That's right. After Nicki was born, she just seemed to hit rock bottom. On the days she felt really bad, Edie or I would watch the baby. Cord wanted to hire a nurse, but Anette wouldn't have it. She wanted to care for her child. She really did."

"Then, Anette was a good mother."

"Yes, even I will admit that. Nicki was never out of her sight for long. I guess that's why the little one's taking this so hard."

Becca brought her concentration back to the present and Nicki. She'd been gossiping too long with Della. Something she didn't normally do, but she was very curious about Anette. And Della had definitely filled in some of the background facts.

"Would you please set a place for Nicki at dinner?" Becca asked.

Della turned from the sink with a startled expression. "She's coming down to eat?"

"Yes," Becca said with more confidence than she was feeling. "I'm going up to see her now, and Della, if you hear her crying or complaining, please don't interfere."

"Does Cord know about this?" Della inquired, wiping her hands on her apron.

"Yes," Becca answered, heading for the stairs. As she walked up, she silently prayed that she could get through to Nicki. She opened the door and found Nicki sitting exactly as they'd left her—and Becca knew she had to use drastic measures to shock Nicki back into the real world. To do that, she had to be strong and keep her emotions in check.

She knelt in front of the rocker. "Hi, Nicki," she said cheerfully. "My name is Becca. I told you that before, remember?"

No response, as she had expected.

"I'm a doctor and I take care of girls and boys. If they don't feel well, I try to make them feel better. Do you feel bad?"

No response.

In Becca's experience, it was sometimes easier for a child to talk through an object like a toy. She focused on the doll in Nicki's arms. "What's your doll's name?"

Again no response.

She sat on the floor in a comfortable position. "I had a doll similar to that when I was your age. My sis—" She stopped as she realized she was about to say *sister*—a minor slip of the tongue. It was so hard to think of Emily as her mother when she remembered herself at that age. Lord, she was getting sidetracked and it was a weird feeling, but one she could handle. "Actually, my mother bought me the doll. She bought me lots of dolls, but I liked that one best. I named her Chocolate because I love chocolate, and I called her Coco for short. Does your doll have a name?" Becca held her breath as she waited.

Nothing.

"It's important for a doll to have a name, don't you think?"

Still nothing.

"She has blond hair like you, so is her name Nicki?"

Nicki rubbed her head against the doll's. "Dolly," she murmured.

"That's nice," Becca said, grateful for a response. She knew that if she kept talking, kept pushing, Nicki would respond in some way. She was hoping for a positive reaction, but she'd take anything at this point. "Does Dolly like to eat?"

Nicki shook her head.

"That's a shame, because Della's prepared this wonderful

meal. I was just down in the kitchen and the smell alone was a real treat. She's made this chocolate pie that has a fluffy meringue about three inches thick. Do you like chocolate pie?"

"No. Go 'way. I don't like you," Nicki said in a defiant tone.

Good, Becca thought. Now they were getting somewhere. She had to keep pushing.

"You don't have to like me, but I've come all this way to see you and I expect you to eat dinner with me."

"I'm not hungry. Go 'way."

Becca reached up, and caught Nicki's face with both hands and forced the child to look at her. "I'm not going away and you're coming downstairs to eat."

"No." Nicki spat the word. "Daddy says I don't have to and you can't make me."

Becca still held her face and looked into those angry eyes. "I'm going to pick you up and we're going downstairs." As she said the words, she got to her feet and gathered Nicki in her arms. This action was met with resistance. Nicki began to cry "No, no, no" and hit at Becca with her free hand and her feet. Becca kept walking; the blows to her face, neck and legs didn't stop her. Halfway down the stairs, Nicki began to scream, blood-curdling screams. Becca still didn't stop.

CORD JUMPED TO HIS FEET when he heard the screams. He ran for the patio door, then halted abruptly when he heard Becca's words. *"Please don't come inside."* He turned and went back to his chair, but the screams continued. What was she doing to his baby? He marched back to the door and stopped again. God, how was he supposed to handle this? He wanted his child to get better, but he couldn't take this. Each scream was tearing his heart out. He grasped the doorknob.

WHEN BECCA REACHED the bottom step she sat down, with Nicki still fighting and screaming in her arms. Suddenly Becca screamed as loudly as Nicki. Nicki stopped and stared at her with tear-filled eyes.

"I can scream as loudly as you," Becca informed her in a calm voice. "So are we going to scream or eat dinner?"

"I don't like you," Nicki muttered, rubbing her eyes.

"I don't like you too much right now, either," Becca replied.

"You're mean," Nicki said crossly.

"I don't want to be mean," Becca told her.

Nicki didn't answer. She still had a death grip on Dolly, who was looking a little worn and tattered. Now was the time for a softer approach.

"Dolly seems so sad," Becca said.

"She is," Nicki told her.

"Oh, that's too bad. What do you think will make her feel better?"

Nicki shrugged.

"Chocolate always makes *me* feel better."

"Candy?" Nicki's eyes opened wide. She was talking, asking questions. That was good—very good.

"Yes, when I've had a long day and I'm tired, a chocolate bar perks me right up."

"It does?"

"Sure does, but even though I love chocolate, chocolate doesn't love me."

"Why?"

"Because when you get to be a woman my age, you have to watch your weight and if I eat a lot of chocolate, my butt gets bigger and bigger."

"You got a big butt?"

Becca laughed out loud. She couldn't help it. Why in the world had she said that? She just wanted to keep Nicki talking, and the words seemed to come of their own volition. How could she correct this?

Before she could gather her wits, Cord came charging in, Della right behind him. Nicki immediately crawled off Becca's lap and ran to her father. He picked her up and held her tight.

"How's my baby?" he whispered.

Nicki pointed a finger at Becca. "She's mean. I wanna go to my room."

Just like that, Nicki had reverted to her old self. Becca got to her feet. Her eyes locked with Cord's. *Don't you dare* was flashing in their depths, and she hoped he got the message.

Cord received the message loud and clear. Thirty minutes ago he would've taken Nicki back upstairs. When he heard her scream, it was a certainty. Then he'd gone into the den and heard Nicki talking to Becca in a normal tone of voice. He couldn't make out what she was saying, but she was interacting with Becca—something she hadn't done with anyone in a long time. Now he had to look at himself. Was he an enabler, as Becca had said? Was he enabling Nicki to be the way she was because he didn't have the strength or the courage to do anything else? Yes, he was. He could see that. Now he had to try some of that tough love Becca had talked about. Nicki's future depended on it.

"No, baby," Cord said with every bit of strength he possessed. "We're eating dinner in the dining room. Della has the table all set." Without another word, he moved toward the door.

"'Kay, Daddy," Nicki said meekly, and laid her head on his shoulder.

Cord let out a long breath. If she'd started crying, he still would have made her, but this was so much easier. Becca was right; he had to be firm.

Becca followed them into the large dining room. As Cord

settled Nicki in her chair, Becca glanced around. The furniture was exquisite and definitely antique. She guessed the late 1800s. The table could easily seat twenty people. There was also a hutch and a china cabinet. The entire set was made of dark wood and decorated with an ornate design that was unlike anything she'd ever seen. The carving had to have been done by hand. She also noticed the china in the cabinet, which was old and very beautiful. She'd bet it wasn't used anymore because of its fragility, but it was a pleasure just to look at.

Becca took her seat next to Nicki, and Cord sat at the head of the table. Della brought the food to the table without a word. Afterward she said, "If you need anything, I'll be in the kitchen."

"Thanks, Della," Cord said, and began to fill his plate and Nicki's.

"I'm not hungry," Nicki said with her arms tight around Dolly.

The silence became strained, and Becca could see that Cord was struggling with himself again. She had to do something, and fast. She did what came naturally—she talked.

"My, this looks wonderful," she said as she dished roast and potatoes onto her plate. "In the hospital, I eat in the cafeteria and it's not the most appetizing food. The vending machine and I are best friends. Of course, it's not very healthy so I try not to indulge too often. But sometimes the mind and the stomach aren't in agreement." As she talked, she mashed Nicki's potatoes with her fork and dipped gravy onto them. Then she lavishly buttered a roll and placed it beside the potatoes.

As Cord watched her, he thought, *Anette used to do that.* She'd make the food appealing so Nicki would eat. Maybe he should've been doing that.

"These potatoes are delicious, don't you think so, Cord?"

He blinked and realized Becca was talking to him. She stared pointedly at his fork, and he realized she wanted him to start eating. He recovered himself and began to do just that.

"Yes, yes, the potatoes are great," he said, following Becca's lead.

"Della said they were new potatoes. Does that mean she grows them?"

"Gus does," Nicki chimed in. Until that moment, she hadn't said a word or even attempted to pick up her fork, but she was avidly watching Becca.

"Gus?"

"That's my ranch foreman," Cord answered, as Nicki didn't say anything else. "He and Della have been here since I was a kid. They live in a small house not far from this one."

"Well, Della can certainly cook. I've never tasted food so good. And this roll—" she took a bite and purposefully swallowed "—is about the best thing I've put in my mouth. I remember one time, my friend Ginger and I decided to make cinnamon rolls. The concept of yeast rising clearly escaped us and our rolls were like pancakes with cinnamon. So I admire anyone who can make rolls like this. It definitely takes talent and patience."

Becca's voice drummed on inside Cord's head. The woman had one button—On—and she rattled incessantly about anything and everything. He was almost ready to scream *stop,* when he saw Nicki reach for her fork. Slowly she began to eat the potatoes, then she picked up the roll and took several bites. Cord kept eating, watching this miracle out of the corner of his eye. Becca's voice hummed on, and it was the most beautiful voice he'd ever heard. He now knew what she was doing—distracting Nicki so she wouldn't feel forced to eat…and it was working. His baby started eating, and before he knew it almost all the food on her plate was gone.

Becca was also watching Nicki closely. She leaned back in her chair. "My, that was the best meal I've ever eaten."

Nicki also leaned back. "Me, too," she said.

Della brought the pie out and set it on the table with a knife and plates. Then she began to collect the dinner plates.

"I'll help you, Della," Becca offered.

"No, you won't," Della was quick to say. "That's my job. You can cut the pie and serve it."

Becca didn't argue. She picked up the knife and cut three pieces. She handed one plate to Cord, placed one in front of Nicki and took the third for herself. She stuck her forefinger in the chocolate and tasted it. "Mmm. That's delicious."

Nicki scrambled to her knees and Dolly fell to the floor. Nicki stuck her finger in the chocolate as Becca had done. "Mmm, it's good," she said.

"Oh, I love chocolate," Becca said as she reached for her fork. "I could eat this whole pie myself."

"It's gonna make your butt bigger," Nicki said as she put a spoonful in her mouth.

Becca almost spit the chocolate onto the table.

"Nicki!" Cord admonished.

"What?" Nicki looked at Cord with big, innocent eyes.

Becca swallowed quickly. "It's okay, Cord. Nicki and I were talking about this earlier. It's really okay." It was an effort to keep her face from turning red, but she managed.

Cord couldn't figure out why Becca was talking to Nicki about big butts. That made no sense. Besides, Becca didn't have a big butt. She was very slim with curves in all the right places and—he put skids on that thought. She was Colton's girlfriend and he'd do well to remember it.

After they finished their pie, Becca smiled at Nicki. "You have chocolate all over your face."

A look as if she'd done something wrong came over Nicki, and Becca wanted to quickly dispel it. "But that's okay because I'll just lick it off." Becca tasted chocolate from Nicki's cheeks with her tongue, and Nicki giggled. "You're like one big chocolate bar and I could eat you up."

"No, don't eat me." Nicki giggled more loudly and it was a delight to Becca's ears. A hospital wasn't going to be necessary; Nicki just needed some tough love. Now she had to make Cord understand that. Finally she reached for a napkin, dipped it in water and wiped Nicki's face.

Anette used to do that, Cord thought again. She always wiped Nicki's chin and cheeks with a napkin—but she'd never lick food from Nicki's face. That was too undignified. And she would never permit Nicki to laugh at the dinner table. Anette had all kinds of ridiculous rules. They had argued about them all the time. He believed children should be allowed to be children, and Anette—

Cord got to his feet. "Let's go into the den so Della can clean up."

"'Kay, Daddy," Nicki said, crawling out of her chair and scooping up her doll. Becca followed them, trying to think of something to occupy Nicki. She didn't want her going to her room just yet. Cord sat in his chair and Nicki climbed onto his lap.

"Let's play a game," Becca suggested.

Nicki frowned at her and that same frown was echoed on Cord's face, but it didn't bother Becca. Nicki needed to act like a normal child.

"I know," she said, a game they often played in the hospital coming to mind. "I'll mention an animal, and you have to act and sound like that animal. The one who's the best animal wins."

Two pairs of brown eyes stared blankly at her. The Prescotts were not cooperating.

"Okay, I'll go first." She thought for a second. "A chicken. I'll do a chicken."

She tucked her hands under her armpits and flapped her elbows like wings, then pranced around the room squawking.

Nicki laughed out loud and pointed a finger at Becca. "You're funny."

Cord was hypnotized by the sound. Nicki had giggled earlier, but he hadn't heard her laugh outright in so long that for a moment he felt winded by the pleasure.

"Okay, funny pants." Becca grinned. "It's your turn. Let's see. A cow. You have to do a cow."

Nicki jumped out of Cord's lap, the doll falling to the floor again. "I can do a cow. I can," she said as she got on all fours and trudged around the den going "Moo, moo, moo."

"That's about the best cow I've ever seen. What do you think, Cord?"

"The very best," he agreed. "Better than any of the cows I have in my pastures."

His eyes met Becca's, and for an instant something seemed to pass between them, but Becca was sure she'd only imagined it.

"It's Daddy's turn," Nicki called, interrupting the moment. "Daddy has to do one. What can Daddy be, Becca?"

Becca eyes gleamed because Cord was clearly resisting the idea. "A horse. I think Daddy should be a horse."

"Me, too," Nicki agreed brightly, and pulled Cord to his feet. He had that *I'll get even with you* look in his eyes, but he got down on his hands and knees and crawled around the room with an occasional "Neigh."

Nicki crawled onto his back and shouted, "Giddyup, giddyup, horsey."

Cord laughed, a sound that came from his heart, and rolled over and held Nicki in the air as her delightful giggles filled the room.

"What the hell's going on here?" Blanche demanded from the doorway, then glanced at Becca. "And who the hell are you?"

"Becca Talbert," she answered stiffly, taking in Blanche's tight-fitting red dress and heels.

"Colton's girfriend? Is Colton here?"

Cord swung to his feet in one easy movement, Nicki held tight in his arms. "No, he isn't."

"Then, what's she doing here?"

Becca bit her tongue to keep a retort from tumbling out.

"I invited her," Cord said woodenly.

"You're fooling around with Colton's girl? I won't have this, Cord."

"Please, Blanche, acting like a mother is out of your league, so give it a rest. I've got to get Nicki to bed." Exhausted from the unaccustomed exertion, Nicki was falling asleep on his shoulder.

"Cord," Becca called after him. "It's getting late, so I'll be going."

He looked back at her. "Could you wait for just a minute? I'd like to talk to you. This won't take long."

"Sure," she said unenthusiastically. Spending time with Blanche was like spending time in a room full of red wasps. Didn't matter what you said or did, you were gonna get stung.

As Cord left, Blanche went over to the built-in bar and poured a glass of scotch. She raised the glass to Becca. "What're you up to, sugar?"

"I don't know what you're talking about," Becca said, reaching for her jacket.

"Sure you do," Blanche muttered. "You're playing my boys against each other."

Becca opened her mouth, but quickly closed it. She wouldn't dignify that statement with an answer. It wasn't any of Blanche's business, anyway. This was between her and Cord.

"Let me give you some advice, sugar," Blanche said, when Becca remained silent. "Stick with Colton. He has the money. Cord's a rancher and always will be. It's in his blood. That stupid Anette tried to change him and get him away from here, but it didn't work." She paused for a second and took a big swallow of scotch. "Aren't you a doctor or something?"

"Yes, I'm a doctor."

"Then, you're not stupid and I'm sure you can see the writing on the wall. Cord has that rugged handsomeness that appeals to women, but sugar, in the dark it don't make no never mind, as my dearly departed husband used to say. So stick with Colton. He has the big bucks."

"Is that what you did, Blanche? Stick with the big bucks?"

A sly smile played across her red lips. "I see you've heard my story. But until you've walked a mile in my shoes, sugar, you don't have the right to judge me."

"I'm not judging you," Becca said, but knew she was. She couldn't imagine why an eighteen-year-old girl would marry a sixty-year-old man—other than the obvious reason. Money.

"Claybourne was a lot like Cord—very handsome even at sixty. I wouldn't have married him, otherwise."

"I'm sure that's a matter of opinion." Becca couldn't keep the words from slipping out.

Blanche was angry. Becca could see it in her glittering blue eyes.

She finished off the scotch and walked over to Becca. "Let me tell you something, sugar. Get your ass back to the city where you belong before the same thing happens to you that happened to Anette."

"Is that a threat?" Becca asked in a barely controlled voice.

"Take it any way you like, sugar, but stay away from my boys." With that, she swept from the room.

CHAPTER THREE

BECCA PICKED UP HER PURSE and slid it over her shoulder. She would really prefer to leave, but she'd promised Cord she'd wait.

He soon returned. "I'm sorry," he said. "I hope Blanche wasn't rude to you."

Becca wasn't sure how to answer that or how to tell a man that his mother was obnoxious and vile, so she said, "I'm sure Blanche is always the same."

"Yeah." He sighed. "She's hard to take on a good day."

Becca retrieved her medical bag thinking the Prescott men had a strange relationship with their mother. "You said you wanted to talk to me."

"It's about Nicki."

Becca had expected as much. That was why she'd stayed, even though Blanche had made her temperature rise. "She's at a critical stage. In the morning it'll start all over again. She won't want to leave her room or eat, but you have to make her."

"I'm not very good at that."

"You have to be, for Nicki's sake."

He gazed directly at her. "I was hoping to persuade you to come here for a couple of days so Nicki can keep progressing. I know that's asking a lot, but I'm desperate. Della and Edie have tried to coax her out of that room with no results. You did it, though, and you had her talking and laughing. I want my little girl back. Please, Becca."

Her stomach turned over at the sound of his saying her name. She hadn't anticipated this, and found herself grappling for the right answer. She knew there was only one—but, still, she hesitated.

"Does Nicki go to school?"

"Anette had enrolled her in a private school in Houston. She started pre-kindergarten, but it didn't last long. After Anette's death, she cried all the time, and the teacher suggested maybe it would be best for her to be at home with a private teacher."

"Did you do that?"

"Yes, I hired Mrs. Witherspoon, who's also a nanny, but she can't get anything out of Nicki, either. Nicki's enrolled for kindergarten in the fall, but I'm not sure how that's going to go."

"Nicki's health is at stake here," she told him. "Nicki has to start acting like a normal child and the adults in her life have to be strong. They—and not Nicki—have to call the shots."

"That's not easy."

"You don't have a choice."

"She responds to you like nothing I've ever seen. I'm just asking for a little of your time."

Becca took a long breath and tried to explain. She didn't want to seem insensitive, but she had to be practical. "Nicki needs to start interacting with the people in her own environment. If she becomes attached to me, it'll only make things worse."

"Okay, Becca, I think you've made your position clear. I'm sorry I asked."

Oh God, this wasn't what she wanted at all! For the first time in her life, she was afraid of becoming too attached to a child—and to the child's father. But Nicki needed help, and Becca had started a course of treatment and she had to see it through…to see Nicki happy again. That was the one thing, the only thing, that mattered. This wasn't about Becca or her feelings. Besides, Cord wasn't interested in her as a woman. He was still dealing with a lot of emotion over his wife's death.

She'd wanted a change, an opportunity to get away from Houston for a while. The ranch wasn't far, but it could be perfect. She'd have the time and peace to sort through all her own discontent.

"What's it like living on a ranch?"

His eyes narrowed. "Pardon?"

"I was raised on the coast and I don't know a thing about cows or horses or the ranching life."

He blinked. "Does this mean you'd consider coming here to help Nicki?"

"If the offer's still open." She smiled. "I'm a sucker for a child in need."

His face relaxed. "Thank you. Oh, Becca, thank you. I know you probably have a hectic schedule, but if you can just fit us in for a couple of hours, I'd really appreciate it."

"Actually, my schedule's open. I have some free time before I begin my practice in July."

"Oh." He seemed shocked. "Then, you'd be willing to stay here and help Nicki?"

She nodded. "Yes, but the nanny stays, too. I want Nicki to realize that I'll only be here for a short time."

"Sure, no problem." He watched her for a moment. "I can't believe you've actually agreed to do this."

"I have an ulterior motive."

He raised an eyebrow. "Really?"

"I've had an exhausting schedule for the past few years and I need a break. A break from city life." *And so many other things.*

"Well, then, I hope this works out for both of us," he said. "There's a pool in the backyard, horses to ride, wide-open spaces, and more cows than you'll ever want to see. You won't be bored."

That was one thing she couldn't possibly be around Cord. For some reason, whenever she was near him her senses seemed magnified.

"I hope Blanche won't mind my being here." One encounter with the woman was one too many, but Becca wasn't going to let her interfere with Nicki's health.

"Don't worry about Blanche. I'll take care of her."

She was sure he would. The relationship between the Prescott men and their mother was an odd one. And she intended to keep out of it.

"I'll be back sometime tomorrow morning," she said as she moved toward the door.

"I'll have Della prepare a room for you—and thanks again for doing this."

She turned in the doorway. "Nicki just needs someone to push her, and I can see you're hopeless in that area."

"Yeah."

"I'll see you tomorrow," she said, forcing herself to walk to her car. She wanted to continue talking to him, to continue… There was something about Cord that touched a place deep within—a place no man had ever reached. Maybe it was the sadness she saw in his eyes or the struggle to help his little girl. Whatever it was, it had made her do an impulsive thing. Staying at the ranch was not in her plans, and yet she'd suddenly found herself volunteering. She didn't regret that impulsiveness. In all honesty, she was looking forward to living at Triple Creek for a few days. Or even a few weeks. Now she had to tell her parents—and Colton.

CORD WATCHED until her taillights disappeared down the driveway. He couldn't believe his luck. She was coming back and she'd be staying here. That was far more than he'd ever hoped for. This was exactly what Nicki needed—someone to help her deal with Anette's death. Lord knows he hadn't been able to do it.

She's coming back was all he could think as he went in search of Della. As usual, he found her in the kitchen.

"Becca gone?" Della asked as she wiped off the counters.

"Yeah," he answered.

"She sure has a way with that child. Lordy, lordy, that was wonderful to see."

"It was," Cord agreed. "Please get the room across from Nicki's ready. Becca is coming back to stay for a while." Was he smiling? He couldn't seem to stop.

"Wow, that's good news! But you're in the room across from Nicki."

"Damn, what was I thinking?"

"Yeah, what were you thinking?" Della repeated with a sly smile.

He'd moved into that room after Anette's death because their old room held too many painful memories.

He looked at Della, not rising to the gleam in her eyes. "How about the room at the end of hall? That's not far from Nicki."

"What *about* the room at the end of the hall?" Blanche asked as she strolled into the kitchen wearing a short black silk robe.

Cord turned to face his mother. "I'm having the room prepared for Becca. She's going to be visiting for a while to help Nicki."

"Really." Blanche placed her hands on her hips. "I don't recall being consulted, and I own this house and this ranch. No one stays here unless I say so."

Cord's eyes darkened. "Becca is staying."

"Don't push me, Cord." Her tone was threatening, and Cord reacted to it.

He stepped closer to her. "You may own this place, but I run it and at a profit that you enjoy. So if you have a problem with my decision, then you have a problem—because my baby needs help and I'll fight you tooth and nail to ensure her well-being."

"Okay, okay." Blanche changed her tone. "Don't work yourself into a lather." She walked over to the refrigerator and got a bottle of water. "This Becca is Colton's girlfriend. Have you forgotten that?"

"Of course not, and I don't see what difference it makes."

"Because you have the hots for her," she answered crudely.

Cord felt the blood rush through his system in raging anger, but he forced himself to remain calm. He wouldn't let her get to him.

"You haven't looked at a woman since Anette died, and your brother's girl is not the woman to start with."

Cord whirled toward the door. "I'm checking on Nicki." He stopped, unable to leave without setting this straight. "Becca is staying here for *Nicki*. That's it. And I don't want you telling her these lies. I'll speak with Colton to make sure he's okay with the arrangement. Other than that, I'd appreciate it if you'd keep out of my business."

"I tried to tell you about Anette. You wouldn't listen to me then, either, and look how that turned out."

Cord ran his hands through his hair in a weary gesture. "Blanche, leave it alone. For God's sake, just leave it alone." He sighed deeply and hurried through the door.

Blanche glanced at Della. "I don't care how old they get, kids never grow up."

"Cord's been grown-up most of his life," Della remarked.

"Don't take that haughty tone with me, Della."

Della's blue eyes became sharp. "Cord's in pain. He's lost his wife and now he's fighting to save his child. Give him a break. Give us all a break." Without a backward look, she followed Cord.

BECCA DROVE TO HER PARENTS' HOME in Bellaire. She parked by the garages and went in through the kitchen, where she came upon Emily and Jackson putting dishes in the dishwasher. Scotty ran through from the den, shouting, "Sissy!" and hurled himself into her arms. She hugged him tight. At eight years of age, he was getting so tall. She could hardly believe he wasn't a baby anymore.

"I got a new computer game. Wanna play?" Scotty asked, his green eyes shining. Like his father, Scotty loved computers, and spent as many hours as he could at a keyboard, or at least until Emily made him go outside and play.

"In a minute, tiger," she answered. "I want to talk to Mom and Dad first."

"Okay, I'll be in my room." He dashed out the door.

Emily hugged her. "This is a nice surprise."

Every time Becca looked at Emily or heard her voice, she felt a surge of love and warmth. They had a strong bond that pain and heartache had not diminished.

Jackson planted a big kiss on her cheek. "How's my girl? Hope you've been getting some rest."

All this love had kept her sane during that dark time, but she sometimes wondered if Emily and Jackson saw her as an adult or only as their little girl. For a parent she was sure that feeling never changed, but Becca knew she had to be more than their daughter. And she didn't know how to explain that. She would just try to be honest and hope they understand.

They sat at the kitchen table. "What do you want to talk about, angel?" Jackson asked.

Becca made an effort not to squirm in her chair. "I just wanted to let you know that I'll be going away for a little while."

"Oh?" Emily raised an eyebrow. "When did this come about?"

"Cordell Prescott called me today," she said slowly. "His daughter, Nicki, still hasn't adjusted to her mother's death. I went out to the ranch to check her over, and she's not doing well. Grief is making her physically ill."

"I'm so sorry to hear that," Emily murmured.

"Colton never mentioned a thing," Jackson said.

"I'll be staying at the ranch, trying to help her."

Emily frowned. "Becca, angel, that's not your field. Cord needs to get her to a psychologist."

"He has, and it didn't work. If I see things aren't improving, then I'll suggest it again. But I feel I can help her."

Jackson patted her hand. "You're very good with kids."

"Thanks, Dad. I'm a pediatrician. I'd better be."

"Becca—"

"I know what I'm doing," she said emphatically, before Emily could say anything else.

"Sure you do," Emily agreed. "I was just hoping that…"

"I'd rest and have fun," Becca finished for her. "Getting away to the ranch will be good for *me,* too, and I need that. A different environment, different kinds of activities… Please try to understand."

"Of course," Jackson said.

"And I'm very fond of Nicki and I want to help her." She got to her feet. "Now I'll go and let Scotty beat me at this new game, which won't take much letting on my part."

EMILY AND JACKSON STARED at each other as Becca left the room. "Do you think Colton knows about this?" Emily asked.

"I don't think so."

"This is so sudden and I—"

Jackson leaned over and kissed her. "Stop worrying."

"It's so hard."

"I know," he whispered. "But I think Becca's feeling the constraints of our love. She's not our little girl anymore. She's our grown-up daughter who can make her own decisions."

"I just want to protect her."

"Me, too, but we've had her for ten wonderful years. I consider that a blessing. Now we have to support her in whatever she chooses to do."

Emily smiled. "You're so wise."

He kissed her again. "And don't forget it."

WHEN BECCA GOT BACK to the apartment, she called Colton and asked him to stop by on his way to work in the morning. He'd been in Dallas and she was glad he was back; she needed to talk to him.

Sleep didn't come easily. Explaining her life to everyone was starting to get on her nerves. She sensed that her parents disapproved, especially Emily, but this was *her* decision, and she hoped it was the right one. Minutes later, it seemed, the doorbell woke her. God, she'd overslept! She grabbed a terry-cloth robe and headed for the door.

Colton stood on the doorstep, wearing an impeccable tailored gray suit and holding two takeout cups of coffee. "Hi, gorgeous," he said with a smile.

"I'm not gorgeous," she muttered grumpily, as she ran her hands through her tangled hair. "I look like hell."

"That's a matter of opinion," he said, as she accepted one of the coffees, mumbling her thanks.

She led the way into her living room. Colton took a seat on the sofa beside her.

"How's the time off going?"

"Pretty good," she answered, sipping her coffee. Cream, no sugar, exactly as she liked it. She told him about her visit to the ranch.

"Damn, I feel terrible," he said. "I haven't talked to Cord in over two weeks. I've been so busy I never seem to have time for anything except work. I knew Nicki wasn't doing well, and I told Cord weeks ago that he should consult you. I never dreamed he'd take my advice."

The Prescotts were not a close family, and Becca knew Blanche was the primary reason for that. She took a deep breath. "I'm planning to spend some time at the ranch, so I can try to help Nicki."

"You are? That's wonderful," Colton said. "If anyone can help her, it's you."

"Thanks." They talked about Nicki and about Colton's business trip, but she was well aware that there was another conversation they had to have. She wasn't quite sure how to bring it up.

"Colton?"

"Hmm?"

"We're good friends, aren't we?"

"The best."

"Have you ever wished that our relationship had turned into…more?"

He moved uncomfortably. "Yeah, but I've always realized that you don't have those feelings for me."

"Oh, Colton." She felt like crying.

"Don't worry about it. Besides, I'm too old for you, anyway." His eyes narrowed. "Why are you mentioning it now? Oh." He answered his own question. "You've been listening to that crazy redhead."

"Don't call Ginger that!"

"She's loony as a bat and always making nasty comments about our relationship."

"She's very outspoken," Becca said in Ginger's defense.

"Yeah." He laughed sarcastically. "But our relationship is none of her business and she'd better keep her opinions to herself."

"You're getting angry for nothing," Becca told him. "I just didn't want you hoping that something was going to happen between us, because I'm not sure what I want and you're too nice a person to keep baby-sitting me. You deserve a—" The doorbell interrupted her.

"Excuse me," she said, and got up to open the door.

Ginger brushed past her. "Look at this," she cried agitatedly. "Look at my hair! It's one big fuzz ball. I can't go to work like this."

Ginger had naturally curly red hair, and on humid days it sprang into a mass of tight ringlets. During the sweltering Houston summers, Ginger was always in a panic about her hair.

"I looked in the car mirror and I couldn't believe it! I just fixed it, and now I resemble the bride of Frankenstein. Your place is close to work, so I came here for emergency repairs. Can I use your curling iron?" Ginger turned and saw Colton. "*You're* here awfully early."

"Got something to say about it?" Colton asked in a hard tone.

"Had nails with your coffee, Prescott?" Ginger returned without skipping a beat, then swung toward the bathroom.

Becca shrugged. "That's Ginger."

Colton stood up, shaking his head. "I don't know how you put up with her."

"We've been friends for a very long time."

Colton looked into her eyes. "Don't worry about us. Don't worry about anything."

"Colton…"

He placed a finger over her lips. "I've got to get to work. I'll call you later, and I'll call Cord as soon as I get to the office." He started for the door. "Thanks for doing this for my family. I know Cord will appreciate it." Becca stared after him.

Ginger came back with her hair looking much better. "Stuffed Shirt gone?"

"Ginger, don't."

"I have to run, anyway."

"Can you wait just a second?"

Ginger glanced at her watch. "That's about all I've got."

Becca told her about the visit to Triple Creek, about motherless Nicki and her father.

"Wow. What's this Cord like?"

Becca groaned. "It's not about Cord. It's about Nicki."

"If you say so." Ginger sighed. "Now, I've *really* got to go."

"Can you water my plants while I'm gone?"

"Sure," Ginger called, hurrying out the door. "Phone me when you're back in town."

As Ginger left, Becca tried to ignore her words. Was she doing this for Nicki—or Cord? *For both of them* was her instant response, and she was getting tired of justifying her actions to everyone. She let out a long breath and went to make fresh coffee.

Fueled by the additional caffeine and new resolve, she called the Prescott ranch. Cord answered it on the second ring.

"Cord, it's Becca."

"Hi, how are you this morning?"

Her stomach trembled at the undertones in his voice, and she wondered why he had this effect on her and Colton didn't. She swallowed.

"Fine. Where's Nicki?"

"In her room."

"Cord." She couldn't keep the frustration out of her voice.

"Della's fixing her breakfast and I was about to go upstairs and get her. I'm not looking forward to this."

"Crying and screaming won't hurt her. Not eating *will*."

There was a pause, then he asked, "When are you coming?"

"In about two hours."

"Well, maybe I'll wait and let you work your magic."

"Oh, no, Cordell Prescott. You go upstairs and bring her down for breakfast. Today is the day she starts to get better, and you have to be strong."

"All right, but if I'm a wreck when you get here, you'll know why."

"Yes, I'll know why. I'll also know you're the biggest softie I've ever met."

"I've been told that."

Another pause. Then he asked, "Do you know where Colton is? I tried his apartment but he wasn't there."

"He was here, and he just left. You should be able to catch him at his office."

All the warm feelings inside him dissipated and he didn't understand why. He knew Becca and Colton were seeing each other. That had been for years, so why, all of a sudden, was he feeling so discouraged by this evidence that they were sleeping together? Could Blanche be right? No, Blanche was never right about anything. His interest in Becca was strictly for Nicki's sake. He would never covet his brother's lover.

"Cord."

He jerked himself to attention as he realized she was saying his name. "Yes."

"I'll be there as soon as I can."

He hung up the phone with a frown on his face. What was wrong with him? Nothing, he told himself. He just felt like this because of Blanche and her crude suggestion. He wasn't attracted to Dr. Becca Talbert. Not at all.

CHAPTER FOUR

BECCA WASN'T SURE what to pack, so she took a few of everything, but mostly jeans and tops. With her suitcases in the living room, she stopped to call Grandpa George—Jackson's father—as well as Rose and Owen. Then she called Dr. Arnold's office to let them know her whereabouts in case they needed to contact her. Hanging up the phone, she decided that part of her problem was the fact that she had to justify her whereabouts to so many people. At her age, she shouldn't have to do that. Their love was overwhelming her. Was that ungrateful? She hoped not. She loved her family, but she needed to be free, to experience life on her own. And that was exactly what she was going to do.

With her bags loaded in the car, she drove toward Triple Creek Ranch. Once she left Houston proper, the scenery along the route was serene and peaceful, so unlike the busyness of the city. Again she parked in the drive near the house and walked to the front door. It swung open before she could ring the bell. A frantic Cord stood there, holding Nicki in his arms. The child's face was buried in his shoulder and she was crying. Cord stared helplessly at Becca.

"Good morning," she said brightly as if everything was normal. "My bags are in the car. Do you mind getting them?"

Cord seemed dumbfounded. "Sure," he answered distractedly, and slowly set Nicki on her feet.

Nicki wrapped her arms around his leg and began to cry louder. "I wanna go to my room. I wanna go to my room."

"Becca's here, baby. Don't you want to say hi to Becca?"

Nicki rubbed her head against his leg. "No. Don't like her."

"You liked her yesterday."

"No, I didn't. I wanna go to my room. Daddy, please."

Becca could see Cord weakening. "Would you get my bags, Cord?"

Didn't she notice he had a child attached to his leg? Then Cord realized this had to be one of her maneuvers to get him out of the way. He disentangled himself from Nicki, but she ran after him crying, "Daddy! Daddy!"

Becca caught her before she could follow him to the car. She carried Nicki, kicking and sobbing, into the house and sat her firmly on the sofa.

"Leave me 'lone," she whimpered, and reached for Dolly.

Becca held her face between both hands, rubbing her thumbs over the girl's wet cheeks. "No, I'm not leaving you alone. I've come to spend some time with you and that's what we're going to do."

"Don't want to."

"Why?"

"'Cause."

"'Cause why?"

"'Cause you're mean."

"We had fun last night. I was a chicken, you were a cow and Daddy was a horse. Remember?"

"Yeah." She hiccuped.

Cord came into the room and set down her bags. As soon as she saw him, Nicki threw out her hands and started to cry again. "Daddy, I wanna go to my room."

Cord took a ragged breath. "Baby, we're not going to your room."

She drummed her legs on the sofa in a temper tantrum. "Daddy, please! Daddy, please!" she wailed.

Becca stood and walked over to Cord, whose face had turned a grayish white. "Just leave, Cord. I'll handle her."

"Becca." Her name sounded more like a groan.

"It'll be all right. I promise." She gently pushed him toward the door. As she did she noticed that two women had come to stand in the doorway, one tall and thin with gray hair, the other short and on the plump side.

Cord looked back at Becca. "This is Mrs. Witherspoon, the nanny."

The plump lady stepped forward and shook Becca's hand. "Nice to meet you, Dr. Talbert."

"And I think you've met my sister, Edith," Cord said. "We call her Edie."

Becca smiled at the older woman. "Yes, it's good to see you again, Edie."

Nicki's wails drowned out her words.

Becca gave Cord a knowing look, and he slowly made his way out the door, preceded by the two women.

Nicki's cries continued and Becca sat beside her. She could understand now why everyone was so reluctant to make Nicki leave her room. This type of behavior was hard on the nerves. She waited for a moment, trying to figure out the best approach to this situation. Her attention was drawn to the doll clutched in Nicki's arms, and she started to talk.

"Dolly, do you know what you and I are going to do today? No? Well, I'll tell you. We're going outside. The sun is shining. The birds are singing. It's a beautiful day. Of course, I'll have to put some sunscreen on you. Your skin's so light and we have to protect it. My skin, I don't have to worry too much about. I just get brown. Still, it never hurts to be careful with the sun. When I was little, I was in the sun all the time. My mother called me a brown-eyed Susan. I never knew what that was, and it confused me. My name's Becca, not Susan. What do you think of that, Dolly?"

The wails stopped, and Nicki opened one eye and stared at Becca. "Dolly can't talk."

"That's a pity because I like Dolly."

"She don't like you."

Becca brought one hand to her chest. "That breaks my heart."

Nicki opened her other eye. "It does?"

"Yes."

"What does that feel like?"

"It feels sad. Does Dolly feel sad?"

"Yes."

"Everybody's sad sometimes, but it's not good to feel sad for too long."

Nicki smoothed Dolly's hair. "No."

Becca knew it wasn't the right moment to delve further, so she got to her feet. "Tell you what. Why don't you and Dolly show me to my room and help me unpack?"

Nicki's eyes narrowed, and Becca was waiting for an *I don't want to,* but instead Nicki scooted to the edge of the sofa. "'Kay."

Becca picked up a suitcase just as Edie returned to the room.

"Let me help you with those." Edie had to be in her seventies, but she was still agile, her posture as straight as that of a younger woman.

"Thank you," Becca said, pretending she couldn't lift the other case. "I think I need help with this one."

"I'll help," Nicki piped up and ran over to Becca. It was the response Becca had wanted. Together, the trio clambered up the stairs.

On the landing, Becca looked around. There was a long hall with half a dozen doors. She remembered Della's saying that Cord had locked up Anette's room. She wondered which room it was. She shook her head; it didn't matter. Still, Anette had died over a year ago, and Becca felt that Cord should have disposed of her things, kept some for his daughter, perhaps given the rest away. Maybe the task was still too painful for him.

"Which room is mine?" she asked to divert her thoughts.

Nicki shrugged.

"The one at the end of the hall," Edie said. "Mine's at the other end, and—" she pointed to a door on the right "—that's Cord's. Blanche has the big suite downstairs."

"Thanks," Becca replied, entering the room. It was elegant with dark furniture and a four-poster bed. The decor was in peach and pale green, and very soothing. She was going to like it here.

"If you don't need anything else, I've got a function at the church I need to attend."

"No, and thanks for helping, Edie."

"Sure." Edie glanced at Nicki, who had crawled onto the bed. "Good luck. Bye, Nicki."

"Bye, Edie."

That was all very polite, but Becca knew it wouldn't last. Nicki had been allowed to do whatever she wanted for too long. When she couldn't get her way, she became angry and defiant. Becca would try to change all that because she knew it stemmed from Anette's death. Inside Nicki was still hurting…and so was Cord.

Becca opened her suitcase and began to put her clothes away in an old-fashioned wardrobe that looked priceless. She loved the antique furniture in this house.

Nicki sat, still on the bed, watching her. When Becca opened her makeup bag and set out the contents on the dresser, Nicki's eyes grew big.

"My mommy had thin..." Her voice trailed off as she realized what she was saying.

Becca sat beside her. "It's all right to talk about your mother."

"No, I don't want to." Nicki hung her head.

"Are you mad at your mother?"

Nicki didn't answer.

"I used to be mad at my mother."

Nicki glanced at her. "Why?"

Becca wasn't sure how much to say, but she went with her gut instincts. "Because she gave me away when I was a baby and I didn't know she was my mother until I was seventeen years old. I did mean and bad things because I thought she didn't love me."

"Did she?"

"Oh yeah."

"How you know?"

Becca placed a hand over her heart. "I know in here. Just like you know in there—" she put her hand on Nicki's chest "—that your mother loved you."

Nicki's eyes widened as she tried to understand what Becca was saying. Becca waited a minute, then said, "It's almost lunchtime. Why don't we go and see what Della's fixing?"

"I'm not hungry."

"Well, I am. I only had coffee this morning."

"I wanna go to my room."

Becca took a deep breath. "Nicki, sweetie, we're not going to your room. Please try to understand that. We'll do anything else that you want—swim, play dolls, swing... anything."

"No, I'm going to my room."

Before Becca could stop her, she jumped off the bed and ran for the door. Becca caught her halfway down the hall and swung her up. Nicki kicked and screamed, and Becca joined in as before.

CORD CAME THROUGH the back door, wiped his boots on the mat and stopped in his tracks. Screams. Oh God, how did he deal with this? He walked into the kitchen and asked Della, "Has this been going on since I left?"

Della looked up from the stove. "No, it just started."

Suddenly the screams stopped, and Cord wondered if he should interfere. He'd wait, he decided; he had to give Becca a chance. He felt sure she knew what she was doing. But it wasn't easy to hear his child in torment.

BECCA AND NICKI EYED each other. Nicki rubbed her eyes with one hand, still clutching Dolly with the other. "Why you do that?"

"Because I don't like it when you scream."

"I don't like it when you scream, either," Nicki muttered crossly.

"Well, then, let's not scream."

Nicki gave her an assessing look. "'Kay."

Becca smiled. It was a very tiny step, and there were so many more. "Ready to go downstairs and have lunch?"

Nicki shook her head. "I'm not hungry."

Another step to take, Becca thought. "That's okay. You can watch me eat." She set Nicki on her feet and they walked downstairs.

When they entered the kitchen and Nicki saw Cord, she ran to him, crying, "Daddy, Daddy, I wanna go to my room!"

It seemed to be a statement Nicki routinely used to get her way. Her room was where she could grieve in peace—but that wasn't happening anymore. Becca would insist on it.

They ate at the kitchen table. Della had prepared hamburgers, homemade French fries and cut-up fruit. Just like last night, Becca didn't force Nicki to eat; she filled Nicki's plate and cut the hamburger into four pieces so she could eat it easily. She poured lots of ketchup on her plate, then left Nicki alone and started on her own food.

"This burger is absolutely delicious," she said as she took a bite.

"Triple Creek beef. It's the best," Della told her.

"It certainly is," Becca agreed. "So you eat the beef raised here on the ranch?"

"Sure do," Cord said. "I won't sell something to a consumer that I won't eat myself."

Beef was something Becca got at the supermarket, not something in her yard. Or was that *pasture?* She didn't think she could possibly eat a cow she was personally acquainted with. But if she said that, Cord would laugh. She was a city girl, not used to country ways. Didn't mean she couldn't learn, though.

"Do you have a lot of cows?"

"Sometimes more than I want."

"I've never even touched a cow."

Cord raised his head. "You're kidding."

"No, like I said, I was raised on the coast. I've touched plenty of fish, but I've never even been near a cow."

A smile curved his lips. "We'll have to change that—give you a close-up view."

As they talked, Nicki started to eat her burger and nibble on the fruit. Cord looked at Becca and smiled. They were making progress, and she was warmed by that light in his eyes.

Della placed a bowl of chocolate pudding on the table.

"Look, Becca, it's chocolate," Nicki said with her mouth full of fruit.

"So I see." Becca grinned and spooned some into their bowls.

Nicki stuck her finger in hers, then glanced guiltily at Cord.

"It's okay, baby, you can eat it any way you want," he assured her.

Which she did. She got it on her face, her clothes and the table. Finally Becca took Nicki upstairs to wash her and change her outfit. The child was falling asleep. Staying up had taken its toll, and now she needed a nap. Becca carefully laid her in bed, covering her with a sheet.

Cord was waiting for her outside the door. Her stomach tightened as she encountered him—his tall lean frame, his rugged features and dark eyes. Funny how her body reacted to him.

"Thanks, Becca. I didn't think I was gonna survive after this morning. She fought me every step of the way. She doesn't seem to do that with you."

"She knows you'll give in," Becca said as they walked downstairs to the den.

"Yeah, but it's so hard to discipline a child when you know she's hurting."

"It'll get better."

"With you here, I know it will. You have a magic touch with her."

"Thank you" was all she could say.

They gazed at each other for a few seconds, then Cord said, "I'd better get back to work. I've got hay being baled and calves that need vaccinating. I'll see you later." He turned, then stopped. "Oh, Mrs. Witherspoon asked if she could have some time off to go see her sister, who's not feeling well. I said I'd have to ask you."

Becca shrugged, amazed that he was clearing this with her. "Sure, as long as Nicki knows she's coming back."

"Good." He nodded and left the room.

BECCA WAS ABOUT TO SIT DOWN in the den, when Blanche breezed in, wearing yet another skintight knit dress.

"I see you've arrived, sugar."

"Yes," Becca said curtly, not wanting a scene with Blanche.

Blanche looked at herself in a mirror on the wall and fluffed her hair, then she turned to Becca. "Let's get one thing straight," she said coolly. "This is *my* house and I've agreed to let you stay here for Nicki's sake. Cord seems to think you can help her, but at the first sign of trouble, your ass is out of here."

"Okay, Blanche," Becca replied in an equally cool voice. "You want to be straight? I will, too. First of all, I do not need a place to stay. I have my own apartment. I'm at the ranch to help Nicki—that's it. You keep referring to trouble, but I have no idea what you're talking about."

"I'm talking about my boys, sugar. Cord and Colton."

"So?"

"You have to be incredibly naive or just plain stupid. Colton's has been seeing you for years and now you're here with Cord."

Becca drew a patient breath. "I am not here with Cord, and Colton and I are just friends."

"Sugar, if I know anything, it's men and women, and they can never be friends. There isn't any such animal when it comes to the sexes."

"Then, you don't know your son because—"

"Oh, please," Blanche interrupted sarcastically. "Colton's been hanging around you all these years for one reason and one reason only. He wants you."

Was that true? She remembered how uncomfortable Colton had been when she'd brought the subject up this morning. She also remembered that he'd said he knew she didn't have "those feelings" for him. Oh God, that meant he *did* have "those feelings"—for her. All these years, and they'd never talked about it until today. They'd always been thrown together at family events, gone to movies and out for dinner, enjoyed each other's company. Maybe she *was* naive, because Gin saw Colton's attraction to her, and so did Blanche. Why hadn't she done something about it? Because they were friends and she didn't want to lose that friendship. Now what? She didn't know. Well…yes, she did. She simply had to let go of Colton so he could find the woman of his dreams. That woman was out there; it just wasn't her.

"I can see you know what I'm talking about," Blanche murmured.

Becca raised a hand to her throbbing head. "Blanche, it may be hard for you to believe, but Colton and I *are* friends. I met Cord at the funeral, and I saw him yesterday for the first time in a year. There's nothing going on between us. I hardly know him. As I already told you, I'm here to help his daughter. Nothing else."

"You're lying to me, sugar, and you're lying to yourself. And I don't think you even know it."

"What are you talking about?"

"Last night when I walked into this room, I saw the way you were looking at Cord and the way he was looking at you. There was enough electricity to jump-start Hoover Dam."

"Don't—"

"No, you listen to me," Blanche cut in. "Cord hasn't looked at a woman in over a year, so don't take those glances seriously. He just needs what all men need, and it has nothing to do with those fairy tales in your head."

Becca's eyes narowed. "You're a very crude person."

"I'm also realistic. You're a doctor with a medical practice, and here you are baby-sitting a five-year-old girl who throws temper tantrums."

"It's much more than that," Becca insisted.

"I don't think so. Cord and that witch, Edie, have just pampered Nicki since Anette's death. They haven't even tried to address the real issue, but I'm staying out of it. I've got better things to do."

Becca frowned. "I can see you love your granddaughter as much as you love everyone else."

Blanche peered at the diamond watch on her arm. "Damn, I've got to run. I'm gonna be late for my luncheon." She whirled toward the door. "Help yourself to my house, sugar, and anything in it, even my son." She threw the words over her shoulder in a baiting tone.

Becca felt the urge to stomp her feet and scream like Nicki. Blanche had that effect on her. She probably had that effect on most women. Becca wondered about her relationship with Anette; from the remarks Blanche had made, it didn't sound like a good one. And how did Nicki fit into the picture? Blanche didn't seem to care for her at all. Becca ran both hands through her hair and sank onto the sofa. The Prescotts were hard to take. She'd only been here a few hours and she was already yearning for the love and closeness of her own family. Maybe you had to leave something before you could truly appreciate it.

Becca leaned against the sofa and tried not to think about the things Blanche had said, but they were pounding through her head. She wasn't attracted to Colton in a sexual way, and Colton knew it. Then, why had he hung around all these years? *Oh, Colton,* she prayed, *please don't love me.* She couldn't bear the thought of hurting him. Colton had told her not to worry, but she did. They had to talk again, and soon.

Enough electricity to jump-start Hoover Dam.

Blanche was right about that. Becca couldn't deny that she was attracted to Cord; it was there every time she looked at him. She couldn't explain it and she sure didn't understand it. He had done nothing to encourage her, except love his little girl. She admired that in him. She'd noticed it the very first time she'd met him—his love, his heartfelt pain and his strength. She genuinely liked Cord Prescott, and beyond that she didn't want to think. Her goal was to guide Nicki through this rough time, then go back to Houston to begin her new life. She'd finally achieved the goal she'd been working toward for almost ten years.

Why wasn't she more excited about it? Why, instead, did she keep seeing two pairs of brown eyes? She was so afraid that Nicki might become attached to her, but what if Becca became attached to Nicki—and to Cord? Oh God, what was she going to do?

CHAPTER FIVE

BECCA RESOLVED to stop thinking about the negatives and do what she'd come here to do. As soon as Nicki opened her eyes, Becca didn't give her time to start crying or begging to stay in her room. She brushed the child's blond curls and put them in pigtails. She grabbed some children's books off the shelves, then carried Nicki—Dolly and all—downstairs, even though the child should walk on her own. When they reached the bottom of the stairs, she set Nicki on her feet, waiting for a temper tantrum. None came. Mainly, Becca suspected, because Nicki was still half-asleep. She took her hand and they walked into the kitchen.

Della glanced up from snapping green beans. "Well, ain't this something," she remarked.

"Could you tell me how to get to the backyard?" Becca asked. "Nicki and I are going outside for a while."

"You can go out this back door or through the French doors in the den."

"Thank you, Della," Becca replied. "We'll go out this door."

"Amazing," Della muttered, as Nicki followed Becca without a word of protest.

Outside, Becca caught her breath. To the right were garages, but to the left was a beautifully landscaped yard. The swimming pool had a cascading waterfall. At the shallow end was a kiddie pool, probably built for Nicki. The large swing set and sandbox, she knew, were also for Nicki. A decorative wrought-iron fence enclosed the yard, and green shrubs and flower beds surrounded it. Through the fence, Becca got a view of the ranch. Nearby were numerous barns and sheds, but her eyes were riveted on the valley below. Cattle dotted the landscape, so many that she couldn't even count them. Two tractors and a truck were moving toward the barns, and in the distance, several riders on horseback meandered among the cattle. It was like something out of a movie, an old western with John Wayne or Gary Cooper. She wondered if Cord was on horseback or in the truck or tractor.

She shook her head and walked to the covered patio. Placing the books on a table, she turned to Nicki, who stood there staring at her with sad eyes. Becca tried to get her to swing, to play ball, to run, to laugh, but nothing worked. This was going to be a long afternoon.

Finally they went in for a snack. Della had milk and cookies waiting. Nicki took a bite and drank half her milk, but that was it. When they went back outside, Becca noticed the books she'd put on the table.

She sat in a lounge chair and reached for one. "How about a story?"

Nicki shook her head. "No, I don't want to."

Becca opened the book, and on the title page was inscribed "To my precious baby, Nicki. I love you. Mommy." She saw that each book had a similar inscription. She wondered if Nicki even knew about it.

Becca opened the first book a little wider. "Do you want me to read this to you?"

"No," Nicki shouted, jerking it out of her hands.

Nicki knew what was written in the book—that was obvious. It was time to talk about Anette. "Your mommy wrote something on one of the pages."

Nicki's eyes grew stormy.

"She wrote that she loved you."

"No, she didn't," Nicki shouted, then added in a pitiful voice, "She went away."

Becca pulled the child onto her lap. She just held her for a moment, suddenly understanding the source of Nicki's pain. Nicki thought her mother didn't love her and that was why she'd left.

She kissed her forehead. "Sweetie, listen to me. Your mother didn't leave you. She was sick and she died."

"She didn't feel good," Nicki mumbled.

Evidently Anette had a lot of those days and Nicki was aware of that, which Becca hoped would make her mother's death easier for Nicki to grasp. "Yes," she said, opening the book, "but she loved you. It says so right here and you feel it in your heart—" she placed her hand on Nicki's chest "—don't you?"

Nicki nodded, then abruptly jumped up, dropping Dolly and running to where some crows were scratching in the flower beds. "No, no, no!" she screamed, shooing the birds away.

Becca didn't know what to think, but she quickly followed. Nicki knelt in the dirt and carefully spread leaves into a neat pile.

"Nicki, what's wrong?"

"They were bothering Goldie."

"Goldie?"

"That's my goldfish. He died, and Daddy and me buried him here. See?" She pointed to a pole in the fence. "Daddy marked a X on the fence so I'd know where Goldie was."

"I see," Becca said, thinking this over. Did Nicki know where her mother was buried? That sense of not knowing where her mother was could result from never having seen her grave. Becca would have to find out about this.

She took Nicki's hand. "Goldie's fine. Come, let's sit on the swings."

Nicki trudged obediently to the swings and sat there with her head down. Becca could only imagine what she was thinking.

"Nicki, have you ever been to your mother's grave?"

Nicki looked at her with big eyes, then shook her head. Becca had thought as much. Cord was trying to protect her, but Nicki needed to see the place where her mother was buried.

"Would you like to go?"

Her eyes grew even bigger. "Can I?"

"Sure, and we'll take some flowers." She made that decision without thinking. Cord wasn't going to like this, she felt sure. Maybe she should've tried to explain it to him first, but it was too late.

"Roses!" Nicki clapped her hands together. "Mommy loves red roses."

Before Becca could curb her excitement, Cord came through the back gate. Nicki immediately ran to him. "Daddy, Daddy," she cried, and he swung her up in his arms.

"How's my baby?" Cord asked.

"Becca and me, we…we…" She twisted her hands in her excitement.

"Slow down so you can tell me," he instructed gently.

"Becca and me, we…we gonna go to Mommy's grave."

"What!" The blood drained from his face and he pinned Becca with a cold stare.

"Yeah, Daddy, and we gonna takes roses 'cause Mommy likes them."

"Nicki, sweetie, you'd better go get Dolly." Becca intervened, knowing she had to get Cord alone. "She looks awfully lonely."

"'Kay," she said, and ran to the patio.

"How could you?" Cord demanded as soon as Nicki was out of earshot. "I never expected you'd do something like *this*. Go to Anette's grave? That's insane!"

"Would you listen to me for just a second?"

"No, I don't think so. I told you there're just so many things I'll tolerate, and this isn't one of them."

Becca brushed back her hair with an angry gesture. "That's too bad, Cord, because Nicki needs to know where her mother is."

"What are you talking about?"

She told him about the books and Goldie, and she could see him calming down. "She thinks her mother left because she didn't love her. She doesn't understand that she's in a grave—like Goldie. She *needs* to see that."

He pulled off his hat and shoved a hand through his hair. "Becca, I—"

"Look at her. She's excited at the prospect."

His eyes caught hers. "The cemetery is such a depressing place."

"It's part of life and you can't shield her from that. Besides, we'll be with her."

The word *we'll* sounded so good to him. What would she say if he told her he needed someone with him when he went there, too? He hadn't been to the cemetery since Anette's headstone was set. After the sadness and loss had worn off, he'd felt angry. He still did. So angry that she'd hurt him and Nicki like this. It seemed impossible to get through those emotions, and he had no real desire to visit Anette's grave. Now Becca wanted him to take Nicki. He didn't know if he could do it.

At his hesitation, Becca said, "I can't take her without your permission."

They continued to stare at each other, and Cord suddenly

realized he didn't have much of a choice. For his daughter, he would do anything—even visit her mother's grave. One thought kept running through his mind: *Becca will make it easier for both of us.*

"Let me go inside and get cleaned up, then we'll go."

Becca smiled, and his chest tightened. God, she was beautiful.

"Thank you, Cord. I know this is hard, but I believe it's what Nicki needs."

"You're the doctor," he said, moving toward the house. "Daddy will be right back," he called to Nicki.

"'Kay," she answered.

Inside, he took a long breath. He'd never realized that having Becca here would be so difficult for him. He hadn't felt the inclination to be with a woman in over a year. At forty-two, he'd thought those urges were gone; looking at Becca, he knew they weren't. But he could control them, and he would. Being Colton's girlfriend put her way off-limits. Not to mention the fact that she was too young. He wouldn't be foolish like his father. Becca was here for Nicki and that was the only interest he had in her. He had to keep telling himself that.

SOON THEY WERE IN CORD'S TRUCK and traveling toward Houston. The truck was a four-door cab with leather seats and every feature available. To Becca's astonishment it rode like a car. Becca sat in the passenger seat, with Nicki in the back.

"We have to get flowers, Daddy," Nicki reminded him.

"Okay, baby," Cord said, pulling into a small flower shop.

Before they could stop her, Nicki crawled out of the truck, leaving Dolly on the seat. "I have to pick them out. I know what Mommy likes."

Cord glanced at Becca, and they slowly followed.

In the flower shop Nicki became shy and didn't say a word.

"We'd like to see some red roses, please," Cord said.

The florist brought out a huge vase of red roses.

Cord looked at Nicki. "What do you think?"

Nicki held up three fingers. "We need three."

Cord didn't know why they needed three, but he paid the lady and she put them in a box. Nicki carried the box to the truck and sat with the roses on her lap.

A few minutes later, Cord drove through the gates of the cemetery, parking near Anette's grave. He gulped a couple of deep breaths, then got out of the truck. Taking Nicki's hand, he made his way to the grave. They stood for a while, staring at the headstone. *ANETTE PRESCOTT* was written in bold letters.

Pain and memories overwhelmed Cord, and he tried to dredge up Anette's face, but he couldn't. It was shadowy; he couldn't make it out. God, what was wrong with him? he thought, panicking a little. He should be able to see his wife's face.

Cord was lost in his own inner pain, so Becca led Nicki to the gravestone. Nicki pointed to the lettering. "That's my mommy's name," she whispered.

Becca knelt down. "Yes, it is. This is where your mommy's buried."

"Oh," she whispered again, her little arms locked tightly around the box of roses.

"You want to put the roses on the grave?"

"'Kay."

Becca opened the box. Nicki removed the roses and placed them, one by one, on the grave.

"You can talk to her if you want," Becca said.

Nicki twisted her hands. "Will she hear me?"

"Yes, she'll hear you."

Nicki stared at the roses, and Becca knew she was nervous, so she pulled the child into her arms. “Go ahead, say what you want to.”

“I brought you flowers, Mommy,” Nicki said in a breathless voice. She glanced at Becca. Becca nodded and Nicki continued. “Red roses that you like. One’s from me, one’s from Daddy and one’s from Becca.”

Again Nicki turned to Becca. “Anything else you want to say?” Becca asked.

Nicki was still twisting her hands, and Becca sensed that now was the time to get everything out in the open. “If you’re mad at your mother, tell her.”

Nicki shook her head. “I’m not mad at her.” She looked at the grave. “I’m not mad at you, Mommy. You didn’t feel good. Do you feel better now?”

A lump formed in Becca’s throat, and her arms tightened around Nicki. “Oh, yes, she feels much better because you’re here.”

She held her for a little while longer, then got to her feet. “Ready to go?”

“Uh-huh.”

Becca stopped when she saw Cord’s shattered expression. He held his hat in his hands, his fingers crushing the Stetson. It was painful to watch. She wondered how many times he’d been to Anette’s grave. From his reaction, not often.

“Cord,” she said tentatively.

His head jerked in the direction of her voice, but all he could hear was Nicki’s words. *I’m not mad at you, Mommy. You didn’t feel good.* He heard the awe and joy she felt at being near her mother again. Why hadn’t he brought her here? Why hadn’t he seen that his child needed to visit her mother’s grave? He felt like a failure as a father because he’d let his hurt and pride get in the way. He had failed Nicki.

"Cord."

He made an effort to collect himself. "Yes."

"Are you ready?"

"Sure."

The drive from the cemetery was quiet, until Nicki started asking questions.

"Becca?"

"Hmm?"

"Is my Mommy 'cared?"

"No, sweetie, she's at peace and she's in heaven." She looked surreptitiously over at Cord, to make sure he approved of that answer. He nodded.

"Becca?"

"Hmm?"

"Is heaven a nice place?"

"Very nice, and no one feels bad in heaven."

"Oh."

On and on it went. Nicki kept asking questions. Cord noticed that she never asked him, just Becca, and he was beginning to feel left out, which was patently ridiculous. But he wanted Nicki to turn to *him*. He wanted to be the one to help her, even though he'd realized months ago that he couldn't. He was too emotionally involved. It took someone like Becca to free Nicki from the doubts and fears caused by Anette's death.

"Daddy."

Cord was so consumed by his own misery that he didn't hear Nicki the first time.

"Daddy!"

"Yes, baby. What is it?"

"Can I have an ice cream?"

He glanced at Becca and smiled. He couldn't help it. His baby wanted to eat. Hallelujah. He didn't even care that it was close to supper.

"Sure," he replied happily.

"I want chocolate on mine. Becca does, too."

"Really?" Cord raised an eyebrow at Becca.

She shrugged. "I have a thing for chocolate."

"Yeah, I think I heard that before." The glint in his eyes made her stomach tense excitedly.

They each had a cone dipped in chocolate, and it was a joy to watch Nicki gobble hers. Cord got ice cream on his mustache, and Becca had the ludicrous urge to lick it off. As he wiped it away with a napkin, her fantasy dissolved into a pleasurable ache.

When they got back to the ranch, Della had supper waiting. As usual, Edie was eating in her room and Blanche was out. They sat at the kitchen table, just the three of them. Nicki hadn't stopped talking during their drive home or during the meal; finally her head started to bob and Becca saw that she was about to fall asleep.

Becca got to her feet. "I'll take her to bed."

"I can put my own child to bed," Cord snapped as he scooped Nicki up.

"Sure," Becca said, wondering what that was about. He seemed put out with her. Maybe he was still feeling emotional over the visit to the cemetery. Whatever it was, she didn't like the feeling that he was upset with her.

CORD STRIPPED NICKI OUT OF her clothes and pulled her nightgown over her head, then held her tightly in his arms. "I love you, baby," he whispered in her hair.

"Love you, Daddy," she answered sleepily.

His child was back. The process of healing had started. He knew there'd still be bad days, but he felt so much better about things. Yet he also felt helpless because he hadn't been able to do this for her, his own daughter. And he'd snapped at Becca for no reason. Oh God, he had to apologize for that.

He gently tucked Nicki in and removed the pigtail bands from her hair. He stood for a moment, staring at his precious child. He could finally see the light at the end of the long, dark tunnel. They were going to make it; he knew that with certainty.

Now he had to find Becca.

DELLA SAID SHE'D GONE to her room, so he went back upstairs. He knocked on her door.

She opened it with a hairbrush in her hand. "Cord," she said in surprise.

"Hi. Could I talk to you for a minute?"

"Sure." She moved aside to let him in.

"I'm sorry to bother you."

"It's okay. I was just brushing my hair before my shower. Something I do every night."

He'd love to watch that ritual, but shook his head to rid himself of those thoughts. "I have to apologize," he said quickly, sitting in a chair positioned near the door.

"For what?"

"For snapping at you and being in a disagreeable mood."

She sat on the bed facing him. "I know this isn't easy for you."

"No, it's not, but that's no reason to get angry at you."

"It's okay, Cord."

"But it isn't," he said earnestly. "I've tried everything I know to help my daughter deal with her mother's death, but nothing worked. Things just got worse and worse. You've been here two days, and she's almost back to normal." He sighed. "I'm thrilled—and deeply grateful—but I don't feel like much of a father."

She hated that look on his face. "I've been trained to deal with children. Sometimes I can read them, other times I can't. I got lucky with Nicki."

"I don't think luck has anything to do with it."

"I'll take that as a compliment."

His eyes met hers. "It was meant as one."

He was the first to glance away. He rested his elbows on his knees and clasped his hands. "You see, I've only been to the cemetery once since Anette died, and that was when they installed the headstone. I've been so angry at her that…"

When he didn't say anything else, she asked, "Is that why you locked her room?"

His eyes swung to hers again. "How do you know that?"

"Della mentioned it."

"Oh," he said in a quiet tone, staring down at his hands. "Partly, I suppose. I didn't want to be reminded of those memories, and I didn't want Nicki going in there and remembering, either." He paused, then added, "I felt the same way about the cemetery. That was selfish on my part. I should have considered Nicki's feelings, but I thought it would just hurt her more."

"Stop blaming yourself. You did the best you could under the circumstances."

"No, I didn't. I never should have married Anette. Ranching life wasn't for her, but a man doesn't think too clearly with his head in the clouds."

He loved his wife. She should be happy about that, but she wasn't. She didn't want him to love… Oh God, she was getting in too deep, too fast. She had to stop this.

"The main thing is that Nicki's getting better," she said to return to a subject she was comfortable with.

"Yes, thanks to you."

Their eyes met again, and for a moment she was lost in feelings she wanted to deny.

"Colton called this morning," Cord said abruptly.

"Oh." Her voice was low and detached.

"I invited him for the weekend. I thought you might like that."

She swallowed. "What did he say?"

"He said he had a lot to do, but he'd try."

"Colton's always busy."

"But he makes time for you, doesn't he?" If she was the woman in *his* life, he'd move heaven and earth to be with her.

She frowned. "My relationship with Colton is hard to explain."

"You don't have to explain it to me."

She didn't seem to hear him. "Colton and I have been friends for ages."

"I know. He's talked about you a lot."

Her eyes grew mischievous. "Don't believe everything you've heard."

"Oh, I think I will," he said, getting to his feet. "I'd better let you take your shower. And thanks for everything."

She stood, too. "You're very welcome."

They stared at each other, and then Cord started to move away, but he turned back. Almost in slow motion he took her in his arms. She wrapped her own arms around his waist and laid her head against his chest. Her heart was beating so fast that she couldn't hear or think. All she could do was feel his hard, lean body, the strength of his arms and the sadness that was such a part of him.

"Thank you, Becca," he whispered, then released her and walked out the door.

Becca felt empty and alone. She wanted his arms back. She wanted all of him. For years, she had waited for these feelings, but she'd never dreamed they'd happen with a man who didn't want her in the same way. She sank heavily onto the bed. Now what?

WHAT WAS HE DOING? Cord berated himself as he strolled to his room. He shouldn't have touched her. But he couldn't resist. He could still feel her softness, smell the scent of her hair. And she was Colton's lover. That truth jolted him and stiffened his resolve to stay away from her. He had to, no matter how he was beginning to feel about her. She belonged to Colton.

CHAPTER SIX

BECCA FOUND that the next few days were easy and difficult at the same time. Nicki was progressing. She was playing, laughing and learning to be a kid again. She didn't mention going to her mother's grave; she now knew where her mother was, and that seemed to satisfy her.

Dealing with Nicki was not a problem. Dealing with her father was. They discussed Nicki every night, and she was so drawn to him, so aware of him, but he was creating a distance between them. He left early in the morning and didn't return until almost dark. He seemed to be avoiding her, and she didn't understand it. He'd been so considerate, even loving, that night in her room. She thought they'd reached a new level in their relationship, but evidently not. If he wanted to avoid *her,* that was fine, but he couldn't avoid his daughter. Things had to change. In fact, a *lot* of things had to change in the Prescott house.

Nicki needed a stable family environment. Becca didn't see any of that. She and Nicki were alone each and every day. When Edie wasn't at church functions, she stayed in her room. Blanche slept till almost noon, then left to go to her club in Houston and didn't get home until Nicki was in bed. Becca was the only person Nicki consistently interacted with, and she needed more than that. She needed grown-ups to guide her and she needed to be with children her own age. Becca planned to talk to Cord about this as soon as possible.

She had told Nicki she'd only be here for a few days and

that Mrs. Witherspoon would be returning. Nicki seemed to understand, but Becca wasn't sure. If Nicki became too attached to her, then her departure would be traumatic. It would destroy all the progress they'd made. She didn't want to think about her own feelings in the matter because they were irrelevant. Besides, she could handle them.

That night, Becca waited for Cord in the den. Every evening he bathed Nicki and put her to bed, then read her a story until she fell asleep. It was their little ritual, and Becca didn't intrude. Nicki needed all the time she could get with her father.

Deep in thought, Cord walked into the den—and stopped suddenly when he saw Becca sitting on the sofa. She was usually in her room by now. At the sight of her in jeans and a knit top, with her dark hair hanging loose around her shoulders, his body tightened with unbelievable need. That reaction seemed to be getting more frequent—which was why he was trying to stay away from her. She was beautiful, fresh, exciting and young, young, young—way too young for him. And she was Colton's. He had to keep saying that to himself, but somehow it wasn't working. God, he was in so much trouble.

"May I speak to you?" she asked when she saw him.

Cord moved to his chair and sat down. "Sure," he replied in a distant voice.

She frowned. "Cord, are you upset with me?"

"No, of course not," he answered in that same tone. "How can I be upset with someone who's given me back my daughter?"

"That's what I want to talk about—Nicki."

"Is something wrong?" he asked urgently.

"Yes, she needs more interaction with her family. Blanche and Edie are never here and you're gone all day."

"It's a busy time with roundup and baling hay."

"You're here on the ranch. Why can't you have lunch with her?"

"It's not that simple. When I have a pen full of calves to be tagged, vaccinated and branded, I can't just drop everything. Besides, I'm miles from the house."

"Don't you eat?"

"Gus always carries an ice chest full of cold cuts for the ranch hands. We have a quick bite and get back to work."

"Can Nicki and I join you?"

"Beg your pardon?"

"If you'll give me directions, I can drive us to where you'll be working."

"This is a ranch. We don't have highways."

Her eyes narrowed. "I didn't think you did."

"If I told you to drive due south for fifteen miles, would you know what I was talking about?"

"Yes, if you gave me a starting point."

God, she was serious—absolutely serious. Anette had lived here for years, and she'd never left the house or the backyard. The cows and horses frightened her, and she found the vastness of the property terrifying. Apparently Becca didn't have that problem.

She watched him for a moment. "Cord, you're acting like you'd rather I wasn't here anymore. If that's the case—"

"No," he interrupted. His emotions were contradictory. He was trying to stay away from her, but he didn't want her to leave or feel as if he didn't need her. "You're the only thing Nicki talks about, and now that she's better, I'm trying to catch up on the work I've put off to be with her. That's all, Becca. You're very welcome here."

Too welcome. That's the problem.

"And you can bring Nicki to where I'm working anytime you want." His eyes held hers. "Can you ride?"

"You mean, like a horse?"

He grinned. "Yeah, like a horse."

"No, I've never been near one."

Another city girl.

He shook off that thought. "We have a couple of Jeeps you can take. You'd ruin your car driving it in a pasture. Can you drive a standard shift?"

"Yes," she replied in a bright voice. "I learned in my dad's old—" She stopped as she realized what she was saying. "I mean, in my grandfather's old truck. Sometimes I have trouble keeping parents and grandparents straight."

She was trying to be lighthearted, but he saw the bewilderment and pain that flashed in her eyes. "Colton told me what happened. That must've been hard for you."

She linked her fingers. "Yes, it was."

Cord felt an overwhelming need to comfort her. He wanted to put his arms around her, the way she'd done to him the day of the funeral, but he couldn't touch her. He'd made a promise to himself.

"I'm sure that's why you're so good with Nicki. You can identify with her pain. You didn't actually lose a mother, but you…"

"Yes, I did," she said quietly. "I lost a mother and I gained my real one. I was confused, and I was angry, especially at Emily because she gave me away. But love has incredible healing powers." She smiled slightly.

"You're incredible." He meant it. Colton was the luckiest man on earth.

"I don't know about that," she said quietly. "I've rarely stayed angry for long. Once I tell the person I'm angry with how I feel, I'm able to deal with whatever's bothering me. Back then, though, I didn't want to talk and I went through a destructive period. Emily was patient and understanding, even though she was hurting as much as I was, which I didn't understand until later. Luckily, we got through that rough time, and I'm grateful for the relationship I have with my parents *and* my grandparents."

Becca couldn't believe she was telling him all this. Maybe it was because she knew he had a compassionate heart and she was consoled by the empathy in his eyes. She glanced down at her hands. "But sometimes I feel…"

"What?" he prompted.

She looked up. "I feel as if they're smothering me. So many people love me and I love them. But I feel pulled in too many directions and I…" She blinked away a tear as she tried to regain control of her emotions.

He got up to sit beside her. He'd said he wouldn't touch her, but he found himself reaching for her hand. Her fingers locked tightly around his.

"At times I still have difficulty figuring out who I am."

His other hand touched her cheek. "You're Becca, a beautiful woman, inside and out."

She smiled through the tears. "I think I've heard that line before."

"From many eager guys, I'm sure." He was suddenly jealous of all those guys.

She took a quick breath. It was so easy to talk to him that she'd told him things she'd never shared with anyone, not even Gin.

"I'm sorry. I shouldn't have unloaded on you like that. I'm not usually so weepy."

"Don't worry about it," he said softly. "After what you've done for Nicki, you can unload on me anytime you want."

She removed her hand from his and brushed her hair back in a nervous gesture. If he kept holding her hand, she was going to kiss him—to experience all those feeling that were about to overtake her. He didn't reciprocate her feelings, though, and that was the only thing that stopped her.

"Nicki," she said quickly to cover her embarrassment.

"That's who we were talking about before I got sidetracked. As I started to say, I feel Nicki needs more interaction with her family, especially Blanche and Edie because they live here."

"We're not much of a family, Becca," he said in a regretful tone, "but I guess you've figured that out. Edie and Blanche have been at each other's throats since the day Pa married Blanche. That's been going on for over forty years, and it's not going to change, not even for Nicki."

"Has Edie always lived here? Has she never married or left home?" Becca thought that if she knew more about Edie and Blanche, she might be able to understand them—at least a little.

"She went to Texas A&M to become a veterinarian. She came home for a weekend to see her sister, who'd been married a couple of years and just found out she was pregnant. They went on a shopping trip to Houston with their mother and were involved in a bad car accident. Edie's mother and sister didn't survive. Edie was injured and spent months in the hospital. She was engaged at the time. Pa said the guy came around for a while, then eventually stopped coming. After Edie recovered from the accident, she never went back to school. She took care of the house and helped Pa. It was just the two of them for several years."

"Then he married Blanche," Becca murmured. "And things have never been the same for Edie."

"That about sums it up. And Pa didn't help matters. He was from the old school, where the man was the head of the household and his decisions were not to be questioned. The women were supposed to be pampered and taken care of. Pa never explained anything to them or tried to help with the transition. He just expected them to accept his decision."

"That must've been difficult for both of them," Becca said.

"Yeah, Edie was twenty-seven at the time, and sharing

the house and Pa with a younger woman didn't sit well with her."

"How old was Mr. Prescott when he died?"

"Ninety-six, and he rode a horse until the day before his death. He got dizzy after riding and I had to carry him into the house. The next day he quietly passed away with Blanche and me by his side."

She could hear the love for his father in his voice. "So your parents were married for thirty-six years?"

"Yep."

"He lived to see all his sons grown," Becca added.

"Sure did. I was thirty-two when he died."

"And the apple of his eye," she said, smiling.

He glanced at her. "Some people say that, and I have to admit Pa and I were close. We both enjoyed ranching, and he taught me everything I know. He argued a lot with Clay and Colton because he didn't understand either of them."

"Did Blanche?"

"Blanche is Blanche and it's hard to explain her, but she's never had much interest in her sons."

"But she was always there for your father."

"Yep, I'd have to say she was."

"Then, that has to count for something."

"Becca, don't go looking for miracles," he told her shortly. "There aren't any in this house."

"Are you sure?"

"What do you mean?"

"I mean, have you asked Blanche or Edie to share in Nicki's life? Like having supper with her in the evenings or just spending time with her?"

Cord rubbed his jaw. "No, because I know it's a waste of my breath."

"Do you mind if I try?"

He shook his head in amusement. "If you can get my

mother to take an interest in my daughter, hell will freeze over, as the saying goes. Blanche is interested in no one but herself. I learned that when I was a kid, but if you want to try, go ahead."

"I will," she said, determined to make some changes for Nicki's sake. "I'd also like to enroll Nicki in a play group. She needs to be around children her own age."

He frowned. "Do you think she's ready for that?"

"Yes."

"Then, I trust your judgment. It hasn't been wrong so far."

"Thank you," she said sincerely. "And tomorrow we'll pay you a visit on the ranch."

He shook his head. "Not tomorrow. It's Saturday and I have to take care of business in town. Besides, Colton will probably be coming for a visit. Don't you want to stay close to the house for that?"

"No. Anyway, if Colton was going to visit, he would've called me," she said, to his surprise.

"He hasn't called you?" He couldn't keep the shock out of his voice. "He's not coming to see you?"

She tucked a strand of hair behind her ear, deciding to set him straight about Colton. "No, we don't have that kind of relationship. Colton was there when I found out about my parents. I didn't like him at first, but he spent a lot of time at our house because of his business dealings with my father. Gradually, I began to like him and we became friends. When he opened an office in Houston, I saw more of him. He'd call and take me out to dinner, to a movie, whatever. Colton and I are friends, very good friends. That's all."

She could see he didn't believe her. "It's true. You can ask Colton."

Cord still wasn't sure about that; however, it really didn't make a difference. Becca was too young for him, anyway. But, oh, she was so damn good to look at and to be with.

Becca got to her feet. "Now, I expect you to be home in time to have supper with your daughter tomorrow. I'm going upstairs to speak with Edie, and I'll talk to Blanche when she gets in."

"You're serious about this, aren't you?"

"Yes."

"Becca, don't expect too much."

"Oh, I do, Cordell Prescott," she said mischievously. "And you'd better remember that."

As he watched her leave the room, he had a feeling that hell was about to freeze over.

BECCA KNOCKED on Edie's door. There was no answer, so she knocked again. Suddenly the door swung open. Edie stood there in a blue cotton robe, her gray hair frizzed as if she'd been sleeping.

"I'm sorry. I didn't mean to wake you."

"I was catnapping." She waved off Becca's apology and tried to tame her hair.

"I just wanted to talk to you for a second."

"Okay," Edie said, and Becca followed her into the suite. There was a bedroom area, a sitting room that held a tiny refrigerator and microwave, and a small alcove complete with a computer and electronic sound equipment. Floor-to-ceiling bookshelves covered one wall.

No wonder Edie stayed in her room; this was her own little world away from her stepmother.

"I wanted to talk about Nicki."

"She's doing so well," Edie said. "I don't hear the crying or screaming anymore."

"Yes, she is, and I'd like that progress to continue."

"Of course, and if I can help I will."

"I'm glad to hear that, because Nicki needs to feel her family's love. And I was hoping you'd join us for supper tomorrow night."

Edie's calm face became hard. "Will the harlot be there?"

"If you mean Blanche, yes, I hope so. I'm asking her, too."

"Then, I won't be there. I'm happy having dinner in my room. I can't breathe the same air as that woman."

"Not even for Nicki?"

Edie remained silent, and Becca knew this was going to be as hard as Cord had predicted. Time to bring out the guilt.

"You love Nicki. I know you do."

"Yes, she's like a ray of sunshine, even though her mother was..." Edie shook her head as if to clear it. "But that has nothing to do with Blanche. She destroyed my life and she destroyed Pa's."

"How did she destroy your pa's? She gave him the sons he wanted."

Edie paled, and Becca knew she was hitting close to home. "And you love those sons. Actually, you raised them, didn't you?" Becca was basing this on what Colton had told her.

"The nanny was incompetent! I was the one who got up with them in the middle of the night. I was the one who rocked them when they were sick. I was always here for them. Their mother wasn't."

"So she gave you a great gift."

Edie's face became rigid. "What are you talking about?"

"I'm talking about Clay, Cord and Colton. She practically gave them to you."

"Because *she* didn't want them."

"But Mr. Prescott did."

Edie's skin turned almost white. "Pa always wanted sons and he let that harlot talk him into—"

"Come on, Edie, even you have to admit she probably didn't have to do much talking."

"No, men that age aren't too discriminating."

Becca wanted to laugh but didn't. She was just glad Edie had a sense of humor.

"Edie, it's time to let go of the resentment and hatred."

"She's a vile woman."

Becca had to admit that Blanche wasn't on her list of favorite people, either, but there had to be a way to pull this family together. "Bottom line, Edie, I was hoping you'd do what's best for Nicki."

There was no answer, so Becca pushed further. "And by staying in your room, you're letting Blanche win."

That got a reaction. "I will *never* let her win!"

"Then, you'll be there for dinner?"

"I'll be there."

Becca had to get one thing clear. "I don't want this to turn into a scene, especially in front of Nicki."

Edie straightened to her full height. "I will behave like a lady, but a harlot is a harlot, no matter how much money is lavished on her."

"Okay," Becca said slowly, thinking maybe she should've left well enough alone. "Tomorrow at six, and thanks. I know you'll make this a wonderful evening for Nicki."

Yeah right, she thought as she left. A barroom brawl was more likely. Two women with strong points of view and neither willing to give in. This could turn out to be awful. Why had she started it? For Nicki. And she'd see it through. Now she had to talk to Blanche, which was going to be as much fun as stepping on a rattlesnake.

FROM HER ROOM, Becca had a view of the garages, and when she saw a flash of headlights she knew Blanche was home. After ten minutes, she went downstairs.

Becca tapped on her door. "Blanche, it's Becca."

"Come in," Blanche called.

Becca entered the room and stopped in her tracks. Blanche stood in front of a full-length mirror preening without a stitch of clothing on. And she made no move to cover herself.

"What do you want, sugar?"

"I…uh…I…" She was at a loss for words.

"What's the matter? Haven't you ever seen a naked woman before?"

"Plenty, but never one without any modesty," Becca replied shortly.

"Come on, Becca, you're a doctor," Blanche said, admiring herself in the mirror. "Have you ever seen a woman my age with a body like this?"

Becca shut the door and walked closer. She found it a little bizarre to be studying Blanche's naked form, but Blanche didn't mind. That was obvious. Her butt was too tight—butt tuck. Her stomach flat—tummy tuck. And her breasts were too pert for a woman of sixtyplus. Blanche had had a lot of work done.

"No, I haven't," she answered. "Not without plastic surgery."

Blanche swung to face her. "How dare you," she spat, and quickly reached for her black silk robe.

"As you said, Blanche, I'm a doctor. I can tell."

"You can't tell a thing. What do you want, anyway?"

"I want to talk about family unity."

"What the hell is that and what business is it of yours?"

"It's about Nicki and the fact that she needs a loving family around her."

"Cord's very loving, as I'm sure you've noticed, and this doesn't concern me. Cord's told me that many times." Blanche sat at her dressing table and began to remove her makeup.

"Don't you want to be involved in your granddaughter's life?"

Blanche met her eyes in the mirror. "Sugar, I'm not the motherly type, nor am I interested in being a grandmother."

Becca could only stare at her. Didn't this woman have any feelings at all? Or was she an expert at masking them?

Blanche didn't miss her disapproving expression. "Is that too cold for you?"

"I just find your attitude hard to understand."

"Let me tell you something, sugar. I grew up fast and hard. My mother ran a beer joint on the outskirts of Houston and we lived above it. I never knew who my father was. I don't think my mother did, either. There were so many 'uncles' and 'special friends' that I lost track. I guess I was about twelve when men started hitting on me. You know what my mother told me?"

Becca shook her head, afraid to even hazard a guess because she had a feeling the answer would taint everything she believed about youth and innocence.

"She said to enjoy it, but to make damn sure I got everything I could out of the man."

Becca tried to keep the shock from her face, but knew she'd failed. Gin's mother worked in a bar and was on husband number five, but she loved Gin and would never suggest she do such a thing. She'd protected Gin from that kind of behavior. Of course, Gin and her mom had problems, but nothing like this.

"So you see, I grew up with what you might call a different kind of love. I don't know the kind of love you're talking about. The only time I came close was with Claybourne. He used to come into the bar, and I could see the way he'd watch me. He never tried anything like the other men. We talked a lot. He told me that when I turned eighteen he was going to marry me. I laughed and said I'd be waiting. He kept his word.

The day I had my eighteenth birthday, he came back and I left with him. I haven't seen the bar or my mother since. I've never regretted marrying Claybourne. He was my ticket out and he knew it. We were always honest with each other. He wanted a son. I wanted freedom. I didn't want to be a mother, but I had the boys for Claybourne. Doesn't mean I don't care about them. Just means I look at life a little differently than other people."

Becca hadn't dreamed she'd get such a glimpse into Blanche's life. She felt great sympathy for that young girl who had never known true love or happiness. But Becca was well aware that her sympathy was wasted on Blanche.

"If you care about Cord, then you must care for Nicki."

Blanche turned to face her. "What are you getting at?"

"Nicki's improved so much, and I think a show of unity from the family would benefit her. All I'm asking is for her grandmother and her aunt to have dinner with her a couple of times a week."

"You want me to sit down to a cozy family dinner with the witch of Triple Creek?"

"With Edie, yes."

"Forget it, sugar. She hates my guts and I despise the pompous twit."

Trying to play on Blanche's heartstrings was futile, since they didn't seem to exist; Blanche required a different strategy. Becca noticed the mirror and immediately knew how to reach her.

"Does Cord know about your many nips and tucks?" She was guessing he didn't.

"It's none of his business."

"Good, then you won't mind if I mention it to him—and Edie."

Blanche stood and tightened the belt on her robe. "Are you trying to blackmail me?"

"Oh, blackmail is such an offensive word. I care to think of it as gentle persuasion."

Blanche's eyes narrowed. "I don't think you know who you're dealing with, sugar."

"Oh, but I do," Becca assured her. "I'm dealing with a woman who's struggled all her life to survive in a world that hasn't been kind to her. She's tough, crude and unbelievably hard-hearted, but underneath I'm hoping she has a tiny glimmer of concern for her granddaughter."

Blanche's eyes didn't waver. "Your hope is in vain."

Becca didn't back down, even though her knees were beginning to feel weak. "Okay," she said. "At least we know where we stand." She moved toward the door and turned back. "Let's see, that's a tummy tuck, a butt lift, breast enhancement and—oh, the face. You've had so much done to the face, I hardly knew where to start. I'm just trying to get this straight. I'm sure Edie will want all the details."

"I don't care what that bitch thinks."

"Fine," Becca said, and continued to the door. She would've sworn that Blanche would do anything to keep Edie from finding out her secret. Maybe she'd been—

"You little bitch."

Becca looked back. "Are you talking to me?"

"You got spunk. I admire that," Blanche said, watching her closely.

"Then, we'll expect you tomorrow night at six. Cord and Nicki will be pleased."

Blanche walked over to her. "Don't let this little victory go to your head, sugar. I'm still keeping an eye on you. Cord's not too wise when it comes to women. He doesn't need another city girl in his life. The last one almost destroyed him."

"You mentioned Anette before. What do you know about her death?"

Blanche took a step closer. "She drank herself into oblivion because she was a weak simpering idiot. Now, get your ass out of my room before I really get upset."

Becca left. She'd pushed enough buttons for one night. But a series of questions followed her to her room. Why was Blanche so bitter about Anette? Was something going on that Cord didn't know about? Blanche had said she'd do anything to protect her sons. How far would she go to accomplish that?

CHAPTER SEVEN

CORD HAD BREAKFAST with Becca and Nicki before he left to take care of his business. Becca worked with Della to plan a special meal for the evening; Della clearly thought she was out of her mind. And maybe she was. She just wanted this family to feel some sort of togetherness instead of the constant tension that seemed to permeate the place.

She and Nicki picked flowers from the backyard for the table and then arranged them in a crystal vase. Nicki wasn't as excited as Becca had thought she'd be. She didn't seem to be looking forward to the evening so much as resigned to it, which Becca didn't understand. Maybe she'd been hoping for too much. She couldn't help remembering the occasions when she and Rose would prepare a special table for Emily. She was always so excited at the prospect of seeing Emily. But then, there was a simple difference between their family and the Prescotts. Love. That was what had gotten them through the difficult times.

Nicki didn't have anything that even resembled a loving relationship with Blanche. She'd probably witnessed more arguments than a five-year-old should. Becca prayed everyone would be on their best behavior tonight.

That afternoon she read to Nicki on the patio. The fresh air was intoxicating, and Nicki fell asleep in her arms. Becca stared at the inscription in the book. The woman who'd written those words loved her child. That was very clear. Then, why would she kill herself and leave that child behind? What had driven her over the edge? Depression—or something else? She shook her head. She had to stop thinking about Anette.

CORD'S DAY WASN'T GOING WELL. He'd planned to pay his feed bills and make sure he had enough corn and milo to last for the month. There were several farmers who supplied him. He just wanted to arrange for the trucks to be at his ranch on specific days to dump the grain. But all the farmers wanted to talk, and then he had to have coffee with them. It was after five by the time he headed back to the ranch. Becca was going to be annoyed with him.

He could remember when he'd had those same feelings about Anette. But this was different. Anette had started laying down rules and schedules she expected him to follow, even though she knew he had ranching commitments; that had made him angry. With Becca, he felt an eagerness to see her again. He shouldn't, but he did. He tried to recall Anette's face. It wasn't there anymore. Everything about Anette was receding in his mind—except her death. That was vivid and clear. So were the emotions that went with it. Conflicting thoughts and feelings ran through his mind.

It was 5:45 when he walked into the kitchen. Becca strolled in from the dining room with Nicki trailing behind her. His breath caught in his throat at the sight of her. She wore a brown knit top and brown print skirt that flowed around her ankles. She looked gorgeous, and he couldn't stop staring at her.

"Hi, you're home," she said with a smile. No anger, no threats, no hurt feelings. Oh, he liked this. A woman who understood.

"Daddy!" Nicki shouted, and ran into his arms.

He noticed the dress and socks and shoes. Her hair wasn't in pigtails or a ponytail. It was hanging around her shoulders in bouncing curls.

"How's my baby?" He kissed her cheek.

"Fine." Nicki hugged his neck, then looked at him with wide eyes. "You should see what we did." She wriggled out of his arms and raced into the dining room. "Come on, Daddy."

It was so good to see his child like this again—full of excitement and life. He glanced at the woman who'd made it happen and his heart swelled with so many emotions that he had a hard time figuring out which were real and which were a result of his gratitude.

"Daddy, Daddy," Nicki called, diverting his attention. He made his way into the dining room, Becca walking right behind him.

Della was arranging chafing dishes on the sideboard and she wore a dress. Cord was disconcerted for a second. Della never wore dresses except to church. She noticed his startled expression.

"I don't know how Becca did it, but she talked Gus and me into having dinner with you." She moved past Cord. "I think I'm in the twilight zone."

Before Cord could assimilate this, Nicki shouted, "Look, Daddy, look."

He swung his gaze to the table, where Nicki was pointing. It was fully set with linen, flowers and candelabras he hadn't seen in years. They used to be on the table at special functions when his dad was alive.

"Becca and me picked the flowers and fixed 'em," Nicki was saying. "Aren't they pretty?"

"Very pretty," Cord murmured, but he wasn't looking at the flowers. He was looking at Becca.

"And we put the ca…ca…I don't know what they're called, but they hold the candles. Della said they belonged to somebody, but I forget."

"Your great-grandparents."

"Oh, I don't know them."

"No, baby, they—" He didn't want to tell her they'd died. He didn't want her to think about Anette. "They lived here a long time ago."

"Oh, I'm glad they left the ca—"

"Candelabra," Becca whispered in her ear, glad that Nicki was now taking an interest in the dinner. Once they'd started putting things together, Nicki's excitement had grown.

"Yeah, candel-la-bra," Nicki said slowly. "Becca and me put 'em on the table."

Becca and me. Cord heard that a hundred times a day and he didn't think he'd ever grow tired of it. He glanced at the woman in question. "I'm going upstairs to get cleaned up. Five minutes is all I need."

"It's okay, Cord," she assured him, evidently hearing the anxiety in his voice.

Was she for real? Why wasn't she berating him for being late? Anette would have.

"I'm not sure everyone will show up. I'm just hoping," she added.

He hurried for the stairs. They'd better show up, he thought, or he was personally dragging them down to dinner. Becca had gone to a lot of trouble and he wasn't having her disappointed.

He showered and dressed in starched jeans and a white shirt. The grandfather clock chimed six as he entered the den. Gus was fixing a drink. With his weathered skin and legs bowed from spending years in the saddle, he looked out of place among the elegant furniture and the beautifully set table. Gus was a cowboy to the core.

"Hey, Gus," he said.

Gus took a swallow of whiskey. "Wondered where you were. If I have to be at this shindig, so do you. Don't know why I let that little filly talk me into this. I just came by this morning to tell Della something, and she introduced me to the doc. Nice woman—and man, can she talk. Before I knew it, I was agreeing to have dinner with the family." He shook his head.

"Becca's very persuasive."

"I'll say, and I hate these ironed clothes. I feel like I've been rode hard and put up wet."

"You'll survive."

Gus tipped his glass. "Not too sure about that. Having dinner with Blanche could be about as much fun as putting panty hose on a bobcat."

"Remember, no scenes tonight. I want this to be perfect for Nicki." *And Becca.*

Becca and Nicki came in at that moment. "I guess we might as well sit down," Becca said in a resigned voice.

Cord knew Edie was upstairs, and if she'd said she was eating with them, then she was. "I'll check on Edie," he said, but before he could make an exit, Edie walked in.

"I'm sorry. I'm running a little late."

"That's okay," Becca told her. "We're just glad you joined us."

"Hi, Edie," Nicki said.

"Hi, and don't you look pretty."

"Becca fixed my hair."

"I can see that."

"Want me to show you where to sit? I know where everyone sits."

"Yes, I'd like that."

"Okay." She took Edie's hand.

Becca glanced at the clock. Six-fifteen. Blanche wasn't coming. At least Becca had tried.

But as they filed into the dining room, Blanche breezed in wearing a cream silk dress with a silver belt fitted over her hips.

"You're not gonna eat without me, are you, sugar?"

"We were just taking our seats," Becca said. She should've known that Blanche would have to make a grand entrance.

"And I know where everyone sits," Nicki put in.

"Aren't you smart?" Blanche responded in a condescending tone.

"Yeah," Nicki answered, not noticing the condescension. "Daddy sits at the head of the table and you sit at the other end. Edie is next to Daddy, then Gus and Della. And me and Becca are by Daddy on this side."

"How sweet," Blanche said in the same tone as she took her seat. "Let me get this straight. Della and Gus are eating with us?"

"Yes, I invited them," Becca told her, trusting Blanche wasn't going to make an issue of it.

"I'm glad I was consulted."

Before Becca could reply, Cord spoke up. "If you were home more and took an interest in the family, maybe you would be. But we're not talking about that right now. We're going to enjoy this wonderful meal that Della and Becca have prepared."

"And me, too, Daddy," Nicki reminded him. "I helped."

"And you, too, baby." Cord smiled at his daughter, then stared at Blanche, warning her not to say one more insulting word.

Della brought out the prime rib, and conversation stopped while all the food was put on the table, then Della took her seat.

"Would you like to say a prayer?" Becca asked Nicki. They had talked about this earlier and Nicki had said she wanted to.

Nicki folded her hands and bowed her head. "Thank you for the food and everyone here. Amen."

"That was very nice, Nicki," Edie said.

"Yeah, kid, you heard that from the mouth of a—"

"Cord would you slice the prime rib, please?" Becca intervened before Blanche could say something hateful.

Cord spared Blanche a glance before he stood to carve the roast. Becca filled Nicki's plate—cutting up her meat, buttering her roll and mashing her potatoes.

"You're just a regular little mother, aren't you, sugar?" Blanche remarked.

"Thank you," Becca said, not reacting to the obvious insult.

"You outdid yourself, Della girl," Gus said. "This meat is succulent."

"It sure is," Cord agreed.

After that, conversation was mundane and the tension seemed to ease, until Blanche asked, "What did you do today, kiddo?"

"I played, and Becca and me picked flowers and fixed 'em for the table."

"Becca's a jack-of-all-trades, isn't she?"

Nicki frowned. "What's that?"

There was silence for a moment, then Cord answered, "That's a person who can do anything."

"Yeah, Becca can do anything," Nicki said, nodding vigorously.

Gus laid his napkin on the table and smiled at Nicki. "Well, little bit, Half Pint's been awful lonely in that pasture. She sure needs riding."

A change came over Nicki and she leaned back in her chair with a sullen expression. "Don't want to."

"But you love to ride, baby," Cord said.

"No, I don't. I wanna go to my room."

Becca was shocked. The child hadn't said that in days. She turned to her. "Nicki…"

"I wanna go to my room," Nicki repeated, and before Becca

could stop her, she jumped out of her chair and ran for the stairs.

Blanche stood. "Well, sugar, looks like you've got a lot more work to do. This has been more fun than I really needed. Now I've got to get to a party at the club."

"To a man, you mean," Edie slipped in.

"Shut your trap," Blanche snapped.

Edie glared at her. "I can say what I want in this house."

"You dried-up old bitch." Blanche went on. "I should've kicked you out the day Claybourne died."

Cord threw his napkin on the table. "Enough! This dinner is over. Just get out of my sight." With that, he headed for the stairs, and Becca followed.

"Cord," Gus called. He looked back. "I'm sorry. I shouldn't have mentioned the horse. I didn't know she'd react like that."

"It's all right, Gus. She's still dealing with a lot of pain."

Not a word was said as they walked up the stairs and into Nicki's room. Nicki was sitting in the rocker with her arms around Dolly. She rarely clung to Dolly these days. Something had triggered a major upset and Becca had to find out what. She hitched up her skirt and sat on the floor in front of Nicki.

"What's the matter, sweetie?" she asked softly.

"Nothin'," Nicki muttered.

"Yes, it is, 'cause you're so sad and when you're sad, I'm sad and so is Daddy."

Nicki didn't say anything.

"Look at me, Nicki."

Nicki raised her head. "I don't want you to be sad, Becca," she cried, and threw herself into Becca's arms.

Becca held her tight, smoothing her curls. "Then, tell me what's hurting you."

Needing to be near them, Cord sat on the floor beside

Becca. Nicki made a dive for him, locking her arms around his neck. "What is it, baby—?" His voice cracked, but he couldn't help it.

"Mommy said...Mommy said..."

Cord's chest tightened. "What did Mommy say?"

"Mommy said she didn't want me to ride. It's not ladylike."

"Oh, baby." Cord held her close, trying to find the right words. "Mommy was scared of horses. You're not. You remember that book we read about Annie Oakley? She rode a horse. And you've seen those old westerns Gus likes. Even in those days, ladies rode horses. There was Dale Evans, and she was a grand lady."

"Then, it's okay to ride a horse?"

"You betcha." He kissed her nose.

"And Mommy won't be mad at me?"

Cord swallowed. "No, baby. Mommy loved you and she could never be mad at you."

"Oh." Nicki thought about it for a second, then she went back to Becca. "Mommy's not mad at me," she told her.

Becca stroked her face and kissed her. "No, Mommy's not mad at you."

She settled back on Becca's lap. "Becca?"

"What, sweetie?"

"Can you...can you..."

"Can I what?"

"Can you ride?"

"No, I've never been on a horse, but I'd like to try."

"Daddy can teach you and...and...you can ride with me."

"I'd like that."

And Daddy would, too, Cord thought.

"Now, would you like to go have dessert?"

Nicki clamped a hand over her mouth. "I forgot." She glanced at Cord. "We fixed a special dessert."

"I'll bet it has something to do with chocolate."

Becca made a face at him. "Actually, it's cheesecake," she said, then added with a grin, "but it's got a caramel-chocolate topping."

Cord got to his feet. "Somehow I knew chocolate would not be left out." He swung Nicki into his arms and reached out a hand to Becca. She placed her hand in his and he helped her to her feet. Her touch was soft, tempting, blocking out everything but the feeling in his heart.

Together they went downstairs. Edie, Della and Gus were in the kitchen eating cheesecake; Blanche had evidently left. Nicki immediately ran to Gus.

"I can ride Half Pint, Gus. Let's go now."

Gus gave Cord a puzzled look.

"Baby, it's dark outside. We have to wait until tomorrow."

She turned back to Gus. "And Daddy's gonna teach Becca how to ride, so she can ride with me."

"Now, ain't that somethin'."

"I'll ride with you until Becca learns," Edie offered.

"'Kay, but I ride fast. Can you ride fast?"

"At my age, I don't do anything fast, but I'll try to keep up."

After that, they sat around the table and ate cheesecake and talked. Eventually Nicki started to nod, and Cord took her upstairs and put her to bed.

The evening hadn't turned out exactly as Becca had planned, but she couldn't help feeling Anette's ghost had finally been put to rest for Nicki. After her shower, she slipped on a big T-shirt and started to get into bed, but the cheesecake had made her thirsty so she went downstairs to get a glass of ice water.

Heading back to the stairs, she thought she saw someone in the den. She strolled in to see Cord sitting on the sofa, his head buried in his hands. There was no light on, but the moonlight streaming in through the large French windows illuminated him clearly.

She walked closer. "Cord, are you all right?"

His head jerked up. "Becca. I didn't realize you were still awake."

"I just came down to get some ice water."

His shirt was pulled from his jeans and open down the front. His boots were lying on the floor. She felt as though someone had punched her in her stomach, and she had a hard time breathing.

She sat on the coffee table facing him, setting the glass beside her. "She's fine," she said, knowing exactly what was bothering him.

"Is she?" he asked in an angry tone. "Anette put so much garbage in her head, and it makes me angry that I allowed it. I never did anything to control her phobias and insecurities. I should've made her get more treatment, for that and the depression. She always resisted…."

"But she loved Nicki. That's very obvious from the inscriptions in all the books."

"Do you think that's normal?"

"Well, I hadn't really thought about it, but I don't see anything wrong with it."

"It seems weird to me, but Anette wanted Nicki to know how much she loved her. I guess it's exactly what she'd do. You see, her mother died when she was a teenager and her father married a woman Anette didn't like. There were arguments all the time, and Anette left to live with an aunt. I met her in Fort Worth when I was there for a cattleman's convention. She was the manager of the hotel where I stayed. It was a wham-bam affair, and I found myself going back on weekends, which I got tired of so we decided to get married. She had no problem giving up her job at the time, but I heard plenty about it later. Anette was looking for a family, and when she found out the Prescotts weren't the ideal American family she became depressed, and then obsessed with having a baby. God, I hated all those tests, but I did everything because I thought it would make her happy. Nothing did, though, not even Nicki's birth."

There was silence for a while. He couldn't believe he was talking so much. "Go to bed, Becca. I'm not in a very good mood."

She knew that. Still, she was reluctant to leave him. "What kind of relationship did Anette have with Blanche?"

"Tense—just like Blanche has with everyone. Why?"

She started to tell him what Blanche had said, but decided he didn't need any more problems. "Just that living here couldn't have been easy for Anette."

"No, but it's not a reason to kill yourself, especially when you have a four-year-old daughter." His voice was full of pain. "God, I just can't get past that. I—"

Becca moved to sit next to him and, unable to resist, she put her arms around him. His reaction was instant and urgent. He pulled her to him and held her tight. For a moment it was just comfort, but slowly other emotions began to take over. His breath on her hair and his hands on her body awakened a deep need in her. One hand stroked the hair at his nape while her other slid to his bare chest.

"Cord," she whispered.

He turned his head and kissed her. His lips moved over hers with an expertise that her body recognized and welcomed. She opened her mouth, and then they were lost in the joy of exploring each other. He pushed her gently into the sofa, his hands caressing her body through the T-shirt. Her senses started to spin, and she knew she'd been waiting for this all her life.

Cord wasn't thinking. He was only feeling—warm and

overpowering emotions he'd thought he'd forgotten. But he didn't think he'd ever felt exactly like this. Wanting someone so badly that he hurt—someone he couldn't have. It was hard to remind himself of that when her soft, tempting hands touched his skin. But he had to. Oh God, he had to.

He tore his mouth away and got to his feet. He ran both hands roughly through his hair. "I'm sorry. I shouldn't have done that."

Becca sat up and straightened her T-shirt. "Why not?" she asked in as steady a voice as she could manage. "We're both adults and if we want to—"

"You're my brother's girlfriend."

She took a deep breath. "I'm Colton's *friend.* I told you that." She was tired of having to explain her relationship with Colton, but she had to make Cord understand. "I've known Colton for ten years and he's never kissed me like that."

Her words didn't ring true. "That day you called from your apartment. It was early in the morning and you said he'd just left. Friends don't sleep together."

"We don't *sleep* together," she said patiently. "He stopped by on his way to work. He was there maybe fifteen minutes."

Cord was thrown. If Colton hadn't kissed her like that or slept with her, he was a fool. *Why?* was his next thought. Had he misread the situation? It didn't matter; he had no right to kiss her. There were too many issues standing between them.

"Becca, do you know how old I am?"

She shook her head.

"I'm older than Colton. I'm forty-two."

"So?"

"I'm too old for you."

"Really?" she mused. "Then isn't Colton too old for me, as well? You're close to the same age."

Her question rattled him. There were only fourteen months

between him and Colton, yet he'd never considered Colton too old for her. Why? Maybe it was because he just *felt* so much older. Or maybe…

"Age has nothing to do with it," she said stiffly. "If you regret kissing me, just say so and stop using every excuse you can think of." She made to walk past him, and he caught her arm.

"My dad was sixty when he married Blanche. A girl young enough to be his granddaughter. I promised myself I would never be that foolish."

"I'm hardly young enough to be your granddaughter or even your daughter. I'll be twenty-nine on my next birthday, which isn't far away. I'm a woman who can make up her own mind. I wanted to kiss you and I think you wanted to kiss me."

Cord didn't say anything. He couldn't. She was getting to him in the worst way, and he had to put a stop to it. "Don't read too much into my reaction, Becca. It's been a long time since I've been with a woman." With that, he walked briskly to the stairs.

Her mouth fell open and she quickly closed it. Of all the— She took another deep breath as anger overtook her. *I'll never kiss you again, Cordell Prescott.* But before the thought left her mind, she knew she was lying.

CHAPTER EIGHT

THE NEXT MORNING Nicki was so excited, Becca could hardly keep up with her. The little girl wore her boots and jeans and she'd found her cowboy hat. Nicki was going riding, and the whole household felt her enthusiasm. They all went out to the corral to watch the big event. Everyone except Blanche.

Cord treated Becca coolly—as if they'd never kissed. Well, if that was the way he wanted it, fine, or so she told herself. But she could still feel his mustache on her skin—provocative, tantalizing…. She harnessed her thoughts. She refused to let Cord hurt her, but she was afraid he already had.

Becca, Della and Edie stood outside the fence as Nicki rode around and around on a black horse Gus had saddled and ready to go. Becca could see why they called the horse Half Pint. She was small and gentle and seemed perfect for Nicki. Cord opened the gate, and Nicki rode out into the pasture. The horse galloped at an alarming speed, and Becca held her breath waiting for Cord to call a halt. But he didn't. He probably knew what Nicki could and couldn't handle. She was acting like a nervous city girl. Wincing, she turned toward the house, thinking Nicki was going to hit the ground at any moment. She saw a curtain fall into place. It was Blanche. She was watching but didn't want anyone to know.

Becca's eyes shifted to the old black truck driving up to the barn. A big man got out, tall and heavyset, and staggered toward them.

"Cord Prescott," he shouted, his words slurred. The man was obviously drunk.

"Get off my property, Bates," Cord shouted back.

Gus immediately got between the two men. Luckily Nicki was busy riding. "You'd better get outta here, Joe," Gus said.

"Not until I say what I come to say," the man snarled. "I spent six months in jail because of you, Prescott, and it's time you got what's comin' to you."

Cord walked closer. "You spent time in jail because you rustled Triple Creek cattle. That was your decision, not mine."

"You didn't have to press charges. I'd have paid you back."

"With what?" Cord muttered. "You were down on your luck because of your gambling and drinking. Besides, a cattle rustler is a disease to ranchers and you got what you deserved. Now get off this property before I call the sheriff."

"You bastard," the man yelled, stumbling to his truck. "I'll get even, Cord. I swear. You'll get what *you* deserve. Just wait and see."

"Is that a threat?"

The man laughed as he got into the truck and fired the engine. In a second he was roaring away from the barn.

"Forget it," Gus said. "He's just drunk."

Cord gazed after the truck. "Maybe, but I'll still let the sheriff know he was here." He shrugged. "If nothing else, he should be taken off the road, drunk as he is."

"Daddy, Daddy, watch me," Nicki called then, and Cord turned back to his daughter.

"Who was that?" Becca asked Della.

"Joe Bates," Della replied. "He used to work here until Cord caught him stealing cattle at night. I didn't know he was out of jail."

"He seems...dangerous," Becca said, rubbing the goose bumps on her arms.

"He is, and I hope the sheriff keeps him away from here."

THE REST OF THE DAY was spent watching Nicki ride. Cord didn't offer to teach Becca, and when he and Nicki went farther into the pasture, she walked back to the house feeling oddly left out. She thought maybe it was time to go home to Houston. She'd done everything she could here; Nicki would be fine without her. That thought did not make her happy.

She called her parents and talked to them and Scotty. Then she called Rose and Owen and Grandpa George. Her parents were planning a family trip to Rockport and wanted her to go, but she hesitated. She needed more time. Time for what, she had no idea. But it felt good to talk to everyone. The conversations confirmed that this was what she needed—time away to appreciate everything she had.

Becca sat on the patio reading medical journals she'd put aside. Her eyes kept straying to the valley below hoping for a glimpse of Cord and Nicki. She was glad Nicki was spending this morning with Cord. She just wished she didn't feel so alone. She thought about Joe Bates and wondered if he meant to harm Cord. The mere possibility sent chills through her body, and she knew her feelings for Cord were getting stronger and stronger. She didn't understand it, since he rebuffed her at every turn.

That evening, they all had supper in the kitchen. It was the meal they should've had last night. Everyone was laughing and talking, and Nicki was the center of attention, chatting on and on about her day. No one seemed to care that Blanche wasn't with them. But Becca did. She was part of this family and needed to be there. Becca knew that was strictly her own opinion. Blanche would not thank her for interfering, so she decided to stay out of it. Besides, she planned to leave soon, and it didn't concern her.

Later, Cord and Gus retired to the den, and Becca could hear them talking about the price of cattle, the delivery of grain and a pasture of coastal that needed cutting. After she, Della and Edie had cleaned up the kitchen, they joined the men. Nicki was curled up in Cord's lap, listening as if she understood every word.

Cord tried to focus on what Gus was saying, but he was having a hard time, since all he wanted to do was turn to Becca and apologize. The day had been dreadful without her, especially since every other word out of Nicki's mouth was *Becca.* He should've saddled a horse for her and taught her the rudiments of riding. But he couldn't. That would mean he'd have to be close to her, and he *had* to keep his distance. He'd made that decision last night and he'd had no sleep as a result. No matter how he tried, he could still feel her hands on his body. And that look on her face—God, he couldn't get it out of his mind. But he had to remind himself that she didn't need someone like him in her life. She was intelligent and beautiful and she had a high-powered career in Houston.

A flash of light from the entry caught everyone's attention.

"Who could that be?" Della said.

Cord immediately thought of Joe Bates and his spine stiffened. The guns were in the gun cabinet, not far away. But he didn't want anything to happen with Nicki in the room. He had to get her upstairs, then he'd deal with Bates.

Before Cord could move, Colton strolled in from the kitchen. "Hey, I wondered where everyone was."

Cord relaxed. With all of today's events, he'd forgotten that he had invited Colton out for a visit.

Becca was surprised to see him, and she jumped up excitedly and hugged him. He kissed her cheek. "Hi, gorgeous."

Gus stood and shook his hand. "Glad to have you home, boy."

Everyone else said hi, but Becca noticed that no one made a move to hug or kiss him, not even Nicki. What was wrong with this family?

Edie patted him on the shoulder and said, "Good to see you. Now I'm off to bed."

Why didn't she stay and talk? She probably hadn't seen Colton in months.

On impulse, Becca hugged Edie. "'Night."

Edie was startled and it showed in her eyes. "Yes, well… good night, all." Nervously she left the room.

"Della and me are gonna mosey over to our house," Gus said. "My easy chair is calling me."

Becca hugged both of them and there was silence for a moment, then Della said, "See you in the morning."

As they left, Cord carefully got to his feet, holding his daughter. "This one's falling asleep, so I'd better get her to bed." If Becca hugged him, he didn't know what he'd do, but he knew there was no way he could get out of this room without her hugging Nicki. Nicki was half-asleep, so maybe he—

"Becca," Nicki whimpered, and that small hope died.

"Right here, sweetie," Becca said, and walked over to kiss her cheek. Nicki reached for her and they hugged tightly. Cord could smell the scent of her hair, and her breasts were pressed into his arm as he maintained a grip on Nicki. God, he had to get out of here.

"'Night," Becca and Nicki chorused.

"Talk to you later, Colton," Cord murmured, and quickly left.

Colton raised his eyebrows. "Do I know how to clear a room or what?"

Becca sat on the sofa and Colton followed. "What are you doing here?" she asked.

"Wanted to see how you were getting on?"

"Your family lives here. Didn't you want to see them, too?"

"We're not your typical family."

"So I gather. Still, aren't you glad to see them? As mad as I've been at Rose, I'm always glad to see her."

"That's because you have a strong family bond. We don't have that."

"Colton." She sighed.

"Let me tell you what it was like in the Prescott house at Christmas. Edie and Pa would wake us up, and we'd come downstairs and open our gifts. Then we'd have breakfast and play with our toys. Blanche made an appearance when dinner was served because Pa insisted. She always had on a fancy negligée and inquired what we'd gotten for Christmas. After that, she spent her time snapping at Edie until a full-blown argument erupted. Believe me, we were glad to get that day over with."

"Your mother is very…unconventional, but Edie was always there for you. Why don't you have any affection for her?"

"We do, but we just don't show it."

"Why not, for heaven's sake?"

"Because we weren't raised that way." He glanced at her with blue eyes so like Blanche's. "What's this about, Becca?"

"It's about Nicki. She should be surrounded by a loving family. She needs that now."

"I'm hardly ever here."

"But just now, you didn't even hug her."

He squirmed uncomfortably. "You may have noticed, I'm not a demonstrative person."

"You hug me."

"Mainly because you hug me first. You've always been like that. You're not afraid to show your emotions."

She was completely dumbfounded. Over the years, had Colton taken her openness and friendliness as something more? No, she was sure he hadn't, but she had to be certain.

She curled her feet beneath her and turned to face him. "Your mother and Cord are under the impression that we have a sexual relationship."

"Really? Where would they get an idea like that?"

"Evidently when you see them you talk about me a lot."

He shifted again. "So? That doesn't mean anything."

"We talked about this in my apartment, and you told me not to worry, but I can't help it."

His eyes met hers. "I know you don't love me."

She touched his arm, still looking into his eyes. "But do you love *me?*"

"Becca," he sounded aggrieved.

"Tell me the truth."

"I could have," he admitted. "Probably very deeply, but do you remember that time we kissed under the mistletoe at your parents' house?"

"Yes," she replied, remembering it quite well. She'd thought that if Colton kissed her passionately, all the other feelings would follow, but it hadn't happened that way. There was only a comfortable warmth between them.

"That spark, the explosion of the senses, wasn't there, and I knew you didn't have those kinds of emotions for me, nor I for you." He leaned his head against the sofa. "Why *don't* we feel that way about each other?"

"Because we're not the half that makes the other whole. That's what true love is. When you can't stop thinking about the other person, when you want to be with him in the worst way, when your heart beats faster at just the sight of him and when you'd do anything to make him happy."

His eyes narrowed. "Sounds as if you've..." He sat up straight. "You haven't fallen for Cord, have you?"

"Colton, I—"

"Cord's not the man for you," he told her swiftly. "His life is so screwed up. Anette hurt him so much, he'll never be the same. I know you're helping Nicki, but leave it at that. Don't—"

"Don't tell me what to do." She stopped him, her voice sounding angry.

"I'm not. I just want you to be happy."

"I will, but I have to find that happiness on my own. I hope you understand."

"Sure," he said slowly.

"And I hope you find a woman who makes you so silly-giddy in love that you can't think straight."

He grunted. "I don't think that's gonna happen. I *always* think straight."

"About business, yeah, but you just wait."

"Luckily, I don't have the silly-giddy capability."

"Life is not all about business."

"I haven't found that out yet."

Becca realized why she and Colton had never worked as a couple. His mind was constantly on business. There wasn't room for anything else. He was right when he said he didn't have a silly-giddy side. He had a dead-serious personality. Someday the right woman would awaken the other part of him. But that woman wasn't her.

The silence stretched between them, and Becca tried to think of something to say to ease the tension. Her mind drifted to her apartment and her plants. She hadn't even thought about them and she wondered if Gin had.

"Have you seen Gin lately?" she asked suddenly.

"The crazy redhead? Of course not. I avoid her at all costs."

"I haven't talked to her since I got here. She's supposed to be watering my plants in the apartment."

"Consider those plants dead."

She tapped him on the shoulder. "Gin's not like that. She's very responsible."

"Yeah, right. This is the same woman who's lost her car keys four times that I know of and the same woman who—"

"Okay, she's a scatterbrain, but that's why she's so much fun."

"More like a nightmare."

"You should get to know her. You have a lot in common."

His eyebrows shot up. "Like what?"

"You both have very unconventional mothers."

"Yeah, now there's something I'd enjoy talking about on a regular basis," he said facetiously, then added, "but I'll check on your plants if you want me to."

"Gin has the key, so just call and remind her." Becca knew she could call Gin herself, but it wouldn't hurt them to get better acquainted. Maybe then they'd stop saying mean things about each other.

Colton groaned dramatically. "I'd rather buy you new plants."

She tapped him on the shoulder again, and they settled into easy conversation like they always did. He told her how he and Scotty were working on a new computer game and how he was thinking of going to Rockport with her parents. Colton was so involved with *her* family. He needed to be involved with the Prescott family—or was that completely outside the realm of possibility?

CORD PACED in his room. He wouldn't go down. He wouldn't. Colton had come to see Becca, and he wouldn't interrupt. He'd give them some time alone. He sat on the bed. Becca said they didn't have that kind of relationship, but she seemed eager enough to see Colton. What were they doing? Kissing, touching… He stood, unable to tolerate the images in his head. It was what he wanted, wasn't it? For Becca and Colton to… Without even realizing what he was doing, he found himself opening the door and hurrying downstairs.

They were sitting on the sofa talking, and his heart slowed. He moved to go back upstairs, but Becca saw him.

"Is Nicki asleep?" she asked in a concerned voice that turned his insides into a quivering mass.

"Yeah, she's out for the night," he answered stiffly. "I was just on my way to the kitchen."

"Why don't you talk to Colton?" she said. "You two haven't seen each other in a while, and I'm sure you have a lot of catching up to do. I'm off to bed." She stood, stretching. "'Night."

Cord watched her leave with a confused look on his face.

"So how's the ranching business?" Colton asked.

Cord collected his thoughts and sat down. "Busy."

"Yeah, that's how the computer business is."

Silence.

"Computer working okay?"

"Yeah, thanks," Cord answered absently. "Keeps track of everything, just like you said it would. It's difficult making time to feed it the information, though. There's so much work to be done on the ranch."

"Have you ever thought of letting the cowboys handle the work and you take care of the business end?"

"The outdoor work is what I enjoy."

"Pa used to say if you were on a horse and had a rope in your hand, you were in hog heaven. I guess that hasn't changed."

"No."

Silence again.

"Heard from Clay lately?" Colton asked abruptly.

"No. Since he moved to Alaska, we don't get to talk much."

"We're a pathetic family. I haven't even seen Clay's girls. They're seven and four, I think. He didn't even bring them to Anette's funeral."

"I guess he felt it wasn't appropriate."

"Hell, we're family. When *is* it appropriate?"

Cord wondered what this was about—and then he knew. Becca. Becca was working her magic. She just didn't understand that the Prescotts weren't like other families.

"Becca's been talking to you," he said quietly.

"Yes, and she's right. We need to be closer."

"Easier said than done."

"Yeah, what am I thinking? We have Blanche for a mother."

They smiled at each other. Cord rested his forearms on his knees. "Can I ask you a personal question?"

"Sure."

"What kind of relationship do you have with Becca?"

Colton rubbed the palms of his hands over his slacks. "That's hard to explain, but I can see it's important to you." He paused, then went on. "Since I'm in the computer business with her father, I've gotten to know her quite well. I've seen her go through the depths of hell and come out smiling. She has that ability—to take what life shoves at her and make the best of it. I admire that in her. She's intelligent, beautiful and strong. From time to time, I've wished our relationship would deepen into something else—but we're just friends." His eyes pierced Cord. "And I don't want to see her get hurt."

"Sounds like a warning." Cord met his look squarely.

"It is. Don't hurt her. She doesn't deserve that."

"I will never hurt Becca," Cord said quietly. "She's worked wonders with Nicki, and I will always be grateful for that."

"Come on, Cord, who are you trying to kid? You're not

asking about Becca because of Nicki. You're asking for yourself. You're interested in her."

Cord stood. "I am, but I'm too old for her."

"Stay away from her then, and let her go back to Houston."

"I wish it was that simple."

"It is. You're not over Anette's death, and you know it. Don't drag Becca into your misery. She doesn't deserve that, either."

Cord didn't say anything. Everything Colton had said was true. Anette's death still weighed heavily upon him. But he couldn't put Becca out of his mind.

Colton got up. "I have an early meeting in the morning. I'd better go."

They shook hands. "Cord?"

"Hmm?"

"Don't encourage Becca. She's an affectionate, outgoing, giving person and—"

Cord broke in. "You don't have to tell me a thing about Becca."

"Good, so I don't have to worry."

"No, you don't have to worry."

Cord went to bed with that thought on his mind. He wouldn't encourage Becca. He wouldn't do anything with Becca—except think about her every minute of every day. That would be his own personal hell. As if he needed another one.

THE MORNING BROUGHT a complete change of plans. Nicki woke him by jumping on his bed. That hadn't happened in so long that for a second he thought he was dreaming.

"Daddy, Daddy, wake up!" she called brightly. "We've got to go."

Cord opened one eye and glanced at the clock. It was four

in the morning. He flicked on his bedside lamp and pushed himself into a sitting position. "What's wrong, baby?"

"We've got to go riding. I'm all ready."

Cord noticed that she was dressed, although her top was on backward and her boots were on the wrong feet. He gathered her in his arms. "It's too early, and Daddy has to work today."

"You promised, Daddy. You promised you'd teach Becca to ride."

God, he was hoping she'd forgotten about that. How should he handle this? "Not today, baby. Daddy has to work." It was a feeble excuse, but it was all he could think of at this hour.

Nicki stuck out her lip. "I wanna go riding."

"Nicki..."

She started to sob, hard and loud.

Cord caught her face in his hands. "Stop that this instant."

At the sternness in Cord's voice, her sobs immediately ceased.

"I'll get Smithy to saddle Half Pint so you can ride."

"But Becca," she whimpered.

Cord took a long breath. "I'll get Smithy to saddle a horse for her and teach her a few things."

Nicki smiled.

He pushed back her tangled hair. "I don't want you crying to get your way. I won't have that. When I won't let you do something, I have a very good reason for it."

"'Kay, Daddy."

BECCA SAT BOLT UPRIGHT when she heard the crying. She quickly got out of bed and ran to Nicki's room. Nicki wasn't there. Her heart jolted against her ribs. Where was she? She noticed Cord's door was open, so she walked in—and stopped abruptly. Nicki was sitting on the bed talking to Cord, who had nothing on from the waist up. Her breath lodged in her throat as she stared at the dark blond hair that curled down his chest.

"Hi, Becca," Nicki said cheerfully. "We're gonna go riding."

Becca blinked. "I thought I heard you crying."

"You did," Cord said, trying to tear his eyes away from Becca in the T-shirt. Her breasts were pressed against the material and her dark hair was mussed around her face as if she'd been making… He cleared his throat. "She was just having a tantrum, trying to get her way."

"What did she want to do? Oh, Nicki, you're all dressed. Sort of."

"She wanted to go riding at four a.m. That's what the crying was all about."

Nicki shook her head. "I not do that anymore."

"Oh," Becca murmured. "Good."

Nicki clapped her hands. "We gonna go riding, and Smithy's gonna teach you. Daddy's gotta work."

Who the hell was Smithy? Then everything became clear. Cord was opting out of teaching her; he'd given the job to someone else. She took large strides over to the bed and plucked Nicki out. "Let's get you back to your room."

"Don't want to," Nicki protested. "I'm not sleepy."

"Then, you can keep me company," Becca said as she bundled the child into her room.

She looked down at Nicki's booted feet. "For heaven's sake, you've got your boots on the wrong feet."

"No, I don't," Nicki answered, pointing at her feet. "That's *my* feet."

Becca smiled as she slipped the boots off and curled up in bed, with Nicki beside her. She started to change Nicki's clothes, but the little girl was already dozing off.

How dare he! How dare he think he could just get rid of her. Just hand her off to someone else because he didn't want to be with her. That made her angry. *Well, forget it, Cordell Prescott, you won't find it quite so easy.*

BY THE TIME SHE AND NICKI went down for breakfast, she had a plan. Cord had said he'd show her the ranch, and she would hold him to it.

Edie was at the breakfast table, to Becca's surprise. Maybe she was making an effort to be part of the family. Becca hoped so.

"Della, do you know where Cord is working today?" she asked as she poured syrup over Nicki's pancakes.

"In the north pasture, in the bottom."

"Can you tell me how to get there?"

Della turned from the sink. "Why?"

"Because Cord said I could use one of the Jeeps to bring Nicki to have lunch with him."

"I see. It's kinda hard to explain."

"I know where it is," Edie told her. "I'll go with you."

"That's great." Becca beamed. "We'll make it a family outing. Want to come, Della?"

"Lord, no. I got too much to do around here."

"Can't it wait? We could pack a big picnic lunch and take it to the guys. Gus would probably like a hot sandwich or something."

"He does like my steak sandwiches, and I could fix chicken salad for us." Della was getting interested.

"Hot dog for me," Nicki piped up with a mouth full of pancake.

"Okay," Della said. "Let's do it. It's been ages since I've watched the cowboys in action."

By ten o'clock, they were packed and ready to go, except for one little problem. Nicki wanted to ride Half Pint. In the end, Becca decided to let her, especially since Edie and Della were with them. Surely they could handle any problem that arose. Smithy, the man who cared for the horses, as Becca found out, wanted to go along, but Becca assured him everything was under control.

There were a few tense moments as Becca adjusted to driving a stick shift again. Della sat in the back, Edie in front. They just smiled tolerantly at the jerky ride. They were very good sports. Soon she got the hang of it and they were off, with Nicki racing ahead on Half Pint.

She followed Della's directions, and they drove through pasture after pasture of cattle. She'd never seen so many in her life. She had to stop repeatedly to let the animals cross the road. They took their time, unafraid of the Jeep. Each pasture was fenced off with a cattle guard so she didn't have to open gates. Becca had thought the trip would take maybe fifteen minutes, but thirty minutes later, they were still driving and there didn't seem any end in sight. Grassland gave way to bushy creeks, and then suddenly they drove into a clearing and Becca knew they'd arrived. Cowboys and cattle were everywhere. Several cattle were milling about in a pen. Cowboys were riding into the large herd in the pasture and separating cows with calves and guiding them toward the pen. A Jeep with a trailer behind it was parked to one side. The lowing of cattle filled the air, and excitement tingled along her nerves.

Nicki galloped to where Cord sat astride a big red-and-white paint horse. The tingling inside her became a jangling of sensations. God, he was so handsome—everything she'd ever dreamed about in a man.

She put the Jeep in gear and drove slowly forward. Cord had noticed Nicki and nudged his horse toward her. Then he saw the Jeep. It was all too obvious that Cord wasn't pleased.

He removed his hat and wiped his hand across his forehead in a weary gesture, and in that instant Becca wished she'd gone back to Houston.

Cord didn't want her here.

CHAPTER NINE

BECCA PARKED THE JEEP near the other one, and they got out. She and Della removed the basket of food and the ice chest with the drinks and set it on the flatbed trailer. Gus rode over, followed by three dogs with mottled blue coats.

"What brings you ladies here?"

"We brought you lunch," Della answered, and Becca was glad. She felt so foolish; she'd come to get back at Cord and that was such a teenage thing. She could see that now. The man had made it plain how he felt, and she had to accept it. When she returned to the house she'd pack her things and leave. She hoped Nicki would understand.

Just then, Cord and Nicki galloped over.

"The ladies brought us lunch," Gus told Cord. "Ain't that nice?"

"Yes, very," Cord replied in a cool voice.

Nicki wriggled down from the saddle, and Becca caught her before she hit the ground.

"Nicki, you know better than to get off your horse without someone to help you," Cord reprimanded. "And never leave your horse untethered. You know better than that, too."

"Yes, Daddy," Nicki said in a pitiful voice.

Cord immediately swung from the saddle and helped her tie Half Pint to the trailer. Becca could see he didn't like snapping at his daughter. She knew it was a reaction to her unwanted presence.

"We got a few more calves to brand, vaccinate and tag,

then we'll stop for lunch," Gus said. "You ladies can watch the fun." Gus clicked his tongue. "Let's go, boys," he said to the dogs.

"That's Gus's dogs—Bubba, Beau and Boo-Boo," Nicki said as she crawled up beside Becca on the trailer. "They're work dogs, so you can't play with them."

"Why is that?" Becca asked.

Nicki shrugged.

Della spoke up. "Gus is very particular about his dogs. They're Australian Blue Heelers and known for their expertise in handling cattle. Gus believes if you pamper them, they won't work, but he pampers them more than anyone."

Becca tried to listen, but her focus was on Cord as he remounted and followed Gus to the pen. A cowboy opened the gate and they rode in, the dogs waiting outside. Within minutes, Cord and Gus had separated the mother cows from their babies. Another cowboy opened the gate on the other side, and the cows were herded into a different pasture. The cows bellowed in an agitated manner and ran along the fence line trying to get to their babies.

Becca's attention was diverted back to the pen as the action started. She noticed a fire just outside the fence with a branding iron stuck in it. Gus and Cord dismounted, then Cord waded in among the calves and grabbed one around the back legs, jerking him to the ground. Things happened so fast that Becca had a hard time keeping up. A cowboy handed Gus the iron and he seared a Triple Creek brand on the calf's hind rump. At the same moment, another cowboy handed Cord a needle and something that looked like a gun. Cord injected the calf and snapped a tag in his ear.

"What's he doing?" she asked Della.

"Vaccinating against disease and putting a tag in his ear to show when he was injected. As soon as a calf's born, a tag with its mother's number is put in its ear. That way, the calves can be identified."

Gus knelt down with his pocketknife. "Gus is castrating the calf to keep him from becoming a bull," Della told her. "When the calf is weaned from its mother, he goes into a feed lot for several months, then he's shipped to the slaughter and packing houses. It's how meat gets into the supermarket."

In a matter of seconds, the whole thing was over. Cord let the calf up, and the cowboys quickly shooed the calf out the gate to his mother. Cord grabbed another and the process started again. It seemed a bit inhumane, but she knew it was necessary. The calves had to be castrated, and the vaccinating kept down disease. As a doctor she understood that. The tag and branding was for identification. Cattle rustling must be a constant danger with so many cattle. Joe Bates's appearance had underlined that particular reality.

It was all fascinating. Cord worked with a speed and expertise that probably took years to learn. Soon the calves were all vaccinated and branded, and Cord and Gus saddled up and rode back to the women, the other cowboys hard on their heels. Della opened the basket and spread out the food. The cowboys professed their thanks as they each took a steak sandwich and a drink. Several spared Becca a knowing glance, but she merely smiled back. They all wore shabby jeans, boots and tattered hats, their skin was leathery from the sun. They epitomized a dying saga—that of the Old West.

Nicki ate half her hot dog and fell asleep. Becca pulled the child against her, letting her nap. She'd had a busy morning.

As the cowboys sat in the grass eating, Della and Edie joined them. Edie seemed to know many of them, since she asked about their families. Cord sat with the group, while Becca sat on the trailer holding Nicki and feeling alone. She couldn't eat; she felt far too miserable.

Suddenly Cord got to his feet and walked toward her. "Let me take Nicki so you can eat," he said brusquely.

"No, she's fine and I'm not hungry."

He sat on the trailer. "Why not?" he asked, more kindly this time.

She couldn't hold everything in anymore. "I know you don't want me here, but I—I wanted to see something of ranching before I left."

Cord felt his throat close up. "You're leaving?"

She hadn't meant it to come out now, in front of everyone, but nothing was going as she'd planned. "Yes, Nicki will be fine and I need to get back to Houston."

He drew a deep breath. "Does this have something to do with Colton?"

Frowning, she tucked her hair behind her ear. "No, it has nothing to do with Colton."

"Then…"

She stared directly at him. "Then, what?"

Cord looked up at the blue sky, saw the bright sun and heard the cowboys talking, but all he felt was the pain in his chest. If she left, his world would come apart. He didn't know much, but he knew that. He was tired of all the confusion, all the aching inside him. Somehow, when he was with her, it wasn't so bad. So letting himself live again couldn't be bad, either.

His gaze swung back to her. "Then, don't go."

She swallowed at the suffering in his eyes, but she had to ask. "Why?"

"Nicki needs time to adjust," he lied with as much dignity as he could.

And so do I.

Becca realized he was lying—but she didn't mind. There was something happening between them, some emotional connection, and they both were aware of it. She could cope as long as he didn't push her away.

"Will you teach me to ride and not pass me off to Smithy?"

A grin ruffled his mustache. "Sure, and I'm sorry about that. I—"

Before he could finish, a rider emerged from the woods and galloped toward Cord. Becca thought it was a man at first, but it turned out to be a woman. She was easily six foot, stoutly built and probably in her late forties. She drew up in front of Cord.

"Howdy, Mona," Cord said.

Mona tipped her hat and stared at Becca holding Nicki.

"Oh, this is Dr. Becca Talbert." He made the introduction. "She's spending some time with Nicki. And Becca, this is Mona Tibbetts. Her ranch adjoins ours."

"Nice to meet you, Mona," Becca said, smiling.

"Likewise," Mona answered. "You seem awful young for a doctor."

"I hear that a lot."

"Glad Cord found someone to help the kid. She's been having a rough time."

"Yeah," Becca said, gathering Nicki closer. "We're working on all that."

"Good," Mona murmured, her eyes moving back to Cord. "That black bull I bought from Hudson has broken the fence and gotten into your pasture."

"Dammit, Mona! I don't want him breeding my cows. He's got a wild streak and I don't want that in my cattle."

"I know, Cord, and I'm sorry. You warned me and I wouldn't listen." She shook her head. "He had such good markings, though."

Cord stood. "Do you know where he is?"

"No, but my cowhands are looking for him. I just wanted to let you know."

"Thanks, Mona. If we run across him, we'll pen him."

"Okay. Just call me." She turned the horse abruptly and rode off.

Nicki stirred and opened her eyes.

Cord poked her in the ribs. "Hey, sleepyhead. How am I gonna make a cowhand out of you if you sleep all the time?"

"Daddy," she said impatiently. "I'm hungry."

"Della brought some homemade cookies, and I believe she has some milk for you." He reached to take Nicki out of Becca's arms and as he did, their eyes locked and everything faded away except for the feeling that flowed between them.

"Daddy," Nicki said again. Cord quickly gathered her into his arms and they walked over to the group still sitting in the grass, listening to Gus tell his stories. Becca didn't hear much. Her heart was singing too loudly.

Soon after that, the guys went back to work, and she helped Della and Edie pack up the remains of the lunch, which consisted of wrappings and empty cans. The cowboys had a healthy appetite. Becca was secretly glad when Della and Edie decided to stay for a while. The cowboys herded more cows and calves into the pen. It was thrilling to watch Cord. He was so natural on the horse, so in control. She couldn't take her eyes off him. The process with the calves started again and time flew by. Soon the last calf in the pasture was taken care of and the portable pens were taken apart and put on the trailer.

"Oh my, look at the time," Della said. "I've got to get back and fix supper."

"Why don't you and Edie take the Jeep?" Cord said. "Becca can ride with me. I want her to get the feel of a horse."

"Sure thing," Della answered. "See ya'll back at the house."

They clambered into the Jeep, which sputtered to life and roared off. Nicki was on Half Pint, ready to go. Becca glanced up at Cord on the big horse. "Is there a correct way to get on this thing?"

Cord's mustache twitched. "Yeah," he said, sliding his boot from the stirrup. "Put your foot in there and swing up behind me."

"Which foot?"

"The left one."

"Put my foot in there and swing up," she repeated. "Just like that?"

"Yeah."

"It's easy, Becca," Nicki said.

She looked up again and Cord seemed a hundred feet in the air. How could this be easy?

Sensing her nervousness, Cord held out his hand. "Come on, give me your hand and I'll pull you up."

That was all she needed. She placed her foot in the stirrup and gave Cord her hand, and with one smooth movement she was on the back of his horse. Her arms locked tight around Cord's waist. The ground had never seemed so far away.

"Becca, you have to loosen your arms. I can't breathe." Laughter edged every word.

She swallowed. "Do you have to?"

"Occasionally."

She slowly loosened her grip, then the horse moved and her arms tightened again.

"Relax," Cord coaxed. "Apache won't do anything I don't want him to do."

Apache! Oh God, she was on a horse named Apache.

Slowly they began to trot, and the movement of the horse reminded her of being in a boat—an easy flowing rhythm she could identify with. Her body relaxed as the creak of leather soothed her nerves and the musky scent of horse filled her nostrils. She reveled in the hard muscles of Cord's chest and back. Oh, she liked this.

The scenery was spectacular with green grasses, tall oaks, birds and cattle here and there. The landscape brought a sense of peace that was unequaled.

"You okay?" Cord asked.

"Yes," she answered. "It's so beautiful out here."

"Yep, there's nothing like it. I've always loved the outdoors. Clay and Colton were different. They preferred to stay in the house and read or play games. I hated school, but they loved it. I didn't like the confinement."

"So what did you do after high school?"

"Went into the army."

That was a surprise. She had assumed he'd never left the ranch.

"It was a learning experience, and what I learned was that I never wanted to be anywhere but on this ranch. It's in my blood, as Pa used to say."

"Why is the ranch called Triple Creek?"

"Three major creeks run through the property. My ancestors were looking for a good water supply and they found it here. There're also some ground-fed springs. Water's important to a rancher."

Becca heard the love and pride in his voice. It was clear that his heart was in this land.

Nicki raced ahead and shouted, "C'mon!"

"She's very good with a horse," Becca remarked. "She takes after you in that."

"Yeah," he replied somberly.

"Why didn't Anette like her to ride? Nicki obviously loves it."

"Because Anette didn't want her involved in anything she couldn't participate in, too, and she was deadly scared of horses. Anette was scared of a lot of things. I guess Nicki was about two years old when I just took her and put her on a horse. Anette was furious. She said if anything happened to Nicki she'd never forgive me. She had this fear of Nicki getting hurt. She was so protective of her.... That's why it doesn't make sense that she'd kill herself. Nothing about her death makes sense."

"It does seem strange," Becca said.

They rode in silence for a while, and Becca wondered what had happened to Anette Prescott. What had made her do such a terrible thing? The truth would probably never be known.

"How you doing back there?" Cord asked.

"Great," she answered, and her arms tightened instinctively around him. Would he ever get over his wife's death? Would there ever be room for another woman in his life?

They rode up to the barns, where Mona and several cowhands were waiting for them.

Mona glanced at Becca on the back of the horse. "Something wrong?"

"No," Cord said. "Just giving Becca a tour of the ranch."

"Oh, well, we found the bull and we've got him in your pen. I'll pick him up in the morning, if that's okay."

"Sure, no problem."

"I'd do it this evening, but we have that cattlemen's meeting tonight."

"Damn, I'd forgotten about that."

"You are going, aren't you?"

Cord sighed. It was the last thing he felt like doing. He'd rather be with Becca. Still... "I'm the president. I have to be there."

"I'll see you tonight, then." She tipped her hat to Becca and rode off, the cowhands behind her.

"Daddy, Daddy, watch," Nicki called.

Cord turned the horse toward Nicki. She threw her leg over the back of the saddle and slid quickly to the ground.

"See?" Nicki smiled. "I can get off all by myself. I'm not little anymore."

"I can see that."

Becca was wondering how *she* was going to get off. If a child could do it, she resolved, then so could she. She did as Nicki had done—swung her leg over the back of the horse and slid to the ground. But she moved too quickly and lost her balance, falling backward. She landed on her rear, feeling more than a little undignified.

Cord dismounted. "Are you all right?" he asked, but she could hear the laughter in his voice. Nicki laughed without restraint, and Becca sent her an exaggerated look of disapproval.

"Yes," she answered, as he helped her to her feet. She brushed off her backside. "I just bruised my pride."

They stood staring at each other. She finally cleared her throat. "Thanks for the ride. I enjoyed it."

"My pleasure, ma'am."

A warm fluttering started in her stomach, and she couldn't tear her eyes away. She wanted him to kiss her so badly....

Nicki leaned against Cord's leg. "I'm tired, Daddy."

Cord looked down at his daughter. "Who's gonna unsaddle your horse?"

"Gus will," she mumbled.

"No, Gus didn't ride your horse. You did. Now you have to take care of him. He has to be rubbed down and fed."

"'Kay, Daddy."

Becca thought that was a little unfeeling, but she knew Cord was trying to teach Nicki about responsibility. She also knew that he'd do most of the work.

Becca made her way to the house, as father and daughter

led their horses to the barn. She wished Cord didn't have to go out tonight. She wanted to be with him.

But there was always tomorrow, she consoled herself.

THE NEXT MORNING Cord hung around the house waiting for Mona to pick up the bull. Becca and Nicki went out to look at the animal. He was massive with enormous horns and he pawed at the ground in anger. Evidently he didn't like being penned up.

Mona drove up soon afterward with a trailer. She immediately began talking to Cord, so Becca left them to their business. Nicki wanted to see Half Pint; hand in hand, she and Becca strolled into the pasture. Half Pint was grazing some distance away and wouldn't come when Nicki called. Nicki ran back to the barn to get a feed bucket.

As Becca turned to follow, she saw the black bull—and he was running directly toward her. Fear shot through her and she fell instinctively to the ground. The bull charged over her. She felt the heaviness and the sweaty heat of the animal, and her breath locked in her chest.

Stark terror rippled along Cord's spine as he saw the bull run over Becca. He dashed over to Apache and jumped into the saddle. "Gus!" he shouted, swiftly turning his horse toward the bull. Gus immediately joined him. The bull charged Apache, but Cord managed to move out of the way. He pulled out his rope and swung it at the bull, and between him and Gus, they drove the bull back into the pen.

Cord had one thought—to get to Becca. She *had* to be okay. He was out of the saddle before Apache came to a stop, and threw himself down beside her. "Becca, Becca," he murmured, gently rolling her over.

"Oh," she moaned, and sat up.

Cord wrapped his arms around her. "Thank God you're

okay." He drew back. "Did he step on you?" He glanced at her body.

Becca brushed grass from her blouse and jeans. "No, I don't think so." Her voice came out hoarse and unsteady.

Cord swept her into his arms and carried her to the barn. Mona hurried toward them.

"Cord, I'm sorry. I have no idea how this happened."

Cord set Becca on a bale of hay. "I want to know how that gate came open and I want that bull off this ranch."

Gus laid a hand on his shoulder. "She's fine, boy. Calm down."

Cord took a long breath. "Mona, I want that damn bull off this property—now. Gus will help you load him. I want him gone. Do you understand me?"

"Sure, Cord," Mona answered, and turned away.

Nicki came running over and crawled up beside Becca. "Oh, that mean bull! I don't like him."

Becca slipped her arms around Nicki, just needing to hold on to someone. Her body was quivering and she couldn't make it stop. Cord knelt down, gazing into her eyes.

"Are you all right?"

"Yeah." She tried to smile and failed.

"Let's get you to the house."

She staggered to her feet but her legs buckled, and Cord scooped her up and started toward the house. Nicki ran behind them.

"What happened?" Della asked as they came through the back door.

"That bull ran over Becca and Daddy's real mad." Nicki spoke up before Cord could.

"Oh my God."

"I'm taking her upstairs."

Once they reached her room, Cord carefully placed her on

the bed. "Are you sure you're okay?" he asked in a worried voice.

"I'm just a little jittery, that's all," she assured him.

Della, Edie and Nicki entered a moment later. Della had a cup in her hand.

"We brought you a hot…" Nicki glanced up at Della. "What is it?"

Della gave Becca the cup. "A hot toddy. It'll calm you down."

"Thanks, Della." She took a sip. It was definitely brandy and something else—and it did calm her. Her body hadn't stopped trembling, but with Cord looking at her so tenderly, she didn't mind.

"I'll be back in a minute," Cord said suddenly, and left the room.

He met Gus at the back door. "Is that bull gone?"

"Yep, and Mona's pretty upset. You were kinda hard on her."

"One blow from that bull's hooves, and Becca could be dead. I don't take that lightly."

Gus removed his hat and scratched his head. "It was a bad thing, but the doc's okay."

"How did the gate get open?" Cord asked.

Gus shrugged. "It wasn't latched properly and that bull's good at finding holes."

"Still."

"It was an accident." Gus watched him for a second, then added, "You've been champin' at the bit lately, and it's time to let that horse run."

Cord scowled fiercely. "What the hell are you talking about?"

"You got some heart-bustin' feelin's for the doc."

Cord didn't say anything because he couldn't deny it.

"I'd better get back to work," Gus muttered. "I'll check

on those calves we worked yesterday and see that Burt gets started cuttin' that hay, 'cause I know *you'll* be hanging around the house."

Cord walked around to the patio and sat down. He rubbed his face with a shaky hand. Gus was right. His heart was about to burst inside with the feelings he had for Becca. He'd never felt like this about any woman. He gazed off to the pool and watched as the sun glistened off the water. But all he could see was the bull charging straight for Becca. He would see that for a very long time.

He could ride and rope with the best of them, but he was powerless to stop a two-thousand-pound bull. That chilling thought had gripped him as he rode frantically for the animal. His only thought was to keep the beast away from Becca—to keep her safe. *Heart-busting'.* Oh God, he loved her. He'd known it in that instant as he felt his heart being ripped from his body. It didn't matter that she was too young. Nothing mattered but the way he felt.

He took a tortured breath. It was a relief to admit it, but beyond that he didn't know what to do. He knew she was attracted to him, but her life was in the city and his was here. He had brought one city girl to Triple Creek, and he'd sworn he would never do that again. Where did that leave them? Becca wasn't like Anette, though. She didn't seem to be afraid of anything.

Yet they were so different, and sexual chemistry couldn't change that. Could love?

CHAPTER TEN

BECCA SPENT THE REST of the day being pampered by everyone in the house, especially Cord and Nicki. She told them repeatedly that she was fine, but Cord insisted she take it easy. She spent the afternoon on the patio and found herself alone for a few minutes. Cord had gone to answer the phone, while Nicki was kicking a ball around.

Blanche came through the French doors with a glass in her hand. She wore tight stretch pants and a tank top. She sat in a chair opposite Becca, the ice in her glass tinkling, and crossed her legs. "Heard you had a little mishap, sugar."

"Yes," Becca said guardedly, wondering where Blanche had heard it because everyone seemed to avoid her.

"Did it scare the crap out of you?"

Becca's eyes narrowed. "What are you getting at?"

"Time for you to go back to the city, don't you think?"

"You've said that to me more than once. Why do you want to get rid of me?"

She met Becca's eyes boldly. "Because you're not the woman for Cord."

"Why, Blanche? Why am I not the woman for Cord?"

"You're not, so leave before anything else happens to you." Blanche stood to go back inside, but Becca stopped her.

"Why do you have to be so…so hard and cruel?"

"That's me, sugar, and you'd do well to remember it."

Becca shook her head. "I don't think that's you at all. It's just a front you put up so no one'll get near you, not even your sons." She paused, then added, "I've seen you looking out the window when we've been doing things."

"In your mind that means what?"

"That you care more than you want anyone to believe."

Blanche gave a fake-sounding laugh. "Oh, sugar, you haven't got a clue about me or Cord. This ranch is his life. Anette couldn't get him away from here and neither will you."

"Is that it? You're afraid I'll persuade Cord to leave?"

From the look on Blanche's face, she knew she was right. Blanche was afraid of losing Cord. Becca moved to the edge of her chair. "I would never ask Cord to leave Triple Creek. He loves this place, and love is about giving, not taking."

"Every love I've known was about taking and it's a lesson that's served me well over the years."

"Has it? Then, why aren't you happy?"

Blanche took a swallow of her drink. "Look around you, sugar. Everything you see belongs to me—and that makes me happy."

"I don't think so," Becca told her. "I think you'd love it if your sons called you Mom. I think you'd love to be part of their lives. That's why you're desperately trying to hold on to the last piece of family you have—Cord."

"Shut up," Blanche hissed, and stormed into the house.

Well, well, well, Becca thought. Blanche loved her sons, but she would never tell them. Why was that so difficult for her? Maybe it had something to do with her upbringing, or maybe she was just afraid. She was certainly afraid of losing Cord; that was obvious from her reaction. But Becca knew that Blanche would never admit it.

THE NEXT FEW DAYS passed quickly. Cord was very attentive and he no longer seemed angry at himself for being attracted to her. She and Cord had very little time alone, however. Edie was now eating every meal with them and even Blanche had made a couple of appearances at the dinner table. On the third evening, they sat in the den and listened to Nicki, who regaled them with stories about her day. Then she insisted on playing the animal game and chose animals that had to be acted out by each person. She said Edie was to be a mule and Blanche a goat. The ladies didn't demur. They played along, and by the time it was over they were all laughing, Blanche as much as anyone. Becca thought this was the way it should be—laughter should always fill this house. And she had to give both Edie and Blanche credit.

Cord kept his word and taught her to ride. The next morning he brought out a reddish mare. "This is Ginger," he told her, rubbing the horse's neck. "She's gentle and affable. You shouldn't have a problem with her."

Becca started to laugh.

"What's so funny?" Cord asked.

"My best friend's name is Ginger."

"I'm sorry, but that's her name."

"I can't call her Ginger. How about…Ginny?"

"Sure, whatever." There was laughter in his eyes. "Come on," he invited. "Rub her head and neck. Get acquainted with her."

Becca did just that. The animal was so gentle Becca couldn't help falling in love with her.

"Okay, time to ride," Cord said. "You sit in the saddle and I'll ride behind you. That way you can learn to control her." She climbed into the saddle without mishap, then Cord swung up effortlessly behind her and they were off at a slow canter.

"A cowboy uses the neck rein technique," Cord told her. "That way, he can hold the reins in one hand and use the other to rope or do whatever he has to." He held both reins in his left hand. "To turn the horse to the right, you merely lay the reins on the right side of her neck and Ginger—Ginny—will go in that direction. Likewise for the left. Pull the reins toward you to stop." He demonstrated, and Ginny reacted instantly to the touch and pull of the reins. She followed his instructions, and it was the most exhilarating experience of her life. With Cord's breath on her hair and his arms around her, she thought she could do this forever.

Each day she got better at controlling the horse. Riding was a matter of balance, which she was learning. She couldn't wait to get Nicki up in the mornings, dressed, fed and to the stables. One of the first things Cord taught her was that if you ride, you take care of your horse and equipment. Handling a saddle wasn't easy, but she was determined and soon she mastered the skill, although Cord or Smithy always ensured she had the belts girded tight. The saddles were kept in the barn on long wooden sawhorses. Each cowboy knew exactly where his spot was and everyone respected the property of others. As Gus put it, *A cowboy don't mess with another cowboy's stuff.*

Becca was beginning to know the cowboys by name: Shorty, Snuffy, Hank, Rocky, Billy Bob, Joe Bob, Clint, Dusty, Big Jim, Little Jim, Burt and Weazel. They were between the ages of twenty and sixty. None seemed to be married, though some were divorced, and they lived in the bunkhouse attached to the barn. Saturday was their night to dress up, go into Houston and hit the bars and dance halls looking for a woman. They talked quite openly about their escapades. Clint and Dusty were the Casanovas in the group, and it was a given that they wouldn't return to the bunkhouse on Saturday night. But the cowboys were always betting on who else would "get lucky."

Becca enjoyed their antics and camaraderie. She realized she should return to Houston, but she didn't do anything about it. She and Cord were becoming closer and closer, and she wanted to spend some time alone with him. With Edie and Nicki around, privacy was nil. Soon, she kept telling herself. It would happen soon. She'd waited a long time to experience these feelings and she didn't have to question her needs or desires.

She knew what she wanted. She wanted Cord.

CORD WENT THROUGH EACH DAY as if in a dream. Becca loved to ride and she seemed to love the ranch and the cowboys. For their part, the cowboys adored her. He had a hard time getting them away from the barn to actually go and do their work. They were all eager to help if she needed anything and they were gonna be some lovesick pups when she left. Not to mention him. Mrs. Witherspoon had called twice asking about her return date, but he'd told her to take a little more time with pay. He kept postponing it, but he knew Becca had to leave. Her life was in the city. He'd sworn he would never put himself in this position again, but Becca was different. She had a big heart and a loving spirit and everyone responded to that—even Blanche. Blanche was now playing with her granddaughter…something Cord had thought he'd never see. Edie was riding again, and they were having meals as a family. All because of Becca.

And his heart, which had been closed for so long, was slowly opening. He wasn't sure what to do about it. He decided to take it day by day, hoping when the time came, that he would have the strength to let her go.

BECCA PACKED A LUNCH prepared by Della and Edie for the cowboys. Della helped her put the heavy ice chest and basket in the Jeep. Nicki, of course, wanted to take Half Pint, and Becca agreed when Edie decided to ride with Nicki. The child was very comfortable on her horse, but Becca worried about the risks she took.

She followed some distance behind Edie and Nicki. They were going to a different part of the ranch today where the cowboys were spraying the cattle with a medication against flies, ticks and other pests. Hooping, hollering and distressed mooing could be heard before they reached the site. The pens were set up in a clearing and cattle were herded in, sprayed and released.

Several cowboys were milling about the campsite. Becca parked the Jeep and joined them, surprised to see Mona there. The older woman apologized for what had happened with the bull.

"It was an accident," Becca told her.

"I know, but I'm just glad you're okay. I took that bull to auction and sold him right away. I should've listened to Cord."

Nicki rode up to Becca and jumped off her horse. "I'm hungry."

"We have to get the food out of the Jeep first. Can you wait?"

"'Kay," Nicki chirped, and ran to Gus to tell him something.

"Cord and I thought we'd never hear that again." Becca laughed. "Now we can't seem to fill her up."

"You've worked wonders with her," Mona said. "Cord's lucky to have a brother with such an understanding girlfriend."

Becca didn't know quite how to answer that, so she didn't. It wasn't any of Mona's business, anyway. Soon the rest of the cowboys rode over with enthusiastic greetings and shy grins. Dusty and Clint hauled the food and drinks out of the Jeep before she had to ask. Cord dismounted and walked toward her. Just the sight of him sent a shock of excitement right down to her toes. She was amazed at how her body reacted to him and no one else.

"I see you don't need any help." Cord smiled as he watched the cowboys quickly spreading out the food.

"I think they're very hungry." She smiled back, lost for a moment in the light in his eyes.

"Hot damn," Gus interrupted. "Fried chicken and biscuits. That Della's a peach of a gal."

"You should be grateful," Becca told him as they sat on the grass. Gus's dogs lay beside him, waiting for scraps. "She and Edie fried chicken all morning."

"Edie, I'd give you a big kiss if I didn't have a wad of chewing tobacco in my mouth."

"No, thanks, Gus. I'll pass," Edie muttered, and everyone laughed.

"Do you know how bad that tobacco is for you?" Becca had to ask.

"C'mon, Doc, don't preach at me."

"I've seen men with half their faces removed because of cancer caused by chewing tobacco."

"Ain't nobody taking part of my face off. I'm dyin' with my boots on. Besides, at my age it's a roll of the dice, anyway."

"Just so you know the dangers."

Gus turned and spit the tobacco in the grass. The dogs sniffed it, then settled back down. "Satisfied, Doc?"

"Don't do it for me. Do it for yourself and Della."

"Right now I'm doing it 'cause I wanna eat fried chicken."

There was another burst of laughter, and then everyone started to eat. Nicki sat in her lap with a chicken leg and a biscuit. Soon her head nodded against Becca's chest.

"My child always seems to fall sleep on you," Cord said.

"I don't mind," Becca said, licking her fingers. She was beginning to love Nicki so much, she wondered how she'd be able to leave her. She didn't want to think about leaving Cord. Tonight, she vowed, they would find time alone to talk and… the *and* part made her feel warm all over.

Mona asked Cord a question and that brief moment was gone. After lunch the cowboys headed back to finish spraying the cattle, but not before they'd helped clean everything up. Mona left, saying she had her own work to do. She apologized again for the incident with the bull. Nicki awoke and wanted her chicken leg, which Becca had ready for her.

Once the cowboys had finished spraying, they dismantled the portable pens and moved on to another pasture. Becca, Edie and Nicki followed the procession, reluctant to go back to the house. Becca enjoyed watching; the horses seemed to know exactly what to do and when, and the rider became part of his horse. One day she wanted to ride like that.

The dogs were also a pleasure to watch. They worked on commands from Gus, darting in and out of the herd, making sure that no cow or calf broke free.

The clouds grew dark, and Cord decided it was time to call it a day. Again Edie and Nicki rode ahead and Becca followed in the Jeep. The cowboys were still collecting the pens and storing them on the trailer. A few raindrops hit the windshield, and Becca hoped they could all make it back to the barn before the rain started in earnest.

The brakes seemed weak. She rounded a curve in the dirt road and applied the brake, but her foot went right to the floorboard. She pumped the brake several times, but it was useless. In her panic, she veered off the road and began to roll into a ravine. She tried to guide the Jeep back, but she was going downhill so fast that her efforts were jerky. She saw the huge oak a moment before the Jeep crashed into it.

Her head hit the steering wheel and sharp pain ripped through her. Everything floated around her in a fog. *God, please, don't let me lose consciousness.* But she couldn't focus, and try as she might, she couldn't stop the blackness that overtook her.

Cord.

CORD LEFT THE COWBOYS at the shed storing the pens, then rode toward the barn, eager to see Becca. He'd only been away from her for a little while, but even that was too long. Tonight he'd make time for the two of them. If he didn't kiss her and soon, he'd go crazy.

Before he could reach the barn, Nicki came charging toward him on Half Pint. "Daddy, Daddy," she shouted, and he immediately knew something was wrong.

"Whoa, slow down, baby," he said, stopping her. "What is it?"

"Becca, Becca…"

"What about Becca?" He had an uneasy feeling in his gut.

"She, she—we looked…and…"

Nicki wasn't making any sense; he was relieved when Edie rode up. "What's going on, Edie?"

"Becca didn't come back."

"What do you mean, she didn't come back?" That uneasiness turned into outright fear.

"We waited here for half an hour or so, then we rode back. We couldn't find her anywhere."

"She has to be *somewhere* between the site and the ranch!"

"I know, but she's not on the road."

"Daddy, where's Becca?" Nicki wailed.

He rode closer and put his hand over hers. "Go to the house with Edie and I'll head out to look for Becca."

"No, Daddy, no! I wanna look for Becca, too."

"Baby, listen to me. It's fixing to pour down rain, and I want you to go with Edie. I'll find Becca."

"You promise."

"I promise."

He nodded to Edie, then turned Apache and rode hell-bent for the shed. "Gus!" he shouted.

"Yeah?" Gus came out of the shed.

"Saddle up."

"What the hell for? It's startin' to rain."

"Becca didn't come back," Cord said urgently. "Something's happened and we have to go after her."

Gus whirled around. "Sure thing. I'll get the boys."

Within minutes they were saddled and ready to ride. Cord gave orders to check the road on both sides from the area where they'd been working to the barn. The rain began, a hard, driving rain, and darkness fell, hindering their efforts. An hour later they still hadn't found her. Cord thought he'd go out of his mind.

"Where the hell could she be?" he asked Gus.

"Don't know. The rain's washed away all the tracks. Ain't much we can do in the dark."

"Like hell." Cord exploded. "If anyone wants a job on this ranch, they'd better keep looking."

"Didn't say nobody's quittin'. We'd all ride through a blizzard for that gal. Just sayin' the weather and darkness ain't helping."

"She's just farther off the road than we think. Let's start again, and remember to tell everyone to fire three shots if—when—they find her."

"They know the signal. Don't worry. We'll find her."

Another two-hour search proved futile. The rain had stopped, but it was difficult to move a horse through the woods in pitch-black darkness. Cord was wearing a slicker but his boots and hat were soaked. Apache was also wet and tired, but Cord kept pushing him on. He *had* to find Becca. He cursed himself for not having had someone drive with her. After all, she didn't know this ranch. He should've taken better— Suddenly a deer jumped in front of them, and Apache reared onto his back legs.

"Down, boy, down." Cord talked to him in a soothing voice,

trying to calm him, but he felt just as nervous as the horse. *Where was Becca?* Fear gripped him like a vise, a fear he remembered well. He'd felt it the day Blanche had said "Something's wrong with Anette." But this was different. This feeling encompassed his heart, his body, his soul. And he knew what it was—love like he'd never known before. He'd admitted it earlier, but now he knew it beyond a shadow of a doubt. Becca was younger and a city girl, but none of that seemed to matter anymore. He just wanted to see her face again. *Oh God, please let her be okay.*

BECCA AWOKE to a throbbing in her head. She raised her hand to her forehead, and pain shot through her. Something dripped onto her hand. Blood. Everything came back with startling clarity. The brakes. The tree. As a doctor, she thought of neck and back injury, but she felt she was safe in that area. There wasn't much she could do. She had to staunch the bleeding; that was her next concern. It was so dark, though. She felt for the glove compartment and opened it, then fished around until she found a rag and something else—a flashlight. She held the rag to her head and wondered where she was and why no one had found her.

She winced as she tried to move, but managed to get out of the Jeep. She trained the light on the vehicle and saw that it was smashed against the tree and almost completely covered with bushes. She didn't even remember running through the bushes. The ground was wet, so that meant it had rained. God, where was she? Should she try to walk? Which way should she go? She saw no alternative and began to trudge up the ravine until she became so dizzy she had to stop. She took a couple of shaky breaths and sank to the ground as the darkness wrapped around her. She held the rag to her forehead and flicked the light on and off hoping someone would see it. The wind whistled through the trees with an eerie sound and lightning flickered across the sky. Another rainstorm wasn't far off.

She remembered another time she'd been in a rainstorm—the day she'd found out she was Emily's daughter. Filled with so many tumultuous emotions, she'd taken Owen's boat out in a storm, trying to run from the truth, but the truth was inescapable—like her love for Cord. She loved him and she had to tell him. Emily had told her she'd know when love was right. She finally understood what Emily meant. There was no indecision or doubt; she knew Cordell Prescott was her soul mate. Now she had to convince him of that...but first he had to find her.

She flashed the light several times, pointing it at the sky, then turned it off. She didn't want to run down the battery. She did that every ten minutes or so. She knew Cord was out there and he *would* find her. She just had to wait.

CORD GUIDED APACHE through the bushes, trying not to think the worst, but if she was hurt and needed medical help, time was running out. An armadillo appeared in front of them, and Cord pulled his horse to an abrupt halt.

He patted Apache. "Just an armadillo, boy." He looked down to see if there were more and noticed something in the bushes. He slid down from the saddle and began to drag the bushes aside. His breath caught in his throat when he saw the Jeep rammed against the tree. The passenger door was open and Becca wasn't inside. He looked in, resting his hand on the doorframe, and drew back as he felt something wet. It had to be blood. Oh God.

He glanced around. She couldn't be far. Then he saw it—a light flashing some distance away. He started to run, following the light. When he saw her, he sped up, then fell down beside her, his heart pounding so fast it was actually painful.

"Becca, Becca." He threw his arms around her. "Are you all right?"

"I bumped my head, but other than that I think I'm fine." Her voice quavered as she spoke. The rain was beginning again, mingling with the blood on her face.

"Are you sure?" He made a quick inspection of her arms and legs. "Nothing broken?"

"No," she breathed, dropping the bloody rag she'd pressed to her forehead. Cord quickly removed his slicker and draped it over them. She nestled in his arms, needing him more than she'd ever thought possible.

The rain beat down on them, but they were cocooned in their own private world. "What happened?" he whispered into her hair.

"I was making a turn and the brakes gave way. I pumped and pumped, but the Jeep wouldn't stop or slow down. Before I knew it, I was off the road careering down the ravine. I remember hitting the tree, then everything went black."

"Oh, Becca." His arms tightened around her. "I don't know what I would've done if anything happened to you."

That note in his voice made her feel suddenly weak. "I'm a little shaken, but I'm okay," she assured him again.

The rain continued to pelt down, but Becca hardly noticed. All she cared about was the man holding her so tenderly. Her hand slid up his chest to the warmth of his neck. Despite the stab of pain, she raised her head, and his lips covered hers urgently. She clung to him, eyes closed, and his mustache felt like velvet against her skin. She wanted him to touch every part of her. She gave herself up to pure sensation, and the world spun away.

Cord was melting into pure need—a need for Becca. Her hands, her softness, blocked out everything except the emotions inside him. His body hadn't been this alive in years.

He heard a sound and jerked his head up.

"What is it?" she asked.

"Someone's calling," he answered in a troubled voice. What was he doing? He'd been so glad to find her, he'd forgotten to alert the others. "It's probably Gus. I've got to let them know you're okay."

He began to get up, but she held on, kissing him passionately. His lips lingered on hers for a second longer. "Becca," he groaned. "You keep doing that and we'll stay lost forever."

"Sounds good to me," she whispered.

His hand touched her face and he drew it back when he felt the blood on his fingers. He scrambled to his feet. "I've got to get you to a doctor."

"Cord."

But he wasn't listening. He whistled and Apache came galloping up. He pulled a rifle from his saddle, then fired three times in the air. The sound ricocheted through Becca, returning her to the world of reality. As always, she and Cord had had a moment—that was it. She'd wanted to spend the night with him, but things had turned out so differently.

Would there ever be time for the two of them?

CHAPTER ELEVEN

CORD SWEPT HER UP into his arms and mounted Apache. How he did that she didn't know, but one minute she was on the ground and the next she was in the saddle. They set off at a slow, careful pace, and within minutes, they were surrounded by cowboys.

"You found her," Gus said. "Thank God."

"Yeah, the brakes went out on the Jeep and she crashed into a tree. The Jeep's in the bushes. I've got to get her to a doctor." With that, he kneed Apache and they took off. She could tell they were going faster than before by the rhythm of her body, but as long as Cord held her, she wasn't afraid. Behind them she could hear the clap of hooves and she knew the cowboys were following them home.

When she saw the lights of the ranch in the distance, a peaceful feeling came over her. Cord didn't stop at the barn. He galloped straight to the house. As he began to lift her from the saddle, Nicki ran from the house, screaming, "Becca, Becca, Becca."

Della, Edie and Blanche were right behind her.

Becca slid to the ground, and Cord caught Nicki before she could crash into her. When he let the child go, Nicki wrapped her arms around Becca's legs. "Where *were* you? We looked and looked. Where *were* you?"

"Baby," Cord said. "Becca had a wreck in the Jeep and I've got to take her to the doctor."

"Oh, are you hurt?" Nicki glanced up at her, frowning.

"I bumped my head and your father thinks I should get it checked out."

"I wanna go, Daddy! I wanna go."

"Now, baby…"

"No, no, no. I wanna go," Nicki wailed.

Becca felt as though the top of her head was about to spin right off, but she had to deal with Nicki. She couldn't leave if the child was upset.

Before she could say anything, Blanche stepped up. "Come on, sugarplum, stay here with us. You'll just be sitting in a stuffy old room at the hospital. Stay here and we'll play that animal game again. Wanna bet I can be a better cow than you?"

"No, you can't. I'm the best cow. Daddy said so."

Cord knelt beside her. "Go with Blanche, baby," he said. "It's way past your bedtime."

"'Kay," she agreed, then flung her arms around Becca's legs again. "You coming back, Becca?"

Becca swallowed and bent down, trying not to wince at the pain in her head. "Yes, I'm coming back."

"You promise."

"I promise," Becca said with a catch in her voice, and kissed Nicki's cheek.

"I love you, Becca."

Becca had to swallow again. "I love you, too, sweetie. Now go with Blanche. I bet she'll make you some hot chocolate if you ask nicely."

Blanche took Nicki's hand, as the cowboys rode up. They were wet and tired and looked at her with woeful eyes.

"Thanks for searching for me," she said shyly. She was wet, muddy and tired, too—not to mention in pain—but she'd never felt so cherished.

Dusty tipped his hat. "Our pleasure, ma'am."

"Yep," Gus said. "You're a sight for sore eyes, Doc."

"Okay, everyone," Cord broke in, taking her by the arm. "I've got to get her to the hospital." He led her to his truck as Gus grabbed Apache by the reins and the cowboys rode to the barn.

Soon they were on the highway to Houston. Becca felt herself drifting off but knew she shouldn't fall asleep.

"Talk to me," she said. "I have to stay awake."

"I was just thinking about the changes you've made in the Prescott house. Blanche is taking care of my daughter." He shook his head. "Never thought I'd live to see that. And she and Edie haven't had a cross word in days. They can actually eat a meal in peace—or close enough. I'm not sure how that happened, but I know you've worked some sort of miracle. And Nicki. I'm so grateful for what you've done for her."

"I guess I'll have to put my magical skills on the market," she said lightly.

"I'd be the highest bidder."

"Why?"

He took a deep breath. "Because I don't want you to leave Triple Creek." Then he quickly added, "But I'd never ask that of you. I know you have a career and a life waiting for you."

"What if I stayed voluntarily?"

The truck swerved to the right; Cord straightened it immediately. "Don't say things like that while I'm driving!"

"It's true." She wasn't ashamed to admit it. "I'd give up everything to be with you."

His hands tightened on the wheel. "I don't want another woman giving up anything for me."

"I'm not Anette, Cord."

No, she wasn't. She was young, vibrant and captivating, and he wanted to spend the rest of his life with her. He stopped at a red light and turned to her, but the words lodged in his throat. "Oh my God," he muttered.

"What?" she asked in a startled voice.

"Your face," he said. "The side of your face is blue and there's blood oozing from one spot. Are you in pain? Why didn't you tell me you were in pain?"

"Calm down. I'm sure it's just a bad bruise."

As soon as the light turned green, Cord made it to the hospital in record time. She directed him to The Methodist so she could at least see someone she knew.

A wheelchair was brought out when they arrived, and a nurse took Becca inside, where Cord filled out the necessary forms.

Before they'd even reached the waiting area someone called, "Becca Talbert, is that you?"

Becca turned to see an old friend. "Hi, Candace. Yes, it's me."

Candace eyed her wet and muddy appearance and studied the bruise on Becca's face. "What happened to you?"

"I had a car wreck. I'm waiting to be seen."

"We can't have that," Candace said. "Come on, I'll take you back and have a look."

"Candace, really it's..."

But Candace wasn't listening. She was already wheeling Becca down the hall into an exam room. Cord followed.

"Candace, this is Cordell Prescott and Cord, this is Dr. Candace Barker." Becca made the introductions.

"Nice to meet you," Cord replied.

"Same here, but I'm afraid I'll have to ask you to step outside while I exam her."

"Sure," he said, glancing at Becca. "Would you like me to call your parents?"

"No, please don't do that."

"Okay, I'll be right out there."

"Thanks, Cord."

After he left, Candace asked, "How did you manage to get rescued by a tall, handsome cowboy?"

"It's a long story."

Candace laughed and began to examine her. Becca felt there wasn't anything seriously wrong, but she had to be sure so she agreed to the tests Candace ordered. Her main concern was getting back to Cord. They'd started to talk in the truck and she wanted to finish their conversation. He'd said he didn't want another woman to change her life for him. But it wasn't about *changing,* in Becca's opinion. It was about accepting, about making compromises and being together. In a matter of three weeks, she'd fallen madly, wildly in love. She hoped Cord felt the same way. He hadn't *said* he loved her.

She had to talk to him.

CORD SAT IN THE WAITING AREA and noticed that people were staring at him. He must look a sight. He was wet and muddy from head to toe. He'd tried to wipe off his boots, but they were still caked with mud. He'd lost his hat somewhere and his hair was slicked back and dark with rain. None of that mattered.

There was a telephone in a corner of the room, and he wondered if he should call Emily and Jackson. No, Becca had said not to, so he had to respect her wishes. But he felt they needed to know she was hurt. God, would this terrible night ever end?

He didn't understand what had happened. They'd never had a problem with that Jeep before. If the brakes gave way, something had to have caused it. He strode over to the phone and called the ranch.

Edie answered. "Hi, Edie," he said. "How's Nicki?"

"She's fine. Blanche is upstairs reading her a story."

Cord was taken aback for a moment. Blanche was reading to Nicki? There was something wrong with *that* picture, but he wasn't going to question it. "Hard to believe, isn't it?"

"I know, and don't ask me what kind of story she's reading 'cause I'm not interfering."

"Thanks, Edie. I appreciate your restraint. Things are definitely changing in our house."

"Becca said it's time to let go of all the bitterness and hatred, and she's right. I'm too old to keep this up. Besides, Blanche is your mother and Clay's and Colton's."

"Yeah," he said, trying to digest this startling revelation of Edie's.

"How's Becca?"

"They're examining her. We'll be back as soon as we can. Is Gus around?"

"He's in the kitchen with Della. They were just fixing to leave. I'll see if he's still here."

Cord waited, and it wasn't long before Gus came on the line. "Hey, Cord. How's the doc?"

"Being examined," he answered, then added, "Gus, would you do something for me?"

"Sure, anything. You name it."

"At first light, get the boys to pull the Jeep to the barn and ask Smithy to go over it with a fine-tooth comb. I want to know why those brakes failed."

"You think it wasn't an accident?"

"I don't know, but there has to be a reason the brakes didn't work. Smithy keeps our vehicles in good running order, and he'll figure out what went wrong."

"Sure enough. We'll get to the bottom of this. You just take care of the doc."

"I will. See you in the morning."

He hung up with a somber expression. He had to have some answers—for himself and for Becca. He ran both hands over his face in a weary gesture, trying not to think about their conversation in the truck. But he couldn't block out her words. *What if I stayed voluntarily? I'd do anything to be with you.*

He wanted to grab at everything she was offering, but he had to do what was best for her. He still felt so confused, so bitter, over Anette's death. Colton was right; he couldn't drag Becca into his misery. But how did he let go of something he wanted with all his heart?

WHEN CORD WAS ALLOWED to see Becca, she was sitting on the side of an exam bed, wearing a bandage on her forehead. Her skin was so pale, it terrified him. His heart jackknifed into his throat, and he knew in that instant that he'd never be able to walk away from Becca. He could remind himself of all the reasons he should, but when he looked into her dark eyes all those reasons disappeared.

"Ah, Mr. Prescott," Dr. Barker said when she noticed him. "Becca has a bad bruise and a slight concussion. She'll be fine in a few days. She just has—"

"I know the drill, Candace," Becca broke in.

Candace winked at Cord. "She's on the stubborn side, so make sure she takes it easy."

"Don't worry. I will."

"I'll sign these release forms and you can be on your way." Candace rolled the wheelchair over.

"I can walk. I don't need that thing."

"Hospital procedure," Candace said calmly. "You know that."

Cord practically lifted her off the bed into the chair.

"Thanks," she said to Candace.

"No problem." Candace smiled. "Working with Dr. Arnold doesn't mean you can't visit us poor souls still here in the hospital."

"I'll remember that." Becca returned her smile.

AS THEY LEFT THE EMERGENCY ROOM parking lot, Cord asked, "Would you like to go by your parents' place?"

"It's the middle of the night, Cord. I'm not waking them up."

"I'm sure they wouldn't mind."

She turned to look at him. "I'm not ten years old."

"I didn't—"

"Are you trying to get rid of me?"

"No, of course not. I just want you to feel better."

"What'll make me feel better is to go home to Triple Creek." The word *home* had slipped out, but she wouldn't take it back. Even without her realizing it, that was what Triple Creek and the people there had become to her.

When they stopped at a red light, she caught his gaze and could almost feel the wall he was trying to erect between them. "Don't do that."

"What?"

"You're trying to think of everything you can to keep us apart—Anette, Colton, my career, my age—and they're simply excuses to mask what you're really feeling."

"I want what's best for you."

Her eyes didn't waver from his. "You're what's best for me."

"Becca." He reached out his hand to touch her face. She linked her fingers with his.

"When my head stops throbbing, we'll talk about this again. But right now, I just want to go home and go to bed."

Cord didn't say another word. He couldn't. Happiness was unfurling inside him with such speed that it made nonsense of everything he was thinking.

WHEN THEY ENTERED through the back door, the lights were on and Blanche was sitting at the kitchen table in a black negligée drinking coffee. She rose.

"How you doing, sugar?"

"A bit of a headache, but I'm fine."

"Well, I'm off to bed." Blanche yawned. "Didn't want to go to sleep in case Nicki woke up."

"Thanks, Blanche," Cord said. "That means a lot to me."

Mother and son stared at each other for a moment, then Blanche walked out of the room.

Cord picked up her cup and sniffed it.

"What are you doing?" Becca asked.

"Seeing what she drinking 'cause she's sure not acting like herself."

"What's that saying? Don't look a gift horse in the mouth."

His mustache twitched. "Yeah, I should leave well enough alone. Now, it's time to get you to bed."

Becca slowly made her way up the stairs with Cord supporting her. When they reached her room, he said, "Just undress and get in bed."

"I can't."

"What?"

"I can't go to bed without a bath."

"Surely that can wait. You're dead on your feet."

"I can't rest or sleep without a bath. I'm filthy."

"All right." He sighed. "But I'm not leaving."

"Fine." She moved into the bathroom and closed the door. Turning on the taps full blast, she stripped out of the dirty clothes. Then she eased into the water. Her body was aching and the hot water felt heavenly.

"You okay?" Cord called through the door.

"Yes. Stop worrying."

"I'm gonna take a shower. Be right back."

"Okay."

Cord rushed to his room, removing his clothes as he went. The wet boots were difficult to pull off, but he managed. He stepped into the shower, shampooed his hair and washed, doing everything as fast as he could because he didn't want to leave Becca for too long. He quickly dried off, slipped into a pair of clean jeans and a T-shirt, then darted back to her room.

He tapped on the door. "Becca, you okay?"

"Yes, but could you hand me my T-shirt? It's in the top dresser drawer."

"Sure." He found it without a problem, opened the door a crack and handed it to her.

"Thanks." As she slipped it over her head, the room spun crazily. She gripped the vanity to keep from falling. "Cord!" came out as a desperate cry.

He pushed open the door and took in the situation at a glance. She was trembling and her skin had gone a pasty white. He gathered her into his arms and carried her to the bed.

Pulling the sheet over her, he said, "Get some rest. Reaction is setting in."

"Please don't leave," she begged.

He nodded and sat down on the bed. "I'll stay until you fall asleep."

"I'd like that." She sighed, then added, "But I don't like that you're so far away."

He didn't, either, but he was trying very hard to keep his head clear, which was a wasted effort where she was concerned. He stretched out on his side and draped one arm over her waist.

With her head beneath his chin, she placed her hand on his chest. Her fingers felt his taut muscles and she drew strength from his closeness. "Oh, yes." She sighed heavily. "I like this much better."

He kissed her forehead. "Go to sleep."

"Cord."

"Hmm."

I love you echoed through her head as she drifted into sleep.

Cord knew she was asleep but he continued to hold her. Whatever she'd been about to say had curved her lips into an enchanting smile. Unable to resist, he gently touched her mouth with his own. She moved against him and every nerve in him came alive. He hadn't thought it was possible to have this overpowering need and love for anyone. With Anette it hadn't been this strong. Or if it had, he'd forgotten, with all the other problems in their marriage. Problems they couldn't work out. Problems that had ultimately led to her death. He never forgot that fact. He didn't want Becca to feel that kind of unhappiness. He knew they were two very different women, yet he couldn't rid himself of those doubts.

At the hospital, when he'd looked into Becca's eyes, he had known he couldn't walk away from her. His feelings for her went too deep for that. But one fear tortured him day and night. Could he make her happy?

Oh, Becca, where do we go from here?

CHAPTER TWELVE

THE NEXT MORNING Becca woke up to a slightly disoriented feeling, which surprisingly was not unpleasant. She reached out her hand, somehow thinking Cord was there, but he wasn't. It was cool where he'd lain, and she yearned for his presence. She pushed herself to a sitting position, brushing hair away from her face. Her body was achy and sore but otherwise she felt fine. Her head wasn't even throbbing anymore.

"Becca, Becca." She heard Nicki shouting a moment before the child burst into the room. Cord followed close behind.

Nicki ran to her side. "Daddy said I can't jump on the bed. Oh..." Her eyes grew big when she saw Becca's face. "Oh, you got an ouchie. Does it hurt?"

Becca leaned over and kissed her. "No, I feel okay this morning." Her voice slowed as she noticed what Nicki was wearing. She had on a red silk gown, and the thin straps had been tied into a knot to fit Nicki's small size. "Where'd you get that outfit?"

"It's Blanche's," Nicki said excitedly. "She let me sleep in it." She ran her hands down the red silk. "Isn't it pretty?"

"Yes, very," Becca said enthusiastically. She glanced at Cord, who was frowning. Their eyes met and she smiled, wanting him to know it was all right for little girls to play dress-up.

He smiled back, and her heart raced.

"Baby." He addressed Nicki. "Becca has to rest today. She can't play or go riding."

"That's okay, Daddy," Nicki informed him. "Blanche is gonna show me how to put makeup on."

"What!"

Nicki's face crumpled at the note in Cord's voice. "She said it was okay."

Cord took a calming breath. "Nicki, you're too young to wear makeup."

Nicki shook her head in agitation. "I'm just gonna *play* with it."

"I'm sure Daddy understands that," Becca said, her eyes catching Cord's and sending a message.

"Yeah," he said slowly, receiving the message and shifting his eyes back to Nicki. "Now it's time for you to get dressed."

"'Kay, Daddy. I can dress myself, then I'm gonna wake Blanche." Nicki ran from the room.

Cord opened his mouth to stop her, then closed it.

"Aren't you going to tell her that Blanche doesn't get up until noon?" Becca asked when she saw the glint in his eyes.

"No." He walked over to sit on the bed. "I think I'll let her surprise Blanche." He dropped a quick kiss on her lips. "How are you?"

She looped her arms around his neck and kissed him deeply in response. He groaned, gathered her close and took the kiss a step further. Delicious warm feelings swirled around them, and Becca didn't want the kiss to end, but Cord began to draw back.

"Much better, I'd say." He grinned.

"Yes, now that you're here." She stroked his shaven cheek and one finger traced his mustache. He caught the finger in his mouth, then kissed her palm and trailed kisses up her arm to her shoulder. Her body quivered from the sensation.

"I could stay here all day," he whispered into her neck.

"There's a thought," she said breathlessly.

"Hmm." He gave her a final quick kiss and got to his feet. "I've got a child to take care of, so stop tempting me."

"Cord, it's all right for Nicki to play with makeup and to wear fancy clothes. That's normal for a girl her age."

"I just don't want her to grow up too fast."

"I know, but Blanche's taking an interest in her is good."

"Yeah, I have to be careful what I wish for." A grin split his face and he added, "Take it easy today. Nothing strenuous. And maybe you should call your parents."

She frowned. "Cord."

"Think about it," he said as he left the room.

Becca stared at the phone, then picked it up with a sigh. She knew her parents would be up and it was probably a good time.

Her father answered the phone; she could tell he was startled by her voice.

"Is something wrong?" was the first thing he asked.

She told him about the accident, and her mother immediately came on the line.

"Becca, are you okay?" Her voice was full of anxiety.

"Yes, Mom, I'm fine."

"Why don't I come out to the ranch and check you over?"

"I'm fine. I just have a bruise on my head."

"Your father and I can be there in no time."

"You're not listening to me," Becca said impatiently.

"I'm sorry. I get a little nervous when one of my children's been injured."

"But I'm fine," she repeated again. "So you've got nothing to be nervous about."

"When are you coming home?" Emily asked, suddenly changing the subject.

"I'm not sure."

"You've been there three weeks and you said Nicki's doing better. Isn't it time to come back to Houston?"

Becca took a long breath. "No, the time's not right. When I decide to leave, I'll let you know."

"You sound annoyed."

"I am." Becca didn't lie or disguise her feelings, as she had so many times in the past. "I wish you'd let me make my own decisions and trust my judgment."

There was a long pause.

Finally Emily said, "I always trust your judgment."

"No, you don't," Becca said. "You're questioning my decision to stay here."

"Only because I want you home where I can take care of you."

"I'm not Scotty's age and I can take care of myself. If I couldn't, you'd be the first person I'd call."

Another long pause.

"I love you, Becca."

Becca blinked back a tear. "I love you, too, but I'm not a little girl anymore."

"You will always be my little girl."

"But now, please, let me be an adult."

"That's so hard, angel."

"I know, but it's what I need."

"Okay, then, I'll try, but you'll have to bear with me if I falter at times."

"I will, Mom. Always."

"Call me when you get back to Houston."

"I will. Bye."

Emily hung up the phone, turned in to Jackson's arms and promptly burst into tears.

"Emily, what's wrong?"

"Our little girl is all grown-up," she sniffed. "She doesn't need us anymore."

His arms tightened around her. "She will always need us, but we have to release our hold—let her live her own life."

"I don't like this part of being a parent."

"Ah, but this is where it gets good. Grandchildren will be next, and I can't wait."

"Grandchildren!" Emily drew back in shock, and Jackson laughed at her. It wasn't long before she was laughing with him.

CORD HELPED NICKI finish dressing, persuading her to wear a T-shirt and shorts rather than the frilly pink sundress she'd originally chosen. They were halfway through breakfast when the phone rang. It was Gus.

"Can you come to the vehicle shed as soon as possible?" he asked.

"What's up?"

"You need to see this for yourself."

"I'll be right there."

Cord left Nicki with Edie and Della, and hurried to the shed. He was sure it had to do with the Jeep, which made him anxious. Gus met him in the yard.

"How's the doc?"

"She has a bad bruise on her head and a slight concussion, but she's going to be fine. Just has to take it easy."

"That's great."

"Did you get the Jeep pulled in?"

"Yep, that's what I want to talk to you about. It didn't take Smithy long to find the problem."

"What was it?"

"The nut on the brake line tubing has been loosened. The brake fluid drained out."

Cord stopped in his tracks and stared at Gus. "What!"

"The nut was loosened," Gus repeated. "There're fresh marks on it. Smithy says it was done recently."

"You mean it was loosened intentionally."

"Looks that way."

"My God, who would do that?"

"I'd say we got a snake in the chicken house."

"But who?" Cord said under his breath as he walked into the building. Smithy showed him the line, and it was plain as day that it had been loosened. Smithy assured him it couldn't have been jarred loose. He'd checked the line last week and the nut was tight with not a mark on it. For a moment Cord was completely staggered. This was *intentional.* But he couldn't let his thoughts run away with him; he had to have more facts.

He walked some distance away, and Gus came with him. "What do you think's going on?"

Gus removed his hat and scratched his head. "Got me. Ain't nothing like this happened around here before."

Cord glanced off to the horses frolicking in the pasture. "Doesn't make sense. Who'd want to hurt Becca? Everyone likes her." He said the words he'd been trying to avoid, to deny. *Someone was trying to hurt Becca.*

"Yeah, maybe that's the problem."

Cord's narrowed his eyes at Gus. "What do you mean?"

"All the cowboys are smitten with her. Maybe one of 'em thought he'd come to her rescue. Be the big hero and all."

Cord shook his head. "That's hard to believe. I trust every cowpoke on this property."

"Me, too, but we have to face facts. We were the only ones around that Jeep yesterday."

"It must've been loosened sometime after it left Smithy's shop," Cord said almost to himself.

"That's what I'm saying. Becca drove straight to the bottom where we were working. No one else came near the Jeep except us, the cowboys and Edie. Mona was there for a little while, but she left when we went to the last pasture."

Cord dismissed them immediately. "Mona doesn't even know Becca, and I doubt if Edie has any idea how to loosen a brake line."

Gus thought for a minute. "Maybe someone wasn't trying to hurt the doc. Maybe they were trying to hurt you."

"What do you mean?"

"Joe Bates." Gus said the name that tied Cord's stomach into a hard knot of anger. "He said he'd get even, and he knows you drive that Jeep occasionally. He's a shifty character, and he could've slipped in and out of here easily. He knows the ranch."

"I suppose," he muttered, trying not to let his anger get the best of him. He had to think this through with a clear head. Still, none of it was logical. Joe Bates was all talk and basically a coward. He knew that if he pulled anything, Cord would come looking for him. But what if he was drunk? He'd been bold enough to show up at the ranch the other day. Surely the man wasn't so stupid as to try something like this. Nevertheless, Cord decided he'd let the sheriff know. But he'd start by questioning his cowhands.

"Get all the boys into the bunkhouse. I want to talk to them."

"Now, why don't you let me do that? I probably can get more out of 'em."

"I'll talk to them personally," he responded in a stubborn voice.

"Don't lose your temper. These are good boys," Gus reminded him.

"Maybe one of them isn't," he said in that same stubborn tone. When Gus began to speak, he held up his hand. "Whatever. Just get them in the bunkhouse—now."

Gus ambled away without another word.

Cord went into his office, which was attached to the tack room, and called the sheriff. Then he walked over to the bunkhouse with a hollow feeling in his gut. He had to get to the bottom of what was happening here. Now that he knew the Jeep's crash couldn't be dismissed as an accident, he had to acknowledge that Becca's life could be in danger. He had to keep her safe and he would do everything in his power to achieve that—even if it meant her leaving the ranch.

CORD ENTERED THE BUNKHOUSE with a dark expression on his face. The house consisted of a kitchen, large living area, two bathrooms and two big bedrooms with four bunk beds in each. The cowboys were gathered in the living area.

Cord didn't sit, nor did he say a word. He'd known each of these men a very long time and for a moment he just stared at them.

Dusty was the first to speak. "What's up, boss?"

Cord took a step closer. "It's about yesterday."

"The doc's all right, ain't she?" Clint asked anxiously.

"She has a slight concussion and a bad bruise on her face, but she's going to be fine."

"Great," Joe Bob put in.

"I want to thank all of you for your efforts in finding her last night." Cord thought he should mention that first.

"Ah, shucks, boss, it weren't no problem," Rocky said.

"What happened? Did she lose control of the Jeep?" Big Jim asked.

"No, she didn't lose control," Cord replied, letting his gaze sweep over them. "The nut on the brake line was loosened."

Cord watched their faces in the shocked silence that followed his words. A minute later, Dusty jumped to his feet.

"What the hell? Somebody did that on purpose?"

"Yeah," Cord replied.

"Well, I'll be a son of a bitch," Hank said. "Tell us who it is and we'll string 'em up."

"I don't know who it is. That's why I'm talking to you."

The silence became suffocating. Then Clint got to his feet. "Are you saying you suspect one of us?"

Gus intervened. "Now, don't go getting' a burr in your jeans. But we were the only ones around that Jeep yesterday, and it's not exactly a secret that you all are smitten with the doc. If one of you did something a little crazy, just tell us. That's all Cord's asking."

"I'll handle this," Cord said to Gus, a little offended that he'd interfered. He turned back to the men. "I'm just asking for the truth."

"Hell, boss," Clint said. "We may be cowboys, but we're not stupid. We can all see the doc only has eyes for you, just like the song says. She's a nice lady and we all like her. Not one of us here would harm her in any way."

"I believe you," Cord said without having to think about it. These men *wouldn't* hurt Becca. "Did any of you notice anything suspicious—anything out of the ordinary?"

"No, we were working," Rocky said, and each man in turn shook his head.

"Any of you noticed Joe Bates around lately?"

"He was at the feed store the other day when I picked up that load of feed," Little Jim muttered. "He said some snide things about you, and I told him if he didn't shut up, I'd smash his face in. He said you'd get what was coming to you."

Cord frowned. "This was on Tuesday?"

"Yeah. Want me to find him and rough him up a little?"

"No, the sheriff will talk to him. And he'll probably talk to each of you. Just be honest."

"Sure," Dusty said, then asked, "You do believe us, don't you?"

Cord nodded. "Yeah," he said, and walked out, Gus on his heels.

Outside, he turned to face Gus. "Next time I'm talking to the boys, please don't interfere."

"I'm sorry. I was only trying to help."

"Gus..." He took a deep breath, not sure why he was so upset. "I'm just—never mind. I have to talk to Becca."

He strolled toward the house, stopping as the sheriff drove up. Cord explained what had happened in more detail and showed him the Jeep. They talked a bit about Joe Bates, then Gus took the sheriff over to talk to the cowboys and Cord headed back to the house. He wanted to tell Becca personally; she deserved to hear it from him.

Before he could make it to the house, Mona drove up, pulling a cattle trailer. Cord could see a bull inside. He didn't have time for this. But he and Mona had been friends since they were kids. Mona and his brother Clay were the same age and she was more Clay's friend than his, but Cord occasionally helped her with ranching problems. He'd tell her what was going on, and she'd understand that he didn't have time to look at a bull today.

"Howdy," he said, as she got out of the truck. Mona was a strong, independent woman, and Cord had always admired that about her. Even after her father died, she'd continued to run the ranch with as much expertise as a man.

Mona glanced toward the sheriff's car. "Something wrong?"

"Yeah, there's been an accident." He told her about the night's events.

"Oh, no. Is Dr. Talbert all right?"

"She's fine."

"I'm so sorry, Cord. I know how appreciative you've been of the doctor's help."

"Not a very good way to show my thanks."

"No, but I'm sure the sheriff will find the culprit."

"Mona, did you notice anything yesterday?"

"I was only there for a little while."

"Did you notice anyone around the Jeep?"

She shook her head. "No, can't—wait a minute. Gus was putting an ice chest in the back as I rode away. But I'm sure that means nothing."

Cord thought about that for a second, but dismissed the possibility. Gus wasn't like that. He only wanted to help Becca. Didn't he? Cord shook his head to clear it of such traitorous ideas.

He glanced at Mona. "You seen Joe Bates lately?"

"Yeah, he was over at my place yesterday asking for work."

"He was?" That might be the answer to all his questions—Joe Bates.

"Yes, but don't worry. I didn't hire him."

"Damn, this is all so confusing."

"I guess I'll leave you to sort it out. I only stopped by to show you this new bull."

"Put him in your pen and I'll try to look at him tomorrow."

"Thanks, Cord, and try not to worry too much."

"Bye, Mona."

BECCA SPENT MOST OF THE MORNING on the phone. Not long after she'd talked to her parents, Grandpa George called, and she knew her father had told him what had happened. He insisted that he didn't want to bother her but just had to hear her voice. She assured him she was fine, and Grandpa George believed her. That was what she loved most about him—his trust in her judgment, his faith in her good sense. She suddenly realized that was the major problem with her parents; they'd never fully believed that she'd adjusted to the revelations that had changed her life. They wanted to be there for her, to comfort her, to help her. But with two such wonderful people, she had adjusted a long time ago. Now they had to trust her to live her own life. Becca felt good about this morning's conversation, in which she'd taken a stand on this very issue. The past, present and future seemed clearer in her head, and Cord had a lot to do with that. He eased her restlessness. And she needed that. She needed Cord.

Later, Rose and Owen called to see when she was coming to Rockport, but she knew they were really asking about the accident. She told them she was okay and that she wasn't sure when she'd make it to Rockport. Not before her birthday, which was in August. They didn't try to dissuade her, and she was grateful for that. She understood that everyone genuinely cared about her well-being, that her family wanted her to be happy. And she finally was. She couldn't wait to see Cord again.

After talking to Ginger, she curled up on the sofa in the den, leafing through a medical journal. Nicki crawled up beside her.

"You don't feel good, Becca?" There was a note of anxiety in her voice, and Becca knew she was remembering her own mother and all the times Anette didn't "feel good."

She kissed her cheek. "I feel great—and you know what?"

"What?"

"I think we need some chocolate. What do you think?"

"Yeah. We need chocolate."

There was a bowl of candy kisses on the coffee table. Becca was sure they hadn't been there yesterday. She reached over and grabbed a handful. She unwrapped one and handed it to Nicki, then popped one in her own mouth.

"Mmm, mmm, that's good." She sighed.

Nicki nodded. "Real good." She stretched out her arms. "It's gonna make your butt *this* big."

Becca made a face. "I sincerely hope not."

Nicki burst into giggles and Becca joined in. She loved this child so much. How was she ever going to leave? She gathered Nicki close and held her tight. A lot had happened in a short period of time, but she knew with overwhelming certainty that her heart would always be here with Cord and his little girl.

CORD CAME THROUGH the kitchen door and stopped short. Blanche and Edie were sitting at the table drinking coffee. It was a sight that took a moment to get used to. There were no hurtful words flying around—just an amicable silence.

Blanche glanced at him. "Cord, you should tell that kid of yours that some people don't get up at the crack of dawn."

Cord suppressed a grin. Blanche wore a lavender negligée, her hair was mussed and her face devoid of makeup. In all his forty-two years, he'd rarely seen that. Blanche never left her room unless she was perfectly dressed, coiffed and made up.

"And maybe you should be careful what you say to her. She was just excited about the makeup you mentioned." He glanced around the room. "Where is Nicki?"

"She's in there bothering Becca, thank God," Blanche groaned. "I don't think my eyes are fully open yet."

"They're not," Edie remarked. "You look like you've been rode hard and put up wet, as Gus would say."

"You're not exactly fresh as a daisy," Blanche shot back.

"It's almost noon and this is as good as I get," Edie added with a touch of humor.

"Okay, ladies." Cord held up both hands. "I need your help."

Blanche eyed him strangely. "Something's wrong, isn't it."

He told them about the Jeep.

"Oh my God," Blanche and Edie said in unison.

"Are you sure?" Della asked.

"Yeah, there's not much doubt about it."

"I tried to warn her but she wouldn't listen to me," Blanche mumbled.

Cord frowned. "What are you talking about?"

"This ranch is not a place for a city girl like Becca."

Cord decided to let it pass. He didn't have time for that conversation and preferred not to hear Blanche's opinions on the matter, anyway. He had to talk to Becca.

"Could you occupy Nicki while I speak with Becca?"

"Okay," Edie said. "I'll take her riding."

"That's not a good idea. The sheriff's still here and I don't want to upset Nicki. It might remind her of Anette's death."

"Oh my." Edie put a hand to her mouth. "This is awful."

Blanche got to her feet. "Go get the kid, Edie, and bring her to my room. I'll find some old makeup and paint her up like a clown."

Edie's eyes narrowed. "I will not take orders from you."

"Don't start," Blanche warned.

Cord intervened. "I'll bring Nicki. And for God's sake, get a grip. I don't need this right now."

"I'm sorry, Cord," Edie said immediately.

"Yeah, whatever," Blanche added disagreeably. "I'll be in my room, and believe me, the kid knows where it is."

"I'll send her along," Cord said a moment before he headed for the den.

Becca and Nicki were sitting on the sofa with their heads together. One blond, one dark. His heart melted as he watched them. Becca had brought so much into this house. She had reached Nicki when no one else could and she had touched him in a way that even now was hard to understand. He knew he'd never be the same. Whatever had happened in Becca's past, she had a great capacity to love, to laugh and to share. Now he had to tell her that someone had sabotaged the Jeep—and possibly tried to kill her. How would he do this?

With the truth. Becca would expect no less.

CHAPTER THIRTEEN

"DADDY," NICKI SHOUTED, and scrambled off the sofa when she saw him. She ran into his waiting arms.

"How's my baby?"

"Fine. Becca and me are eating chocolate. Want one?" She held a candy kiss in her hand.

"No, thanks, but Blanche might. She's looking for you."

Nicki frowned. "She was grouchy when I waked her."

"Well, she's in a better mood now and she's getting out some makeup."

"Oh boy." Nicki wriggled from his arms. "I'm gonna get pretty." She glanced back at Becca. "Wanna come?"

"No, sweetie, but you have a good time."

"'Kay." She charged out the door to Blanche's room.

Cord sat beside Becca. He removed his hat and laid it on the sofa, then turned to look at her. His heart constricted at the sight of her bruised face. He gently touched it with the back of his hand. Who had done this to her? Through him swirled anger, which he had to control.

She caught his hand and kissed each finger with slow thoroughness, and for a moment he forgot everything but her. "Becca," he said huskily. "We have to talk."

Something in his voice alerted her. "What is it?"

He linked his fingers with hers. "I had the Jeep pulled to the shed, and Smithy took a look at it."

"Did he find out what was wrong with the brakes?"

Cord nodded but he didn't say anything else.

"Well?" she prompted.

"Did you notice when the brakes got weak?" he asked.

"They worked fine going down there, but when I started back they weren't holding too well, and finally they didn't hold at all."

"I see."

She watched him for a few seconds. "Cord, what are you trying not to tell me?"

He looked directly into her eyes. "The nut holding the brake line was loosened and the brake fluid leaked out."

She blinked. "Loosened? What do you mean?"

"Smithy checked the vehicle last week and everything was fine. Someone loosened the nut."

"On purpose?"

"That's what it looks like."

She took a moment to digest what he was saying, but it was all so unreal. "Who would do that?"

"I don't know. The sheriff's talking to all the cowboys."

Her eyes widened. "The sheriff is here?"

"Yes, I want to get to the bottom of this, but I don't want you to worry. It wasn't necessarily intended for you. Anyone could've been driving the Jeep—including me."

"That doesn't make me feel any better," she said shortly. "Oh, no! Could it have been that Joe Bates?"

"Becca—"

"It could have, couldn't it?" she interrupted. "That's why the sheriff's here."

"Maybe," he admitted. "We're not sure. I..."

She could see he was having difficulty with the words, so she slid her arms around him. "What is it?"

"I just have this bad feeling," he whispered into her hair, not even realizing he was pouring out his heart. "It's the same feeling I had when I found Anette. I couldn't find any answers then, but I knew something wasn't right. Just like I know something's not right now."

"You said anyone could've been driving the Jeep."

"I think it's best if you go back to Houston." The words slipped out before he could stop them. Becca's safety mattered more than his need for her.

She drew back. "You want me to leave?"

He kissed her cold lips. "That's the last thing I want, but we have to do whaterever will keep you safe."

"I feel safe with you."

"Becca, please—"

"I'm not leaving," she said in that stubborn voice he'd heard before.

"Becca…"

"No, I mean it. I'm not running away like a frightened animal. If someone doesn't want me here, then they'll have to tell me to my face."

"Why do you have to be so stubborn?"

"That's just me."

"I know," he replied, shaking his head.

"Besides, I'm not abandoning Nicki. She's so much better, but I have to prepare her before I go."

Who's going to prepare me?

Nothing was said for a moment as Cord wrestled with his conscience. He wanted her out of harm's way, but he didn't have the strength to force her to go.

"Cord, I'm not Anette," she said calmly. "It takes a lot to scare me. I'll admit I'm a little afraid, but not enough to run away and hide."

He didn't say anything—just held her hand so tightly that it went numb.

"I know you have a lot of unresolved issues and feelings about Anette."

"Yeah," he admitted in a tortured voice.

This was the right moment to mention something that was bothering her. "Why haven't you done anything about Anette's things? Nothing's been touched since her death."

"I couldn't stand to go in there," he said brokenly.

"It's time," she whispered. "Go through her things. Put her to rest for good. You said you didn't have any answers about her death. Sorting through her belongings might give you the peace you need."

"This isn't about Anette. This is about your safety," he said in a frustrated voice.

"You said you had the same bad feeling about both."

He took a long breath. "Yeah, and I wish I could make it go away."

"You have to start somewhere."

"I can't go into that room." His voice was so low that she barely heard him.

"Yes, you can," she insisted. "You want answers about Anette and I think that's where you'll find them."

He frowned.

"Her whole life on this ranch is probably in that room. I'm sure you'll discover that she loved you and Nicki. It's time to recognize those feelings and put them behind you. It's time to live again." She kissed the corner of his mustache. "I want you to live again—with me."

"Becca." He covered her mouth with his own. She opened hers and gave him everything he wanted and more.

Della cleared her throat from the doorway, and they immediately drew apart. "The sheriff is in the kitchen."

"Be right there," Cord said in a hoarse voice. He gazed into Becca's darkened eyes. "You have a knack for getting me completely sidetracked."

"Nice, isn't it?" She smiled provocatively.

"I'm sure the sheriff wants to discuss the accident. Are you up to it?"

"Yes." She smoothed his mustache with her finger. "And I'm serious about Anette's room. It has to be done."

"I'll think about it," he conceded as he got to his feet and helped her up.

Becca knew they had no future without resolving the past. And she desperately wanted a future with Cord. The intentional tampering with the brake line was something she had to face, too. She had an eerie feeling that this incident and Anette's death were connected. How, she had no idea; it wasn't a rational conclusion. But she sensed that the place to start was Anette's room.

THE DAY PASSED IN A BLUR. The sheriff questioned them all, but there wasn't much anyone could tell him. Becca had seen no one suspicious around the Jeep and neither had Edie. The sheriff believed Joe Bates was probably the perpetrator. He didn't feel any of the cowboys had reason to do such a thing. He intended to find Joe Bates and see what he was up to.

Becca felt better, but she could see Cord was still suspicious. She knew his emotions were tied to Anette and she had to get him past that. She *had* to talk him into entering Anette's room.

Soon after the sheriff left, Nicki walked into the kitchen, and all Cord and Becca could do was stare. She had on a red dress of Blanche's that came down to the floor and she tottered on high heels. Beads adorned her neck and arms, and long silver earrings dangled from her ears. Her face was heavily made up and a purple streak had been sprayed in her blond curls.

She held out her arms. "Aren't I pretty?"

Cord couldn't speak.

"Yes, sweetie, very pretty," Becca said in a whisper.

Cord found his voice. "What's that in your hair?"

"Color. Ain't it neat?"

"No, I don't like it," Cord said before he could stop himself.

Nicki's bottom lip began to tremble.

"What Daddy means is that it's different," Becca said. "Once he takes another look, I'm sure he'll like it." She gazed pointedly at Cord.

"Yeah...yeah..." He spoke slowly, knowing what Becca wanted him to say, but the words were like sawdust in his mouth. He couldn't see his little girl behind the glitz and glitter.

Edie entered the kitchen and stopped dead in her tracks, her eyes on Nicki. "Oh my Lord."

"Look at me, Edie," Nicki called.

"Is it Halloween?" Edie whispered in Becca's ear.

"Nicki's been playing dress-up with Blanche," Becca explained.

"Oh my Lord," Edie said again.

"My sentiments exactly," Cord murmured.

Blanche breezed in at that moment. "Well, sugarplum, did you dazzle everyone?"

"I don't think *dazzle* is the correct word," Cord told her.

"Daddy doesn't like my hair," Nicki informed Blanche.

"Ah, your daddy's a cowboy and they like simple things. But you and me, we're movers and shakers."

"Yeah." Nicki beamed, obviously glowing in her grandmother's attention. "We move and shake. I'm gonna show Della." Nicki stumbled for the den.

"Have you no sense?" Edie hissed when Nicki left.

Blanche stepped close to her. "You know, Edie, I could

spruce you up, too, but it's kinda hard making a silk purse out of a sow's ear."

"And it's hard to make a lady out of a harlot," Edie shot back.

"Time out," Cord said loudly. "The main thing is that Nicki's happy." He paused, then added, "In the future, Blanche, try not to get so…overenthusiastic. I'd better find her before she breaks her neck in those heels." Cord hurried out with Edie behind him.

"How you feeling, sugar?" Blanche asked when they were alone.

"Much better."

Blanche pulled out a chair and sat down. "I guess it helps that Cord's so attentive."

Becca shook her head. "I'm not letting you goad me. But I'm proud of the interest you've taken in Nicki."

"Don't read too much into it, sugar."

"Oh, but I do."

"Then, that's your problem," Blanche said. "If I were you, I'd get the hell outta here before anything else happens."

"Is that another warning?"

Blanche's eyes met hers. "Take it any way you want, but that brake line was tampered with for a reason. It was intended for you or Cord. Either way, it's not good. You'd be better off in Houston."

There was a tone in Blanche's voice she hadn't heard before. "Are you worried about me?"

Blanche stood. "Sugar, I don't worry about anyone except myself. You're the worrying type, though, but you won't have to worry about the kid. I'll look out for her. Just go where it's safe." She disappeared out the door.

Well, well, Becca thought. Did wonders never cease? Blanche was afraid of showing emotion. That was why she'd left so quickly, but she couldn't hide her fear from Becca. Did Blanche know more than she was saying? Becca had a feeling she did. But what?

CORD AND BECCA HAD TO WASH and rewash Nicki's hair to get the purple out. After the second scrubbing, Nicki insisted she didn't want "no more of that stuff." Cord tiptoed out of the room a little later as Becca was reading Nicki a story. Nicki drifted off to sleep, but he still wasn't back. Becca put the book away, glancing at the inscription. Again she felt that a woman who loved a child this much would not intentionally kill herself. It had to have been an accident. But tampering with the brake line wasn't. God, why did she keep putting the two together? They'd happened so far apart and they weren't related in any logical way. Then, why couldn't she shake the ominous feeling?

Becca had a quick bath and put on a big T-shirt. She studied her face in the mirror and saw that it was much improved. The bruise was fading and the swelling had gone down. She'd always been a fast healer.

She went into the bedroom, wondering where Cord was. They hadn't said good-night and she was hoping that just maybe they'd spend this night together. She hadn't expected him to leave so suddenly. Where was he?

CORD STOOD AT HIS BEDROOM window, staring out into the darkness. His mind seemed numb, overwhelmed by the confusion of his thoughts. Was someone out there trying to hurt Becca? Or were they trying to hurt him? He didn't have any answers—just like before. *Everything* was just like before. The not knowing was the intolerable part. What was out there that he couldn't see? And *why* couldn't he? If there was a traitor on his property, he had to know. Around and around his thoughts went, until he threw back his head and clenched his fists. He had to know.

The place to start is Anette's room.

But that had nothing to do with Becca, he told himself. Then realization dawned. In a way, it did. Until he resolved his feelings about the past, he had no future. And all he could see in his future was Becca. All he *wanted* was Becca. Cord knew what had to be done—and he was finally ready to do it.

He opened a drawer and took out a key. A key from the past. The key to the room he'd shared with Anette.

BECCA SAT CROSS-LEGGED on her bed, trying to read an article she'd been working on all day. But her eyes kept straying to the door. Was Cord not going to say good-night? She couldn't believe how much that hurt her.

Just as she became absorbed in the article, there was a tap at the door. Her head jerked up, and she smiled as Cord stepped into the room.

"Hi," he said, walking over to the bed and taking in her smooth legs. A warmth settled in his loins, but he forced himself to ignore it. First things first. "I've been thinking," he said as he sat down.

"Have you?" She ran her hand across his broad shoulders, loving the way his muscles tensed.

He caught her hand. "Yes, and you're right."

"About what?"

"Anette's room."

She hadn't expected this. "You mean…"

"Yes. It's time for me to get rid of her things and close that door of my life forever."

"Oh, Cord."

"I've been so angry with her that I couldn't go in there.

Now I feel I can, and I want to do it while Nicki's asleep, but I need your support."

"Of course." She squeezed his hand.

He raised an eyebrow. "Ready?"

"Now?"

"Yes. I've got two big boxes in the hall."

"Okay," she said, getting off the bed. When he decided to do something, he meant business. But she was so glad. Cord needed to be free, and this was the beginning of that freedom.

She followed him down the hall to the locked door, where two boxes waited to be filled with the remnants of Anette's life. When he removed a key from his jeans and opened the door, a smell of dust and something Becca couldn't define greeted them. Cord flipped on the light, and for a moment they both stood and stared. The room was decorated in pink and deep blue, and the floral bedspread on the king-size bed was tumbled as if someone had recently been sleeping on it. Pictures of Nicki covered one wall, but Becca's eyes were drawn to the dresser. Three bottles of whiskey were still there—two were empty, but the third had about a fourth of the liquor still left. Becca realized that was the source of the foul smell. The room had a sense of doom about it.

Cord felt a suffocating sensation and he wanted to run, to forget he'd ever shared this room with Anette. He remembered the many arguments, the temper tantrums and the tears. Bad feelings about his marriage threatened to overtake him. Then he noticed the pictures of Nicki and the panic eased. Anette had given him Nicki, and he could never regret that. There *had* been good times, but they were so hard to remember, because the pain had darkened even those.

Aware of his turmoil, Becca slipped an arm around his waist and went into his arms. Without her shoes, she barely came below his chin. "Are you sure you want to do this?"

she said into his chest. His heart was beating so fast that she couldn't even count the rate.

"Yes," he muttered, and knew that he did. It was time. Gently releasing her, he pulled the boxes into the room. Without any real organization, he started opening drawers and throwing clothes into the boxes. Becca joined in until they'd emptied the dresser and armoire. Cord scowled at the whiskey bottles, then slammed them to the floor.

"Damn her, damn her," he cried in a strangled voice. "How could she do this to Nicki?" All the emotion he'd been trying to hold back suddenly burst forth.

Becca immediately hurried over to him and held him tight. "I don't think she knew what she was doing," she told him.

He clasped her just as tightly for a second, then let her go. "Sorry. I just lost it when I saw the bottles." His hand trembled as it touched the dresser. "I don't know where they came from. We didn't keep liquor in our room, and the whiskey's not a brand Blanche stocks downstairs, so Anette must have bought them herself."

Becca knelt and picked up the bottles, which hadn't broken. As she did, she noticed something against the dresser. Several pills were lying on the carpet, almost hidden in the deep pile. "Look," she said, picking one up. "There're pills on the floor and they're an antidepressant. I recognize the tablet."

Cord glanced at the pill and drew a deep breath. "She must've been taking as many pills as she could and following them with liquor. All this time, I was hoping it was an accident, but it must have been intentional."

"I suppose," Becca murmured in a weak voice.

"What? You don't think so?"

"I just keep remembering the books she bought for Nicki and the inscriptions. It's hard for me to imagine a woman with that much love abandoning her child, but depression alters personality."

Cord sucked air into his lungs and released it. "I'm glad I did this. I know she committed suicide for some reason of her own. A reason I wouldn't understand. But now I have to accept it, even though I'll always wonder if I could have changed things."

"Probably not," she said. "So you have to stop blaming yourself."

"Yeah, I've carried that burden around for too long."

"I agree," she said. She lifted the jewelry box on the dresser. "I'm sure you want to save this for Nicki."

"Yes, I put Anette's wedding and engagement rings in there after the funeral. I definitely want Nicki to have those."

Their wedding picture stood on a corner of the dresser. Cord picked it up and placed it in a box.

"Cord," she admonished. "I'm sure Nicki will want that, too." She knelt by the box and retrieved it, then studied the two people in the photo—a much younger Cord in a suit and tie, but still just as handsome and stirring to her senses. Anette was blond and very pretty. Nicki looked a lot like her.

Becca touched the photo. "So you like blondes?"

There was a note of uncertainty in her voice, and Cord wanted to reassure her. He knelt behind her, pulled her hair away from her face and gently kissed her neck. "Not anymore," he whispered.

She leaned back against him, and he slipped his arms around her. "Oh, that was the right thing to say," she teased.

"It's the truth." He kissed the side of her face as she rested her head against him.

"Still, I think you need to keep the photo for Nicki."

"Okay," he said. "But I believe her memories of her mother are fading. These days all she thinks about is Becca, Becca, Becca. You've overshadowed all the pain in her life." His arms tightened around her. "Just like you've overshadowed all the pain in mine."

"Oh, Cord." She turned in the circle of his arms and met his lips with a need that was unequaled by anything she'd ever felt. When that need was about to consume them, Cord drew away and scooped her into his arms. "Let's continue this somewhere more comfortable."

"But we haven't finished the room."

"We'll finish it in the morning," he told her. "Right now, all I want to do is love you."

CHAPTER FOURTEEN

HE CARRIED HER TO HER ROOM and placed her on the bed. His lips found hers while his hand slid beneath the T-shirt to her breasts. Pinpoints of pleasure shot through her as his thumb gently massaged, then his lips followed. The feather-light stroking of his mustache against her skin sent her senses spiraling out of control. She never dreamed it could be like this—she couldn't think, she could only feel.

"Oh, Becca," he whispered. His lips trailed down her abdomen. "I want to take it slow and make this perfect for you, but it's been so long for me, I don't know if I can. I've never wanted anyone the way I want you."

She had to tell him the truth. She forced herself back to reality, which wasn't easy with her body pulsing at a new rhythm.

She swallowed. "I want you just as much. But..."

His tongue stopped its exploration of her navel and he raised his head. His hair was disheveled from her hands and his eyes were glazed with passion. "But?"

"This will be my first..." She couldn't finish. Admitting such a thing at her age was embarrassing, somehow.

"Are you saying..."

She nodded.

He immediately tried to pull away, but she held on to him. "Oh, no, Cordell Prescott. You're not doing that to me. This is *my* choice, my decision. My mother always told me I'd know when the time was right. The time is now and the man is you. Do you know why?"

He shook his head, mesmerized by the fire in her eyes.

"Because I love you."

He closed his eyes and sagged against her. "Oh, Becca."

"It's true," she told him. "My heart flutters when you walk into a room. My knees get weak when you smile at me. I hurt when you hurt, and I can't stand the thought of being apart from you. There's a special connection between us. I don't know how it happened, it just did. Yes, you're older than me and more experienced, but you are my soul mate."

Cord felt his heart beating in unison with hers. They *were* one. He'd felt it for a very long time. But could he take from her what she was so willing to give?

He drew back and stared into her darkened eyes. "I've made so many promises about you. I promised myself I wouldn't get involved with Colton's girlfriend or someone so young, and most definitely I wouldn't fall for another city woman. But I broke all those promises."

She kissed the corner of his mustache, his cheek, and then her tongue tantalized his ear with gentle strokes.

"Becca." His head tilted toward her as the emotions she engendered in him overshadowed his doubts. He took a deep breath. "I have a feeling I'm going to break another one."

She smiled and rained kisses along his neck to his jaw. Her lips met his in a long, heated kiss and her hands quickly unbuttoned his shirt, her fingers reveling in the taut muscles before she unfastened his belt.

"Wait." He breathed raggedly. "I have to take off my boots."

"No problem." She laughed as she slid to the floor, grabbed a boot and began to pull.

"A cowboy's dream," he remarked. "A woman to remove his boots."

"I thought a cowboy's dream was to have a woman warm his bed."

"Ah, they're one and the same thing." Cord grinned. "First she removes his boots, then she warms his bed…among other things."

The task completed, Becca stood and removed her T-shirt. "I can do *other things*." She met his grin, which slowly turned to an expression of awe.

"My God, you're beautiful," he whispered. He reached for her, pulling her between his legs. His lips found her sensitive breasts and then he quickly removed her panties, and his lips and hands tantalized her body until her knees buckled and they fell back onto the bed.

She helped him out of his jeans, and his body was hard, firm and aroused. Her hands touched and explored and excited feelings she'd never experienced before. "Becca, are you sure? I don't think I can—"

Her finger covered his lips. "I don't want you to stop. I want you to love me."

He cradled her face in his hands and gazed into her eyes. "Do you know how much I love you?"

She smiled the most beautiful smile he'd ever seen. "No, but you can show me."

"Becca, Becca." His tone was ragged as he rolled her onto her back.

He was gentle and tender, just as she'd known he would be. The first thrust of pressure tightened her muscles, then Cord kissed her deeply and her body melted into a shimmering receptacle. The next thrusts she accepted with unbound pleasure that echoed through every nerve ending and intensified until she cried his name with an urgency that carried her to a realm she'd only dreamed about. Cord moaned his release a moment later, but they held on to each other, still needing that closeness.

"Are you all right?" he said, his breath warm against her neck.

"Oh-h, yes. Cowboys definitely do it better."

He grinned at her. "How do you know? You have nothing to compare it with."

"Oh, I just know." She smoothed his hair back. "That's why I waited so long. I've been waiting for you."

"Becca..."

"Don't ruin this moment with regrets," she warned.

He kissed her softly. "I won't. I've just never met anyone like you before."

"Good." She sighed. "Now I just want to go to sleep in your arms and feel your breath on my skin."

He moved to the left side of the bed and pulled her in to him. "That can be arranged."

She snuggled against him. "Thank you," she whispered.

"I'm the one who should be saying that." He kissed her neck. "Go to sleep, my Becca. I'll be here when you wake up."

She fell asleep with that thought in her head. *He will be here.*

Cord got up and turned off the lights. When she murmured softly, he gathered her back in his arms. Tomorrow he'd probably have those regrets and curse himself for taking something so precious from her, but tonight he would cherish this moment and this woman.

BECCA WOKE UP to a lethargic achy feeling and it was a wonderful sensation. She stretched languorously and reached for Cord. He wasn't there. *Oh, no.* He'd said he'd be here. He couldn't have—then she spotted him in the bathroom shaving, and her heart rebounded.

For a few minutes she just watched him. Shaving cream was slathered across his chin and he was methodically shaving away a night's growth. All he had on was his underwear. Light brown hair covered his lean body in all the masculine places—places she'd explored last night. A warm ache dissolved in her lower abdomen as she remembered his gentleness. Their lovemaking was everything she'd ever thought it would be, and she was so glad she'd waited for Cord. Sex with love was exactly as Emily had told her—more than a physical act, it was a coming together of two hearts, bodies and souls.

Her hands ached to touch him. She slipped out of bed and walked naked into the bathroom. She curled her arms around his waist from behind, drew in his tangy masculine scent and kissed his back. "Good morning."

Cord's whole body jerked alive at her soft touch. He wiped shaving cream from his face with a towel and turned to her. His breath caught in his throat at her sheer loveliness. Her hair was mussed, her eyes bright, and she was beautiful to her soul. He didn't know how he'd got so lucky, but he wasn't going to question his feelings anymore. They were too damn good.

"Good morning," he murmured as he kissed the fading bruise on her face. Then his hands caressed her smooth shoulders and worked their way down her arms to her waist and pulled her nude body against him. He leaned against the cabinet, holding her close, marveling at all the emotions that tripped through his body—emotions that had been dormant for too long.

His eyes slid to her breasts. "When I saw you in tight jeans, I thought that was as good as it got. Then I saw you in that big T-shirt with those gorgeous legs and I knew it couldn't get any better than that. But this—" he kissed each breast lingeringly "—is my favorite. You without a stitch on is pure heaven."

Her body shivered with delight as she stood on tiptoes and linked her hands behind his head. "I kind of like you that way, too."

"Do you?" He grinned mischievously.

"Mmm." His lips smothered the sound against her mouth

in an open, revealing kiss that she welcomed. "I like that, too." She giggled as she felt his hardness against her.

He groaned and the kiss deepened. Her fingers tangled in his hair and his hands were equally at work on her body. Slowly he turned, and they moved toward the bed, still in each other's arms. They tripped over his boots and fell backward onto the bed laughing. But the laughter died as more urgent demands took over. Cord kissed, touched and caressed until everything spun away but the love that bound them together.

Later—how much later she wasn't sure—she lay in the crook of his arm, savoring this special time with the man she adored. Nothing would ever equal the experience of finding love and having it returned. She suddenly knew what her restlessness was all about—Becca the woman had been struggling to emerge…and now she had.

"I don't want to, but I've got to go," he said with a tremor in his voice. "I'd have a hard time explaining to Nicki what I'm doing in your bed."

She turned her head and kissed him. They hadn't talked about the future, but they would. In the meantime, their love would grow until it encompassed everyone around them. Last night had been a big step, and each step now would guide them toward the future.

Cord hurriedly slipped into his jeans and grabbed his boots and shirt from the floor. "I'll get Nicki up and fed so you can take it easy," he said. "Then I'll ask Edie and Smithy to take her riding, 'cause I want to finish cleaning out Anette's room." He reached down and softly kissed her warm lips. "Oh," he muttered. "If I don't go now, I'll never get out of here. See you later." Another quick kiss and he was gone.

She pushed up against the headboard and sat for a long time with her arms around her waist, just enjoying these wonderful new feelings. Cord loved her and she loved him. But she felt an uneasiness, a vaguely unsettled sensation, which she knew must be related to Anette's death. She had to put that out of her mind. Cord had finally accepted it; that was the main thing. Today they'd clear out the rest of Anette's things and, as Cord had said, close that door forever. After that, they'd talk about the future. Instinctively, she realized that Cord would not want her to give up her job—just as she'd never ask him to leave this ranch. She could easily commute. It would take her thirty to forty-five minutes to get to work each day, depending on traffic, but she wouldn't mind. She'd do a lot more to be with Cord.

A smile spread across her face, and she knew she had to talk to someone. She picked up the phone and punched in Gin's number. It was early, but she knew Gin would be getting ready for work. Not that she planned to tell her every little thing. She just wanted to tell her best friend that she'd finally fallen in love. Madly, deeply, forever in love.

The phone rang several times, then a sleepy voice came on the line. "Hello."

Becca was startled. That wasn't Gin's voice—but she knew it well. "Colton, is that you?"

"Becca?" He sounded just as startled.

"Yes."

"Oh—you're...probably wondering what I'm doing here."

"No, I—"

He broke in. "I...uh, Ginger's having a problem with her car and I stopped by to help her."

Becca frowned. Colton was lying. He didn't know a thing about cars and he'd be the last person Gin would call. Wouldn't he?

"I'm glad you could help her," she said for lack of anything else to say. "Is Gin there?"

"Yeah, yeah, she's right here."

There was a moment of strained silence. "Hi, Bec," Ginger said, her voice tentative.

"Has the world stopped turning and no one told me?" she asked in a teasing manner.

"What do you mean?"

"You asked Stuffed Shirt for help. That has to mean something drastic."

"Well, stuffed shirts are good for something." Becca heard a muffled laugh. "I've got to go," Gin added quickly. "I'm running late. I'll talk to you when you get back to Houston."

Becca hung up the phone with a smile. Something was definitely going on between Colton and Ginger. And they didn't want her to know about it. Why? She was happy for them; she had to make that clear as soon as possible.

SHE AND CORD DIDN'T GET TO Anette's room until later in the day. Nicki clung to Becca, not wanting to do anything without her. Becca figured this had to do with her injury, and she spent the morning reassuring Nicki. They played games, read stories and laughed. She didn't want Nicki to lose any ground. Becca knew it was time for Nicki to be in a play group, which would help prepare her for school in August.

After lunch, she and Cord walked to the stables with Nicki and Edie. They watched her ride for a little while, then headed back to the house. Smithy promised to keep an eye on Edie and Nicki.

They held hands and couldn't seem to stop smiling. Blanche gave them a knowing look, as did Edie and Della—but that was fine. Everyone could see they were in love.

In the hall Cord pulled her into his arms and kissed her deeply. "I've been wanting to do that all day."

"Me, too," she whispered against his lips.

"We could go to your room," he muttered hoarsely.

"We could," she agreed, "but let's finish Anette's room first…."

"Good idea," he said, moving down the hall. "I don't want to think about this anymore after today."

As Becca followed, she remembered the pictures of the Prescott men. She'd never asked Colton, but she wanted to know. "Cord, why are there no portraits of Prescott women?"

He shrugged. "I'm not sure. It just seems to be a tradition to hang portraits of the men."

"That needs to be changed," she said in a tight voice.

He raised an eyebrow. "Does it?"

She poked him in the ribs. "Yes, and I'm sure Blanche and Edie would agree."

"Oh God, I can feel a family uprising about to start."

"It doesn't seem fair to me," she went on, ignoring him. "Prescott women have produced Prescott men, so..."

He gave her a quick kiss. "It isn't, but nothing in this family is done the way it should be."

"That needs to be changed, too."

He shook his head. "You've already changed a lot of that, and if anyone can change the portrait situation, you can, but for now, let's concentrate on Anette's room."

They worked until they had everything in boxes. Becca noticed that all of Cord's things had already been removed from the room. Cord taped up the boxes of clothing and accessories and carried them to the garage to be taken to a charity. Anette's purse and several small photo albums were still in a drawer, and Becca couldn't help flipping through the albums. There were pictures of Cord, Anette and Nicki and their life together. Anette's expression was often tense, and she was smiling in only a couple of the photos. She seemed to be constantly unhappy. Becca assumed that was a result of her depression—Anette's obvious anxiety and inability to feel happiness.

Cord said he didn't want the albums, so Becca added them

to the things they were saving for Nicki. She didn't know what to do about the purse so she handed it to Cord. Dumping its contents on the bed, he pulled out the credit cards and license to destroy. The makeup and miscellaneous items he threw in the trash. Photos, he put in with the albums. He picked up an envelope and tore it open. Inside was a letter.

Becca leaned over his arm to read.

Stop bothering me and making those vile insinuations and remarks. I can't take any more. If you don't stop, I'll tell Cord. I'm serious. You don't frighten me. A

"What does that mean?" she asked.

Cord shook his head. "I have no idea and there's no address on the envelope." He took a long breath. "Someone was bothering her. Who? And why? God, this is so bizarre."

She rubbed his arm. "I know, and I guess there's no way we'll ever find out."

He tossed the letter onto the bed. "That's what makes me so damn angry. I just want to know."

Becca wrapped her arms around him, wishing she could give him some answers. All she could offer was comfort. "Let's finish up and get out of here," she suggested.

"Sounds good to me," he murmured in a distant voice, staring at the letter.

She left him with his thoughts and stepped inside the walk-in closet. At the bottom she found two handmade quilts.

"These are so lovely," she said, picking up one of the quilts. "Who made them?"

"Anette," he answered solemnly. "The doctor thought it would be good for her to have a hobby. She really enjoyed it for a while, then she just lost interest."

"We definitely have to keep these for Nicki," she said,

gathering up the quilts. As she stood, she noticed something that had been concealed beneath them. "What's that?"

It was a small metal box. Frowning, Cord took it into the bedroom. "I'm not sure. I've never seen it before." He laid it gingerly on the bed.

Still holding the quilts, Becca stood beside him and they both stared at it. "Is it locked?" she finally asked.

Cord sat down and tried the lock, and the lid popped open. There were papers inside. He took a deep breath for strength. He didn't know what these papers were, but somehow he felt they were going to change his life. He wanted to slam the lid and throw the box away, but he couldn't. He had to face what was in the box—for himself, his child…and Becca.

He withdrew the first paper and unfolded it. Setting down the quilts, Becca sat next to him and read the document. "It's your marriage license," she said.

"Yeah," he murmured with relief. Maybe this wouldn't be as bad as his gut was telling him. The next paper was Nicki's birth certificate. At the bottom was a large document. Cord slowly unfolded it and as he began to read, his body started to tremble and he couldn't stop the anger that coursed through him.

"What is it?" Becca asked worriedly.

"It's Pa's will." The words were low and bitter.

Becca's first thought was to wonder what Anette was doing with Claybourne Prescott's will; her second was to ask why Cord was so angry. His hand clenched the paper and a look she'd never seen before came over his face.

"Cord." She placed her hand on his arm. "Tell me what's wrong."

"This says…" He had to swallow before he could continue. "This says the ranch was left to me and Edie. Clay and Colton were given trust funds, and Blanche a monthly allowance."

"Oh." Becca suddenly understood what was wrong. "Did you never see your father's will?"

"Yes, but it wasn't anything like this. Everything was left to Blanche, and his children received trust funds." He paused, staring down at the will. "You see, Blanche Duffy and Claybourne Prescott made a deal. He would leave everything to her if she married him and gave him a son. The will was drawn up when Clay was born—and that was the will I saw. This one throws me."

"Oh," she said again.

"This is dated twenty years ago."

"Then it was made later than the original will," she said. When she noticed the shock on his face, she wished she hadn't spoken.

He stood and started to pace. "Looks that way, but what the hell was Anette doing with it? She never mentioned a thing about Pa's will. What does this *mean?*"

She got up, too, and flung her arms around his waist, stopping him in midstride.

"I don't understand any of this," he mumbled into her hair.

"I don't, either, but there *has* to be a reasonable explanation," she told him.

"Yeah," he muttered, his eyes dark. "And I know exactly where to get it." Still clutching the will, he grabbed the letter from the bed and stormed out of the room.

"Cord," she called, but he was gone. Becca could guess where he was going—to find Blanche.

CHAPTER FIFTEEN

CORD CHARGED INTO THE KITCHEN, where Della was dicing onions. "Where's Blanche?" he asked abruptly.

"In her room, I think." She eyed him strangely.

"Go outside and find Edie and tell her to come to the house. And please stay at the stables with Nicki."

Della put down the knife. "What's wrong?"

"Just do as I ask. I'm not in the mood for a lot of questions." Cord knew his voice was hard but he couldn't help it. Inside he was a cauldron of emotions.

"Sure, sure," Della said as she headed out the door.

Cord turned and saw Becca standing in the doorway with a worried frown. His stomach churned with the love he felt for her, but it didn't diminish the other emotions. "I have to handle this in my own way," he told her.

"I know," she said. "Just try not to lose your temper."

He went down the hall and banged on Blanche's door. "I want to talk to you now." When there was no response, he banged again. "*Now,* Blanche."

He joined Becca in the den and paced as he waited for his mother. She finally arrived, dressed in a tight black dress and heels. She was obviously getting ready to go out.

"What the hell's the rush?" she complained, staring at her red nails.

"You want to explain this to me?" He shoved the will in her face.

"What is that?"

"Pa's will. His last will and testament," Cord burst out. "It reads a little differently from the one we saw after his death. So I think you'd better explain—and fast."

Blanche's skin took on a grayish hue. "Where did you get that?" she asked, sinking onto the sofa.

"I found it in Anette's room."

"That bitch. She said she was gonna destroy it."

Cord took a jerky breath and tried to maintain some control. "What was Anette doing with it in the first place?"

"She was looking for Nicki's birth certificate for school and came across it in my safe. I'd left the damn thing open."

"Why didn't she tell me?" He couldn't understand that. Why would Anette keep this a secret from him?

"You're the last person she wanted to know."

"What!"

"Think, Cord," Blanche said. "If you found out you owned half this ranch, she knew you'd never leave. Her main goal was to get you away from here. My secret was safe with the snotty little—"

"Shut up!" Cord shouted. "So this is Pa's last will?"

"That's it," Blanche said in an impertinent tone.

"And the will you showed us?"

Blanche remained quiet.

"Tell me!" he shouted again.

"That was the will Claybourne drew up when Clay was born," Blanche said.

"And? Dammit, Blanche, you'd better tell me what happened because I'm losing my patience."

"After...after you boys were grown, Claybourne changed his mind. He went to the lawyer one day and changed everything, then told me what he had done. He said Clay and Colton weren't interested in the ranch, and you and Edie were. He said I would always be taken care of and I didn't have to worry. But I did. I wanted to leave him because he'd broken our deal, but I had nowhere to go and I'd never see my boys again. I..." Blanche turned away, her shoulders heaving.

Cord gave her a minute to recover; he needed one, too.

"I didn't know what to do." Blanche continued. "I knew Edie wouldn't let me stay here. So I did the only thing I could. I used the first will."

Cord sucked air into his tight lungs and realized he was still holding the letter from Anette's purse. "Explain this."

Blanche frowned. "I don't know what that is."

"You were bothering Anette—threatening her—and she couldn't take anymore. You pushed her over the edge."

"Now, wait a minute," Blanche said indignantly. "I didn't threaten her. She's the one who threatened me. I don't know what that letter means, but it has nothing to do with me."

Edie came in, and Becca caught her and held a finger to her lips.

Cord glanced at his older sister and decided he could only deal with one thing at a time. "So let me get this straight. Pa left me and Edie the ranch, and you took it upon yourself to lie, to deceive us."

Blanche clasped her hands, twisting them nervously. "I didn't have any choice," she mumbled.

"What are you talking about?"

"I gave up my life for Claybourne and all he left me was a pitiful allowance. I couldn't live on that. I had to do something and—"

"A pitiful allowance?" Cord interrupted harshly. "A whole family could live on what he left you. You have free room and board and the ranch pays for your Cadillac and credit cards. What else do you need money for?"

Blanche stared at the big diamond on her hand. "It was more than that."

"How?"

She looked directly into his eyes. "I haven't been a good

mother. Hell, I haven't been a mother at all, and Edie hates me. You two would've kicked me out before Claybourne was ever buried. This ranch has been my home since I was a girl." Her voice quavered on the last word.

Cord ran both hands through his hair. "You believed I would kick out my own mother?"

"Yes," she said without hesitation.

Cord swallowed hard. "I lost track of the number of times Pa said to me, 'When I'm gone, son, look out for your mother. Take care of your mother, son.' Do you think I would go against anything he ever asked of me?"

"I didn't know," she said weakly.

"He cared about you, and if you'd given any of us a chance, we would have, too."

Blanche trembled and she seemed to have difficulty breathing. "When Claybourne and I talked about getting married, he said he'd leave everything to me if I gave him a son. Over the years, Edie has made that look as if I was a greedy bitch out to get everything Claybourne had. It was Claybourne's idea, but in truth it was the only reason I agreed to marry him. I wanted freedom from the men and the bar, and I wanted a better way of life. Claybourne said he'd treat me like a queen. He said I wouldn't have to lift a finger. And he kept his word. He treated me better than I'd ever been treated in my whole life and I began to care for him. It wasn't just a bargain anymore, it was real, but I didn't know how to tell him that.

"When I got pregnant with Clay, I was nervous. I was still just a kid and I didn't want to be a mother. I didn't know anything about it. All I knew was how to tend bar. Claybourne said not to worry, he'd take care of everything. After Clay was born, he whisked me off to a spa for a month to recover and hired a nanny for the baby. He was just so grateful to have a son. He did the same thing with each child. I never had a chance to bond with my babies. I never...I never got to hold my babies."

Silence stretched for endless seconds and Cord had difficulty absorbing the heartfelt words. "Did you really want to?" he finally had to ask.

Blanche met his gaze. "Yes."

"Then, how could you do this to me—and Edie?"

"I was fighting to stay here," she said quietly. "That was my only reason."

"Why hold it over our heads for years?"

Blanche twisted her hands again. "Because...that's the only way anyone noticed I was here."

The emotion in Blanche's voice startled Cord, and he was at a loss for words.

"You horrible, horrible woman." Edie broke in, unable to stay quiet any longer. She glanced at Cord. "Is it true? There's another will? Pa left me half the ranch?"

Cord handed her the will.

"Oh God. Oh God," she said, and started to cry. "I thought he'd forgotten about me. But he didn't. He knew how much this ranch meant to me. Oh God, I can't believe it." She sank unsteadily into a chair and stared at Blanche. A sly smile tugged at her lips. "Well, the tables have turned. And you're right, Blanche. I want you out of here as soon as possible."

Blanche got to her feet. "Gloat all you want, Edie," she said. "I could've kicked your ass out of here when Claybourne died, but I respected his wishes. I gave you just as much money as my boys, and I put up with your holier than thou attitude not out of the kindness of my heart, but because I knew Claybourne wanted it that way. All these years you've alluded to the men in my life. Well, after I married Claybourne, I was faithful to him, and there hasn't been anyone since his death. Hell, I not only gave him a son, I gave him three. So believe all the bad things you want. You've always looked at me as the enemy, as someone who took your place with your father. You never looked at anything from my point of view. I was young and a stranger in your house. I knew I had to be strong to survive. I did a terrible thing with the will, and I'm not apologizing for it." She took a breath and continued. "You've taken far more from me than I've ever taken from you. So gloat if it makes you feel better."

"What do you mean, I took from you? I never took a thing!"

"You took my babies," Blanche said quietly.

"Because you didn't want them."

"I wanted my babies, but I just never knew how…" Blanche blinked back a tear and Becca could see she was fighting not to cry, still struggling not to show any emotion. "Christmases were the worst. Claybourne just assumed I didn't want to be part of the festivities. I always watched you boys open your gifts from the hallway." She looked at Cord. "I gave you your first saddle—the one with the silver on it. I had a hell of a time dragging it into the house. Claybourne thought Edie bought it, and Edie thought Claybourne bought it. One never questioned the other. I also bought Clay and Colton their first computers. There were always presents from me under the tree, but no one ever knew and I—" Her voice cracked and she shook her head.

She'd bought him the saddle; that was all Cord could think. He remembered how excited he'd been when he saw it. He'd loved that saddle. He'd used it until he got too big for it, and Nicki used it now. *Blanche bought the saddle for him.* He'd never even dreamed his mother thought about him. His emotions were overwhelmed by so many new feelings.

"I'll pack my things and get out of here," Blanche added in a rush.

"No one's going anywhere," Cord said, and Becca couldn't have loved him more than at that moment.

"Sit down, Blanche," he added. "We have to sort this out." He looked at Edie. "I know how you feel and I also know you're not hard-hearted. Blanche has a lot of explaining to do and we're both going to listen." He turned back to Blanche. "How did you get Pa's lawyer to keep the second will a secret?"

Blanche moved uncomfortably. "After Floyd Dawson drew up the will, his job was done. Claybourne didn't ask him to keep it or to see that his wishes were carried out. Then Claybourne put the original in the safe, but he didn't destroy the old one. I didn't know what I was going to do when your father passed away—and then I saw both wills. Claybourne and I had made a deal, and I decided to stick to our agreement. It wasn't something I consciously planned. I was desperate and I did it before I could really think about it. I was home free until that stupid Anette started snooping around."

Cord closed his eyes briefly. "At this point, Blanche, it would be in your best interests to make an effort to stay on my good side. Snide remarks about Anette aren't accomplishing that."

"I want her out of here, Cord," Edie said, her voice hard.

"Let me handle this, please," he said to Edie. Then he addressed Blanche. "So Dawson knew about the second will and said nothing."

"It's not his job to enforce it."

"Morally, ethically, it's his job! Hell." He shoved a hand through his hair.

"She needs to be in jail," Edie said. "She's committed a crime. I know she has."

"Edie," Cord said sharply, his eyes never leaving Blanche. "We made this easy for you, didn't we, Blanche?"

"Yes. After the funeral, Clay and Colton were eager to get back to their jobs. They looked at the will and said to let them know when I'd taken care of everything." Blanche let out a long breath. “And you were so broken up over Claybourne’s death, you didn’t want to talk about wills or anything else. You let me handle all the details.”

“Do you know why that was?”

Blanche shook her head.

“Because we trusted you,” Cord said. “I trusted you not to do something like this to me.”

Blanche bit her lip, and Cord could see she was wrestling with her conscience. He was glad to learn she had one.

“We all knew about the first will,” he went on. “We’d heard the story all our lives. And we also knew how much Pa loved you. It never crossed our minds that he’d change his will.”

Blanche pushed back her hair nervously. “He never believed I loved him. He thought someone so young couldn’t love a man his age. I didn’t love him at first, but I grew to love him more than I’d ever thought I could. I wouldn’t have stayed here, otherwise.”

“Ha,” Edie interjected.

Cord ignored Edie, trying to take in everything he was hearing. This Blanche was throwing him. This Blanche had feelings. He was angry with her, yet he found he couldn’t maintain that anger. Still, through all the tumultuous emotion, he had to be clear on one thing.

“I’m not sure what to believe right now, but I want you to tell me the truth about Anette.”

Blanche gave him a puzzled frown. “What about her?”

“The letter. Did you have anything to do with it?”

“No! I wouldn’t lie to you now. Whoever Anette wrote that letter to, it wasn’t me.”

Cord was unsure and needed more detail, more corroboration. “You’re the one who found her. What made you go to her room?”

“When I got in that day, Della and Edie had Nicki in the

kitchen and Nicki was crying, wanting her mother. I asked where Anette was, and Edie said she'd been in her room most of the day. I decided the lazy bi—" She paused and changed her tone. "I decided she wasn't getting away with that. She was gonna take care of her kid. I found her on the floor with the whiskey bottles and the pills. I immediately called you, and you rushed her to the hospital. That's all I know. I never realized she drank so much."

"Maybe because you made her life a living hell," Cord snapped.

"She wasn't the saint you thought she was," Blanche shot back. "What do you think she did when she found the will? Did she tell you? No. She held it over my head, threatening to tell you, and she enjoyed every minute of it. Finally I told her to go ahead—that would put an end to her dream of leaving. She knew I was right and she didn't have to write me a letter to tell me that. Whatever we had to say to each other, we said face-to-face."

Cord sighed tiredly. "Where did the liquor come from?"

Blanche blinked. "What?"

"The liquor that was in our room is not the kind that's kept in this house. Where did it come from?"

"How would I know? She did have the ability to buy things. Wait a minute—" Blanche's eyes narrowed. "Are you saying *I* bought her the liquor?"

"I'm not saying anything. I just want answers."

"Well, I don't have them."

Silence. Cord stared at his mother and tried to piece everything together, but nothing was fitting, nothing made sense. He sighed again. Before he did anything else, he had to sort out the will.

"Edie and I have to talk," he finally said. "And I have to

call Clay and Colton. Everyone has to know the truth, and we have to deal with it."

"Fine," Blanche said. She turned and left the room. Becca followed her.

BECCA FOUND HER SITTING on her bed, twisting the rings on her fingers, a broken expression on her face.

Blanche glanced up as Becca stepped into the room. "If you've come to add your opinion, sugar, you'd better hurry because I'm not gonna be around much longer."

"You don't know Cord very well if you think he'd make you leave," Becca said. Blanche had done a terrible thing, but Becca understood her motive and she knew Cord did, too. Her whole life, Blanche had been fighting to survive, and keeping the will a secret was just another instance of that.

"Yeah, well, what I know about my sons could be stored in a thimble."

"Then stop trying to alienate yourself from them."

Blanche gave her a puzzled look. "What are you doing here, sugar?"

"I'm not really sure. I'm so angry at what you've done to Cord. He's suffered so much over Anette's death and he doesn't need this. But somehow…" Becca paused, unsure of her next words. "Somehow I understand why you did it."

"Oh, please." Blanche laughed scornfully.

Becca let that pass. "Just tell me one thing."

"What?"

"Do you know anything about Anette's death?"

"I told Cord I don't, and I'm not lying about that."

For some reason Becca believed her. She'd had a lot of doubts about Blanche and she wanted to resolve them. "Ever since I've been here you've been trying to get me to leave. You've even made insinuations about something happening to me. Why?"

Blanche stared at her rings, then raised her head, her eyes holding Becca's. "Cord and I have had our disagreements, but he's the only son I have who even knows I'm alive. As long as I had control, I could keep him here. But the moment I saw you together, I knew you had a different kind of power over him. A kind Anette never had. You could take him away from here—away from me. He didn't deserve another city woman screwing up his life. I wanted to protect my son from any more pain."

Becca had already guessed most of this, but she was relieved to hear Blanche admit it.

"Yet you've hurt him." Becca couldn't help saying it.

"Yeah." Blanche flipped back her hair. "That proves what a good mother I am, doesn't it?" She spoke in a careless tone, but her attempt at indifference didn't fool Becca.

"Three little words could solve all your problems."

"And what would those be?"

"I love you."

Becca expected a comeback, but none came. The broken look returned to Blanche's face, and she seemed to be struggling for composure.

"Let your sons know you love them," Becca urged. "Love can work miracles."

When Blanche didn't respond, Becca walked out. She was sympathetic—surprisingly so—to the older woman, but her main concern was Cord and what he was going through. How would he handle this? Whatever he decided, she knew she'd be there for him—no matter what.

CORD SAT FACING HIS SISTER, searching for the right words. Before he could find them, Edie spoke.

"I want her gone."

"I know you do, but please understand that she's my mother." Cord didn't know why he was pleading Blanche's case, but that biological bond was there and he couldn't ignore it.

"She was never a mother."

"Maybe because she was never given the chance or maybe because she didn't know how." He rubbed his hands together. "Did she really give me the saddle?"

Edie shrugged. "I didn't buy it. Like she said, I assumed Pa did. I suppose she could have."

He gripped his hands tightly together. "I think we need some time to cope with all of this."

The phone rang, and Cord knew Della was outside with Nicki.

"Excuse me," he said. "I'd better get that." Edie seemed lost in her own thoughts, so he stood up and went to the kitchen to answer it.

"Triple Creek Ranch."

"Cord, this is Sheriff Reyes."

Cord quickly collected his thoughts. "Hi, Sheriff. Found out anything yet?"

"Yeah, we located where Bates is living. His girlfriend said he was out taking care of business, although she couldn't give us any details. We're still watching the place, but I wanted you to be aware of what's happening and to be on the lookout for him. He might show up again, because I have a feeling the business he's talking about is you. All my sources say he really has a grudge against you."

"Thanks, Sheriff. Don't worry, he's not getting near me or my family."

"Give me a call if you even spot him."

"I will."

Cord hung up and walked out onto the patio. He sat down, burying his face in his hands. The world seemed to be crashing in on him. Last night his life had seemed full of potential; his future had promised happiness. He had found something so precious in Becca. But now he'd discovered that his mother had betrayed him and Bates was out to get him. He didn't know how much more he could take, especially if Becca was hurt in the process. He'd do anything to keep her safe, and he wasn't letting her out of his sight until Bates was caught.

He surveyed the landscape, the ranch. He had put his heart and soul into this place and now it was his—and Edie's, too. In the end, that was what Pa had wanted. Somehow, that didn't make him feel better. How could his mother do this to him? And Anette? He didn't understand her part in this. She knew how much he loved the ranch. Why wouldn't she tell him what she'd learned? Was Blanche's accusation true—that Anette was trying to manipulate him into leaving Triple Creek?

The unanswered questions were tearing him apart.

BECCA HURRIED INTO THE DEN looking for Cord, and found Edie silently crying. Becca's heart went out to her. Two stubborn women and both wanting the same thing—to be loved. She knelt by Edie's chair and hugged her.

"He really loved me." Edie choked out the words. "I thought he'd forgotten about me, but he loved me." Edie clutched the will in her hand, so Becca knew what she was talking about.

"Of course he loved you. You were his daughter," Becca told her softly.

"After he brought *her* here, things changed. I became invisible to Pa and I hated her."

"*Hate* is a very destructive word."

"It's how I feel, especially after what she's done to Cord."

"But Cord will forgive her," Becca said confidently.

Edie wiped her eyes. "You seem sure of that."

"I am." She placed her hand over her heart. "Because I know him in here. He'll never be able to turn his back on his mother."

"She's an awful person," Edie muttered.

"Have you ever given yourself a chance to get to know her?"

"No, and I don't want to."

"Let go of the bitterness, Edie. Don't be the one to tear this family apart."

Edie stared ahead with a defiant expression, and Becca got up and left her with her memories. The Prescott family was hurting, and try as she might, she couldn't bring them together. Maybe she was trying too hard. She had to let it happen naturally; she couldn't force them to love one another.

She finally found Cord on the patio. He was staring off into space with a shattered look on his face. His sorrow and confusion wrenched her heart, and she opened the door and went outside to him. When she slid into his lap, his arms gripped her tightly.

"How could she do this?" he whispered.

"For love," she murmured, tangling her fingers in the hair that curled into his collar.

"What?"

"Power and control is love to Blanche. Somehow, by having control, she thought she could keep her boys coming back here and she'd be able to keep you under her thumb. Blanche hasn't had much love in her life, and she did everything she could to hang on to the little she had. She used devious methods, but she was desperate."

"Don't ask me to forgive and forget," he said stubbornly.

"That's exactly what I'm asking you to do."

"Becca..."

"When I found out that Emily was really my mother, I was so angry and hurt. I lashed out at everything and everyone around me. I wanted to hurt Emily and Rose like they'd hurt me, but when I saw the pain in Emily's eyes and saw what my behavior was doing to her, I realized that bitterness was an emotion that could destroy us all—if I let it. I didn't want that. I loved Emily and Rose and knew they were fighting just as fierce a battle as I was. Once we forgave each other, everything else fell into place."

He stroked her hair. "I'm so sorry you had to go through that, but this is different."

"No, it isn't," she insisted. "Blanche is your mother, and no matter how angry you are, you can't change that."

"No, no, I can't," he muttered. "I still can't believe she bought me that saddle. I was with Pa when I saw it in the store. I said I wanted it, and he said I was too young for a saddle like that. I'd have to wait until I got older. Then, there it was on Christmas morning. A gift from Santa."

"So he must've told Blanche about the saddle," she mused. "And he had to have known she bought it."

"I suppose."

"He probably knew her better than anyone—knew how afraid she was to show her feelings."

"She wasn't afraid of Pa. I've seen her get in his face when she was displeased with something."

"Like what?" she asked. She could imagine Blanche standing up to almost everyone, but she couldn't see her standing up to Claybourne Prescott.

Cord didn't answer, and she glanced at his face, which had gone a grayish white. "Cord," she said in an urgent voice. "What is it?"

"The arguments," he whispered. "The arguments were about us. I remember one time—Clay must've been about sixteen, and Pa wanted him to work on the ranch but instead he was building computers in his room. When Pa found out, he was furious. He said he was going to throw the computers in the creek and take a rope to Clay to beat some sense into him. Blanche got between them, and I can still hear her words. She said, 'Don't you dare. If you touch one hair on his head,

I'll leave you.' Pa stormed out of the room, but afterward he was more open-minded about Clay's computer skills. I'd forgotten about that. And there was the time Colton tried his hand at smoking. He set his bed on fire, and Pa was livid at his stupidity. Pa took his belt off and said he was gonna teach him a lesson. Blanche took the belt away from him and said he wasn't hitting Colton and that Colton would be grounded for a month and wouldn't get an allowance until the damages were paid for. Pa never liked his decisions questioned, but he gave in to Blanche."

"Did you father ever hit you?"

"No, he had a bad temper and always did a lot of threatening, but he never hit any of us."

"Maybe because he knew Blanche wouldn't stand for it," she remarked. "In her own way, Blanche was there for each of you when you needed her."

"I never saw it that way back then, and neither did Clay or Colton."

"Maybe it's time you did."

He cupped her face and kissed her gently. "I wish I had your loving spirit."

She kissed him back, and for a minute they were lost in each other. He rested his forehead against hers. "Oh, I needed that."

"Me, too."

"Cord."

"Hmm?"

"Blanche didn't destroy the second will."

He pulled back to look at her. "What do you mean?"

"It was the original. So why didn't she destroy it? No one ever would have known, but something in Blanche wouldn't let her do that. It's called character. Granted, Blanche had to dig deep to find it, but she did. I wonder if your father left both wills in the safe as a test for her."

"Maybe," he murmured. "But I can't think about it anymore."

Blanche was a contradiction that tied him in knots. Who was the real Blanche? He didn't know, and maybe he'd never understand what motivated his mother. But he was very clear on one thing: Becca was the stabilizing force in his life. She brought him joy, and she gave him perspective on the whole family mess. For now, he would just concentrate on her.

He held her tighter. "The sheriff called a little while ago. They located Bates's address, but he wasn't there. Sheriff Reyes wants us to be on the lookout for him. Evidently Bates has been spouting off to everyone that's he's gonna get even with me."

"Then, he was the one who tampered with the brake line?"

"That's the way it's looking, and I don't want you going anywhere without me or someone else." He kissed the side of her bruised face. "I could kill him for what he's done to you."

"We'll just let the sheriff handle it, and I'll stick to you like glue." She pressed herself against him. "Oh, yeah, I like that idea."

He growled deep in his throat as his lips found hers, but the sound of someone coughing discreetly drew them apart. Mona was standing some distance away, watching them.

"I'm sorry," she said. "I don't mean to interrupt, but no one answered the door."

"That's all right," Cord said as he straightened.

He made no move to get up and Becca saw no need to get off his lap. Their relationship was intimate, and she certainly didn't want to keep that a secret.

"Blanche and Edie are dealing with a lot right now and I guess they didn't feel like answering the door," he explained.

"Is something wrong?"

Cord told her about the will.

"Cord, I'm so sorry," Mona said. "How could Blanche do that?"

"I'm still trying to figure it out."

"But I am happy for you. I know how you feel about this ranch."

"Thanks, Mona."

"When you didn't come by today, I knew there had to be some kind of problem."

"Damn, Mona, it completely slipped my mind. I'll try to get over there in the next couple of days."

"No hurry. Just take care of your family first."

"I will."

"Goodbye." Mona tipped her hat. "Dr. Talbert."

"You've known Mona for a long time?" Becca asked, as Mona walked away.

"Since we were kids. She and Clay are the same age. She had a crush on him when they were younger and she still asks about him."

"But Clay didn't feel the same way?"

"No, he preferred feminine blondes."

"Really? Must be something in the Prescott genes."

He grinned. "Not entirely. These days, this Prescott prefers dark hair and dark eyes and…" The rest of his words were drowned as she kissed him.

"And a lot of that," he added in a whisper.

Becca settled against him, feeling content. "Mona seems so stern and…sad."

"She's had a very difficult life," Cord said. "She was the only child of a man who wanted a son, which he never bothered to hide."

"I thought she *was* a man the first time I saw her."

"Sometimes she thinks she is. She runs her ranch better than almost any man I know. A few years back, she fell in love with a guy at the feed store. I told her what the hell, go for it, but then she found out he was married and she was devastated for weeks. Since then, I think she's given up on any chance of love or marriage."

"That's such a pity."

"Becca, Becca, Becca!" They could hear Nicki shouting as she came through the gate, her ponytail bouncing. Becca got up and met her halfway, and Nicki ran into her arms. "You should've seen me," Nicki gushed. "I roped. Gus is teaching me. Gus said I was fast as greased lightning."

Becca kissed her cheek. "I'll bet you are." Her nose twitched as a pungent smell reached her nostrils and she noticed the dirt—or something else—on Nicki's jeans.

"What's that smell?"

Nicki brushed at her jeans. "I fell in the dirt when I jumped off Half Pint."

"I think it was more than dirt, little bit," Gus said from behind.

"It don't matter," Nicki said, then spotted Cord. "Daddy, wait till you hear!" She immediately ran to Cord.

Cord held her close. "I heard, baby."

"I can rope real good," Nicki mumbled into his shoulder.

Cord just continued to hold her. He loved his child with all his heart, just as he loved the woman staring at him with those sparkling, gorgeous eyes. He was truly blessed. The anger inside slowly eased as he realized that. It was hard to stay angry when he had so much. Somehow, he had to find a way to keep this family together. He knew that was what Becca wanted and now he wanted it, too. Truly wanted it, in a way he never had before.

"Let's get you cleaned up," Becca said, and took Nicki's hand.

"Gus said he ain't seen nothin' like it. He said..." Nicki was chattering away as they went into the house.

Gus removed his hat. "What's goin' on, Cord?"

Cord told him about the will.

"Good God Almighty, what's wrong with that woman?"

"It's a big mess" was all Cord said.

Gus shook his head. "By golly. Ain't this somethin'?"

Cord didn't want to tell him Blanche might have been harassing Anette. He still wasn't clear on that.

"Yeah, but there's someone else I want to talk about," he muttered.

"Who?"

"Joe Bates."

"Have they found the bastard?"

"No, but they found where he lives. His girlfriend said he was out taking care of business and the sheriff feels that business might be me. So I want everyone to be on the alert."

Gus stood. "Don't worry. He won't get past us again."

"Thanks, Gus, and I'd like to apologize for snapping at you the other day."

"No problem. We were all wound tight about the doc."

"I just can't stand the thought of someone hurting her."

Gus patted him on the shoulder. "Yeah. Well, ain't nothin' gonna happen to the doc as long as we're around. You can take that to the bank."

As Gus walked off, Cord hoped he was right. He'd feel a whole lot better when Joe Bates was caught.

CHAPTER SIXTEEN

THAT NIGHT, after they'd put Nicki to bed, Cord and Becca sat in the den curled up on the sofa. Blanche and Edie were in their rooms. They hadn't even come to supper. Nicki kept asking questions about it; she'd gotten used to Edie and Blanche eating with her. Cord just told her they had other plans for the evening. Nicki was disappointed because she'd wanted to tell them how well she could rope. That was the only thing on her mind, and she didn't notice any tension in the house, which was a relief to Cord.

Becca ran her fingers through Cord's hair. "What are you thinking about?"

He kissed the palm of her hand. "I called Colton and Clay while you were reading to Nicki."

"How did they react?"

"They were shocked, but both said basically the same thing. Pa left them a trust fund, which they got, and they're satisfied with that. They said that whatever Edie and I decide to do about the ranch is up to us and they'll support us. But we plan to meet and discuss it. Colton asked about you. Evidently your father mentioned the accident."

"What did he say?"

"His usual warning. Also that it's time for you to return to Houston, but he didn't seem as adamant as before."

She told him about the phone call to Ginger and that she thought Colton and Ginger were sleeping together.

"That's your best friend?"

"Yes, and Gin and Colton are always at each other's throat. I guess they finally found something not to argue about."

He looked into her eyes. "Are you happy about that?"

She smiled. "What do you think?"

He kissed her deeply, then asked in an aching voice, "What am I going to do about Blanche?"

She stood and took his hand. "Let's go upstairs and forget about Blanche and everything that's happened today. Let's just think about us. Tomorrow things might look different."

Arm in arm they went up the stairs. Inside her room, he took her into his embrace. "I love you," he said. "I can't get through this without you."

That was all she needed to hear. Somehow they'd survive this—as long as they had each other. They still hadn't talked about the future; that was for later. There were too many other things that took precedence. At the moment, Houston seemed a lifetime away.

THE NEXT MORNING Cord was up and dressed before she even woke. She stirred, and he kissed her lips.

"I'll get Nicki up for breakfast, then I'm going into town to talk to Pa's lawyer. He's got a lot of explaining to do."

She sat up. "Okay, but I'll miss you."

His eyes strayed to her breasts and he kissed each one slowly, his mustache a brush of delight. "If you don't stop, you'll never leave," she teased.

"I know." One last kiss, and he was strolling toward the door. At the door he added, "Don't stray too far from the house. Gus and the boys are on the lookout, but Bates could be anywhere."

"I won't," she promised as she headed for the bathroom. After getting dressed, she went down to the kitchen, looking forward to a cup of strong coffee. Nicki was there munching on cereal and telling Della about her roping at the same time.

"Morning, sweetie." She kissed the top of Nicki's head, then filled the largest mug she could find with fresh coffee.

"I'm gonna rope again today, Becca. Gus said I could, and you can watch me 'cause I'm real good. Gus said so."

Gus entered the kitchen. "How you doing, Doc?"

"Fine, thanks, Gus."

He glanced at Nicki. "Ready to go, little bit?"

"Yep." Nicki slipped out of her chair and looked at Becca. "C'mon."

"I'll finish my coffee and be right behind you."

"'Kay." She ran out the back door and Gus followed.

Becca watched as Della nervously wiped the table. "Della, are you all right?"

She faced Becca. "What's gonna happen to this family? Everything was going so well, but now—how could she do that to Cord?"

"I can't condone what Blanche did, but I don't think she meant to hurt anyone. She wanted to remain part of the family and she was afraid there wasn't much chance of that if the will surfaced. She should have trusted Cord, though. I thinks she knows that now."

"It's just awful, and so is the stuff with Joe Bates. What else is going to happen?"

Becca put an arm around her shoulder. "Nothing. The Prescotts are due for some good luck. Now I'd better check on Nicki. She might have Gus all tied up."

She got a partial smile out of Della. As she walked to the stables she wondered if Cord was at the lawyer's yet. She hoped he could find some answers to help him sort through this.

Several of the cowboys waved and she waved back. Dusty rode up. "You feeling better, ma'am?"

"Much better, and tell all the boys thanks for searching for me."

"No problem, ma'am. Have a good day."

He rode off, and Becca climbed onto the fence. Gus and Nicki were some distance away on horses. Gus twirled a rope over his head and swung it at a post. It circled the post swiftly and accurately.

Nicki had a much smaller rope, but she guided Half Pint toward the same post and swung the rope like Gus. Wobbly it landed on the post. "Did you see, Becca?" she called excitedly. "Did you see?"

"Yes, sweetie, I saw."

"I'm like greased lightning Gus says."

"Gus should know." Becca stayed for a while longer. Sometimes Nicki hit the post, sometimes she didn't. The misses didn't count, but the hits drew lots of shouting. Becca suspected she'd learned that from Gus.

Watching Nicki, she suddenly had the urge to call her own mother. She hadn't talked to her since the accident and needed to hear her voice. She felt deeply grateful for the love they shared; being around so much bitterness had made her realize what their lives could've been like if they hadn't had the strength to forgive. Cord, too, would forgive his mother, she thought. When he was ready, when he'd worked through his anger and his sense of betrayal.

"Sweetie," she called, "I'm going to the house to make a phone call. I'll be right back."

"'Kay," Nicki yelled, not taking her eyes off Gus.

Becca made her way to the house, where she met Della at the back door, clutching a large purse. "Today's my grocery day," Della explained. "See you later."

The house seemed eerily quiet as she walked upstairs. Edie and Blanche were still in their rooms. She started for the phone, then saw Anette's albums lying on her dresser. She'd been planning to store them for Nicki, but with everything that had happened she hadn't had the chance. On impulse, she picked them up and sat on the bed. The first two were typical photos of a family. The third one wasn't an album at all. It was some sort of journal. There were notations in what she recognized as Anette's handwriting. Becca settled back and began to read.

> I hate this place. Why can't Cord see that? Why doesn't he take me away from here? If he loved me, he would.
>
> She scares me. Every time I see her, my skin crawls. She says nasty things and I don't know how to respond. Why can't she just leave me alone?
>
> I want to tell Cord, but I can't. She said she'd get even if I did—that she'd hurt my baby. I have to keep Nicki away from her.
>
> Little by little she's driving me crazy. The pills don't help anymore. I have to tell Cord. He's the only one who can stop her.
>
> I love Cord and I love Nicki. Why can't I fight back? Why am I so weak? She's evil. I know she's evil.

There were more entries, all of them much the same. Becca slowly closed the album. "Oh, Blanche, what have you done?" she said under her breath. She had championed Blanche, thinking there was some good in her, but the woman had obviously driven Anette to her death by her abrasive behavior. How could Becca have been so wrong about her? Maybe she *was* evil. But Becca rejected that idea. She'd seen a side of Blanche no one else had—her vulnerability. Something wasn't fitting here.

The troublesome thoughts went around and around in her head. She placed the albums on the dresser again and wondered what to do about them. Cord had to see these, but she didn't want to cause him any more pain.

As she struggled with what to do, she remembered the

quilts Anette had made and went along to Anette's room to retrieve them. She put the quilts and everything they'd saved for Nicki in a box and stored it in her closet. She left the journal on her dresser; Cord had to see it, she decided.

She called her mother and talked for half an hour or so. As she hung up, she heard a sound—a loud *thump*. She thought Nicki might have followed her into the house, and quickly opened her door to check. She was startled to see Mona in the hallway.

"I knocked, but there doesn't seem to be anyone around," Mona said.

Becca wondered why she hadn't just left instead of coming into the house uninvited. "I'm sorry, but this isn't a good time," she said in a cool voice.

Wordlessly, Mona pushed her way into the room and locked the door.

"Wait a minute! I—"

"Shut up," Mona screeched in barely controlled rage.

Becca took a couple of steps away from her.

"You couldn't leave him alone, could you?"

Becca shook her head. "What are you talking about?"

"Cord. You just had to have him."

"My relationship with Cord is none of your business."

"That's where you're wrong, *Doctor*." She said the last word with disdain. "I've waited all my life for Cord and I'm not waiting any longer. I took care of that mousy thing he brought home from Dallas and now I'm gonna take care of you."

One thing registered on Becca's mind. "What did you do to Anette?"

"I warned her that if she didn't leave, I'd hurt her."

"And you did, didn't you?"

A sinister smile tugged at her thin lips. "Yeah, it took me years, but I got rid of her."

Anette had been writing about Mona, not Blanche. It had

been Mona all along driving Anette to the edge—but did Anette take that final step herself?

Becca moved back still farther. "How did you manage that?"

"It was easy. I made her swallow as many pills as I could, then I forced liquor down her throat until she passed out. I should've done it years ago."

She said the words with such joy that Becca began to tremble. The woman was insane. Insanely in love with Cord. And Becca was locked in this room with her.

Mona saw the fear in her eyes. "You've got a right to be afraid. You should've left when I let that bull out of the pen."

"You did that?" She gasped.

"Yeah, Cord was so busy staring at you, he didn't see me undo the latch."

"And the Jeep?" she asked shakily.

She nodded. "I rode off, but I walked back. Everyone was at the pens. The cowboys were so eager to show off for you that no one noticed when I slipped under the Jeep. All it took was a couple of twists with a wrench."

Becca was speechless. It wasn't Joe Bates—it was Mona. She knew words were futile because the woman had completely lost touch with reality. But Becca had to talk. That was what she did best. She had to talk until someone came to help her. *Cord, please hurry home.*

"But it didn't work." She found her voice. "It only drew Cord and me closer."

"Shut up!" Mona yelled.

"Cord hasn't fallen in love with you in all these years and it's not going to happen, even if you kill me."

"He will. You're young and pretty and you've turned his head. When you're gone, he'll come to me."

"He didn't when Anette died."

"Shut up," Mona yelled again. "I'm tired of listening to you."

Becca swallowed, desperately searching for a way to keep Mona talking. "You said you've been waiting for Cord all your life, but wasn't it Clay you loved first?"

"Yeah, I had a thing for Clay, but he wasn't a rancher and I knew he wasn't the man for me. Cord was different. We have the same interests, and he cares for me. Clay never did."

"Are you sure Cord cares for you?"

"Yes," she replied smugly. "I made up this story about a guy at the feed store I was seeing. I told Cord the guy was married, and Cord got very upset."

"He was upset that you might get hurt," Becca said, remembering the story Cord had told her. "Cord has a very soft heart, but he doesn't have those feelings for you, and you know it. That's why you made up that story."

"Stop talking," Mona shouted, pulling a large syringe from her pocket.

Fear became something real and vivid, and if someone didn't come soon Becca didn't have many choices. Mona was so much bigger, and the hope of holding her off was a pitiful dream.

"One injection and you'll die a peaceful death."

"What's in the syringe?"

"Just can't stop with the questions, can you?" Mona sneered sarcastically. "But since you're so curious, I'll tell you. It's sodium pentobarbital—a euthanasia solution."

"Where did you get something like that?"

"I had a problem a couple of months ago with a few cows having deformed calves. The vet left the drug with me in case it happened again. That way I could put the calf down myself. You see, the vet trusts me. Everyone does."

"There'll be an autopsy. Cord will find out what you did."

"It can't be traced to me," Mona retorted. "I told the vet I used it. It's all on paper. Besides, Joe Bates worked for a vet once. He knows how to get the drug. Everyone'll think he did it."

"You won't—"

The words were cut off as Mona grabbed her by the hair and threw her onto the bed. In an instant, Mona had straddled her, clamping both of Becca's hands in one of hers. Mona was strong, and Becca's attempts to break free were futile.

Mona laughed, a cruel sound. "Go ahead, Doctor, fight until you don't have any breath left. In a minute it won't matter, anyway."

"You can't do this," Becca said in a shaky voice. "Think about Nicki. She can't take losing someone else. She's just a little girl."

Mona removed the plastic cap on the needle with her teeth and spit it on the floor. "She's a nuisance and I'll have to find a way to get rid of her, too. Ship her off to school or something 'cause I'm not having her whining around me."

"You bitch!" Becca shouted. "You conniving, evil bitch." She bucked and twisted and turned, determined to get away, but then she saw the needle coming toward her and she screamed with every ounce of strength she had.

BLANCHE STROLLED INTO the kitchen and poured a cup of coffee, then started for the den, coffee in hand, to add a spot of brandy. She stopped abruptly and stared. Edie was lying on the floor, blood oozing from her head.

"Oh my God," Blanche cried, dropping the coffee. It splattered all over her slacks and feet, but she didn't notice. She threw herself down and raised Edie's head. "Edie, what happened?"

Blood soaked through Blanche's clothes as she cradled Edie in her arms. She jumped up and ran into the kitchen for towels and wrapped them tightly around Edie's head. "Edie, can you hear me?"

Edie moaned.

"What happened?"

"I…came down…and someone hit me. A big person."

"Oh God, you're bleeding so bad. I've got to get you to a hospital."

At that moment, Cord walked through the back door, feeling a lot better. Dawson had confirmed everything Blanche had said—even her fear of being kicked out of the house. Cord had had a few choice words to say to him, but the lawyer had said he'd merely made out the will. Claynourne hadn't asked for him to enforce it. He'd said Blanche had shared a few confidences with him; that was all. He wasn't privy to what she'd decided to do. He'd figured it was a family situation. And Cord realized it was. The thing, though, was that Blanche hadn't lied to him about any of this. It meant a lot, but right now, he just had to see Becca.

He stopped short as he entered the den, then dropped down beside Blanche and Edie. "What the hell happened?"

Blanche wrapped another towel around Edie's head. "I'm trying to stop the bleeding," Blanche cried. "Call 911!"

Cord grabbed the phone from the table and dialed. "They're on the way." He saw that Blanche was soaked with blood and that her hands shook as she held the towels tight. He put his hands over hers.

"What happened?" he asked again.

"I don't know." Blanche choked out the words. "When I came in, I found her like this. She said someone hit her—a big person."

A big person. Joe Bates.

Fear shot through Cord. "Where are Becca and Nicki?"

"I don't know. I don't know," Blanche sobbed. "Cord, I think she's lost consciousness."

Cord felt Edie's pulse. "She's still breathing. Stay with her until the ambulance gets here. I've got to find Becca."

As Cord stood there, a scream echoed through the house. "Oh my God, what's that?" Blanche asked.

But Cord had already left, taking the stairs three at a time. He tried Becca's door; it was locked. Stepping back, he swung at the door with his booted foot. It splintered away from the frame and he shoved it aside and stepped in. For a second he stood motionless, unable to believe what he was seeing. Mona was holding Becca down and trying to inject something in her arm. Becca was fighting like a hellcat.

Cord grabbed Mona by the shoulders and jerked her away from Becca.

"Don't come near me. Don't come near me," Mona screeched in a voice Cord had never heard. She held the needle in front of her like a weapon.

Cord didn't know what was going on, but his main concern was Becca. He reached out an arm and gathered her close, keeping an eye on Mona. "Are you all right?" She was trembling severely, so he tightened his hold.

"Yes, yes, now I am," Becca said in a hoarse voice.

"What's this about?"

"She killed Anette and she was trying to kill me," Becca managed to say.

"What!"

"It's true," Becca whispered. "She made Anette swallow pills, then she poured liquor down her throat until—"

"Why? Why would you do that?" Horrified, Cord stared at Mona. Her eyes were glazed and she had a feverish look.

Mona didn't answer. She took the needle and drove it into her own arm.

"Mona!" Cord shouted but it was too late. The medicine in the syringe was gone. Her eyes rolled back as she crumpled to the floor. Cord released Becca and knelt beside the woman.

"Why, Mona? *Why?*"

"I've waited and waited…all my life. I'm the only…woman for you. I love…you." Her head fell sideways.

Cord knelt there in shock. He and Mona were friends; they'd always been friends. He'd never led her to believe anything else. They had never even kissed, so he didn't understand how she could have these feelings for him. Yet she'd killed Anette and almost killed Becca. How could he have been so blind? Pain ripped up from his abdomen and gripped him—so tightly that his breath locked in his chest.

Two arms slipped around him, and he clasped Becca's hands, taking the strength and comfort she offered. After a moment, he got slowly to his feet and they moved away from Mona. "Are you sure you're all right?" he asked.

"Yes, a little shaken, but I'm fine."

"It's been Mona all along," Cord said quietly. "Joe Bates had nothing to do with any of this."

"No," Becca responded. "She let the bull out and loosened the brake line hoping to scare me away. And it seems she'd been harassing Anette for years, trying to get rid of her. The letter in Anette's purse was to Mona." Becca picked up the journal from the dresser and showed it to Cord.

Cord read for a minute then slammed it shut. "God, why didn't Anette tell me? Why did she let this go on? I don't understand."

"I think she wanted to be strong enough to handle it on her own. Also, Mona threatened to hurt Nicki if she said a word to you."

"Oh, no…"

Cord's words were cut short by the sound of sirens. "God, Mona must have hit Edie before she came up here. She's bleeding heavily. Blanche is with her. We'd better see how she's doing."

They ran down the stairs, where they found Blanche still

holding Edie's head in her lap. Blood was everywhere. Becca immediately sank down beside Edie and took her pulse. "Was she talking to you?" she asked Blanche.

"Yes."

"Did she make sense? Did she knew where she was?"

"Yes."

"Her pulse is weak. Edie, can you hear me?" Becca asked loudly.

"Yes." Edie opened her eyes and then slowly closed them.

"The ambulance is here," Cord told her, running to open the front door.

The paramedics hurried through with a stretcher. Becca introduced herself and explained the situation. "She's received a sharp blow to the head. She's floating in and out of consciousness, but she's coherent. She'll need a c-collar and a back board to guard against trauma to the neck and spine. And I need a 4X4 to bandage her head."

"Yes, ma'am," the paramedic responded, and within minutes they had Edie in the ambulance.

"I'm going with you to apply direct pressure to stop any bleeding."

"We're trained to do that."

Becca sent him a glance that brooked no argument. "All right, let's just go," the paramedic said with a sigh.

Blanche sat there trembling, and Cord helped her to her feet. "Is she gonna be all right?" Blanche asked in a trembling voice.

Becca glanced back and made an instant decision. "Come with me, and we'll make sure she's okay." Blanche went with her meekly, not speaking.

"I'll call the sheriff about Mona and take care that Nicki doesn't see any of this," Cord told Becca as she stepped into the ambulance beside Edie and Blanche. "I'll see you at the hospital."

The ride in the ambulance was a silent one. The paramedics gave Edie oxygen and started an IV. Becca checked her vital signs and found they were stronger.

"Becca, are you sure she's alive?" Blanche asked. "She's so still."

"Yes, she's just very weak, but Edie's tough."

"Tough as an old boot," Blanche remarked, but Becca noticed that the resentment usually in her voice wasn't there anymore. Could something good come out of this tragedy?

AS SOON AS HE'D CALLED the sheriff, Cord dashed out the back door, needing to find Nicki. He had to know she was okay. He met her running to the house and his first thought was relief that she hadn't come sooner. Breathing hard, he scooped her into his arms. *His little girl was safe.*

"Daddy, you're squeezing me too tight," Nicki complained.

"Sorry, baby." He loosened his hold immediately. "I'm just so glad to see you."

"I've been roping." She held out both hands. "My hands are getting red, and Gus said we had to stop."

"That's a good idea. You don't want blisters on your hands."

"'Kay, Daddy. Where's Becca? I want to show her my hands."

His heart felt heavy. He had to tell her something. "Edie had an accident and Becca went to the hospital with her."

"What happened?" Gus asked. He'd been standing there watching.

Cord took a breath and lied. "She fell and hit her head."

"Oh, she got an ouchie?" Nicki asked.

"Yes, she's got an ouchie, and Daddy has to drive to the hospital to check on her. So I want you to go with Gus and—"

"No, I want to go, too," Nicki said in a sullen voice.

"You can't, baby. The hospital isn't a place for children. I'm sure Gus will take you riding until Daddy gets back."

Nicki frowned and played with a button on his shirt.

"C'mon, little bit," Gus said in a cajoling voice. "Let's ride to the bottom and visit the boys. Why don't you show me how fast you can ride?"

That did the trick. Her eyes grew bright and she slipped from Cord's arms. "I can ride real, real fast. You'll see!" With that, she was racing to the stables.

Cord started to call her back, but Gus said, "Don't worry. Smithy's at the barn. He'll watch her. What's going on?"

Cord told him about Mona.

"God Almighty! Mona? I can't believe it."

"Yeah, it takes some getting used to."

The sheriff drove up with a second ambulance behind him. As Cord had directed, they parked at the front of the house. "I've got to go. Just take care of my child and get her away from this. I don't want her to see a thing."

"I will, and phone when you have news about Edie."

Cord hurried back to the house and opened the front door for the sheriff and the coroner. Within minutes they had Mona's body bagged and out of the house.

"There'll be an inquest into Mona's death," the sheriff said. "It's routine, but it has to be investigated."

"I understand."

"I'll call off my boys on Joe Bates."

"Yeah," Cord said in a distant voice.

"Mona Tibbetts." The sheriff shook his head. "I never would've thought it. She seemed like such a nice lady."

"She had us all fooled."

"You just never know," the sheriff said as he walked out the door.

Cord rushed upstairs to straighten Becca's room. The

sheriff's men had removed the syringe, but he wanted to ensure that there were absolutely no signs of what had happened.

He picked up the journal. Why hadn't he known what Mona was doing? Was he so insensitive to Anette's needs that he'd dismissed everything as her paranoia? He sank onto the bed. He had, in effect, helped Mona kill his wife. The truth of that hit like lightning, searing everything inside him. He couldn't give in to those feelings now. Later, they'd tear him apart. But now he had to get to Edie—and Becca.

CHAPTER SEVENTEEN

CORD MET BECCA AND BLANCHE as Edie was being taken up to her room. They'd had to give her blood, and the doctor said it was a good idea if she spent the night. Edie was groggy, but awake. Her head had been stitched; she was going to be fine.

Becca slid one arm around Cord's waist. "You okay?" He didn't answer, and she knew he wasn't. She could feel him distancing himself from her. He had so much to deal with, so much to assimilate, and she hoped he wouldn't push her away.

She didn't have time to think about it as they got Edie settled into a room.

Blanche tucked in the blanket on Edie's bed.

"Why are you being so nice, Blanche?" Edie said crossly. "You're not staying at Triple Creek."

Blanche paled and took a step back from the bed. Becca inhaled a deep breath. It was like dealing with two children, which was something she was good at.

"That's not nice, Edie," Becca told her. "If Blanche hadn't applied those towels to your head, you would've lost a lot more blood and you might not have made it."

"Why didn't you just let me die, Blanche?" Edie asked. "It would've been to your advantage."

"Honestly, Edie, it never crossed my mind. It should have. I'm surprised it didn't."

"Me, too," Edie murmured. "You're still leaving Triple Creek," she added as an afterthought.

"I know, Edie."

"As soon as possible."

"I know."

There was a pause, then Edie asked, "Where will you go?"

"I'll probably get an apartment in Houston. I've never been on my own before. It'll be a new experience."

"An apartment?" Edie thought about that for a minute. "I don't think Pa would want you living in an apartment."

"Well, Pa's not here, now is he?" Blanche said cheekily.

"Enough!" Cord said angrily. "I've had it. I'm tired of all the fighting and bickering. It stops *now.* I can't deal with any more. Blanche isn't going anywhere. She's staying at Triple Creek. Pa would want it that way and frankly so do I. Blanche is my mother. Even though I have a hard time with what she did, she is still my mother. Do you have a problem with that, Edie?"

"No. No, I guess not," Edie answered quietly.

"I've got to get some air," Cord said, and strode out of the room.

"What's wrong with him?" Edie asked.

Blanche started to tell her about Mona, and Becca quickly followed Cord. She found him in a waiting area, pacing.

"Cord," she said softly. She moved to put her arms around him, but he backed away. A tiny fear took root inside her.

"Is Blanche ready to go?" he asked in a cool tone. "I've got to get back to Nicki."

She tried again. "Cord."

He held up a hand. "No, Becca, I don't want to talk. I just want to go home."

Becca watched him for a second and knew he was fighting a

battle within himself. She would give him time. But she wanted to hold him, to comfort him, and it was so hard not to.

"I'll get Blanche," she said, and walked away.

LIKE THE JOURNEY in the ambulance several hours before, the ride to Triple Creek was silent. No one spoke a word and the silence was getting to Becca. Cord was shutting her out. She could feel it as strongly as the heart beating inside her. He was in pain and he needed to share that pain in order to assuage it. How did she make him see that?

Nicki was excited at their return and had a million questions. She couldn't understand why Blanche and Becca were so dirty. The blood had dried to a dark stain, and fortunately Nicki thought it was dirt. Blanche and Becca went to get cleaned up and left Cord with all the questions.

Supper was another silent event, except for Nicki's chattering. Afterward, Becca took her upstairs to put her to bed. Cord didn't follow. The broken door to Becca's room had been removed and Nicki didn't notice that it was missing. As Becca was reading Nicki a story, Cord came in to kiss his daughter good-night.

Cord looked at Becca. "Can I see you downstairs?"

"Sure," she said. When she'd finished the story, she joined him in the den. She sat on the sofa and Cord paced in front of her.

She held her breath waiting for his words because she sensed she wasn't going to like them.

Cord knew what he had to do, but the words wouldn't come. In his head he had it all worked out; his heart was another matter. When he closed his eyes, he could see Mona about to inject Becca with the needle. If he'd been a few seconds later, Becca would be dead—like Anette. Because of him.

Suddenly, he turned and said, "I want you to go back to Houston."

Becca bit her lip, trying to maintain control of her emotions. "Why?" she asked simply.

"Because it's what I want."

"Why?"

"Dammit, Becca, you don't belong here!"

Her eyes met his. "Then, why do I feel as if I do?"

They stared at each other for endless seconds, then he dredged up every ounce of courage he possessed and said, "You don't. You belong in Houston with an elite circle of friends. You're not cut out to be a cowboy's wife."

Her eyes didn't waver from his. "Then, why am I in love with a cowboy?"

"I want you away from this place," he shouted. "There's nothing but pain and suffering here. Can't you see that? I couldn't for so long, but I can now. I killed Anette. I couldn't see what Mona was doing to her. I should have. I should've been there for her. I won't hurt you like that. I'd die before I let that happen."

Becca stood. "Then, why are you hurting me now?"

He drew a ragged breath. "I'm not, and you'll see that in time."

"I won't," she said. She tried to touch him, but he backed away.

"No, don't touch me" came out as a strangled plea, and she knew nothing was going to change his mind. She tried desperately to restrain the tears that were threatening to overtake her. But she wasn't leaving without a fight.

"So Mona wins."

"What?" He seemed disconcerted.

"She wanted to break us up and she's doing exactly that."

He blinked. "That kind of logic might work on Nicki, but not on me. I can't handle you being here. I just can't take any more. Go, please."

She wanted to argue with him or throw a temper tantrum

like Nicki, but she could see how badly he was hurting. He needed time to adjust to the turbulent events that had happened. And she told herself again that she would give it to him. Even though she didn't want to. Walking away from the man she loved would truly be the hardest thing she'd ever have to do.

He turned to leave the room.

"Cord," she called.

He stopped.

Please, he prayed. *Just go.*

"I'm not leaving without saying goodbye to Nicki. She's been through too much—I can't desert her. She has to understand and accept why I'm leaving."

"I know that, and I wouldn't expect any less of you." With that, he left the room, and Becca's heart broke into so many pieces that the pain became unbearable. She sank onto the sofa and began to cry.

CORD WALKED QUICKLY to the barn and flipped on the light. He grabbed a bridle off the rack, then moved to the gate. He whistled and Apache came trotting up. Slipping the bridle over his head, he guided him into the barn. As he slung a saddle onto Apache's back, Gus strolled in.

"What're you doing?" Gus asked.

"Nothing," Cord muttered.

"Shouldn't you be at the house with Becca and Nicki?"

"There is no Becca anymore," Cord said as he swung into the saddle.

Gus frowned. "What're you talking about? Cord, what's wrong with you?"

Cord didn't answer. He pulled his hat low and kneed Apache. As the horse cantered out, Cord embraced the evening's warmth. He gave Apache his head and they headed toward open range at a full gallop. Faster and faster Apache ran, and his hooves hitting the ground were the only sound in the darkness. They cut through the air like an arrow—sharp and steady. On and on Cord rode, driving the horse as well as himself. He had to keep going. He had to keep the memories at bay.

Apache was panting and sweaty when Cord finally pulled up. He sat for a moment rubbing Apache's neck. "Sorry, boy. I'll let you rest."

He slid from the saddle to the grass, walked a few yards away and sank to the ground. He buried his face in his hands, unable to ignore the truth any longer. He had almost gotten Becca killed. He couldn't get that thought out of his head. He loved her and wanted to make her happy, but he had endangered her life. Just like he'd endangered Anette's.

He couldn't drag Becca into his misery. She deserved better than that. Colton had warned him; he should have listened and not gotten involved with her. Now he was hurting her, but she'd get over it. She had a brilliant career waiting for her and she'd find the right man in Houston. *He wasn't the man for Becca.* He lay back on the cool grass and watched the dazzling display of stars. A coyote howled mournfully in the distance, echoing the pain in his heart. He wasn't the man for Becca, he told himself again and again. Even if she was the woman for him.

BECCA HURRIEDLY TRIED to wipe away the tears as Blanche walked in, but she didn't succeed.

"What's the matter, sugar?"

Becca didn't see any reason to lie. "Cord asked me to leave."

Blanche's eyes grew big. "You're joking."

"No, he's all torn up about Mona and Anette. He's blaming himself, and I can't reach him."

"Hell's bells, you're not leaving, are you?"

"Yes. I can't stay here if he doesn't want me to. And if I can't reach him, our love means nothing."

"Sugar, give it some time and it'll work itself out."

She wiped away another tear. "I'm not sure. I have to be back in Houston in a few days, anyway. I was just hoping not to leave under these circumstances."

"Cord loves you. I know he does."

"Yeah." She blinked back more tears. "But I don't think he'll let himself remember that." She took a breath. "Would you do me a favor?"

"Sure, sugar, anything."

"I have to tell Nicki in the morning and I'd appreciate it if you were there for moral support. I'm not sure how she's going to take it."

"I'll set my alarm. I'll be there."

Becca swallowed. "Also, would you be there for her when I'm gone? She'll need someone besides Mrs. Witherspoon."

"Sure, sugar. I'm getting into this grandmother thing."

"Thanks, Blanche." She stood. "Now I'd better go pack."

"Becca," Blanche said, and Becca turned.

Suddenly Blanche hugged her. "You know something? You're the only woman I've ever really liked."

Becca was thrown for a second, but she returned the hug and hurried away. She had to or she'd cry her eyes out.

BECCA DIDN'T SLEEP MUCH. She'd packed all her things; everything was in her car. The only thing left was to talk to Nicki, and she wasn't looking forward to that. But it had to be done.

She was hoping she'd have a chance to talk to Cord one more time, but he was nowhere in sight. He didn't show up for breakfast, and she wondered where he was. It wasn't like him to miss getting Nicki ready in the morning, but then, Cord wasn't acting like himself. She'd thought they were soul mates and could reach each other on any level, but pain had obliterated the bond they shared. There had to be a way to get it back. The love she had for Cord wasn't going to disappear.

Becca took Nicki into the den and pulled the child onto her lap. Blanche stood in the doorway.

"What're we gonna do today?" Nicki asked, and Becca's throat closed up.

Becca rubbed her little arm. "Remember when I first came here and I told you I was a doctor and I took care of girls and boys like you?"

"Uh-huh."

"Well, it's time for me to go back to my job."

"Why?"

"Because those girls and boys are waiting for me to take care of them."

"But you take care of *me*." Nicki's bottom lip began to tremble.

Becca kissed her cheek. "You will always be my favorite patient, and Blanche will bring you to see me and you can call me anytime you want."

"You bet, sugarplum," Blanche said heartily as she came in and sat down. "I'll load you up in the Caddy and we'll head to town. You can see Becca's office and you might even meet some of those kids Becca treats."

"That's a marvelous idea," Becca said, remembering the play group she'd been thinking about for Nicki. "There's a play group in my building, and you can come and play every day or whenever you like."

Nicki twisted her hands. "There's kids there? Kids I can play with?"

"Yes."

"But…"

Becca could see Nicki wasn't quite sure; her eyes were already bright with tears. *Don't cry, Nicki,* Becca was praying.

If she cried, Becca knew she wouldn't be able to leave. Tough love really was tough when the heart was involved.

"You know what, sugarplum?" Blanche said. "I've got this red feather boa that would look super on you, and I bet I could find some red high heels, too."

"Oh boy!" Nicki's eyes lit up and she slid from Becca's lap. "I can wear your heels?"

"You betcha, but you'd better give Becca a hug before she leaves."

Her little arms encircled Becca's neck. "I love you, Becca."

Becca fought back tears. "I love you, too, sweetie."

Blanche led Nicki away. At the door Nicki waved at her and Becca waved back, her heart in her throat. Nicki wasn't going to cry, but *she* would if she didn't get out of here soon.

She ran into the kitchen and hugged Della.

"I'm so sorry," Della said. Becca had told her the whole story.

"Sometimes things don't work out the way we plan."

"We'll miss you."

"Bye!" Becca ran out the door to her car.

She backed out and headed for Houston and her life. But she couldn't help thinking that the scene in her rearview mirror *was* her life—the only life she wanted.

CORD WATCHED HER LEAVE from an upstairs window. She was gone. She was safe. His heart wobbled inside him, but he was doing the right thing. They'd had a moment out of time and he would never forget it. But his loss would torture him for the rest of his life. That was exactly what he deserved.

BECCA WENT DIRECTLY to her apartment and unpacked, but she was restless. She suddenly had to see her mother. She drove to the clinic, but Emily was with a patient so she waited in her office. There was a family photo of the four of them on Emily's desk. Becca picked it up, staring at the smiling faces. They were happy, and she needed that happiness right now.

Emily entered the office and stopped, her surprise almost comical. "Becca! What are you doing here?" she asked in a startled voice. "Oh, it's so good to see you," she said as they embraced.

Emily drew back. "Your hair's longer and you look… different."

"How?" Becca asked.

"I don't know, but…" Emily gazed into her eyes. "You're all grown-up."

"Yeah, Mom. I don't even say *jeez* anymore," Becca said with a touch of mirth. "I'm all grown-up."

"I guess I've never really accepted that before."

"No, I don't think you have."

"Oh my, I have a grown-up daughter." Emily pushed dark hair away from Becca's shoulder. "And she looks so sad."

Unable to stop herself, Becca burst into tears, and Emily held her tight.

"What is it, angel?"

"I'm in love and…and it hurts."

Emily seemed to need a moment to absorb this, then she led Becca to a chair and got her a glass of water. "Tell me all about it."

Becca didn't leave anything out. She told her mother every detail except the intimate part, which belonged to her and Cord alone.

"Oh my." Emily brought a hand to her chest. "I'm so thankful you're okay, and your face has healed nicely, too."

Becca took a sip of water. "I know you and Dad will be upset that Cord's older, has a marriage behind him and a five-year-old daughter—but I love him and I love Nicki."

"Your father and I want you to be happy. That's all we've ever wanted for you."

Becca frowned in puzzlement.

"What is it?" Emily asked.

"All these years I've been trying to be the daughter you wanted. I didn't want to disappoint you again."

Emily pulled up a chair and faced her. "Angel, you have *never* disappointed us."

"Yes, I did," Becca refuted. "When I found out you were my mother, I did all those crazy things to hurt you."

Emily gently removed the glass from Becca's grasp and set it on a table, then she took her daughter's hands in hers. "That was a traumatic time for all of us. You wouldn't have been human if you hadn't responded in some way. You had so many emotions to get out of your system." She squeezed her hands. "You have never disappointed Jackson and me," she said again. "Our love is unconditional." She eyed Becca for a moment. "Did you choose medicine because you thought I wanted you to?"

Becca considered that and she had to be honest. "In part, I guess I did. I always wanted to be like you, but I enjoy being a doctor and I don't regret that decision."

"I'm glad, because you're very good with kids."

"For a while now, I've felt this restlessness and I couldn't figure out what it was."

"Have you figured it out now?"

"Yes." She looked at her mother. "I'd fit myself into the mold of being Emily's daughter. Your little girl. But the woman in me was clamoring to be released. I kept pushing her back, because deep inside I believed that once the *woman* surfaced, I'd lose something precious."

"And did you?"

"No." Becca smiled. "I gained so much more. And I know that no matter what happens, you and Daddy will always be there for me, whether I'm a little girl or your grown-up daughter."

Emily patted her hands. "Yes, we will."

"Oh, Mom, love is hard."

"Yes, but it also brings great rewards."

"I'll try to remember that."

"You're coming to dinner and I don't want to hear any excuses. Scotty hasn't seen you in ages and Grandpa George is in town."

"Yes, I've missed everyone, and I can't wait to hold Scotty." She needed to hold Nicki, too—and most of all, Nicki's father.

Cord, how can you do this to us?

THE NEXT FEW DAYS weren't easy. Becca had trouble sleeping and she didn't feel like eating. She talked to Nicki and to Blanche every day; the child was doing fine. Becca was grateful for that. Blanche said Mrs. Witherspoon hadn't come back and that Cord kept Nicki with him most of the day. When Nicki wasn't with him, she stayed with Blanche. Becca didn't know why he'd chosen to do this, rather than rehire the nanny or send Nicki to a play group, but she was sure he had a reason—one that made sense to him, anyway. Blanche also said that Edie was home and recovering well. The Prescotts had gone on without Becca, and she'd never felt so alone in her life. She had her family, but Becca—the woman Becca—needed a whole lot more.

She called Gin several times but was unable to reach her. The Fourth of July arrived, and Becca planned to stay home in her apartment, but the family was having a barbecue at her parents' so she went. She enjoyed seeing everyone. When she got there, Emily, Rose and Aunt Maude were in the kitchen preparing lunch. Jackson was at the grill keeping an eye on the meat. Grandpa George and Owen were playing ball with

Scotty. So Becca sat on the patio swing by herself, staring off into space and wondering what Cord and Nicki were doing. Did they miss her?

Jackson sat down beside her. "When I see that look on your face, I really want to hurt Cord Prescott," he said.

She glanced at her father. "But you won't," she said with certainty.

"No, because I love you too much."

"Thanks, Daddy," she murmured.

There was silence for a while. Then she asked in a low voice, "How do you feel about Cord and me?"

"When your mother first told me, I wasn't too happy," he confessed. "It was the age issue, but after I thought about it I changed my mind. I know Cord, and he's a good man. I guess what I'm saying is that the only thing I want is your happiness and if Cord makes you happy, then I'm all for it."

"I love him, Daddy," she said softly.

"I know."

"I never thought love would be like this—with such incredible highs and devastating lows."

"Angel, we all go through it. Just give Cord some time to get over this. And remember, once you find true love, never let it go."

She managed a smile. "This is from personal experience?"

"You're damn right it is," he replied strongly. "I thought I'd die when your mom pushed me away after we found out you were our daughter."

"But you got through it?"

"Yeah," he said. "It took time, but now we have you and Scotty…and so much more."

Her parents had endured much, but now they were happy. Would things work out as well for her and Cord? She honestly didn't know.

She turned to face her father, knowing she could talk

about anything with him. "You've known the Prescotts a long time."

"I met Clay in college. He was younger than me, but we became good friends."

"Did you ever meet the older Mr. Prescott?"

"Yes, lots of times. He gave Clay his share of the money to start our computer company. He'd come every couple of months to see how we were doing."

"Did Blanche come with him?"

"Sure. I don't think he went anywhere without her."

"What was she like then?"

"Same as she is now," he told her. "Rough around the edges. She said what was on her mind and couldn't care less if it offended anyone, but Mr. Prescott adored her. She was so much younger than him, but they got along really well."

"What was Mr. Prescott like?"

"Well…" Jackson thought for a minute. "He was his own man—did things his way. Didn't care what people thought. At times he was hard and overbearing, but he loved his sons. Whenever he came to San Antonio, he'd throw Clay into a panic with all his instructions on how we should run the business. But when he left there'd be tears in his eyes as he shook Clay's hand and asked if he had enough money to pay the bills and eat. He didn't want Clay doing without."

Becca ran her hand along her bare leg. This was what she needed—to talk about Cord and his family. "Mr. Prescott didn't ever hug him?"

"No, he wasn't a very demonstrative person."

She remembered Colton saying the same thing about himself, so it must be a Prescott trait. But Cord was very loving, and so gentle with Nicki. That was probably what had first attracted her.

"Tell me what Cord was like when you met him."

"Young, handsome and hardworking, and the ladies always

gravitated to him. Clay and I decided it was the cowboy thing."

"Oh, I don't think I want to hear that."

Jackson lifted her chin with his fingers. "Cord was so unassuming, he never suspected all the ladies were interested in him."

"Yes, he's like that," she said quietly. "He never knew Mona cared for him in a romantic way."

"That's not his fault," Jackson was quick to point out.

"I know that, but how do I make *him* see it?"

Jackson took her in his arms. "Just let the wounds heal, angel."

"But, Daddy, this is so hard."

"It'll get better," he promised. "Now, why don't you go relieve Dad and Owen? Scotty's making them run far too fast."

"Okay." She brushed away a tear. "Thanks for talking to me. I needed that."

"I know," he replied with a father's wisdom.

BECCA WENT TO WORK in Dr. Arnold's office and settled into a routine. Dr. Arnold was a well-known pediatrician and several doctors worked under her. Becca was honored to be one of those doctors. As the newest member of the team, she took patients who couldn't get in to see the other doctors. Slowly she was meeting the little patients and getting to know them. The days were busy, but nights were agonizing. She kept waiting to feel the feathery touch of Cord's mustache or to wake up and see him in the bathroom shaving, but each morning she felt a little more alone and a little more empty.

Early one morning, Ginger breezed into her apartment and slammed her purse on the bar. "Well, so you're back in town and I'm the last one to know."

"I called several times," Becca told her.

"Oh." Gin looked surprised. "I went out of town for the Fourth. So…how are you?"

"Things have been rough lately."

"Colton told me what's been happening. Are you okay?"

Becca sat on the sofa and curled her feet beneath her. "I'll never be the same again."

Ginger eyed her strangely as she sat down, too. "You seem different."

"Pain does that to a person."

"You're in pain?"

"Yes, right about here." She placed her hand over her heart.

That strange look turned to guilt, and Becca knew what was on Gin's mind—her affair with Colton.

"This isn't about Colton, Gin. It's about Cord."

Ginger crossed her legs nervously. "I don't know what you're talking about."

"Colton and I are friends like I've always told you," she said tolerantly. "We've never shared a passionate kiss and we've certainly never slept together."

"That has nothing to do with me!"

"Really? Then, why is your face almost as red as your hair?"

Ginger glanced up; their eyes met and they burst into laughter.

"I'm sorry," Gin murmured. "It just happened."

"What are you apologizing for? I'm happy for both of you."

"It's your fault, anyway."

"My fault?"

"Yeah. Colton called to see if I'd been watering your plants and that made me mad as hell, so I gave him a piece of my mind. Then he stopped by your place while I was here and we got to talking and he offered to take me out to dinner. I surprised myself when I accepted. After that, one thing led to another. Colton's very nice once you get to know him." Her eyes grew dreamy. "I make him laugh and he makes me take life more seriously."

"I assume going away for the Fourth was with Colton."

"Yeah," Gin said in a hesitant voice. "Are you *sure* you're okay with this?"

"Yes, I'm fine," Becca assured her. "Colton isn't the Prescott who's broken my heart."

"Cordell Prescott is a fool."

Becca's face darkened, and Gin immediately backpedaled. "I know he's gone through a lot, but can't he see how much you love him?"

"Right now, he's suffering so much I don't think he can see much of anything."

There was a long silence, then Becca suggested, "Why don't we go out for dinner tonight?"

"I'm sorry." Gin's face fell. "I have plans to meet Colton at his place, but you can come with me. I'm sure he'd be glad to see you."

"No, thanks, I'm not in the mood to be a fifth wheel. Besides, I have some medical reading to catch up on."

After Gin left, Becca quickly got dressed for work, but her mind was filled with thoughts of Cord. How long would the pain last? How long before the ache inside her disappeared? How long was a lifetime? Forever. She would feel this way forever, or until Cord was back in her life.

CHAPTER EIGHTEEN

CORD STOOD WATCHING Nicki play from the den. The sheriff had called and said that Mona's death was ruled a suicide. Apparently they were trying to locate a distant cousin who would inherit the Tibbets ranch. Also, Bates and his girlfriend had moved to Montana. It was over, the sheriff had said, but Cord knew it would never be over for him.

His gaze shifted to Blanche, who was sitting in a lounge chair also watching Nicki. That was the only good thing that had come out of this mess. He and Blanche had gotten closer, and Blanche now helped him with Nicki. They were still waiting for Clay to fly home so they could have a meeting about the will. But in the meantime, Edie and Blanche were getting along. He hadn't heard one argument lately. They were pulling together as a family—just like Becca had wanted them to. God, why couldn't he stop thinking about her?

He hardly noticed when Blanche came in. All he could see was Becca's face, her eyes, her smile. He was walking a tightrope of emotion and didn't know how long he could stay balanced. But he was afraid he was going down and could do nothing to stop himself. He focused on Nicki. His daughter was all that kept him sane.

"Cord, where are you?" Colton yelled from the kitchen.

Cord turned as his brother came into the den. Colton walked straight up to him, his right fist connecting with Cord's jaw. Cord wheeled from the blow.

"How could you?" Colton said through clenched teeth. "I told you to leave her alone. Becca doesn't deserve this."

Cord's eyes darkened. "The first punch is free, but if you try it again, I'll knock you on your ass."

The two brothers faced each other. Cord was the taller, bigger one, but Colton had blood in his eye.

Blanche immediately got between them. "Stop this right now! Nicki could come in any minute."

Cord swung away and went through the French doors to the patio.

Blanche placed her hands on her hips. "Your brother's in pain. Can't you see that?"

"I'm not really worried about his pain," Colton said angrily.

"Yes, you are. That's why you're here. You know Cord and Becca are right for each other. I understand that's hard for you to accept but—"

"If he loves her, how can he do this to her?" Colton broke in.

"Think about everything Cord's been through. In time, he'll realize he can't live without her."

"I don't know. He's stubborn as a mule."

"Maybe, but I hope you got all the anger out of your system."

Colton rubbed his knuckles. "No, and I think I broke my hand."

"Come to the kitchen," she said. "I'll make you some coffee and put ice on it."

Blanche walked away, but Colton just stared after her with a perplexed expression.

Blanche glanced back at him. "What's wrong?"

"I don't think I've talked this much to you in all my life. Who are you? I don't know this person."

“I’m your mother and you’re my son, and that’s how we’re gonna act from now on.”

“Oh,” Colton said, and followed her into the kitchen.

CORD PUT NICKI TO BED, and luckily she didn’t mention Becca. Every time she did, he shriveled up inside. And tonight he’d almost reached the end of what he could tolerate. Colton had a right to be angry, and the bruise on Cord’s jaw was a small price to pay for what he’d done to Becca.

He went down to the kitchen and discovered Blanche there.

“Sit down,” she said.

“Blanche, I’m not—”

“Sit,” she ordered. “I have a few things to say and you’re gonna listen.”

He took a seat.

“How long are you gonna blame yourself for Anette’s death?”

“Leave it alone.”

“No, I won’t,” Blanche told him. “I don’t think you even realize how disturbed Anette was.”

“What are you talking about?”

“Did you finish reading this?” She set the journal in front of him.

He pushed it away. “I don’t want to see that again.”

“That’s too bad, because you’re listening to what it has to say.”

“Blanche…”

But Blanche was reading from the book. “‘I should tell Cord, but I won’t. He says he loves me, but he might take Mona’s side. If he does, then I’d have to kill them both because I’ll never let her have him. I need more pills. Maybe then these thoughts will go away.’” Blanche laid the book down. “Does that sound like a person you could help? She was on medication when you met her. You knew that. Her condition only got worse. Her pregnancy might have been a factor, but she wanted the baby. And Mona didn't help matters. But you certainly had nothing to do with that."

Cord didn't say a word.

Blanche went on. "You've always been a very kind person. When you met Anette, she had practically no one and she wanted a family. You gave her that, but Anette needed a lot more. You got her psychiatric help, but it wasn't enough." Blanche was silent for a moment, then added, "You can't stop living because of what happened. Let it go. Put it in the past where it belongs."

Cord got up and left the kitchen without a backward glance. He walked to his room and fell fully clothed onto the bed. Memories of Anette consumed him. Blanche was right; he'd been kind to Anette. She'd seemed so lost and alone, and he'd wanted to help her, but she had other problems he hadn't really considered. After they were married, her depression and paranoia grew worse. How much Mona had to do with that, he wasn't sure. Obviously Anette and Mona were engaged in some private battle he wasn't even aware of. Why couldn't he see what was happening right under his own nose? Because they'd made a point of keeping it from him. And there was nothing he could have done to change that.

The truth of that jolted him and he sat up. *He couldn't have changed a thing.* But if he'd known how Mona felt—that thought wouldn't let him go. He'd known Mona all his life. The kids at school had teased her and he'd told her she was pretty. He'd done it out of kindness. Just to make her feel better. Could that have been the start of her infatuation with him? Had she read more into it than he'd actually intended? He didn't see how, since there was no romantic involvement between them and Mona was some years older. She'd even been smitten with Clay. He'd dated other women and the only interest he and Mona had in common was ranching. They'd never touched or kissed. How could she have deluded herself that their friendship was something more? He'd never encouraged her in that way.

Still, for whatever reasons, she'd developed an obsession with him. Why hadn't he seen the signs? Mona had spent too much time at Triple Creek. She'd relied on him to help her make decisions—or pretended to. And he'd fallen for it. But anything he'd done, he'd done out of kindness. Around and around went the thoughts until he felt as though his head would burst.

His emotions were wavering dangerously, taking him places he didn't want to go.

Just when his capacity for strength had reached its limit, he glanced down and saw his boots, and suddenly Becca's face swam before him.

A cowboy's dream. A woman to remove his boots.

The memory of her smile eased the turbulence inside him, but he couldn't complete the circle by accepting her in his life. He wouldn't hurt another woman—especially Becca.

He got up and ran down the stairs to the stables. He was saddling Apache when Gus walked in wearing his boxer shorts and boots. He held a shotgun in his hand.

"God Almighty, boy! I thought we had a prowler."

"Go back to bed, Gus. It's just me."

"Where you going?"

Cord swung into the saddle. "Go back to bed."

Gus rubbed his bald head. "You gonna ride that horse to death."

Cord signaled Apache and they shot out of the barn.

"Or yourself," Gus muttered. "When's all this gonna end?"

BECCA LOVED HER JOB and all the kids she saw. They were so innocent and trusting, and depended on her to make their aches and pains go away. She'd hoped that once she threw herself into her work and submerged herself in other people's problems, the pain inside her would ease, but it didn't. Each day that passed without a message from Cord made her heartache worse.

The bright spot in her life was Nicki. Blanche brought her to the play group three days a week, and Becca made sure she had time to spend with her. Nicki was always so thrilled about visiting her, and she chatted on and on about everything. When she mentioned Cord, Becca's heart fluttered with something that wasn't going to disappear—love. Almost a month had gone by, and if it hadn't been for her work, Becca would have been overwhelmed by grief and disappointment.

On Monday morning of the Fourth week, she stopped by the hospital to check over a newborn, a healthy little boy. No problems and all his vitals were strong. She told the mother to call the office and they'd set up scheduled appointments for the baby. When she reached the clinic, the nurse informed her they had a full morning. It started with three-year-old Casey, who had a cold; the mother was worried because it wasn't clearing up. The child was in day care and exposed to all sorts of things. Becca couldn't do anything about that, but she assured the mother her little girl was fine and that she would get better. Next was two-year-old Eric, whose ear was red and swollen. The boy was constantly pulling on it. Becca quickly saw the problem—a dried black-eyed pea was stuck in his ear. Becca was able to extract it without admitting him to the hospital. And another two-year-old, Noah, had a rash all over his body. His hands, feet and face were not affected. It took a while for Becca to figure it out. Finally she asked if he had any new pajamas. The mother said yes, he'd gotten some for his birthday. She prescribed an ointment for the rash and told the mother to get rid of the pajamas. The boy was allergic to the fabric.

Her days were mostly the same, caring for babies and children. Occasionally she dealt with teenagers. Today she saw a fifteen-year-old girl who'd been sick with vomiting for a week. The mother insisted she had the flu and needed something for it because the girl couldn't miss any more school. Becca gave the girl, Katie Adams, a thorough exam and ran some tests. She suspected Katie was pregnant. The mother was very domineering, and Becca could see her daughter was afraid of telling her. While Mrs. Adams went to get coffee, she talked with Katie, who admitted she was pregnant. Becca told her she had to tell her parents. What followed was a big scene. The mother screamed and yelled, but it didn't change the fact that the girl was pregnant. Becca set up counseling for them, hoping they could work things out.

It was one of those days she was glad to go home.

JULY HAD TURNED into August, and she'd still heard nothing from Cord. Her family went to Rockport, but she stayed in Houston. She had to be here if Cord called, but she finally realized that wasn't likely to happen. She had a decision to make. She could go on waiting or—or what?

Then she discovered a certain fact that changed her whole perspective. Her body had begun to tell her something and she knew what it was. She and Cord hadn't used any protection when they'd been together. Doctor or not, she hadn't even thought about it. Love had blinded her to that need. She took a pregnancy test and confirmed it: she was having a baby. That knowledge sent her into orbit with delight, then just as quickly brought her down to earth. How did she tell Cord? He was dealing with so much already, and she had no idea how he'd take the news. She definitely would not tell him with the intent of getting him back. Cord had to decide that on his own.

She sat on the sofa with her hand on her flat stomach and

knew she wanted Cord's child with all her heart. "We'll be fine," she whispered. "I love you already and your father will, too, but I'm not sure there's time for him to realize that before you're born."

She thought of the fifteen-year-old and so many girls like her. Sex came with a price—responsibility. Emily had told her that once. Maybe that was why she'd waited so long. At her age, sex was a choice she'd made consciously and with full awareness. She could handle the consequences.

She considered Emily and what it must've been like to be pregnant at seventeen. Becca was older, self-supporting, mature, but what if she'd been seventeen and unmarried—and had to face Rose? Becca trembled. For the first time, she could really imagine the fear and turmoil Emily must have experienced. It was a revelation.

"Don't worry." She patted her stomach. "You and I will never be parted." But, oh, she didn't think she could wait eighteen years, as her mother had, for Cord to rejoin their lives.

She curled up and wondered how her parents were going to react. A smile spread across her face. There would be no harsh words or judgments, because she was their daughter and they loved her. She'd tried so hard to be perfect for them, but she didn't have to be. They loved her just the way she was—faults and all. And they'd love her baby.

HER BIRTHDAY came and she spent it with her family. She wasn't very good company, but no one seemed to notice. She just kept thinking she was twenty-nine, pregnant and alone. The thought didn't depress her; it gave her something to look forward to—the birth of their child.

Nicki started classes in Houston at the private school Anette had wanted her to attend. Nicki was eager to have Becca meet her teacher. So far, Becca had managed to put her off.

Blanche had also enrolled Nicki in ballet classes. The school was having a party to allow students, teachers and parents to meet each other, and families were welcome. Nicki had begged her to come, and Becca couldn't tell her she wasn't part of the family. It didn't help that Blanche kept insisting. Becca said she'd have to check her schedule, but she'd already decided she couldn't go. Cord would be there, and if she saw him she'd fall to pieces. Her emotions were very precarious these days.

The night of the party, Colton and Ginger stopped by. Colton frowned at her. "What? You're not dressed." She had on jeans and a knit top.

She knew exactly what he was talking about. "I'm not going."

"You have to. Nicki's expecting you."

"Colton..."

"So what if Cord's there?" Gin said. "Thumb your nose at him. Come on, I'll pick out something sexy for you to wear." Gin disappeared into her bedroom.

Becca turned to Colton. "I can't do this."

"Sure you can, gorgeous. Just smile and everything'll be fine."

Still she hesitated.

"I'm mad as hell at Cord," Colton told her, "but I can't even imagine what he's going through. I know one thing, though—you're the only person who can reach him. He has to see that life goes on. One look at you is all he needs."

She smiled. "I never knew you were a matchmaker."

"I'm not. I'm just trying to help two people I care about."

"Bec, are you coming?" Gin called from the bedroom.

Colton raised an eyebrow. "You'd better go. You know how she is when she gets going on something."

She hugged him. "I'm so happy for you and Gin."

"You were right. I needed someone to make me laugh.

Ginger makes me feel like the kid I never was, and it's a wonderful feeling." He paused, then looked into her eyes. "For so many years I thought my future was with you but…"

"We'd have been miserable together," she finished for him.

He grinned. "That about sums it up. Now, what's it gonna be? Are you planning to let Nicki down?"

"I would never let Nicki down," she said, and it was true. As Gin had said, so what if Cord was there? She had to see him eventually, and tonight was a good time to start. She couldn't keep the excitement from rushing through her at the prospect.

SHE DECIDED—or rather, Ginger decided for her—to wear a maroon slim-fitting dress with a short-sleeved jacket. Ginger said she didn't need the jacket, but she wore it, anyway. The dress was low-cut and she didn't want to appear—well, she wasn't sure so she wore the jacket.

When they arrived, the party was in full swing. Little girls in tutus were running everywhere. A teacher introduced herself, and Colton told her they were the Prescott family. Before the teacher could say anything, a screech was heard.

"Becca, Becca, Becca."

Becca bent and caught Nicki as the child hurled herself into her arms. "Look at me." Nicki ran her hands down the pink tutu. "We got them today and the teacher said we could wear them. Don't I look pretty?"

"Beautiful." Becca kissed her cheek.

"Watch, I can do this already."

She stood on tiptoe and raised her hands above her head. She tried to turn and toppled backward, but Colton caught her.

"You need more practice, munchkin," Colton teased her.

"Yeah," Nicki said, not deterred for a moment. "Come on.

Daddy, Blanche and Edie are over here." She caught Becca's hand and pulled her forward.

CORD SAW HER COMING—saw everything about her with painful clarity. She looked as beautiful as she did in his dreams, and he wanted to run, to put as much distance between them as he could. But his feet stayed rooted to the spot and his eyes followed her across the room. There was something different about her, but he couldn't determine exactly what it was. Her dark hair was longer and hung enchantingly around her face; however, that wasn't it. Her body seemed fuller—or did it? He wasn't sure. God, he remembered what it was like to touch those breasts, those hips. He had to get out of here. He couldn't do this. But his feet wouldn't move.

BECCA SAW HIM and her insides melted with a need that only he could create. He wore dark slacks and a white shirt with his Sunday boots and hat. He held a glass of punch in one hand and there was a distant, brooding look in his eyes. He was so handsome.

What do I say to him? She had to say something.

She hugged Blanche and Edie, then turned to face him. They stared at each other for several seconds. Without realizing it, she placed her hand protectively on her stomach. Her tongue was thick and the words wouldn't come.

What do I say to him?

"How are you?" he finally asked.

Awful. Without you, I'm awful.

Before she could answer, Nicki broke in. "Becca, look." Becca tore her eyes away and glanced at Nicki, who was holding a pair of tap shoes. "I'm gonna take tap dance, too. These make lots of noise."

"I bet they do."

After that, the liveliness of the party took over. She shook hands with teachers and parents and met some of the little girls. Two of them were her patients, and she visited briefly with their parents. All the while, she avoided looking at Cord. She'd thought they would be able to talk but that barrier was still there. He wasn't letting her near him, and she didn't know how to break through. She didn't understand how she could love him so much, yet still be unable to reach him.

CORD SIPPED HIS PUNCH and watched her. He wanted to look away but he couldn't. Becca was talking to several little girls, Nicki in the center; he noticed that Nicki wasn't letting anyone get too close to Becca. They were all drawn to her like a magnet, just as he had been.

Ginger walked up to him. "I don't think we've been properly introduced, but I'm Ginger Daley, Becca's friend."

He spared her a quick glance. "Yes, I know who you are."

Ginger followed his gaze to Becca. "She's always been like that. Just about every time we went to the mall, there'd be some kid who'd gotten separated from his mother and we'd spend our afternoon searching for her and making sure the kid was okay. And the baby-sitting jobs. I think our teenage years were spent with Becca taking care of every kid in Rockport. I can't tell you the number of Saturday nights that ticked me off. But that's Becca." She took a sip of her punch. "I could probably stand here all night listing Becca's good qualities, but I believe you already know them."

"Yeah," he murmured. He knew all about Becca, and he didn't need another person telling him anything. He glowered at her. "Is there a point to this, Ginger?"

"There sure is," she replied without hesitation. "You're an idiot, Cordell Prescott."

His eyes narrowed. "Excuse me?"

"You've been through hell. So what? A lot of people have.

Get over it. Can't you see you have heaven waiting for you?" Without another word, she walked away.

If one more person tried to interfere in his life, he was going to snap. He didn't need… Becca raised her head and their eyes met across the room. All he could see was pain. Deep, inner pain.

Pain he'd caused.

All the emotions he kept locked up came pouring into his heart. He couldn't breathe for a moment and he had to force himself to inhale deeply. He was at the crossroads of his life and he knew it. The past still had a strong hold on him, but there was nothing he could do about it. He finally saw that. The present, though, the pain he saw in Becca's eyes and the pain he felt in his heart—that was something he could change. *You have heaven waiting for you.* Suddenly the mist around him cleared. The past would not keep him a prisoner.

His heart leapt with this awakening. Circumstances had clouded his judgment and blinded him to what was important in his life. He'd no control over Anette or Mona. He had done everything he could to help his wife, but she'd chosen to keep secrets from him. He had no power over that. And he certainly had nothing to do with Mona's insane behavior. It was all so clear now, and he knew what he had to do. And he had to do it immediately.

He walked over to Colton. "Could you take Blanche, Edie and Nicki home? I have somewhere to go."

"Sure, but what the—"

Cord didn't wait to hear the rest. He strolled quickly to the door.

Becca saw him leave and her heart sank. He couldn't even stay in the same room with her. All her hopes died. He wasn't going to give them a chance. She had to get away before the tears took over. She kissed Nicki goodbye and used her cell phone to call a cab. Colton wasn't too pleased, but she had to be alone to deal with the fact that the life she wanted with Cord was only a fairy tale—as Blanche had once warned her.

CORD DROVE TO THE CEMETERY and walked to Anette's grave. He stood for a long time breathing in the warm August air. The wind picked up and blew stray leaves around his feet. He was no longer overwhelmed, but he had to confront his emotions concerning Anette. That was the only way to put all this behind him. He remembered when he and Becca had brought Nicki here. Talking had helped his child; maybe it would help him, too.

He remembered the words Nicki had said and they echoed his own feelings. "I'm not mad at you anymore," he whispered from his soul. For so long he'd been angry at Anette for what she'd done. But now he understood that she hadn't killed herself. Mona had murdered her. He sucked air into his lungs. He couldn't let that destroy him because there was nothing he could have done to change it. Nothing. He couldn't go on blaming himself, punishing himself.

"I'm not mad at you," he repeated, and the rest of the hurt began to leave him. He put his hat on his head and walked back to his truck.

BECCA UNDRESSED and slipped on a T-shirt, then curled up on the sofa. The tears she'd been holding back suddenly burst forth, and she cried for herself, for Cord and for everything that was lost. She knew Cord was softhearted and felt things deeply, but she'd believed he would find his way back to her. Tonight that hope had dwindled to nothing. He was going to continue blaming himself for everything. He refused to let himself live again.

She sat straighter and dried her tears. She wanted to call her mother and tell her about the baby. She had to tell *someone.*

But she wanted to tell Cord first. A baby was probably the last thing he wanted to hear about, though.

She curled up again. She couldn't help thinking that unhappy pregnancies ran in the family. Rose and Emily had both gotten pregnant out of wedlock. Why was it that history had a way of repeating itself? But this baby was very much wanted….

THE RINGING OF THE DOORBELL woke her. Groggily she sat up and pushed hair away from her face. It was after twelve. Probably Colton and Ginger making sure she was okay.

She got up and looked through the peephole, and her whole body froze. Cord was standing outside. Was something wrong with Nicki? That was the only reason he'd be here, the only reason she could think of. She quickly opened the door.

For a moment they just stared at each other. He wore the same clothes he had at the party and clutched his hat in one hand. "Can I talk to you, please?" he finally asked.

"Sure," she answered, moving aside to let him in. "Is it Nicki?" She could hear the anxiety in her voice.

"No, she's fine."

He was so much taller, and without her shoes she was reminded of that. His mere presence in her apartment took her breath away.

He noticed her red and puffy eyes. "Have you been crying?"

She tucked hair behind her ear and didn't know quite how to answer that—so she didn't. "Cord, why are you here?"

He twisted his hat. "I'm not sure where to start," he said. "But this thing with Anette and Mona hit me pretty hard."

"I know that."

"When I thought Mona could have killed you, too—well, I just couldn't handle it. I hurt every woman who's ever loved me and I couldn't handle that, either. I felt so much guilt and blame that it overshadowed everything."

Becca's heart started to beat with alarming speed.

He raised his head and she saw his eyes. The pain was gone. Thank God, the pain was gone.

"Tonight when I saw you, I realized I'm still hurting you. I can't do that anymore, either."

"You can't?"

His eyes held hers. "No, I love you and—"

"Don't say that." She broke in fiercely, surprising herself. "How can you love me and still hurt me? Anette didn't hurt me. Mona didn't hurt me. *You* did. You hurt me and…" Emotions overwhelmed her and she couldn't go on.

"Please, forgive me," he said in a tortured voice. "I do love you. You may not understand why I had to send you away, but at the time it was the only thing that made sense to me." He paused, then added, "I love you, Becca. Nothing will ever change that."

At the look in his eyes and the passion in his voice, everything in her crumbled away, the anger and the grief and the hurt. All that remained was the love. She threw herself into his arms and words were stilled as their lips met in hungry, aching need. Cord lifted her off the floor as the kiss went on and on. She wrapped her arms around his neck, her fingers tangling in his hair, giving herself up to this moment, his kiss.

Somehow they were on the sofa and she wasn't sure how they'd got there. All she wanted to do was hold him, touch him…and love him.

"Oh, Becca." He groaned as his hands slipped beneath her shirt to her breast. "I'm been starving for this, dying for you."

"Then, why did you push me away? That hurt so much."

He rested his forehead against hers. "It's hard to explain, but when I found out about Mona and Anette, I felt a terrible guilt. It was eating me alive and I didn't want to drag you into my agony. I wanted you to have a normal life, away from the insanity that plagued me."

She kissed the corner of his mustache. "I have no life without you."

"I finally realized that, too. About myself, I mean. After everything that happened, I didn't think I deserved one, but now I do—a life with you."

That was exactly what she needed to hear. Her world suddenly righted itself. Except for one thing…

"Say you love me and forgive me," he whispered.

"I love you and I forgive you," she answered, and for the next few seconds there was only blissful silence as their lips met. She didn't want this to end, but she had to tell him. "We have to talk," she said in a hoarse voice.

He shook his head. "No talking or thinking. I just want to love you."

She wanted that, too, and it was tempting to wait and tell him later. But they couldn't start their life that way. She had to be honest.

"We have to talk," she repeated in a stronger voice.

Her voice got his attention, and he drew his lips away. "What is it? What's wrong?"

She didn't know how to tell him, so she said the first thing that came into her mind. "You haven't mentioned marriage."

He seemed to relax. "I assumed we would. Isn't that what you want?"

"Yes, but it would be nice to be asked."

"Oh, I'm sorry," he said and stood up. "I'll be right back."

Startled, she asked, "Where are you going?" But he was already out the door. She didn't know what to think, but he'd said he'd be back. So she waited.

In a minute, he *was* back. He laid a box of chocolates and a dozen long-stemmed white roses in her lap. Then he got down on one knee and took her hand. “Rebecca Talbert, will you marry me?”

She pushed the candy and roses aside and made a dive for him. “Yes, yes, yes,” she said as they kissed long and deep, then she asked, “Where did you get the candy and roses?”

“I brought them as a peace offering.”

“Very wise.”

They kissed again and Cord settled back on the floor, against the sofa, with her on his lap.

“You sure you don’t want to rethink that decision? I come as a package deal—Nicki and the rest of my crazy family.”

“And one more,” she said softly, leading up to what she had to tell him.

“One more what?” His tongue found the sensitive area behind her ear.

“One more child.” She tried to keep her senses clear, but that was hard to do with Cord’s breath on her skin.

“Child? What child?” he asked in a hazy voice.

She swallowed. “Our child.”

“We don’t have a child.”

“In about seven months wc will.”

The room suddenly became very quiet, and she rushed on. “Now, Cord, don’t freak out on me and please don’t go all silent. Let me reach you.”

“You’re pregnant?” His voice came out low and shaky. “How did this happen?”

She lifted an eyebrow. “Want me to give you a biology lesson?”

“No, I mean…are you okay?”

“I’m fine.”

“But this is too soon for you.”

“I’m ready for a baby—your baby.”

“Oh, Becca.” He cradled her head in both hands. “I love you so much.”

"Then, you're okay with this."

"I'm so happy I could walk on water. A new life. A new beginning. That's what I need—with you and our family."

They kissed slowly, then held each other close. "I love you, Cordell Prescott," she said, and for several heavenly moments not another word was spoken.

Slowly she reached for the chocolates. "Do we eat these chocolates and make love, or make love and then eat the chocolates?"

He took the box out of her hands and smiled. Soon the whole world faded, leaving just the two of them in a private universe of their own making. Shadows of the past might appear from time to time, but their love, strong and lasting, would now have the power to chase them away.

EPILOGUE

Two years later

BECCA PUT THE FINISHING touches to the table. The flowers, candelabra, china and linen were perfect—just the way she wanted it. It was Thanksgiving and both families, Cord's and hers, were coming. It was the beginning of a new Prescott tradition, and she enjoyed preparing the house and getting a meal ready. She paused for a moment, thinking back, and gave thanks for everything in her life.

She had married Cord a month after that August night, in a small chapel with family and friends. She'd worn her mother's wedding dress, even though it was tight around the waist. Her parents reacted exactly the way she'd known they would to the pregnancy—lovingly and supportively. Rose was another matter. Even though she'd tried to hide it, she wasn't pleased, but she adored her great-grandson. The day she had Cordell Jackson Prescott was one of the happiest of Becca's life. Nicki was infatuated with her little brother; Becca and Cord wanted Nicki to be comfortable with him, and she was. It helped, too, that she was the big sister.

Becca had a hard time adjusting her work schedule. She'd spent so many years becoming a doctor and she loved it, but she loved her family more. So she compromised. She worked full-time until C.J., as they called their son, was born. Now she worked four half days, and was on call one weekend a month, to assist Dr. Arnold. Sometimes it turned out to be more than that, and Cord was understanding. He didn't want her to give up her work. And it helped that he was always close to home.

They had renovated the second floor. They'd ripped out walls and made a new master suite and nursery. Becca now felt as if she was a part of this history in the house. She, Blanche and Edie had hung portraits of all the Prescott women in the upstairs hall. Cord smilingly approved of their efforts.

Colton and Ginger had eloped a year ago and spent a lengthy honeymoon in Europe. She and Ginger were now sisters-in-law. That seemed so natural, given how long they'd been friends.

Della came in wearing a flowered dress and white apron. "What do you think?" Becca asked, surveying her handiwork.

"Just beautiful." Della sighed. "Everything's so different around here. It's a pleasure to come to work these days."

Becca put an arm around her waist. "And it's a pleasure to have your help. Maybe one of these days I'll learn to be as good a cook as you."

"Mommy, Mommy," Nicki called.

On their wedding day Nicki had asked, "Are you my mommy now?" Becca had replied, "Yes." From then on, Nicki had called her Mommy. Anette had receded in her memory. Anette's portrait—painted from a photograph—hung upstairs, and they put flowers on her grave during holidays, but she knew Nicki had very little recollection of her. In a way that was good, but Becca didn't want her to completely forget her real mother. The things she'd saved from Anette's room were in a sealed box in her closet. At the appropriate time, she and Cord would give them to Nicki.

Nicki burst into the room, her blond curls everywhere. "Daddy can't do my hair right, Mommy. I want you to fix it. I want to wear these, and Daddy doesn't know how they work." She held out the hair clips Blanche had sent her from Paris.

Blanche and Edie were now traveling together. Two women who had spent years hating each other had become traveling companions. They still argued from time to time, but their arguments were trivial, almost as though the habit was too deeply ingrained to stop. Forgiveness had come slowly to the Prescott family, but in the end it had arrived.

Clay had finally flown home and he, Cord, Colton and Edie had sat down with Blanche to work out the details of the will. There were no recriminations against Blanche. Her sons did their best to understand her motives. Then Edie shocked everyone by saying she was satisfied with a trust fund. She was too old to run a ranch and it really belonged to Cord. It was enough that Pa had remembered her. So Cord gave up his trust fund, which was divided among Edie, Colton and Clay, and he took full possession of the ranch. Everyone seemed happy with that arrangement, and all the boys were finally getting to know their mother. Blanche had changed so completely that the hard, crude person Becca had first met was nonexistent. Once Blanche had learned that she didn't have to own everything for the family to care about her, she realized what a fool she'd been and what a treasure she had in her sons. Edie was just tired of the long battle and gave in gracefully. After spending two weeks in Europe, the two women had traveled to Alaska to see Clay, Nina and the girls. They were all flying home for Thanksgiving.

Becca combed Nicki's hair and secured the clips. "How's that?"

Nicki looked in the mirror over the buffet. "Just like I wanted," she said, studying herself.

Nicki was starting to take an interest in her appearance. Poor Cord. He wasn't ready for this—and neither was she.

Apparently satisfied with her hair, Nicki turned to Becca. "When are Blanche and Edie coming home?"

"Colton and Ginger are picking everyone up at the airport, so they should be here in about an hour."

"I'm glad 'cause I miss them."

"Me, too, sweetie."

Secretly she knew that Blanche and Edie traveled—at least in part—to give them time as a family. She'd told them they didn't have to do that, but they didn't listen to her, and Becca loved them all the more. She'd been raised as an only child and she wanted to belong to a big family. Now she did, and she couldn't be happier.

"Scotty and me can go riding after dinner, can't we, Mommy?"

"Yes, but remember your cousins from Alaska will be here, too, so you have to include them." Nicki and Scotty were "buddies," as Nicki put it. Becca had worried about the two being jealous of each other. At first they were, but that soon ended. Nicki was taken with Scotty's computer skills, and Scotty was amazed at Nicki's riding and roping ability. They were always eager to show the other new things.

"Okay," Nicki agreed.

Childish screeches could be heard a moment before C.J. flew into the room without a stitch of clothing except for his cowboy boots. He threw himself at Becca's legs and peeked around her to his father standing in the doorway.

At the sight of Cord, Becca's heart fluttered with excitement. It was the same every time she saw her handsome cowboy. He hadn't changed a bit in two years, except that the sadness in his brown eyes had been replaced by a joy that was echoed in hers.

With a smile, Becca ruffled the blond curls on her son's head. "Cord, our son doesn't have any clothes on."

He walked farther into the room, laughter filling his eyes.

"While I was working on Nicki's hair, he took his pajamas off and put on his boots. Before I could think of a way to get his pants over his boots, he darted out the door. I'm gonna have to bring my rope to the house so I can lasso him. Might be the only way I can keep up with the boy."

As Cord drew closer, C.J. screeched again and ran into the den.

"God Almighty, boy, you're naked as a jaybird." They could hear Gus, and Becca groaned.

"I'll get him," Nicki said.

Cord kissed the top of Nicki's head. "Thanks, baby."

Cord stared after her as she chased C.J. "She's only seven and I'm afraid to blink. If I do, she'll be all grown-up."

Becca wrapped her arms around his waist from behind. "Oh, I think we have a while yet."

"Yeah," he murmured. "When I remember what it was like a couple of years ago, I get cold chills."

"That's all behind us."

He turned in the circle of her arms. "Your parents call you *angel* and you really are." He bent his head and softly kissed her as she leaned in to him.

"You're gonna get so lucky tonight," she murmured wickedly.

"I get lucky every night," he teased. "I have to be the luckiest guy on the planet." And he was. The situation with Anette and Mona had almost destroyed him, but Becca's love had saved him. Every day when he woke up with Becca in his arms, he knew he was truly blessed.

She watched his face. "You're in a good mood."

"I guess I am," he admitted. "I never thought we'd have family occasions in this house. Now the whole Prescott family and yours will be here. I'm very grateful for that. And Clay's thinking about moving back to Texas. It would be wonderful if we were all together again."

"Yes, it would," she said. "It would give our kids a chance to grow up with their cousins."

"I think Blanche has a lot to do with their decision."

"Probably, and since Nina's parents have passed away, they want their girls to be around family. Clay's girls think Blanche is cool."

He caressed her face. "I think *you're* cool. And beautiful, brilliant, loving and…"

She kissed the vee in his shirt and traveled upward.

"Oh," he moaned. "When you do that I get completely sidetracked and—" Just as his head dipped toward her, they heard more screeching and laughter from the den. Nicki was still chasing C.J. trying to catch him.

Cord gave her a quick kiss. "I'd better corral our children."

"Cord, why can't we make C.J. understand that he has to wear clothes?" she asked woefully. C.J. didn't like clothes. He preferred to run around in nothing but his boots.

"Beats me. I never had this problem with Nicki."

"I don't know where he gets it from," she said. "I was always very discreet as a child." She poked him in his ribs. "He probably gets it from you."

"Uh, I don't think so. I don't remember preferring the buff."

She looked into his eyes. "Why is it I can handle other children, but not my own?"

He stroked her cheek with the back of his hand. "He's not even two years old. Give it time. He won't be doing this in a few years. Isn't that what you'd tell a worried parent?"

"Yes." She sighed, knowing he was right. It wasn't anything to worry about. "One of us had better get him dressed before company arrives." As the words left her mouth, the doorbell rang.

They could hear C.J. running in his boots to the door.

"Oh, no," Becca muttered.

"Relax," Cord said. "Everyone's seen him without his clothes on." Then he took her into his arms and kissed her deeply. Her arms crept around his neck as she returned the kiss. As always, they were in their own world.

"I love you," he whispered against her lips. "Just wanted you to know that before the craziness of this day starts."

"I love you, too," she whispered back. "You've made me so happy. I'm glad I waited for you."

"Me, too. I never thought it was possible to be this happy," he replied. "You've changed my whole life—not to mention my whole family."

She smiled into his eyes. "I never dreamed I'd fall in love with a cowboy."

He settled his hands around her waist. "How's the experience so far?"

"Exciting, stimulating, fulfilling, passionate—and you'd better keep it that way."

"I promise, for the rest of our lives." He sealed that vow with a searing kiss. "Now we'd better go rescue whoever's at the door from our naked son."

Arm in arm, they strolled to the front door. Becca had finally found the passionate love she'd been looking for. Like Emily, she would love one man—forever.

* * * * *

THAT COWBOY'S KIDS

Debra Salonen

For my mother and father,
who gave me time to dream.

For Paul, who gave me time to write.

CHAPTER ONE

"How much longer, Daddy?" Heather asked plaintively.

Tom Butler stifled a sigh. "Five more minutes, punkin," he said without consulting his watch.

"That's what you said five minutes ago," Angela grumbled, her words muffled by a thick wad of long dark hair.

Tom glanced at her. His twelve-year-old daughter, a spooky mixture of limbs and emotions, sat folded into a tight ball up against the passenger door of his pickup truck. With artistic finesse she winnowed out one ebony strand from the rest of the waist-length tresses and threaded it between sullen lips.

Grazing on hair, he thought, one more thing no one had warned him about.

"Don't worry, Thomas. You're doing just fine," Janey Hastings had told him at dinner last night after Angel stormed off in a huff over some imaginary slight. Janey and Ed, who were more surrogate parents to Tom than mere employers, had been his lifeline these past four months, his tether to sanity. Sadly, next Monday the Hastingses would be off fighting demons of their own. Janey's last mammogram showed a questionable spot, and her doctors had ordered her to Stanford.

"It's a phase," Janey had said sagely. "Just love 'em—that's all that matters. Don't sweat the small stuff. After all," she'd said with an understanding smile, "it's every teenage girl's goal to drive her father crazy. My granddaughters were the same way. I was sure Peter was going to send them back here to live with me until they were old enough for college."

Tom knew how much Janey missed her sons—Edward lived on the East Coast, Pete and his family in Colorado. Ed missed them, too, but he had Tom to fill the gap—a surrogate son to run the Standing Arrow H, the ranch and orchard operation that was Ed's passion.

Angela sat up suddenly and jammed the inch-thick soles of her ugly black boots against the truck's already cracked dashboard. "Why do we have to do this, anyway? It's stupid."

"Feet down, please," Tom said, keeping his tone level. It had occurred to him more than once these past few months that dealing with a teenager was like breaking in a two-year-old colt—you do everything slow and careful and keep body parts out of kicking range. "It's what the judge wants, honey, you know that." They'd been over the issue a dozen times in the past two days.

Her feet didn't budge. "Well, I ain't gonna talk to no therapist. I ain't crazy."

Tom leaned across Heather, who seemed to shrink from the cross tone of her sister's voice, and gently tapped Angela's shin. "Don't say 'ain't.'"

"Don't hit me," she bristled, pulling back.

Tom sighed wearily and gazed out the cracked windshield of his half-ton Ford. Angel's moods changed faster than the weather. Some days she was Little Miss Homemaker, fixing tuna casseroles or macaroni and cheese on Tom's two-burner hot plate; some days she sat glued to his small, black-and-white television watching whatever crap the talk shows aired. Tom hadn't been too pleased with Judge Overman's edict that Heather and Angel see a counselor, since it meant prolonging the bureaucratic umbilical cord wrapped around his neck, but a therapist might help.

"Daddy, I hav'a go potty," Heather said in a tiny voice.

His heart lurched painfully. Poor Heather. No mood swings for her. His bright little poppet had changed from a bubbling, fearless five-year-old at Christmas to a shadow person afraid of the wind.

"We're going right in there, sweetie," he said, pointing to a low white stucco building with a small, discreet sign beside the door. "I'm sure they have a bathroom. Can you hold it?" She'd been wetting the bed ever since her mother's death five months earlier.

Heather's head bobbed tentatively. He put his arm around her and pulled her tiny body close. He'd have given ten years of his life to turn back the hands of time. Maybe if he could have talked Lesley into staying with him, she'd still be alive.

Why, Les? Why didn't you stay? He knew the answer. The love they'd shared had been enough to produce two daughters but not strong enough to close the huge gap in their dreams and ambitions.

Despite their divorce, Tom always respected the way Lesley set goals for herself and met them, goals that didn't include horses, cows and everything else that went along with being a cowboy's wife. At first, he'd hated her for taking away his children, but she'd made sure Tom always had contact with his daughters. Even after she married Val, she'd invited Tom to spend the holidays with them.

Thank God for that, Tom thought. At least he wasn't a stranger to his daughters. Bad enough he was a single parent who didn't know the first thing about raising little girls.

"She's late," Angel complained.

Tom checked his Timex. "One minute to go."

A maroon Honda sedan drove into a parking place two spots away and stopped.

"Maybe that's her." Tom fished a scrap of paper out of the pocket of his jeans.

Angela snatched the paper from his fingers. "Abby Davis," she said, reading the name on it aloud. "Abby. Probably short for Abigail. What a dorky name! Sounds like an old-maid schoolteacher."

"You'll hold your tongue, miss, and I mean it," Tom said, his voice sharp. Beside him, Heather trembled like a wet pup. Tom gave her a comforting squeeze. "She's a victim's advocate. She helps people. The judge seems to think we need some help, and I think maybe he's right."

Angela's eyes filled with tears, making Tom instantly contrite. She was a great kid, she just had too damn much on her plate.

"Besides," he added, trying to lighten the mood, "it's not her fault about her name. Look what your grandma did to me. Thomas Richard Butler. My dad used to say Mama tried to name me after all her boyfriends—every Tom, Dick and Harry, only Harold wouldn't fit on the birth certificate." His mother, the shyest, most self-effacing woman he'd ever known would blush like a schoolgirl when Walt Butler teased her, but Tom knew they both enjoyed the banter. Tom was happy to see his effort earn a weak smile from Angela, but the strand of hair went back into her mouth. He swallowed a sigh. One battlefield at a time.

"DECISIONS, DECISIONS," Abby Davis muttered softly, willing herself to get out of her car when every instinct in her bones told her to put it in reverse and drive.

Abby eyed the unremarkable postwar bungalow that housed VOCAP, the Welton, California, Victims of Crime Advocacy Program. Her home-away-from-home for the past seven years. "Go or stay?"

Without meaning to, Abby took in the large, mud-splattered truck parked nearby. Normally, she might have wondered about its three occupants. It was impossible not to notice the solemn expressions of a family in trouble, but they weren't her problem, she told herself.

She had enough problems of her own. Like turning thirty and realizing her dreams were withering on the vine.

Daniel had left her with few options.

"It's a lack of *dinero,* Abby," her boss, Daniel Kimura, had told her over pasta primavera at the upscale downtown restaurant where he'd taken her for a birthday lunch. "You know how much we need you. You're the heart and soul of VOCAP, but I fully understand your position. You're intelligent and ambitious, and we're guilty of exploiting your goodness and humanity without fully compensating you in either money or title. But my hands are tied thanks to those greedy, short-sighted bastards in Sacramento."

His ebony eyes flashed contempt, making Abby wonder whether the rumors about his own political aspirations were true. Well, why not? A third-generation Asian-American with an admirable record as a district attorney, he had good face. And the camera loved him.

"You deserve better, Abby. It hurts me deeply that I can't give you what you need."

"What are you going to do if I quit?"

"Weep." Whoever called him a cold fish—probably Melina—hadn't shared garlic cheese bread and two glasses of Chablis with him. By the time they split the obligatory brownie sundae, listened to off-key waiters and several curious diners singing her the birthday song, Abby was almost feeling sorry for him.

Almost. Daniel would return to his desk, a highly polished cherry-wood model dwarfed by the size of his office. Abby, on the other hand, was expected to swallow the party line and return to her closet-size cubicle from which she ran the agency that helped victims of crime rebuild their lives. Her modest salary was capped because she didn't have her college diploma, which she'd missed by one semester when she'd pitched in to help after her predecessor got pregnant. Her one-semester job of acting supervisor—the title of supervisor being reserved for the fully accredited—turned into a seven-year stint.

Stay or quit? Abby loved her job, but lately she'd begun to feel as if it was taking over her life. Maybe it was time to go back to college and take a stab at law school.

Ruefully acknowledging that any major decision would have to wait until she could take stock of her finances, Abby opened the door and climbed out. Besides, she had a one o'clock appointment. Some guy whose ex-wife had been killed in a robbery five months ago. The file arrived that morning and, although she'd only had time to glance at it, she'd noticed the court-ordered counseling for two minors. Well, maybe she'd assign the case to someone else because it was time for Abby Davis to move on with her life.

"No more Ms. Nice Guy," she muttered. Lifting her chin, she marched ahead, forgetting about the labyrinth of busted concrete distributed in her path courtesy of a massive root from the shady but messy mulberry tree that was allowed to grow unimpeded in VOCAP's front lawn. The lawn-service budget was an early casualty.

The heel of her left pump disappeared into a San Andreas-size crevasse; the right one snapped out of sympathy and down she went.

"Damn it all to hell," Abby said under her breath, dusting off the quarter-size hole in the knee of her panty hose.

Torn between tears and a temper tantrum, she didn't move until a deep, polite voice asked, "Are you okay, ma'am?"

Abby looked up to see whom fate had designated to share her humiliation. A cowboy. Even if he hadn't been wearing formfitting jeans, dusty boots and a turquoise and pink canvas shirt, she'd have pegged his profession. Blame it on the slight bow in his legs, the Clint Eastwood squint of his sky-blue eyes shaded by a pearly white hat or the Yosemite Sam handlebars framing tight, serious lips.

"Anything broken?" he drawled. Not a southern drawl, more of a western-music sound. Not that she was all that familiar with either; it was a gut feeling, and it did weird things to her gut.

"Nothing worth suing over. Unfortunately," she muttered, twisting the heel, which made a 180-degree turn but remained attached to the shoe.

"I've been nagging Daniel for months to get this sidewalk fixed," she said, more to herself than him. "Tight budget, he says." She snorted. "Tight something else if you ask me."

His very faint chuckle made a rift of gooseflesh break out on her arms, thankfully hidden by the plum-and-cream plaid suit, which undoubtedly would now show scuff marks on several unbecoming places.

"May I help you up?" That he even asked put him in a class of men Abby had heard of and read about but assumed was extinct: the gentleman.

"Um...sure. Thanks."

He didn't touch bare skin, just the clothed arm below her elbow. It seemed to be enough for him to levitate her to an upright position. Abby was pretty sure she had nothing to do with the process since her knees suddenly had as much substance as the whipped cream on her brownie sundae.

"My heels," she explained, in case he was inclined to put a different spin on her wobbliness.

He nodded, just a bit. An economical motion that probably made dogs round up whole herds of cattle and women whip up batches of biscuits and gravy.

"Thank you," she said formally. "I'm not usually this clumsy but it's my birthday." *Aargh, how lame is that?* "I had wine at lunch." *Nice, Abby. Now he'll think you have a dependency problem.* "With my boss." *Shut up, already.*

Her hero was saved from trying to make a polite response to any of her ramblings when a young voice asked, "Are you Abby Davis?"

Abby fought the blush that engulfed her. It was one thing to be a klutz anonymously, but now her humiliation was public. "That's me." Under her breath, she added, "Unfortunately."

The cowboy apparently was blessed with better than average hearing since the hanging-down parts of his mustache twitched.

"My dad's here to see you, and my sister needs to use your bathroom."

For the first time, Abby noticed the two little girls standing in front of the pickup truck. The older child's coloring was darker than her father's, almost Mediterranean, but the family resemblance was borne out in the eyes—old beyond her years. Abby guessed her to be eleven or twelve; she would be a beauty some day soon—probably too soon to suit her father. The younger girl, maybe five or six, was a miniature angel with a halo of white-blond hair and big blue eyes that looked everywhere but at Abby.

Abby's embarrassment evaporated. Children in need were her special weakness.

"Then let's go," she said, taking a wobbly step forward. "Our rest room has green and purple fish on the walls." She bent down to the younger girl's height and whispered, "With orange lips."

The child looked up at her father, who scooped her into his arms like a feather on a breeze. "Let's go see," he said in a gentle voice that made Abby's heart flutter as if touched by the same breeze.

Abby led the way. After three toddling steps, she kicked off her shoes. The shredded panty hose would be next. "If you know my name, I should know yours, but I'm at a loss," she said over her shoulder.

"I'm Angela Butler. My dad's Tom Butler," the older girl said, joining her at the lead. "He has an appointment with you at one o'clock. Some old-fart judge ordered it."

Aah, Abby thought, the name from the file.

"Is your real name Abigail?" the girl asked with a challenging look at her father.

"Nope. Abner," Abby joked, sensing some undercurrent between the two.

"What?" the girl squawked, nearly losing her balance on a hunk of sidewalk.

With youthful nimbleness, she regained her equilibrium before Abby could grab her arm. "Just kidding. That's what Gabe Calloway called me in fifth grade until I popped him in the nose." She caught the sudden movement of Tom Butler's mustache—a frown, she assumed, and tried to make amends. "Not that I condone violence, of course, but in this case, he, um, well, anyway, to answer your question, my father wanted to name me Abigail after his grandmother, but my mother said that sounded too much like an old-maid schoolteacher, so they settled on Abby, instead."

The older girl flashed her father a smug look that left Abby baffled, but she pushed the matter aside when they reached the building's metal-reinforced door. No matter how many times she walked through this portal, she always shivered, remembering one very close call two years earlier.

"Are you cold?" the little girl asked, catching what few adults ever saw.

At eye level in her father's arms, Abby could see the remarkable blue of her eyes and the sadness that left smudge prints under each eye. Poor baby, Abby thought, but she smiled reassuringly and opened the door wide enough for the family to file past. "No, sweetie, but thank you for asking. This door just gives me the willies. It used to be a pretty glass door, but one day a very angry man came and broke it."

Tom Butler's mustache quivered again. Another frown, she sensed. He waited politely for her to enter.

Yep, a gentleman.

Abby scooted past him and paused in the small foyer beside Angela. The original foyer had been twice as big, with a picture window and two couches that gave it a homey look, but added security measures, including video cameras and electronic passkeys, meant less room for the people they were supposed to serve.

"Why'd he do that?" Angela asked. "I thought you helped people."

Abby stifled a sigh. A big part of VOCAP's focus was helping victims of domestic abuse. The man who took out their door—and very nearly Abby's head—wanted his wife and family back. When Abby wouldn't give him either, he took his anger out on her. She'd managed to get away and call the police. The door wasn't so lucky.

"We do. But sometimes people aren't ready to be helped." That her chipper tone, meant to shore up her own flagging morale as much as reassure her new clients, came off sounding like a cheerleader on the Mickey Mouse Club was confirmed by the girl's look of scorn.

She won't be easy, Abby thought, but who could blame her? Trust isn't easily given by someone whose world's been shattered by violence.

AFTER SETTLING HIS DAUGHTERS in the cheerful waiting room, Tom followed Abby Davis into her office. "Make yourself at home," she said. "I'll be right back." Tom lowered himself carefully into the square upholstered chair squeezed into a niche opposite a cluttered desk. Perched precariously to one side of the desk was a computer screen.

While the entry and hallway of the building sported large posters proclaiming the rights of victims, particularly women and children, this office revealed an attempt to promote serenity. A climbing plant with variegated leaves framed the room's single window, which faced the parking lot; two watercolor paintings of unstructured seascapes lessened the impact of metal bookshelves crammed with textbooks and stacks of files.

Tom was becoming a bit of an expert on mid-level bureaucratic office decor—he'd seen more than his share over the past five months. This had to be one of the smallest, yet classiest, offices yet. He particularly liked the hubcap-size, self-sustained waterfall that muffled the sound of the computer.

The machine's drone reminded him of what lay ahead: another retelling of the story, bringing to mind images safely stuffed in the recesses of his head—until fatigue or sleep brought down his guard.

Why even bother? What can these people do? Can they bring back Les? Can they take away Heather's nightmares or make Angel smile again?

Fighting off a wave of despair, Tom reminded himself why he was here—the court order. It might be a hopeless waste of time, but he didn't have any say in the matter. His rights had pretty much vanished the minute some junkie looking for drug money had put a gun to his ex-wife's head and pulled the trigger.

With a hoarse cough, he swallowed the gagging sensation in his throat.

A moment later, Abby Davis entered the room. Barefoot. She'd discarded her broken shoes and damaged hose. She seemed flustered, as if the lack of shoes somehow diminished her professional armor, leaving her vulnerable.

Tom studied her. Clear skin, pale from her indoor job. A few tiny lines starting around the eyes. She wore no makeup, except for a ruddy lipstick.

She was a nice-looking woman, even if her taste in clothes

didn't appeal to him. The severity of the cut and length of the jacket pretty well hid what looked like a trim rear end and shapely waist; the color was something he'd have buried once he made sure it was dead.

"Okay," she said, sliding into the upholstered desk chair. She folded her hands primly on the desk between them and asked, "How can we help you?"

Help. A word he'd come to deplore. He stifled a jolt of anger, reminding himself, as he had Angel, this was the way it had to be.

"This ain't—isn't—for me. I'm here for my girls," he said with as much civility as he could muster.

He looked away from the sympathy he saw in her greenish-gold eyes. He didn't need sympathy; he needed someone to tell him how he was going to make a life for his daughters without screwing things up. He only knew one way to live his life, and it hadn't been good enough for their mother, how could he expect it to be good enough for them?

If she read deeper implications into his response, she chose to ignore them. "The girls will be fine in the waiting room. We've got the hottest video games around, and Becky Barton's great," she said, mentioning the young black woman she'd introduced to him in the waiting room. "She's a student volunteer. She works with victims all the time."

Victims. Tom swallowed hard. Not a word he ever thought would apply to him.

"I apologize for not being more prepared, but your file just arrived this morning." She picked up a piece of paper from her desk and studied it.

He knew how to save them both some time. He'd repeated the story so often it was beginning to sound like a fairy tale. A bad fairy tale. "My ex-wife, Lesley Ahronian, Heather 'n' Angel's mom, was killed January 7." His mouth filled with a rancid taste. The finality of saying those words never failed to get to him.

"A robbery?" she asked, her voice businesslike, detached.

"She was getting money from an ATM machine. The guy who did it got a hundred and eighty dollars. They found one of the twenties under her body along with the receipt for two hundred bucks."

Val told him the bank's security camera provided a horrific record of the event. Although the image wasn't perfect, it produced a suspect, a drug addict with a long history of violence. Whether or not it would be enough to convict him of murder remained to be seen.

"Heather was in the car when it happened," he added gruffly, trying to keep that horror from engulfing his last bit of sanity.

A grimace of anguish flashed across her face.

"She was asleep. The guy tried to steal the car, too, but the alarm scared him off." Even saying the words made his stomach work closer to his throat. What if…?

"Where was Angela?" Her matter-of-fact question put him back on safe ground.

"At a friend's house. Val, Lesley's husband, picked Angel up after the police told him about Lesley. There was some initial confusion because the car was registered to their business and Lesley didn't have any ID on her. The police took Heather into protective custody," he said, recalling the terrible anguish of that weekend.

The attack happened Thursday night, but because of his stupidity, Tom didn't find out about it until late the next morning. One of Ed's friends flew Tom down south, but by then Tom was too late to see the judge and no one would let him near Heather without a judge's decree.

"You do have legal custody." Tom could tell she tried to keep it from sounding like a question, but it still irked him.

"They're my kids," he snarled.

She glanced up at his tone. "Sometimes when a woman remarries, her new husband adopts the children." Her voice sounded soothing, the way he'd talk to a skittish colt.

She had no way of knowing what a sore subject this was, especially after his recent trip to court. "It was suggested. Once," he said pointedly.

Valentino Ahronian was a decent guy who made every effort to be friends with Tom but Tom just couldn't get past the idea that Val had something that belonged to Tom—his family. Of course, he would have hated the breakneck pace Val and Lesley had chosen, but that didn't stop him from resenting the man who'd married his ex-wife and who saw Tom's children on a daily basis while Tom was relegated to the background—a shadow father trotted out on special occasions and for two weeks in summer.

"Are there any custody issues I should know about? Is Mr.—" she consulted her page in a quick nod that set her blunt-cut pageboy dancing near her jawline. Her hair was thick and shiny, about the color of his favorite roan mare "—Ahronian out of the picture then?"

"No," Tom answered, wishing he had a better handle on his feelings where Val and the girls were concerned. "He calls. The girls still have feelings for him."

Compassion deepened the gold in her eyes, as if she could feel the torment he went through every time Val called. Tom forced himself to look away. "But, Val's got his hands full trying to keep his business running. Lesley was the guts of their operation."

She kept reading and Tom sensed when she came to the most recent entry. She didn't make any outward sound or sign, but Tom felt her flinch, inwardly.

"Last month, Lesley's mom filed for custody," he said,

trying his best to keep his tone level. "Ruby Pimental's got a few problems of her own, and Les's death hit her hard. Somehow, Ruby got it into her head I killed Lesley and she wasn't about to leave her grandchildren with a murderer. She found some crook of a lawyer to take her case, and we had to go to court." Tom would never forget that horrible scene in court when Angel rushed to his defense, calling her grandmother every name in the book.

"It got thrown out, but the judge decided the girls might need some help coming to grips with their loss." Court words. He'd heard them so often they almost made sense. Sense. How could anyone make sense of something like this?

She looked at him, her eyes dark with emotion he couldn't interpret. "Violent crime is like a bomb going off in your world. Pieces fly every which way. Survivors wander around in shock, wondering how or if they'll ever get back to the place they'd been in before it happened."

She wasn't saying anything Tom didn't know, but her empathy touched him in a way he hadn't thought possible. Chubs and Johnny Dee had tried to console him; their wives had sent casseroles and cakes. But Tom didn't want sympathy or food. He wanted to know if this pain would ever get easier, but he wasn't brave enough to ask. What if it didn't?

"Some people call what we do here 'triage,'" Abby said, making an encompassing motion with her hand. "We patch you up so you can start to pick up the pieces of your life and move forward. For some, it means walking them through our convoluted judicial system. For others, it's a matter of finding the right resources to rebuild their lives. Violence marks you, but it doesn't have to destroy you, or define the way you live your life from that point on."

Something inside Tom reached out for the invisible lifeline

she was offering. After months of slogging through the guilt and shock that were weighing him down, he felt as if he might have found a way out of the pit.

"Trust me, Mr. Butler, things will get easier. You have to take it one day at a time." She spoke slowly, as in prayer. "And if that's too overwhelming, then one hour at a time. If that doesn't work, one second at a time.

"You keep breathing," she continued, "even though it hurts like hell. You make yourself eat, even though every bite tastes like dirt, and you sleep when your body can't stay awake any longer."

Something about the way she spoke made Tom realize she was speaking from personal experience. This woman knew loss; she knew grief.

She took a breath and added softly, "You and your daughters are facing some big changes. Painful changes."

She reached out and touched Tom's hand, taking him by surprise. He hadn't even realized his right hand was gripping the laminated desktop. Her fingers were cool and soothing like an evening Delta breeze after a scorching summer day. "We can help…if you'll let us."

Something pulsed inside Tom's heart. Hope. A stranger was reaching out to help him shoulder the fearful responsibility of raising daughters who barely knew him and came from a strange world that he didn't know at all.

Tom's daddy had taught him not to expect something for nothing. "What's it cost?"

She withdrew her hand and reached into a side drawer of the desk, giving Tom time to regain his composure. She smiled brightly. Had he only imagined her dark memories? "Our service is free, Mr. Butler. The citizens of California got fed up with criminals walking around after serving a few days or weeks for their crimes, while the people they hurt took years to get their lives back together. They told the courts to impose stiffer fines and put that money into a fund to help victims and the people who witness crimes."

She blinked twice and cleared her throat. "Judge Overman has ordered counseling for Heather and Angela. The first thing we have to do is find the right person to help your daughters get past this horror."

We. God, it felt good to share his burden with this stranger.

"I have someone in mind. Donna Jessup. She's great with kids, but counseling is a highly subjective matter and not everyone connects with the same person, so we can try several. With your permission, we'll try Donna first."

Tom nodded. He felt as if he'd made the first forward motion since that January morning when he woke up in his truck with a highway patrolman knocking on his window.

While Abby made the call, he rose and stretched. He wondered how anyone could stand to be cooped up in a four-by-five cubicle five days a week on a regular basis. He didn't understand it any more than he understood why Lesley had chosen the hustle and bustle, smog and crime of the big city over clean air and open spaces.

"Done," she said, reaching across the desk to hand him a piece of paper with a name, address and phone number all set out in neat, loopy penmanship. "Donna will see you at four this afternoon."

He nodded. "Thank you."

She deflected his gratitude with a casual wave of her hand. Reaching beneath the lip of her desk, she pulled out a sliding table holding a keyboard and mouse. "Now. Let's get you into our system."

Tom shuddered. The last four months had proven how suffocating the octopus arms of the "system" could be, but his peaceful anonymity was a small price to pay for his daughters' welfare.

She typed diligently for a few minutes, glancing between her faxed copy and the screen. She seemed engrossed in her work, her lips pursed in a half frown. Tom recalled that she'd mentioned today was her birthday. Thirty, maybe? Lesley would have been thirty-five in September.

"How are you doing for money?"

Her question took him by surprise. "Excuse me?" he said stiffly.

A blush engulfed her cheeks. "I'm sorry. I've been doing this so long I sometimes let my agenda get in the way of good manners."

She took a deep breath then said, "What I meant to ask in a more sensitive way was, has this been a terrible financial drain on your resources? We have some discretionary funds available and state programs such as food stamps that can help."

Tom knew she was simply doing her job, but she hadn't grown up with Walt Butler's prejudice against the dole. Tom turned sideways to look out the window. In the parking lot his ancient truck stood out like a mule among thoroughbreds. This was going to be the year he bought a new one. Was.

"My daddy always said the dole is what ruined many a good man, and we Butlers do it ourselves or we do without."

She typed and talked at the same time. "I can appreciate that sentiment and I don't mean to sound condescending, but if you need to spend your days making sure your daughters feel safe and loved, how can you be out doing whatever it is you do? What do you do, by the way?"

"I manage a ranch, 'bout twenty miles south of here. We run a few head of cattle and have a couple of hundred acres of almonds. My boss, Ed Hastings, covered for me when I was getting the girls moved up here, but now I'm back full time," he said.

Finances were tight, but when weren't they? So far, he hadn't had to sell any of the broodmares he and his friend, Miguel Fuentes, were raising on the side, but he'd damn well do that before he accepted a handout from the government. Miguel would understand. He and Maria were pinching pennies, too, what with the new baby coming.

"Okay, fine," she said, pushing the keyboard back beneath her desk. At that moment a printer sitting atop a gray plastic shelf to Tom's right came to life. "But if it happens that you can't manage as well as you'd like, I hope you'll let me know. We have a wide array of programs, including low-interest loans for things like remodeling or adding rooms to homes. Sometimes when you add a couple of new bodies to a house, space becomes a problem. So just keep it in mind."

She had to stretch across the desk to reach the paper ejected from the printer. Tom reached for it, too. Their fingers met momentarily, and she jerked her hand back as if scalded.

A moment of stiff silcnce was shattered by a scream, piercing and high-pitched like a small wounded animal caught in a trap. Heather. Tom bolted through the doorway. Too many nights he awoke to the bloodcurdling horror of that cry. He raced down the corridor, almost taking the waiting-room door off its hinges.

Heather was seated on a worn, oval carpet between a low wooden table capped with children's books and a lumpy couch where Angela slouched, a handheld electronic game loose in her fingers. Becky Barton, the young volunteer, was kneeling beside Heather trying to comfort her.

Tom dropped to his knees beside them and scooped Heather into his arms, babbling nonsense words in a tone that always soothed a frightened horse. "Shh, baby love, it's okay. Your daddy's got you, and nothing bad can happen." He rocked her back and forth until the cries wound down to hiccups.

Keeping up his monotone he made eye contact with Angel, who shrugged her shoulders, indicating she didn't have a clue about what had upset her sister.

Becky gave him a sympathetic smile, but appeared as bewildered as Angel.

When Heather's sobs subsided, he used his cuff to wipe the wet tracks streaking her chubby red cheeks. She blinked as if not sure where she was.

"Hey, sweetness, what happened?"

Her bottom lip shot out, trembling.

"You got scared?"

She nodded then buried her face in his shoulder.

Right or wrong, Tom had been running on instinct. Like a wounded animal, he'd taken the girls and gone to ground. He'd protected his daughters the only way he knew how, by isolating them from the world. Maybe that had been a mistake. Instead of getting better, Heather seemed to be sinking deeper into a pit of despair.

He rose, Heather's warm little body plastered to him like a bandage. "Maybe we should see that doctor right away."

Abby nodded. "I'll call ahead and see if she can take you earlier than four."

But will it do any good? Tom's frustration weighed heavily on him.

As if reading his thoughts, Abby said, "Believe me, Mr. Butler, it won't help Heather to keep things bottled up."

She laid a gentle hand squarely on his daughter's little back. She probably didn't feel Heather's sigh, but Tom did.

Abby led the way to the exit, pausing at her office to give Tom her business card. "My home number is there. Feel free to call if you need anything." She smiled. "Please don't give up on us," she said softly. Whether to him or Heather, he wasn't sure.

"ARE YOU READY for a good time, birthday girl?" a voice called, echoing in VOCAP's empty hallway.

Melina Orozco, Abby's best friend and co-worker, had two missions in life: find a man to make her mother happy and have a good time to make herself happy.

"Just give me a minute. I have one more call." Abby smiled as she dialed the number.

Since it was after normal office hours, Donna picked up. "Hello."

"Hi. It's me. How'd it go this afternoon?"

"You mean with the handsome cowboy and his two darling daughters?"

Despite the light tone in her friend's voice, Abby knew Donna was a complete professional. She'd been Abby's therapist at one time, and they were still close. "Did you connect? Are you going to continue seeing them?"

"Abby, dear, you know I can't discuss my patients with you. Besides, one hour with two traumatized little girls and a worried father pacing just beyond the threshold didn't give me a lot to work with. I've suggested therapy twice a week and participation in Rainbows." Tomorrow's Rainbows was a ten-week peer counseling session in Fresno.

"And he went for it?"

"Yes. With some reservations. Apparently the logistics are tricky—the new Rainbows session will be on Thursdays at six-thirty. Not the best time for him, I gather, but he said he'd work it out."

"Great!" Abby had sensed Tom Butler's reluctance to reach out for help.

"Interesting man, isn't he?" Donna asked conversationally.

Abby knew the ploy. "I called because I was concerned about the children. Not the father."

Donna laughed. "So you think. But I know you, dear heart, and you want to help them all. You're the queen of fix-it."

"That was the old Abby. From now on, it's me first. I'm thinking about quitting to go back to school this fall to get my law degree. Earn the big bucks."

Donna was silent a moment then said, "You have to do what's right for you, Abby. Just be sure it's for the right reasons. Thirty is not old."

After saying their goodbyes, Abby considered her friend's words: the "queen of fix-it." "Not this time," she muttered. She'd do her best to help Tom Butler and his daughters get back on their feet, but if they were still in the system by the end of summer, she'd arrange for another advocate to take over. She couldn't afford to keep putting the needs of others before her own happiness.

"DON'T START READING without me, Daddy," Heather said, scooting off the double bed she shared with Angel.

Angel rescued the bottle of nail polish that almost tipped over when the mattress jiggled. "Damn it, Heather, you're gonna make me screw up," Angel snarled, ignoring the look her father gave her. She knew he disliked swearing, but she didn't care. She had a right to swear. Her whole damn world got turned upside down and she was supposed to like it? Not even.

Frowning, she concentrated on applying a second coat of polish to her toenails. Cat-puke green, her father called the color. Like she cared what he thought; he didn't have a clue about what was cool. He was just a cowboy, living in this shack out in the middle of nowhere. Angel liked it okay when she came to visit in the summer—it made for great stories to tell her friends. But summer was one thing, actually living here was something else. And she was pretty sure she hated it.

"Whatcha need, punkin?" Her father called as he dropped into the spot Heather had vacated.

Angel rescued her polish a second time, growling under her breath.

"A drinka' water," Heather answered, skipping out the door like the little kid she was. She'd started wetting the bed right after the police gave her back. The weekend-long ordeal must have scared Heather pretty bad because she was acting more like a three-year-old than a kid who'd turn six in August. Angel felt bad for her, but it was hell sharing a bed with a bed wetter. "Why don't you just put her in a diaper?" she grumbled.

She felt her father's warning frown.

"Go ahead and get your drink, sweets," he told Heather, who stuck her tongue out at her sister. "Remember what Dr. Jessup said? This'll get better soon."

Angel pictured their encounter with the therapist that afternoon. Right at first Angel thought the woman looked more like a hippie bag lady than a doctor. She had more beads resting on her broad bosom than some department stores had for sale.

"How long will this take? A couple of weeks? A month?" her father had asked, pacing like a cat stuck in a doghouse.

Angel actually liked the room; there was a "safe" feeling about it. In a way, it reminded her of her mother's office back home.

"There's no credible timetable for grief, Mr. Butler," Dr. Jessup told him. Her voice was kind, it made Angel feel warm inside. "There is, of course, a recognized grief process, a pattern of predictable steps we go through toward healing, but no formula that says you should be done with stage one by week three. It just doesn't work that way. It would make my job so much easier if it did."

When she smiled, Angel saw something she liked. Honesty.

Nobody was ever honest with kids. They all act like we're a bunch of babies who can't understand what's happening.

Angel understood most of what had happened. Her mother and Val had a fight. Angel had tried eavesdropping but they'd stayed in their bedroom, which was half a flight higher at the end of the hall. When her mom came and got her, Angel had seen tear streaks on her face, but Lesley had refused to talk about it. All she said when she'd dropped Angel off at Caitlin's house was, "It's grown-up stuff, honey. It'll be all right."

Well, it wasn't "all right." When Val came and picked Angel up early the next morning, he said her mother had been attacked when she stopped at an ATM machine. Angel didn't believe him at first. Her mother was such a stickler for safety. How could she have been that stupid? Angel wondered for the millionth time.

Now, not only was her mother gone, but so was their life—their real life. And Angel was pissed as hell.

"Angel-babe, please try to cut your sister a little slack," her father said softly. "She's doing the best she can. We all are," he added under his breath.

Angel knew that. None of this was his fault. He was a good guy who tried real hard to make things okay for them. And things had been going along pretty good until her crazy grandmother decided to sue for custody. Damn judge. Angel knew how hard it was on her dad's pride to have to go to that victims' place today—even if the lady there was nice enough, and sorta pretty.

"I know," she said, regretting her rotten humor. It wasn't Heather's fault she was having bad dreams. Angel had a few, too.

"Like the lady said, we just gotta take this one day at a time," he said, reaching out to touch her shoulder.

Angel closed her eyes to keep back the tears that seemed right on the verge of coming out nearly every minute of the day. She wanted to scream and hit things. Hurt things. She wanted her old life back. She wanted to go home, but she was stuck in this valley forever.

Angel shrugged off his touch and didn't say anything. Her mom always told her if you can't say something good, then don't say anything at all. The way things were going, Angel figured she'd never have to speak again.

CHAPTER TWO

ABBY CLOSED the refrigerator door on the last of her groceries. Saturday mornings weren't what they used to be in Welton. Traffic in the once-sleepy central valley town was beginning to rival the Bay area—quite different from when she first moved into Billy's house on Glendennon Court.

Actually, the three-bedroom bungalow had belonged to Billy's mom until she passed away, and Billy had left it to Abby in his will. Janice Eastburn, Billy's mother, had been a neighbor when Billy and Jarrod, Abby's brother, were classmates and best friends in high school, but once Billy joined the marines, she'd sold their house in Fresno and moved to Welton, where she took a job in a dentist's office. She lived alone until diagnosed with lymphatic cancer, then Billy moved home from Hawaii to help her. He wasn't back three weeks before she died.

Billy, Abby thought, pausing before the open cupboard, a box of Grapenuts in her hand. A familiar buzzing sensation bloomed in her chest like the beginning of a cold. Her memories of him were so jumbled—some good, some horrible—she was tempted to lock them out, but Donna had taught her to accept any memories that came. "Shove them in a black hole and they'll fester like pond scum," Donna warned her patients.

Resigned that she was having a "Billy moment," Abby set down the cereal and picked up her new "Thirty Isn't Old—I'm just 21 with 9 years' experience" mug and poured herself the last of the morning's coffee. After taking a sip of the aromatic brew, she pulled out a stool at the counter and sat down. Tabby, her overweight cat, rubbed against her ankles, hoping no doubt for an après-breakfast snack. Abby ignored him, focusing instead on the past.

Poor Billy, she thought wistfully, he didn't really stand a chance where I was concerned. I put him on a pedestal not even a superhero could keep from falling off.

She tried to picture herself back in 1988, when Billy came home from Hawaii. A nineteen-year-old college coed, fifteen years his junior, Abby doubted if she'd recognize that silly, naive girl who didn't know the first thing about love…or grief. She learned fast.

Abby, who was just a baby when Billy and Jarrod were in high school, had grown up on Billy stories, from his bad-boy image in high school to his heroism in Vietnam. Jarrod called him "G.I. Bill," since all Billy ever wanted to do was be a soldier. According to Jarrod, Billy's greatest fear was that Vietnam would be over before he got there.

Taking a sip of coffee, Abby pondered the start of her hero worship. Honors English, she thought, bracing her chin in her palm. Each student selected someone local who had made a significant personal sacrifice for someone else. Since Billy lost a leg while helping to evacuate civilians at the close of the war, Abby felt he qualified.

Jarrod gave her Billy's address in Hawaii. Abby wrote him twice, but he didn't write back. So, Abby interviewed Billy's mother, instead.

If Abby had been older and less idealistic she might have been able to separate truth from wishful thinking, but as it was she drew a picture of Billy in her head and so it stayed. When he returned home to help his mother, Abby was already halfway in love with him, even though she never really knew him.

And she wasn't disappointed when she accompanied her family to Janice's funeral. Hawaii had given Billy a sort of "Baywatch" mystique: tan and weathered, a sun-bleached ponytail and wide, muscular shoulders from using crutches—he was the embodiment of a hero. Someone with a more experienced eye might have caught the jaded look in his eyes, the lines of dissipation from ten years of drinking and carousing.

Abby sat back on the stool and looked around her bright, cheerful kitchen. It's so weird that he's gone and I'm still living here. What would my life have been like if he had returned my letters? What if he'd told her his story the way it was, not the way his mother had perceived it?

Instead of a heroic amputee who lost his leg through a selfless act of bravery, Billy had stumbled out of a bar into the path of panicky citizens trying to flee their dying country. Knocked to the ground, he was too drunk to get out of the way of an army truck that backed over his foot, crushing his ankle. Chaos and confusion resulted in less than perfect medical treatment, which led to a series of infections and months of hospitalization. When gangrene set in, Billy agreed to a partial amputation of his foot. Unfortunately, a staph infection resulted from the operation and he nearly died. By the time he woke up, still in pain despite heavy medication, he discovered three-quarters of his leg had been removed to stop the infection from claiming his life.

Bitter and addicted to painkillers, he accepted a disability settlement and hooked up with two ex-Marine buddies in Hawaii who needed some capital to open a bar. Billy drank most of his share of the profits, but his disability income kept him solvent and he tended bar just often enough to hit on lovely young ladies eager to ease his pain.

Abby believed his mother's death was an epiphany for Billy. As their relationship evolved, Billy told Abby about his life in

Hawaii—the drugs and alcohol and the women. He insisted on being tested for AIDS before he would consider making love to her, and even then he always used a condom. Billy said he wanted to put the past behind him and straighten out his life. Who better to infuse him with energy and hope than an idealistic college student?

Who better, indeed? Abby thought ruefully, tracing the printing on her mug. Maybe he'd have succeeded in turning his life around if she hadn't been so full of hero worship. How could any man live up to that, especially a man who felt his whole life was a sham?

"Abby? Are you home?" a voice called from the front of the house.

Another voice from the past. "In the kitchen, Landon," Abby said with a sigh.

Landon Bower, her ex-boyfriend of eleven months, had a habit of dropping by for advice on his new relationship with the beautiful, if difficult, Deirdre.

Dancer lithe, boxer light, he made his usual flamboyant entrance, sliding across the terra-cotta floor tiles on stocking feet. He always took off his shoes inside a house, claiming it his birthright since he was born in Japan. Abby believed it was because he never had to wash his own socks.

"Hi, beautiful birthday girl." Gallantly bowing, he offered her a thick bouquet of white daisies, pink carnations and yellow spider mums.

"My birthday was last week."

"I know. I forgot." He flashed what his mother called his "guaranteed-to-make-women-love-me smile." She'd sent Abby a birthday card, much to Abby's surprise. When Abby and Landon broke up, his mother told her, "You'll regret this someday, Abby. Landon is a wonderful person." Abby wasn't sure if she was trying to convince Abby or herself.

"I'm sorry, girly-girl. You know how I am about dates.

Hence the blooms. When we were living together, I always got away with murder if I brought home flowers." He frowned. "I wish that worked with Deirdre."

Abby rolled her eyes. Sometimes she couldn't believe she'd cohabited with him for as long as she had. Donna called it Abby's self-imposed penance. "I told you at the time, a dog would have accomplished the same thing—companionship and utter dependency, but no, you had to bring Landon home," Donna liked to tease.

"Why can't Deirdre be more like you, Ab?" Landon asked.

Abby moved to the sink, ostensibly to tend to the flowers. She liked Landon, but she was tired of being his sounding board for his new girlfriend. *Another area of my life that needs work.*

"Don't blame Deirdre because she's not a pushover like me." Abby tried to keep her tone light, she'd been wallowing—at least, wading—in self-pity too much the past week.

Landon gave her an inquiring look. "I prefer to think of you as a softhearted person," he said, sounding as though he meant it.

Abby smiled for real. Landon could be very sweet when he wanted to be. They'd lived together for almost four years. But their feelings for each other never blossomed into the real thing. Not that it surprised Donna.

"He doesn't engage your emotions—the ones you locked up after Billy," Donna told her. Abby wasn't sure such a man existed, or that she would want to meet him if he did.

"So, how's work?" Abby asked, changing the subject.

Landon walked past her to pull out the stool she'd been sitting on. As he passed, she could smell his cologne. Canoe. The one she'd picked out for him at Macy's. Did Deirdre know it was Abby's pick?

"Abby," he groaned, dropping his face into his hands, "my

life sucks. I think it started going down the toilet when I left you. Is it possible we made a terrible mistake?"

One small part of her danced in triumph. Yippee. Somebody needs me and worships me and wants me. The adult part of her, the thirty-year-old, groaned. "Landon, our breakup was mutual. Granted, you had someone waiting for you, but I needed you to leave. I needed the space to find answers about myself."

"What'd you find out?" His tone seemed sincere, not skeptical like her mother's.

"Lots of things." *Liar.* "I know I let people take advantage of me." *Most people. Except for certain cowboys who have too much pride to ask for help.* One silly little part of her had expected a call from Tom Butler all week. When it didn't materialize she was oddly deflated.

"But, no more," she said, pounding her fist on the counter for emphasis. "I've made up my mind to stop being so… accommodating."

He fought a smile—she could see him trying—but eventually it burst through. "Abby, you don't have a prayer. You're the kindest person I know. Maybe you are too nice for your own good, but you don't have it in you to be any different."

Before Abby could respond with an infuriated retort, the phone rang. She snatched up the receiver, glaring at Landon—to his obvious amusement. "Hello," she snarled.

The voice on the other end was not the one she'd been hoping for. She listened mutely, before saying, "I'll be right there."

TOM CAREFULLY CLOSED the screen door of the bunkhouse behind him. Heather was napping—for how long was anybody's guess. Every time she closed her eyes, her little body drooping like a wilted flower, Tom prayed she'd sleep for hours, but so far no luck. Sometimes, only minutes later, she'd wake up shrieking from dreams too terrible to remember.

As far as Tom could see, their initial three meetings with the therapist had been as productive as milking a bull, but Dr. Jessup did have a special way with kids. Tom had sat in on Friday's session. Angel had chatted easily like the self-absorbed teenager he remembered from last summer. She described in detail the outfit she wore to her mother's funeral—Tom couldn't even recall whether or not he wore clothes that day. Heather snuggled into a comfortable spot on Dr. Jessup's lap and silently fingered the woman's chunky wooden beads.

On his way out, Dr. Jessup told Tom, "I think it might help if the girls felt more connected to their home. Maybe a little decorating, hang up their posters or pictures, rearrange the furniture."

Before Tom could explain about their living conditions, she added, "Angel told me things are a bit crowded at the moment. Why don't you give Abby Davis a call? She can work bureaucratic magic when it comes to remodeling."

Like a seed from Eve's apple, the temptation was planted. And grew.

"Angel," he called softly through the paint-splattered mesh, "come here."

It took her two minutes to cross the twenty-foot room, but she came.

"It's a beautiful day. Don't you want to do something? I could saddle Jess. You haven't ridden since you got here."

She shook her head. "I'm reading." She held up a paperback novel, then turned away and plopped down on the lumpy couch before he could say anything.

The frenetic chatter of cartoons erupted from the small, snowy screen of his television set. "Still only black and white?" Angel said that first night back at the ranch, after her mother's funeral. "Daddy, those were around in like the Stone Age, for heaven's sake."

Her complaint went no further…yet, but it was only a matter of time. Nothing about his humble abode, once the ranch's bunkhouse, came close to matching Lesley and Val's two-story, 2,800-square-foot home.

"Did you finish your social-studies paper?" he called.

The words "Of course" accompanied a deep sigh of disgust.

Angel was a good student. Her accelerated class, which was part of a year-round school system, was due to go off-track two weeks after Lesley's funeral, so her teachers were not concerned about her absence. They'd passed her without a second thought. The local principal suggested letting her make a fresh start in the junior-high program that fall, instead of putting her into a sixth-grade class where she would be bored. Tom agreed, but he adamantly opposed giving her an additional five months of vacation, so both girls were enrolled in an independent study program.

So far, Angel's only complaint was the lack of a laptop computer, apparently a tool she used to borrow from her stepfather. Last week, the young woman who brought the girls their lessons suggested the possibility of doing homework "on-line." Tom, who'd heard horror stories about on-line predators, squashed the idea. His daughters could make do with pen and paper. Besides there was no extra money for expensive electronic equipment.

Rosie and two of Tom's cow dogs suddenly started barking. Tom squinted toward the road. The walnut trees that backed up all the way to the highway cut into his line of vision, but he spotted a dust devil whirling out of the gravel as a vehicle raced down the driveway.

The ranch, some 650 acres, was divided into irrigated pastures for grazing, and three sections of almonds. The advent of drip irrigation made it easier and less expensive to plant uneven terrain, and Tom knew it was only a matter of time before "cowboying" was a thing of the past. Ed loved his cows, but he was a practical businessman, too. Tom figured if he learned anything from the last four months it was: nothin' stays the same. Tom kicked up a little dust as he walked out into the drive that separated his place from Ed and Janey's newer ranch-style home. The Hastingses' home sat on a slight knoll, offset by a nice green lawn and flanked by an almond orchard on three sides. Tom's house was set in what amounted to a pie-shaped hunk of land between the driveway and the permanent pasture. His place faced the barn and corrals, but an ancient mulberry and semicircle of straggly lawn kept it from being too austere.

"What now?" Tom muttered, feeling an all-too-common burning in the pit of his stomach.

The rumble of a truck engine gave Tom a face to put with the sound. He shoved his hands into the front pockets of his jeans and waited to direct the driver away from the house before the dozen young horses in the paddock beside his bedroom window took it in their heads to get excited. He didn't want anything to wake Heather.

A bevy of barking dogs raced alongside the vehicle as Tom pointed toward the shade of the barn. The truck rolled to a stop. John Dexter Moore—Johnny Dee to his friends—killed the engine and climbed out of the '94 Ford half-ton.

"Hey, Tom. How's it goin'?"

Tom made a "so-so" gesture. Johnny motioned for him to follow him to the back of the truck. He lowered the tailgate and hopped up, dragging a small plastic cooler to his side. When Tom sat down beside him, Johnny reached inside the cooler for a beer and offered one to Tom.

After their last get-together—the night Lesley was killed, when nobody could find him at home because he was passed out cold in his truck—Tom couldn't bring himself to accept the offering. He shook his head.

Johnny was a Hulk Hogan kind of guy with receding blond hair and a heart of gold. He and Tom had been friends since childhood. He knew Tom as well as anybody and apparently had no trouble guessing what he was thinking. "It wasn't your fault, man," Johnny told him. "You didn't know. None of us did."

Tom would have liked to use his friend's solace as it was intended: to let him off the hook, but guilt had its own plans for him—slow torture.

"Hell, you didn't even want to go with us. Chubs 'n' me had to twist your arm."

When Tom bumped into his old friends that fateful night in January, he was on his way home from a week in the mountains. Ed leased a thousand acres of rangeland in the foothills. Since things were slow on the farm, Tom had combined a little fence repair with some fishing. Maybe he'd been hungry for social contact as well as real food, because it didn't take much arm-twisting to get him to the bar.

"You only stayed 'cause of what was happening with me and Beth," Johnny said, kicking the gravel.

Tom caught something different in his friend's tone, and realized sheepishly it had been three weeks since they'd talked. "How's that working out?"

Johnny lifted his substantial shoulders and let them fall. "She moved home, but we're not sleeping together. She's calling it a cooling-down period. Like I was some overheated stud. Like we even had sex often enough before she left to get worked up about."

Tom understood exactly where Johnny was coming from. His own first reaction to Lesley's departure had been nine-tenths bravado and one-tenth paralyzing fear. If he kept up the bravado long enough and made it real loud, he'd thought, maybe no one would see his pain.

"That's a start. At least you can talk face-to-face instead of long distance."

"The kids hated Fresno. All their friends are here."

Johnny crushed the empty can and tossed it on top of a pile of greasy tools in the pickup bed. He cracked open another. "How're you fixed here? Beth said to tell you she's sorry she hasn't made it over, but if you need a woman's touch to give her a holler. I think she meant in the kitchen. She'd better've meant in the kitchen."

Tom grinned at his friend's tone. "That's Angel's domain. We may eat quesadillas more often than I like, but I wouldn't want to hurt her feelings. But, as to that other kind of touching…" His teasing ended when Johnny's elbow connected with his side.

"Need a TV? We got an extra. It's a twenty-four incher."

Rubbing the tender spot on his rib cage, Tom shook his head. "Ed and Janey offered one, too, but things are a little crowded with all the girls' stuff, and we don't get enough stations using rabbit ears to make it worth it."

"That reminds me—how's Janey doin'?"

Tom looked away. Squinting, he could make out the snowcap on the distant mountains. It wouldn't last long—last week had three days over ninety degrees.

"Hold that thought, I gotta pee," Johnny said, hopping down to scurry toward the back of the barn.

Resting against the side of the truck, Tom closed his eyes and thought about Janey. It broke his heart to see her ill. More than anyone else, throughout this whole ordeal, she'd remained a rock, always positive and frank. She was the one person he could trust with his despair, his self-doubts, his fears.

Janey's illness brought back memories of his mother—fit and spry one week, hospitalized the next. Gone before he knew it. The doctors never did figure out what took her; a viral infection was their best guess.

Tom read all the breast cancer pamphlets the doctors gave Janey. The disease sounded treatable if caught early. He sure as hell hoped she could beat it. Not only did he love her, but the girls thought of her as a surrogate grandmother. He wasn't sure any of them could handle another loss so soon.

"Janey's gonna make it," Ed told Tom yesterday when he returned home for some of Janey's personal belongings. "They did a lumpectomy, and now they want her to take chemo and radiation to make sure they kill everything."

The late-afternoon sun had cast harsh shadows across Ed's face, emphasizing the lines of worry and fear. Tom saw a vulnerability he'd never seen before. "Janey says she can beat it and I believe her," Ed continued. "But I also know we're going to make some changes around here. Big changes."

Tom's heart lurched. He'd seen more changes in the past four months than he thought he could handle. He craved stability but knew he had to respect Ed's wishes. Tom owed him more than he could ever repay. After all, Ed had backed him when Tom broke his arm and couldn't rope, and Ed and Janey had been there to pick up the pieces of his heart after Lesley left, too.

Ed's face twisted in pain, as if picturing his wife in the hospital room. "Janey never complains, but I know she had it in her mind to do some traveling when we retired. Go visit her sisters. See the boys." Ed's voice faltered over the last.

Tom knew how disappointed Ed had been that neither of his sons wanted anything to do with the ranch he'd spent his entire life building. Edward, an architect in New Jersey, rarely called or visited. Peter, an advertising executive in Denver, kept in touch and visited at least once a year, but his relationship with his father was always tempered by disappointment and hurt feelings.

"I'll only say this once, Tom. You know you're like a son to me. You 'n' me think alike when it comes to the land. I'd feel real good about selling this place to you on a contract to deed." When Tom started to say something, Ed placated him. "Don't get your back up about the money, boy. That'll work out in the wash."

Tom's heart swelled from the compliment Ed was paying him, but he wasn't sure he could accept. "Ed, we've both got a lot on our plates right now. You took care of the whole show when I needed you, helping out now's the least I can do. Let's focus on getting Janey well before we worry about anything else, okay?"

They'd left it at that, but Ed was adamant about making some changes, starting with remodeling Tom's place to give the girls more room. "Janey's been harping about that for months. If that lady at the victims' place can help, then give her a call and start the ball rolling. I'll pay for everything. Just get it done."

When Johnny returned, Tom told him, "Janey's doin' up pretty good. Next week she starts chemo or radiation, I can't remember which, but she told Ed to get me started on remodeling. We're supposed to add another bedroom and bath to the bunkhouse before she gets back."

Johnny nodded enthusiastically. "Good idea. Believe me, you can't have enough bathrooms when there are women around. And any girl over the age of four constitutes a woman when it comes to bathrooms."

Tom cleared his throat and spat onto the dusty ground. Another bad habit to break. "You ever hear of a place called VOCAP?"

Johnny thought a moment then snapped his fingers. "Sure. The victims' place. They helped out after Maria's cousin got killed, right?"

Tom nodded. "I talked to one of the advocates last week,"

Tom said, picturing Abby Davis's reassuring smile. For some reason, he'd found himself drawing upon that smile more than once this week for a little comfort and reassurance. "She set the girls up with a grief therapist, and she said she could help us out with other things, like remodeling."

"Great. How are the girls doing?" Johnny asked.

"Heather's still having nightmares, but Angel's doing okay." At least, she didn't bite my head off when I asked about her homework. "But they miss their mom."

The two were silent a moment, then Johnny said, "I still can't believe she's gone, Tom. So young 'n' pretty."

Tom's throat began tightening up, the way it did whenever he pictured Lesley's funeral. "Funny thing about death—you know it's real. You say all the words and watch 'em lower the coffin into a hole, but she's still alive in your mind. Laughing, arguing, being pissed off." He forced a chuckle. "And nobody could be more pissed off than Les."

Johnny nodded so emphatically he spilt beer in his lap. "Remember the time you an' me was coming back from that roping in Elko and she thought we stopped off to gamble? Hell's bells, man, I thought she was gonna take off your head before you showed her the check for your winnings."

"She was mad a lot back then," Tom said evenly.

"She was a beautiful woman, Tom, and I know you're not supposed to speak ill of the dead, but I remember thinking it was awful cold of a person to move out on a guy when she was carrying his kid. Although in all honesty, I never pictured Lesley Pimental settling for anything in or around this valley."

Tom's thoughts went back to the summer after his mother died. He'd had three successful years on the roping circuit and had managed to make a name for himself. He took time off to help his father settle her estate. He'd met Lesley, who was working as a receptionist in the lawyer's office handling the probate. Although Tom had known Lesley in high school, she was three years his junior and he hadn't seen her in years. His knees almost buckled when the tall, slim beauty got up from behind her desk and walked over to him, telling him how sorry she was for his loss. A quick hug cinched it—he was in love.

They were married in late September. That winter Tom's father gave him money from the proceeds of the estate to buy Hall's Golden Boy—Goldy—a quarter horse Tom had had his eye on for several years. It had baffled both husband and son that the quiet, demure woman they thought they knew so well had somehow hoarded a modest sum and invested it in gold. Tom knew his mother would have appreciated the poetic irony of using the money to buy a roping horse named Goldy.

"When I heard you two was getting hitched, I figured it was because you were a big-name roper." Johnny wiped a spot of condensation on his beer can. "You were doin' pretty good till you busted your arm."

Johnny was right about some of it, Tom thought. Their first couple of years of marriage were great, cuddling together each night in a single sleeping bag on the sweet hay in the horse trailer. Then, the year after Angel was born Tom fell off the tailgate of his truck and landed wrong—a silly misstep that fractured his arm in three places.

The doctor told him there was a good chance he'd never rope professionally again. When his sponsors found out about his arm, they pulled out. Tom would've lost his truck if not for the kindness of his old boss, Ed Hastings, who made him foreman of the Standing Arrow H.

The arm healed, but by then Tom had lost his taste for the constant travel, competition and pressure. Lesley hadn't; she kept after him to start roping again. "You haven't even tried, honey," she'd say. "How do you know you won't be good again? You don't lose a skill like that."

Tom watched a shiny blue fly march up his sleeve and sighed. "Life's funny, Dee. If I'd kept on roping, I might still be married, and Lesley would still be alive. I sure as hell would have more to my name than a fourteen-year-old truck and a few head of breeding stock."

"You got the house on Plainsborough Road. The one Miguel's rentin' from you."

"You know I bought that house for Les. I bought it with the money from Golden Boy."

Both men sighed.

"Man, that was a horse," Johnny said. "Musta killed you to sell him."

Tom shrugged. "I figured just because I didn't want to rope no more didn't mean he had to quit. When that guy from Calgary offered cash, I snapped it up." Tom started to spit but changed his mind and swallowed instead, almost choking. Johnny pounded on Tom's back until Tom held a fist up between them.

"So, why don't you move over there instead of fixing up this place? It's three-bedroom, ain't it?"

Tom hesitated, recalling with photographic clarity the look on Lesley's face when she realized the little farmhouse, with its covered porch, white picket fence and row of primroses—his midnight effort—wasn't a rental like all the others. She looked at him with tears in her eyes and whispered, almost like a prayer, "Not Goldy?" Tom's heart felt as if it had been squished by a truck tire. But she made an effort and put on a good face. For a couple of years, anyway. Long enough for him to fall in love with one daughter and make a second.

"I can't just kick those poor kids outa there. Maria's got a baby comin'," he said. "So I guess we'll give remodeling a try. Maybe give Abby Davis a call."

ABBY SLIPPED through VOCAP's back door, locking it behind her. Her mind was reeling as she headed to her office.

At Daniel's unexpected call, she'd raced over to the district attorney's office, anticipating a change of heart—but not this kind. Her illusions of a pay raise and a promotion came to a screeching halt the minute Daniel told her about his imminent divorce.

Knees weak, Abby sank into her chair, replaying their conversation in her head.

"Hi, Abby, thanks for coming. Have a seat."

She selected a butter soft leather armchair she secretly coveted. "No problem. What's up?"

His handsome, squarish face showed signs of stress. He heaved a long, portentous sigh. "This is a bit awkward for me, and I want you to know you're the first person within the office I've told. I didn't want to say anything during business hours. You know how the taxpayers are about public servants conducting personal business on their time." His laugh sounded fake, his tone held an edginess that made her uneasy.

"This isn't business business, then?" Abby asked, oddly unnerved to be alone with Daniel in his office on a bright, cheerful Saturday morning. To calm her nerves she focused on the Kimura family portrait, which hung prominently to the left of his desk. In it, Daniel stood behind his wife, Marilyn, who was seated between their children, Robert and Rebecca.

"No, it's not. But what I have to tell you will, inevitably, affect our business relationship," Daniel said, pausing dramatically. "But it's my hope that the news will have a positive effect on our…friendship."

Friendship? Daniel was her boss, not her friend. They'd had shouting matches over budgets; they constantly argued about protocol; they vied for turf where judicial interests overrode the interests of her clients, but the bottom line always came down to power. Daniel had it; Abby didn't. Did that constitute grounds for friendship? She didn't think so. She held her tongue and waited. What he told her next nearly blew her out of the leather armchair. "Marilyn and I are getting a divorce."

Since Abby's mouth dropped open, Daniel probably thought she was going to speak, but any words she might have wanted to say were lost in utter shock. After a minute, he went on. "This has been a long time coming, but we kept things quiet until after the election and Becky's wedding. Robert's back at Stanford. Becky and Troy are still on their honeymoon. Marilyn thought this was as good a time as any. She filed yesterday. It's public record now."

Still not sure why she was being made privy to this, Abby's grip on the soft leather arms tightened when Daniel rose and walked toward her. He paused before her, his expensive cologne following like a well-trained dog. He rested his hip on the edge of the desk and gave her a long, meaningful look. "Abby, you and I have always had a strong working relationship. I didn't realize how much you meant to me—personally—until you started talking about leaving," he told her.

Since her mind couldn't process this totally unexpected turn of events, she stalled. "Daniel, if I'd known you were going through such a rough time, I wouldn't have mentioned anything. It's not like I'm turning in my resignation tomorrow. Even if I do decide to leave VOCAP, it won't be right away."

The intensity of his stare made her squirm.

"Besides," she said, her voice catching in her dry throat, "a new case fell into my lap last week. A man whose ex-wife was killed and a judge decided his daughters needed..."

Daniel's eyes narrowed. "You always go for the hard-luck cases, don't you?" he said, interrupting her.

"It's my job," Abby said, hating the defensive tone in her voice.

Daniel leveled an inscrutable look at her. "But you do it with all your heart, Abby. That's what makes men fall in love with you."

The strangled sound that came from her throat was part laugh, part cry. "You make me sound like a real femme fatale." His ridiculous assertion was made all the more ludicrous by her outfit: faded gray leggings, scuffed deck shoes and one of Landon's discarded J.Crew sweatshirts.

Even in jeans and a polo shirt, Daniel looked professional. And attractive. She and Melina had always joked about Daniel's political sex quotient, but that was when he was safely married and off the market.

Confused and unnerved, Abby beat a hasty retreat, sprinting across the parking lot to the safety of her office. As she rocked back and forth in her chair, one part of her wanted to laugh—could a woman whose sexual history included just two men be considered a heartbreaker? Another part wanted to weep—how did she always manage to attract the wrong type? First a depressive, then a womanizer. And now, her boss—and the ink wasn't even dry on the check to his divorce lawyer.

The blinking light of her answering machine caught her eye. Out of habit, she pressed the play button and received another shock.

A masculine clearing of the throat preceded, "Um…Ms. Davis. This is Tom Butler. I was in last week to see you. With my daughters." There was a pause. Abby could picture the man, his discomfort wearing hard on his soul. "You mentioned something about helping out with home improvements. I think maybe I might like to take you up on the offer. The sooner the better, I guess. I'll be waiting to hear from you."

Abby sighed. Damn. What was it about that man's voice that made her want to do the two-step? She didn't even like country-western music.

CHAPTER THREE

ABBY TOOK her eyes off the road to glance at the basket of goodies on the passenger seat. She felt like Little Red Riding Hood. Home visits were an integral part of her work, but a first visit was always awkward.

For reasons she couldn't quite discern, she was more nervous than usual. She'd worked with hundreds of families and usually managed to maintain a certain level of detachment—you needed it to keep from going crazy—but something about this family touched her more deeply than she cared to admit.

Maybe it stemmed from witnessing poor little Heather's anguish. Maybe it was because she could identify all too easily with twelve-year-old Angela's loss. Abby had been eleven when her grandmother died. Grammy had lived with them since the day Abby came home from the hospital, and her death rocked the foundation of Abby's life.

Abby's mother had returned to work when Abby's older brothers were eight and thirteen. Two years later, when Abby came along, Grace Davis's decorating career, which she'd put on hold to stay home with her sons, was just taking off. The boys didn't need a full-time mother at home, but a new baby did. Fortunately, Grace's recently widowed, impoverished mother-in-law, Agnes, agreed to move into their home and care for Abby.

Abby had adored her grandmother with all her heart. She'd been utterly devastated when Agnes died, suddenly, after exploratory surgery. No, Abby had no trouble empathizing with Angela Butler's pain.

That, Abby told herself, was why she wanted this to go smoothly. Which was why she'd called her sister-in-law, Robyn, that morning. When Abby asked Robyn for the scoop on her kids' likes and dislikes, Robyn laughed out loud. "You want to know what's in with preteens? Why? Are you in the market for a couple? I'm taking offers."

Abby explained about Tom Butler and his daughters, trying to downplay the depth of her own interest.

"What kind of bribes are you looking for?" Robyn asked, her tone teasing. Robyn and Matt constantly razzed Abby about letting her work take the place of a real life.

"Not bribes—gifts."

"Whatever. Well, listen, candy never fails, but you have a single father who may not remind them to brush every night, which might lead to cavities. Stay away from healthy stuff, they'll think you're a real tweek."

"Is that anything like a geek?"

"You got it." She paused. "How 'bout videos? You may not have noticed, but my two are so evolved they can watch a video and do homework at the same time. Charles Darwin would have been impressed."

Abby chuckled, adding the word to her list. "Like what? Disney?"

"Good for the little one. Kiss of death for the teen. How 'bout *Little Women?* Winona Ryder's hot."

"What if they don't have a VCR?"

"Good grief, where do they live? The backwoods of Tennessee?"

"On a ranch."

"If they have electricity, they have a VCR. Trust me. No parent can function without one."

Abby made a note to take along the TV from her bedroom.

It had a built-in VCR. She'd tell Tom, who probably wouldn't accept it as a personal loan, that it was a standard VOCAP practice.

Abby was about to make her goodbyes when Robyn said, "I talked to Grace this morning."

Abby's breakfast flip-flopped in her belly. She loved her mother—in the abstract, Hallmark kind of way, but the two couldn't be in the same room for a minute without Grace saying something or doing something that left Abby feeling "lacking."

"That's nice," Abby said noncommittally. "I guess that means they're back from their cruise. Did Dad hate it? He was sure he'd die from golf-withdrawal."

"I talked to him, too. He said it was fun, but he was glad to get home. Grace said she tried calling you on your birthday, but no answer. Hot date, perhaps?"

Abby had listened to her mother's message—a slightly off-key rendition of "Happy Birthday"—on her answering machine when she returned home from her celebration with Melina, but hadn't gotten around to calling back. "Melina and I went out. We had key lime pie margaritas. Can you imagine such a thing?" Abby asked with forced cheer.

Robyn made a gagging sound. "I can imagine barfing them up. Yech! Your mother's right, girl. You don't have a social life." Before Abby could mount a defense, Robyn said, "Grace is worried about you, kiddo, and so am I. I keep picturing you home alone with only that obese cat for company."

"Tubby is not just any cat. He's a thirty-pound feline sumo wrestler." Robyn's snort did not sound amused. "Besides, Landon drops by off and on." Whoops. Tactical error.

"Jesus, Abby, does he bring his new girlfriend along, too? Are you a masochist or what?"

Abby toyed with the plate of stale birthday cake she intended to feed to the birds. Robyn was right; Abby needed to get on with her life in more ways than one.

"Listen, Abby, I know you hate it when I try to fix you up, but there's a guy I want you to meet."

Abby groaned, wetting her finger to pick up German-chocolate crumbs.

"Don't do that," Robyn scolded. "He's really neat."

"That's what you said about Garvin."

"Gavin. Forget about Gavin. He was a mistake."

"Yeah, a genetic mistake."

"Hush. You're going to like Adam. He's not a computer droid, he's a headhunter."

"Oh, there's a lovely image. Is he four foot six with a bone in his nose?"

Robyn laughed. "He's over six foot and very cute. Just wait. You'll see. I've invited him to the Memorial Day barbecue." Abby groaned. She'd have tried to come up with some creative excuse, like sudden-onset leprosy, but right now she was anxious to get on the road. "Well, pal, I'd love to hear about your little matchmaking business, but I gotta run. Duty calls."

"That's another thing your mother said," Robyn told her, not taking the hint. "You're letting that job take the place of a real life. This is Sunday. You should be doing something fun—bike riding, in-line skating, sharing the comics with some handsome hunk." Robyn paused, then giggled. "Dang, I'm starting to make my own life look like hell. I was on my way to clean the toilets when you called."

Abby laughed, grateful she didn't have to muster her usual defense. She wouldn't admit it to Robyn, or any other member of the family, but lately her life did feel empty, devoid of passion. If it weren't for the Butler case, she might have spent the whole afternoon weeding her garden and watching videos. Alone.

CALL IT WORK, Abby thought fifteen minutes later as she turned off the main highway onto a traffic-free side road, but at least this way I'm driving down a country road on a beautiful late-spring day to spend time with a family that needs my help.

She pushed a button on her armrest to lower the window. Warm, fragrant air filled the car. Alfalfa, she thought, confirming her guess when she spotted a recently cut field of green. Although Abby grew up in Fresno and attended a parochial high school, she had friends involved in 4-H and Future Farmers of America. Her best friend, Kate Petersen, lived on a ranch that bordered the San Joaquin River. Some of Abby's fondest memories were of riding horses along its tree-lined banks and flirting with the cowboys who worked for her dad.

As the road turned southeast, toward the foothills, Abby tried to work out what was bothering her most: her family's interest in her affairs, or the knowledge they might be right. Again. Her sweaty hands slipped on the steering wheel. She wiped them on her jeans and pushed up her sunglasses. She fought the urge to speed up since she wasn't familiar with this part of the county and didn't want to end up in an irrigation ditch.

The directions she'd scribbled on the sticky note had seemed pretty straightforward when Tom dictated them to her last night. She'd deliberated about returning his call on a Saturday night, but, in the end, curiosity won out. He didn't seem at all surprised that she didn't have anything better to do than return phone messages on a Saturday night. She would have been annoyed if not for the honest pleasure she heard in his voice. Her heart had done the funniest little back flip.

Nervously chewing on her bottom lip, Abby consulted her sketchy map. "This has to be more than four miles," she muttered.

The flat, agricultural land, leveled to allow flood irrigation of tomatoes, corn and peppers, had given way to undulating land that sported green shafts of bunch grass and scattered groups of black and brown cattle. Interspersed in the mixture were orchards of almonds, walnuts and pistachios.

"Oh, here we go," she said, spotting the names on two large, steel-gray mailboxes. The bigger of the two bore the word "Hastings" stenciled on the side; the smaller wore the tag "Butler."

She turned off the paved road and slowed down to accommodate a washboard of ripples. On either side of the hard-packed road ran a strip of natural grass, already turned its summer gold. Parallel to the road were two irrigated pastures, home to several dozen head of cattle. Beyond the pastures, Abby spotted silvery-leafed almond trees and, in the distance, a newly planted orchard laid out in precise rows with white, milk carton-like boxes protecting the young saplings.

The driveway curved to the right and appeared to circle back at the top of a slight rise. A grove of mature walnut trees on the left obscured her view. A scouting party of four or five dogs raced between the stout, mottled trunks to meet her. She hastily rolled up her window, muting the raucous furor that might have scared her off if Tom hadn't declared the dogs friendly but barky.

As the driveway completed its S pattern, she looked for Tom's yellow pickup truck but couldn't spot it. An expensive-looking silver-and-blue truck was parked cockeyed in the driveway of a long, low California-style ranch house to her right. An artsy steel sign set amid the riotous glory of red, white and blue petunias defined the owners as "Hastings," with an arrow making up the left-hand upright of the H.

With her foot barely touching the gas, Abby scanned the area. Her impression was of neatly organized obsolescence. No high-tech vehicles or fancy implements in sight, just well cared for tools of the trade. A tractor, its huge tires caked with mud, stood to one side of a massive, weathered red barn. A small group of horses vied for a front-row view in a corral attached to the narrow, faded redwood shed to her left.

"Well," Abby said, trying to decide where to go.

A movement at the door of the shed caught her eye. A wave. She hoped. Either that or the glint of the sun off a gun barrel, she thought sardonically. After all, the building would have been right at home in an Old West movie where tired ranch hands bunked down for the night after a long day of fighting off rustlers.

The door opened all the way and Abby saw Angela Butler step out. No gun in hand. Abby pulled into the graveled, semicircular driveway, parking beneath a brutally trimmed mulberry tree. As she turned off the engine, she saw Angela motion the dogs away. Abby opened the door and got out, taking a deep breath of pure, country air. The distinctive smell of horses and recently irrigated soil made her smile.

"Hi, Angela," Abby said, not bothering to close the car door. She left the basket of goodies, including her pan of hastily prepared Rice Krispie treats, on the seat. Donna had warned Abby to proceed with cautious diplomacy on Angela's turf. "I wasn't sure this was the right place. Where's your dad's truck?"

Angela, barefoot, in baggy jeans and a cropped T-shirt, didn't budge from her spot on the crumbling concrete stoop. Her thin shoulders lifted and fell. "A neighbor called. Some cows got out. He tried calling you, but you'd already left."

"No problem. It's a gorgeous day and I'm happy to be out of the house. Is Heather here?"

"She pitched a fit when he started to leave so he took her with him."

Abby understood the disgust she heard in Angela's voice. On one level Angela probably would have liked to be able to pitch a fit of her own, but as an almost-teenager she had a certain image to maintain.

"Five is pretty young to have to face something like this, but in some ways it's even harder when you're twelve. People don't expect a five-year-old to cope, but when you're older…" She didn't fill in the rest. Angela's quick, probably involuntary nod showed the girl agreed.

"I brought some things I thought you might be able to use. Want to help me carry them in?"

Angela's tentative smile was cut off by an epithet so explicit it made Abby gape. The girl exploded off the stoop like an Olympic sprinter. "Rufus," she screeched, "if you ruined anything, I swear I will kick your skinny ass. Go home, you good-for-nothing son-of-a-bitch. Ed's gonna put a leash on you if you don't stay home."

Abby spun around, following the girl with her gaze. With athletic grace, Angela dived for the car door and reared back with a wriggling armful of puppy. The dog, a black Lab almost half her size, slithered out of her hold and dashed away.

Abby hurried to check the damage.

"They weren't brownies, were they?" Angela asked, her voice low and tense, holding up an empty pan. "Chocolate ain't good for dogs. I'd rather kill him myself."

Abby stared at the pan, too surprised to quite make sense of what had happened. "No. Rice Krispie treats."

"Goddamn it!" Angela swore. "I really like those. Why does everything have to get ruined?"

A quiver in her voice made Abby look up in time to see tears tumble over the rims of Angela's eyes. Without thinking, Abby put her arms around the slim, shuddering shoulders and drew her close. It was on the tip of her tongue to offer to make more treats, but she knew the root of these tears couldn't be fixed by a trip to the store.

How well she knew! A wraith, older than Angela but just as

anguished, hovered peripherally, breathing life into memories too well hidden to be anything but ghosts.

TOM WAITED beside Abby's Honda while she leaned inside to grab the clipboard she planned to use to make notes about everything that was wrong with his living accommodations. He'd jokingly suggested she'd need more than one pad, but Abby had smiled serenely and replied that her forte was getting more from less.

Tom could believe it, too. By the time he and Heather returned from a hasty fence repair, Abby and Angel were measuring the interior of the bunkhouse with a broken tape measure he kept in the kitchen drawer. Before he knew it, Abby had Heather holding one end and Angel the other, somehow turning the process into a game that had both girls laughing.

Now his daughters were happily ensconced in front of the nineteen-inch color television with built-in VCR—on loan from VOCAP, Abby told him—watching the movie *Babe*. She'd given the video to the girls claiming it was an old one she'd grown sick of, but Tom spotted the telltale cellophane wrapping on the floor of her car.

"Got it," she said, returning to an upright position.

Tom liked her better that way. It took too much willpower to keep his gaze off her shapely rear end, which looked every bit as good in blue jeans as he thought it would.

"I make myself these detailed lists so I won't forget anything, then I go off and forget my list," she said, brushing her hair away from her face. "I must be getting old."

"That's my excuse," Tom said, thinking he really liked her hair. The style fit her face and the color picked up highlights of copper he'd missed that day in the office.

Her smile wavered. "Thirty is not all that young, by today's standards."

"Lesley would have turned thirty-five in September," he said without thinking.

He regretted his words when he saw a dark shadow pass across her face. She was much too gentle and caring to have to deal with all this horror. From the first moment he saw her stumble in front of her office, he'd felt a need to reach out and sweep her away to someplace safe. It was a foolish notion since she seemed perfectly happy in her job and able to juggle other people's problems with a magician's finesse.

"She was lovely," Abby said, her tone somber. "Angela showed me her picture."

For reasons he couldn't explain, Tom felt the need to make her understand his feelings toward his ex-wife. "Les and I split up before Heather was born. She hated this life. Wanted action and went looking for it.

"People are like horses. Each one's got a certain nature and there's no changing that. I knew when I married her what she was like." He sighed and looked across the irrigated pasture to the foothills muted by the afternoon haze. "I guess maybe she thought she could change my nature."

"You were both very young," Abby said softly.

"I guess. She was full of dreams. Her only mistake was thinking I could make them come true," he said, unable to keep a smattering of bitterness out of his tone. "She tried hard when Angel was little, but it just got to the point where she wasn't happy no matter what..." He left off the words "I did." No use making it look like it was all Lesley's fault. He'd played his part by being bullheaded and inflexible.

"So she moved to the city," Abby said. "Did that make her happy?"

"I guess. She made good money. Had a big house, nice things." He chuckled wryly, looking over his shoulder at his home. "Heck, this place could fit in one of her bathrooms.

She even had a TV in the master bathroom. Can you imagine watching television in the tub or on the—whatever?"

She smiled but didn't say anything. Maybe she had one in her bathroom. He felt himself flush. Maybe everybody but Tom Butler had a television set in the toilet.

Consulting her notepad, she asked in a professional tone, "Do you own or rent?"

"Neither. Ed Hastings owns this place, and I'm his foreman. We have a sort of lease-option arrangement. His sons aren't interested in the ranch, and he doesn't want to see it broken up after he passes on."

She nodded, which made the sunlight dance off the rich shiny texture of her hair. "How does he feel about remodeling?"

Tom recalled his conversation with Ed half an hour earlier at the mailboxes. Ed was returning to the hospital.

"I saw a car go by earlier," Ed hollered over the drone of the diesel. "That the gal from VOCAP?"

"Yep," Tom said, hating the despondency he heard in Ed's voice. Ever since Janey's diagnosis, Ed seemed tired and distracted.

"Good," Ed said, mustering a little enthusiasm. "I talked to Ralph Miller this morning." Tom recognized the name of the lawyer he and Miguel had used to set up their partnership agreement. Ralph was an old friend of the Hastingses. "He says we should set up a limited power of attorney so you can run things when I'm not around. I'll be back Thursday to settle it."

"Whatever you want, Ed. Just keep us posted on Janey."

Ed nodded, his lips tight. "Tell that VOCAP lady to pull out the stoppers and get going on the addition. It'll give Janey something to look forward to."

To Abby, Tom said, "Actually, Ed would like to see us get started as soon as possible."

"Great. I'll send a contractor out next week. He'll be able to come up with some plans and a dollar figure, then I'll find the money."

Tom cleared his throat. He hated talking money with her, but the subject always seemed to come up. "Ed plans to cover the building costs."

Her eyes lit up with a smile. "That's wonderful, but..." She hesitated, looking at the sheaf of forms on her clipboard as if searching for some hidden answers. "If you don't need a low-interest loan, you don't really need me, do you? I mean, I'd be happy to help, but—"

"Well..." It wasn't in his nature to ask for help, but Tom didn't know what else to do. "I've never done this before and I don't even know where to begin."

There was understanding in her sudden smile. "I have," she said, leaning back against her car. She folded her clipboard against her chest, innocently enhancing the shapeliness of her breasts against her plain white shirt. "I completely remodeled my house four years ago. Talk about a learning experience!"

Her lips pursed thoughtfully. Tom couldn't help noticing how full and attractive they were. Had he noticed that before?

"You said you're going to be running the ranch alone while the Hastingses are at Stanford, right?" Tom had been forced to explain about Janey's cancer treatment when Heather blurted out earlier, "Janey's real, real sick and her doctor lives in a big city so she had to go there. She might have to buy a wig."

He nodded.

"Well, I doubt if that will leave you much time to oversee a project like this, will it?"

Before he could answer, Abby put out her hand and touched his arm. Her fingers barely skimmed his skin, but Tom felt the contact all the way to his toes. "I think this is where my famous 'interceding on your behalf' comes into play," she said, her tone sounding faintly amused. "I'll call a contractor friend of mine tomorrow. Okay?"

Tom nodded, more relieved than he could imagine. Until that moment, it hadn't even crossed his mind how he was going to handle the myriad aspects of remodeling, from subcontractors to design. Thank God, Abby Davis had offered to take this on.

Impulsively, Tom asked the question that had been on his mind ever since she called him back to set up this meeting. "Do you do this for everybody? Make a home visit on a Sunday afternoon?"

A rosy color flashed across her features and she lowered her head to scribble something in her notebook. "I had the time and it seemed like a good idea to get the ball rolling."

"Why?"

She looked up, confused. "Why is it good to get going?"

"Why do you have the time? Why aren't you spending it with your family?"

She shrugged. "My parents live in Palm Desert and my brothers and their families live—"

He didn't let her finish. "Why aren't you married?"

She looked stunned for a second then threw back her head and laughed. The sound made the horses scatter edgily. "Wow, you cowboys don't pull any punches. My father asks me the same thing all the time, but you kind of expect that from a dad."

Tom waited.

She lifted one shoulder and let it fall. "I've lived with two men." She grinned wickedly. "Sounds scandalous, doesn't it? But one was too sick to marry and the other too flaky." She sighed and looked toward the field beyond the barn. "Donna says one was darkness, the other light. Too much of either isn't healthy. I guess I just haven't found that perfect balance."

Tom knew all about balancing acts. At times, he felt like a man juggling land mines on a tightrope.

Abby made a few more notes then opened the door of her car. "I'll call you as soon as I have a meeting set up with the contractor." She cocked her head as if listening for something. Tom heard the sound of a movie sound track. Abby seemed pleased. "Tell the girls goodbye for me. I always hate being interrupted when I'm watching a movie."

"Thanks," Tom said seriously. "For everything—the movie, the TV—"

She waved off his gratitude. "No problem. I'm glad to help. And I'm excited about the addition. Remodeling gets in your blood, you know."

Tom watched her drive away. It wasn't his nature to take to people right off—his mother called him a watchful owl, but he liked Abby Davis. He liked her cheerful candor, even if he sensed a somber undertone.

Humming under his breath, he went inside, intending to start supper. Sunday was his night to cook. So far the girls hadn't complained, but he'd stretched his culinary repertoire about as far it went—quesadillas, egg sandwiches and macaroni and cheese. Tonight, he planned to make chili. From a can.

As he headed for the kitchen, Heather sat up from her sprawled position on the couch and motioned for him to come over.

"What is it, baby-love?"

"Sit with me."

Grinning, he plopped down beside Angel and hauled Heather into his arms. She giggled and squirmed for a few seconds before quieting.

"How's the movie?"

"Okay," Angel said, her tone filled with ennui. "We saw it at the Cineplex near our house."

"I like Ferdinand," Heather said. "He's a duck."

Despite himself, Tom found his gaze drawn to the bright, clear picture. He was curious about the movie Abby had selected.

Angel passed him a bowl of popcorn.

"She's pretty cool, you know," Angel said.

"Ms. Davis?" Tom asked, his voice neutral.

Angel rolled her eyes. "You're so old-fashioned, Daddy. She said to call her Abby."

"Oh."

Angel kept her eyes on the screen. "She said her mother is an interior decorator, I mean, designer. That's what they call them now. She's going to get us some magazines and books so we can design our bedroom. Cool, huh?"

Tom didn't want to burst her bubble, but, despite Ed's largesse, there were finances to consider. "We'll see. It's a ways off, sweetheart."

"I know," she said with a petulant frown. "But Mom always said it doesn't hurt to dream."

Tom closed his eyes. Lesley was dead, and he had a ranch to run and two children to raise. He didn't have time to sleep, much less dream.

MONDAY MORNING Abby raised the cup of aromatic herbal tea to her nose and inhaled, hoping the cinnamon-apple scent could soothe her jangled nerves. She'd spent the last several hours on edge, worrying about what to say to Daniel if he suddenly called or, worse, showed up.

He was an attractive man, but Abby knew the risks of getting involved with a boss, not to mention someone going through an emotional upheaval. Daniel was neither light like Landon nor dark like Billy, but he was stuck in a gray area that he wouldn't be clear of for months, maybe years.

"Wow!" Melina exclaimed, popping her head around

Abby's door. "Did you hear the latest? Marilyn booted Daniel out. She's keeping the house and the Mercedes. God, he loved that car."

Abby flinched. Gossip was one of the least attractive parts of working in a small office.

Melina's perfectly waxed eyebrows shot up like parentheses turned sideways. "You knew this, didn't you? He told you Friday, and you didn't tell me." Her tone was hurt and accusing.

"No. He didn't say a word," Abby said honestly.

"Then how'd you know?"

Abby stifled a sigh. "He called me Saturday and asked me to meet him in his office. I guess he wanted me to know before the gossip hit the fan, so to speak."

It sounded plausible to her ears, but apparently Melina heard something different. She stepped into Abby's office and closed the door. Taking the seat across from Abby, she said, "Oh my God."

"What?"

"He has the hots for you."

Abby smiled at Melina's dire tone. "Don't be silly. He's at a vulnerable point in his life, and I'm a reliable associate. Everybody cries on my shoulder, why should Daniel be any different?"

Melina shook her head, making her thick, wavy hair dance across the black suede lapels of her red-and-white checkered suit jacket. "No, Abby, it's more than that. Otherwise, why didn't he meet you at a coffee shop or someplace public? He wants more than your shoulder for comfort."

Abby took a deep breath. "Forget it, Mel. Even if that were the case, I'm not getting involved. I know a dangerous proposition when I see one. I'm sticking to my original plan."

"You're leaving." Her friend's tone was so downcast, Abby reached across the desk and squeezed her hand. They'd hit if off the minute Melina interviewed for the job of associate counselor. Daniel had lobbied for a man with a bachelor's degree in human resources. Abby had insisted they needed someone bilingual, as Melina was, but secretly she wanted another woman on staff and she liked Melina's bubbly personality.

"Eventually. Not right away," Abby reassured her friend.

Melina pursed her lips—theatrically red today. "I wanted to ask you about that. Roy told me about your new case—a cowboy and his kids. He said you're handling him personally."

Melina's choice of words made Abby blush, so she took a swig of tea to hide her face. "You and Roy both have full loads, and your cruise is coming up pretty soon, right? I figured I was the logical choice since the Marshall case just closed."

Abby gazed at the pale liquid in her cup. If she was serious about changing her life, now would have been the perfect time to start downsizing her caseload instead of volunteering to oversee a three-to-four-month-long remodeling project. But the look of desperation she'd seen in Tom Butler's eyes had robbed her of the ability to think straight.

Melina frowned. "Does this have anything to do with the fact that he's a hunk?"

Abby laughed. "Tom Butler is many things, Mel, but I don't think he considers himself a hunk. He's good-looking… in a country kind of way, but plain. No frills. No vanity or pretensions."

Abby watched Melina's facial expressions as she weighed Abby's reply. The young Hispanic woman was prone to drama, always seeking deeper motives for someone's actions. "Would you say he's the exact opposite of Daniel?" she asked.

"Pretty much. No suit and tie in Tom Butler's closet."

"And he's nothing at all like Landon."

Abby frowned. She didn't like where this was leading. "You could say that."

Melina took a deep breath. "Abby, my friend, my mentor, my mother's idea of a role model, I know I don't have to remind you of this. You are the consummate professional, the standard-bearer for all advocates, the Saint Joan of—"

Abby snorted. "What are you getting at?"

Melina sat forward. "Abby, you can't get involved with this guy. It's unethical."

Abby jerked her hands free. "Who said anything about getting involved?"

Melina rose and put one hand on Abby's shoulder. "You did." Her tone held a Mother Superior quality.

Abby gaped. "I did not." Her own tone sounded just like Angela Butler arguing with her sister.

Melina sighed. Although four years younger than Abby, she was vastly more experienced in the ways of romance. "Abby, I know you. I can tell you like him."

"So? He's a nice man. He cares about his kids. He doesn't kick dogs. What do you want from me?"

With a gentleness she'd seen Melina employ with children who came to her broken and bruised, her friend said, "I want you to be careful. I know you'll work yourself to the bone for this man—this family, but in the end, they will heal and move on with their lives. They always do."

The truth of her words sunk into Abby's flesh like acid.

"This is what we do, remember?" Melina said as she prepared to leave the office. "We help them get their lives together so they can go forward, then we disappear into the past, like old friends who moved away. You're the one who told me you have to hold something back, otherwise this business eats you up inside."

For several minutes after Melina left, Abby gazed out the window. Her grandmother always said the truth was hard to swallow, but it was better than a bellyache from a lie. The truth was she *was* attracted to Tom Butler...and his daughters. But

Melina was right about something else as well. Abby was a professional and she could do her job without breaking her heart in the process. She had to—three other hearts were at stake.

CHAPTER FOUR

TOM HURRIED into Ed's office, a small, cluttered room at the back of the ranch house. He caught a scent of stale coffee and looked at the coffeemaker sitting on the file cabinet—gray globs floated atop an inch of black goo.

A glance at the Caterpillar clock above the room's lone window told him he had forty-five minutes before Maria Fuentes returned with the girls. When she'd picked them up at eleven, he'd given her a grateful hug. "You have no idea what a lifesaver you are. Your husband and I are going to be up to our knees in mud all day."

In typical Maria fashion, she'd waved off his gratitude. "My niece's school sponsors this festival every year. I'm hoping the girls will meet some kids their own ages. I grew up on a ranch, I know how hard it is to make friends, but I had eight brothers and sisters to keep me busy. Besides," she said, ushering his daughters to her '87 Toyota wagon, "you've done so much for Miguel and me."

"Maria," Tom said, uncomfortable with the praise. No matter how many times he told the young couple they were doing him a favor by renting his house on Plainsborough Road, they insisted on treating him like a hero.

Tom had known Maria's family most of his life. He'd played football with her older brothers in high school, and there wasn't a man around he respected more than Ernesto Garza, Maria's father.

Maria, the second to youngest of nine, met Miguel Fuentes

on the sorting line at a local cannery the summer after her high-school graduation. Although, at the time, he barely spoke English, Miguel had ambition and drive. When Maria introduced him to Tom, Tom felt an immediate bond. Ed agreed to give him a chance, and Miguel had proved his worth every day for the last four years.

Maria scolded Tom with her eyes. "Miguel and I can never repay you, Tom. When other landlords were afraid to rent to us because of our…little problem, you handed us the key to your beautiful little house—no first and last months' rent, no deposit."

Their problem was an arsonist who had never been caught. The police theorized that whoever set fire to their duplex was a hired torch courtesy of Boyd Johnston, who was in prison, serving a life sentence for murdering Maria's cousin, Adelina.

It was during the sentencing hearing that Maria's family turned to Abby Davis for help. Thanks to her impassioned plea, Adelina's baby daughter, Celeste, went home to her mother's family instead of to Boyd's parents. Two months later, Maria and Miguel returned home from work one day to find their house reduced to ashes.

At first, Tom had worried that opening his and Lesley's house to the Fuenteses would stir up old ghosts, but Maria had redecorated in her own style, and it filled Tom's heart with pleasure to see horses grazing in the pasture behind his small white barn. Collaborating on a shared dream, Tom and Miguel pooled their resources to buy three broodmares. By trading horse training for stud fees, they were now into their second year.

Tom yanked on the back of Ed's oversize desk chair. He heaved himself into its tweed padding. When he shuffled aside a mound of unopened mail, Tom noticed an envelope from an insurance company. He'd promised to look into group policies for Miguel. Ed paid top dollar but didn't offer benefit packages.

The phone beside his elbow rang. Its partner attached to the fax machine across the room echoed in unison.

"Tom Butler."

"Tom? I tried the house, but Angel didn't answer so I thought I'd leave a message on the machine."

Abby! Tom rocked back in the chair and kicked out his legs, hooking his boots on the corner of the desk.

"Maria took the girls to a school function this afternoon. I didn't even ask about it." He frowned, stroking the coarse, comforting texture of his mustache. "Does that make me a bad father?"

Her light, melodic laughter eased some weight inside him. If he closed his eyes he had no trouble picturing the smile that went with that laugh. "Yeah, right," she said dryly. "Maria Fuentes could take those kids to a biker bar and they'd be safe."

"I forgot you know her. From her cousin's case, right?"

"Yep." The lightness went out of her voice. "One of the hardest cases I've ever worked, but Maria was a rock, even when it looked like the judge was going to award custody to Boyd's family. But the good news is—Celeste is doing great."

Tom stared at a cobweb arching from the file cabinet to the overhead fluorescent-light fixture. He needed to hire a housecleaner before Janey got back, but he was too tired to think about it. "It was an awful time for Maria. She and I have talked about the parallels of what happened to Adelina and Lesley. Two mothers. Both murdered. Maria even suggested I come see you, but I thought I could handle things myself."

"Tom, you need to remember that it's okay to ask for help. You had nothing to do with the violence that created this situation. You're a wonderful father, but even the best parent needs a break now and then. I think it's terrific that Maria has the girls. It'll be good for them, too."

Tom closed his eyes. The praise felt good, even though he didn't want to admit it. "I'm a little worried about Heather," he told her before he could stop himself. "She had a really bad dream last night—worse than usual. It took hours to get her back to sleep."

"Good," Abby said, catching him off guard.

"Good?"

"Believe it or not, that may be a sign of progress with Donna. Be sure to mention it when you take the girls in tomorrow. Is that why you sound so tired?"

She can tell? "That, and I was up at four. Miguel had some problems with one of our irrigation pumps. Out here, water is money."

"So you raced out to the field in the middle of the night with practically no sleep and fixed the pump. Sounds like a job for SuperCowboy."

The humor in her tone made him smile. "I didn't fix it. That's P.G.&E.'s problem—well, it will be once I get this fax off to them. That's why I'm in the office. I hooked up a temporary unit and diverted the water to another field so it wouldn't go to waste and we were back in business."

"Then you went home and took a nap, right?"

Involuntarily, Tom hooted. "What planet do you live on?"

"I was being facetious." She paused, and Tom could picture a serious look settling on her face. He'd noticed her habit of taking a few seconds to compose her thoughts before delivering a serious message. "You know, Tom, sleep deprivation is a dangerous thing. For one thing, you could be too tired to cope with the girls."

Before he could protest, she asked, "You operate heavy machinery, right? Tractors? Farm implements? The kind where one slip could cost you life or limb?" When Tom didn't answer, she continued, "At the very least, when you get run-down, you enhance your chances of getting sick. And that wouldn't do any of you any good, either." He could hear the concern in her voice.

He started to answer, but she beat him to the punch. "Tell you what—why don't you let that fax wait until tomorrow? Just rock back in that big comfy chair of Ed's and close your eyes for a few minutes. A catnap's better than nothing at all."

The suggestion caught him off guard and he had to admit he felt as tired as he could ever remember. His eyelids drooped; his arms felt too heavy to hold the phone. "Wait a minute," he said, surfacing above the waves of fatigue that were pulling him down. "How do you know Ed's chair is comfy?"

Her musical giggle made him smile. "Quit procrastinating. Angel and I used the fax to send my mother a rough sketch of the floor plan yesterday. That chair could house a family of five. I almost stole it. Just close your eyes and let go," she coaxed. "I'm hanging up."

"Wait," he feebly protested. "Why'd you call?"

"It can wait till tomorrow. I'll meet you at Donna's when you take the girls to their session. Sweet dreams." She hung up.

Tom put down the receiver with a deep sigh. As fatigue carried him into a black, dreamless state, his last thought was of Abby, a sweet-voiced siren who cared about tired, lonesome cowboys.

NO MAROON HONDA.

Tom scanned the parking lot one more time, but clearly Abby wasn't waiting for him at Donna's as planned. He swallowed his disappointment and parked the truck, letting his children's chatter wash over him without hearing a single word.

He'd gotten a fairly decent night's sleep—only one mild nightmare for Heather—and he'd been looking forward to telling Abby how much the nap she'd suggested had helped him. Twenty short minutes had been enough to put a smile on his face when Maria brought the girls home. They'd actually played Chutes and Ladders after dinner until bedtime and he'd still had enough energy to tackle paperwork. All in all, it was a nice evening and he wanted to thank her. He wanted to see her.

Donna met them at the door. As usual, she had her hands behind her back and a grin on her face. "Hello, my young friends. Which hand today?"

Tom didn't know if this was part of their therapy or just a ploy to get in their good graces, but she always had some small treasure or goodie waiting when the children arrived. As usual, Angel let her little sister pick first, a generosity that both amazed Tom and made him very proud. As always, Heather chose the left hand.

Donna produced two perfect Bosc pears.

"Thank you," the girls chimed in unison.

"You're most welcome. Now settle down at the table and I'll be right there." She waited until they were seated, then partially closed the door. "Tom, Abby called a minute ago. She tried to reach you at home but you'd already left. Something came up and she couldn't meet you here."

"No problem."

Donna studied him a second. "Are you getting enough sleep?"

He smiled. "Almost enough. Abby helped."

Donna's eyes showed surprise. "She did?"

"She told me it's okay to take a nap when you need it and to let other people help with the kids."

Donna's smile looked less reserved. "She's right, of course. And it is important that you look after your health during this difficult period. Your daughters need you to stay healthy. If you were a woman, I'd tell you to treat yourself to a trip to the beauty parlor for a little pampering." She let out a small sound of impatience. "What a sexist remark! Tom, go find a beauty parlor and treat yourself to a little pampering. That's an order from your health-care professional."

Chuckling, Tom left the building at a loss as to how to fill his time. He was childless and off duty for the next hour and a half. He usually spent the time running ranch errands, but since he'd planned to meet Abby, he'd left his paperwork on Ed's desk.

Idly choosing the path of least resistance, he wandered along the sidewalk of the small, shady strip mall. A striped barber pole at the far end of the complex caught his eye and he headed toward it.

Angel had been threatening for weeks to trim his hair in his sleep. His eagerness slowed as he neared the doorway. The original barbershop had metamorphosed into a beauty parlor. Outlined in brightly painted flowers, the rose and gold printing on the front window promised Glitzing, Acrylic Nails, Perms, Facials and Aromatherapy. Tom lowered his chin and started to pass it by when he noticed a hand-scribbled sign that read "Walk-Ins Welcome."

The scents that assailed his senses were far more caustic than anything his barnyard produced. His nostrils twitched and he almost turned around but braved the threshold. If this was aromatherapy, those New Age people needed their noses examined.

"Hey, sugar, come on in. My name's Jackie. We don't bite unless you ask us real nice." The person attached to the throaty drawl was a caricature composite of Mae West and Lucille Ball. A good two hundred pounds, the red-haired woman wore shiny pink bicycle pants and a baggy top sporting two dancing purple poodles with pink polka-dot bow ties. "What can we do you for, honey?"

"Haircut," Tom croaked, glancing around the room in case he needed a weapon or quick escape. The shop's other two occupants consisted of a matronly-looking woman with a helmet of skinny blue plastic rollers who was receiving a manicure by an elfin Asian woman of incalculable age.

"Well, hand over your hat and park your butt in that royal-blue throne, cowboy, and we'll give it a go."

Tom cringed when she tossed his good, white felt hat carelessly on a magazine-strewn coffee table, but he obediently walked to the indicated chair. He eyed its reclined back wedged up tightly to a sink with an indentation about the right size for a neck, and said, "Just a haircut, ma'am. I washed it this morning."

Grinning, the woman chomped on a wad of chewing gum with enough snap to mimic gunfire. "Indulge me. It's all part of the price—sixteen bucks."

Tom lowered himself into the chair and leaned back. With a speediness that amazed him, Jackie secured a plastic bib around his neck and aimed a tingly spray of warm water at his head. Tom closed his eyes, relaxing to the feel of her fingers massaging his scalp. The apple-scented lather smelled good.

"Nice, isn't it?" Jackie said. "Men don't know what they're missing at barbershops and I can tell this is your first time in a beauty parlor, right?"

Tom was too lethargic to answer. He grunted.

As she worked some apple-scented lather into his hair, she asked, "So what brings you to these parts, stranger?"

"My daughters see a…doctor in the building across the way."

"Oh, really? I know one of the doctors over there. Her name

is Donna Jessup. She's cool. She helped out my son when he was nineteen. Had a little drug problem."

"Is he better now?"

"Yep. Goes to Narcotics Anonymous faithfully and finished college. He and his girlfriend just had a baby. I told him if he didn't get off his duff and marry that girl, I was sending him back to therapy, but he said people don't get married for the same reasons these days. A kid isn't a reason enough? Who knows? Maybe he's right. I married his father for that reason and look where it got me—bruised, battered and divorced."

She squeezed the excess water from his hair and dried it briskly with a big fragrant towel. Her touch held a mothering quality he liked.

"You married?" she asked, pushing a lever that sat the back of thc chair upright.

It took Tom a minute to get his bearings. "Not anymore."

"Over here, doll." She led him to a silver-flecked padded plastic chair on a hydraulic lift.

He sat down warily and eyed his wet image in the mirror. Surrounded by an oval of round white bulbs like in the movies, the image of a wet-dog cowboy in the silver-flecked chair looked ridiculously out of place, yet something about its air of glamour made him relax, as if he were preparing for some unannounced play.

"You share custody with the mom, huh?" Jackie asked.

Tom looked at her in the mirror. Kind eyes were hidden beneath an outrageous layer of mascara and black eyeliner. She was real, he decided, even if the color of her spiky locks wasn't.

"No. She died. The girls are getting some counseling to help them deal with it."

"Well, good for you," she said, grasping his shoulder in a supportive way. "What a smart dad you are! I lost my mama when I was nine, and my daddy sent me to live with my aunt.

She was a good woman but she had four kids of her own and I didn't make it easy for her. I was mad at my mama for getting sick and dying, mad at my dad for sending me away, just mad at the world, I guess. I think my life would have been a lot different if I'd had someone to help me see it wasn't anybody's fault."

She straightened up, suddenly all business, and spun Tom around to face her. "Now, what are we doing here, son? Way I see it is we have two choices—same ol' same ol' or something a little radical. Which is it gonna be?"

"I could probably stand a little change." Even as he said the words, Tom had a feeling he was going to regret his choice.

She rewarded him with a big smile. "Then close your eyes, honey, and let Jackie go to work."

Tom lost track of time. When Jackie suggested losing the mustache he'd groomed and pampered since the early days of his marriage, he shrugged with cavalier ease but drew the line at glitzing, whatever that was.

"Okay, honey," Jackie said with a flourish, spinning his chair to face the mirror. "Open your eyes."

Tom did. He searched the mirror for a familiar visage but found a stranger sitting in the chair with silver stars. He blinked. So did the man across from him. Oh my God.

"Well, what do you think? Am I a genius or what?"

Jackie's infectious triumph helped take the edge off the severity of the change. This person didn't look like him, but he didn't look bad. In fact, he looked younger and more... current.

"I think my twelve-year-old will love it."

Jackie winked. "So will your twenty-five-year-old and your fifty-year-old. Trust me, Tom, you're a hunk."

The other two occupants voiced their approval. The grandmother went so far as to volunteer for a date, if her husband of fifty-one years gave his okay. Tom let the knot in his stomach relax. What would Abby think?

AS FAR AS Abby was concerned, Al Carroll was a god. Or the next thing to it. Fifty-five. Bald. Built like a bull terrier with suspenders, he made miracles happen. She'd seen his work dozens of times over the years, starting with the remodeling of her home. He'd transformed her dark, moody ranch-style house into an open, sunlit bungalow.

She couldn't wait to turn him loose on the Butler house.

Originally Abby had planned to meet Tom to go over some remodeling ideas, but when Al had called and said he had a couple of hours free, she'd jumped at the chance to meet him on-site.

"Not good," Al said, kicking his booted toe at the crumbling foundation. "Why do people build without footings?"

"How bad is it?" Bad meant money.

"I've seen worse. We'll just make sure not to involve the county suits in that part of the process. This newer stuff is acceptable."

Abby trotted along, trying to see what Al discerned in the weathered plank siding and moss-covered shingles. "I'd suggest putting gutters on the whole building when we do the addition. Saves some settling and might help shore up this area. Landscaping helps, too."

Abby scribbled notes while swatting flies. "He's going to have to move the horse pen, right?" she asked, more prayer than question.

"Makes sense. That area is already level and if you go the other direction you run into septic problems."

Good. She had a feeling that Tom had agreed to this addition out of both a sense of doing the right thing for his daughters and a dire need for privacy and space, but she knew he wasn't crazy about the changes it would entail.

She glanced at the slim watch on her wrist. The family should be back from Donna's any minute.

"What about this area?" Al called, catching Abby staring at the road.

She hurried around the corner of the building, nearly stumbling over a pile of firewood debris. A huge ax protruded—Paul Bunyanish—from a circle of wood. An image of Tom chopping wood on a cold morning, muscles taut beneath his worn flannel shirt, caught her off guard.

Al gave her a moment's scrutiny. "You okay? You oughta get some boots if you're gonna be out here in the country."

Abby looked down at the beige heels that accented her outfit: off-white Liz Claiborne silk and wool-blend suit with sculpted shell and nude hose. Not quite Eva Gabor in *Green Acres,* but close. She'd only been here twenty minutes and already there was a paw print on her skirt and some sort of vegetation on her sleeve.

At that moment, the thunderous roar of a diesel engine combined with a cacophony of barking filled the air. The faded yellow pickup rolled to a stop around the corner from where Abby and Al were standing. Angel appeared at Abby's side almost before the sound of the engine died.

"Wait till you see Dad," she whispered breathlessly. "You won't believe it."

Abby caught her breath. Angel's impish grin could be read as good or bad, you just never knew with girls this age. Abby leaned around the corner and nearly lost her balance again. Heedless of slivers, she anchored one hand on the rough siding.

"Ohmygod."

The mustache was gone. He'd left his hat in the truck, and his hair—what was left of it—was short. And wavy. And gorgeous. The shorter locks were full of rambunctious waves, which glinted like tempered bronze. This new look, even with a strip of slightly lighter skin tone above his upper lip, was more mature, more polished. Except for the faded denim shirt and scuffed blue jeans, he could have been a *GQ* magazine model. He should have been. "Wow."

"Cool, huh?" Angel enthused. "Do I have the, like, most with-it dad in the whole world, or what?"

"Absolutely. He gets my vote. Doesn't your daddy look great, Heather?" Heather, who was in Tom's arms, hadn't taken her eyes off her father's face, as if she expected him to turn into someone else while she watched.

"Daddy lost his mistash," Heather told Abby. "He went for a walk while we were at Dr. Donna's and some genie stole it because it was so pretty the genie wanted it for his wife."

Abby laughed and couldn't resist throwing her arms around the pair of them and giving them a hug. "Well, I'm glad I'm not married to that genie. Can you picture me with a mistash?"

Heather giggled and wiggled to get down.

Abby dropped her arms and backed up a step, suddenly self-conscious.

"Daddy says I get to pick a kitty from the new ones that were born in the barn. Wanna help me pick one?" Heather looked up at Abby expectantly.

Abby was grateful for the diversion. "I'd like that a lot."

Tom leaned down and planted a kiss atop the springy blond curls. "Mama cats sometimes hide their babies, punkin. Why don't you go find them and Abby'll catch up?"

"Okay, Daddy."

As Heather trotted off, Abby eyed Tom more circumspectly. "I do like it. But I have to admit I'm a little jealous. I go into the beauty parlor and come out the same, every time. You go in Tom Selleck and come out..." She searched for the right celebrity's name. "Tom Cruise."

Angel shook her head. "Naw. Too smooth. How 'bout Nicholas Cage?"

"Too extreme. Sean Connery?"

"Too old."

Tom coughed. "Would you like to introduce me to your friend?"

Abby's cheeks heated up as she realized Al was watching this exchange with bemused puzzlement. "Oh, sorry. Tom, this is Al Carroll, the best remodeling contractor in the business. Al, Tom Butler, homeowner."

"And movie star," Al said dryly.

Tom shook his hand. "Not exactly. I knew there was a reason I always went to the same barber all these years."

"Me, too," Al said, passing a freckled hand over his bald pate. Everyone laughed.

All awkwardness behind them, Tom and Al set off around the building with Angel at their heels, discussing the project. Abby started toward the barn but gave herself a moment to compose her scattered sensibilities. It was only a haircut, for heaven's sake.

TOM LIKED Abby's favorite contractor. The man knew his stuff and had some excellent ideas. In fact, talking to Al Carroll energized him. This project underscored the realization that the girls were here permanently and it was up to him to make a home for them.

Abby will understand, he thought. When Al Carroll left, Tom headed toward the barn.

As he walked, he thought about the look on Abby's face when she saw his haircut. To be honest, Tom had to admit her reaction hadn't hurt his ego. Donna had been reserved about his new look until she saw how the girls responded. Tom had been a little worried about what Heather might think, but she'd stroked his smooth cheeks and kissed him without reservation. "Where'd your mistash go, Daddy?"

He invented a story that made her laugh and she was fine

with the change. Donna told him, "I'm pleased. I see this as real progress. She's comfortable that you're here for her and nothing about that is going to change. This is very good." Then, before he left, she winked and said, "Not to mention it looks great. Very debonair."

Tom entered the barn quietly. He didn't want to disturb any important girl talk. He was also curious about why Heather had included Abby in the choosing of a kitten.

He heard a quiet murmur of voices and stepped closer to the yellow glow of the light he'd suspended over a stacked pyramid of hay bales.

"I used to have lots of kittens of my own when I came up here to visit Dad in the summers," Tom heard Angel say.

He peeked over the railing of the empty horse stall. Abby was perched on the edge of a bale beside the two kids, who were sprawled on their bellies trying to see inside a hollowed-out area between the stacks.

"Those summers alone with your dad must have been very special," Abby said, trying to peer over their shoulders without losing her balance. "My brothers were ten and fifteen when I was born. My grammy told me they thought my being born was the worst thing that could have happened, that I'd ruin everything."

Tom smiled.

"Did ya? Did ya ruin everything?" Heather asked, ignoring the nudge from her sister.

"Just the opposite. Turns out I was a built-in babe magnet. The boys took me everywhere. All the girls would come around and 'ooh' and 'aah.' Nothing like a cute little toddler to break the ice."

"Didn't you have any sisters?" Heather asked.

Abby shook her head. "Not until later on when my brothers married. Robyn and Patrice are my sisters-in-law and I love them like sisters. Matt and Robyn have two kids, Megan and

Patrick—you're right between them in age, Angel. And Jarrod and Patrice just had a baby, Chloe, right before Christmas."

Angel sat up, cross-legged; she eyed Abby intently. "Dr. Jessup says you have great mothering instincts. How come you don't have any kids?"

Tom's pulse jumped. He almost interceded to admonish Angel. He was stopped by a curious flash of pain that crossed Abby's face before she camouflaged it by poking at a piece of moss on the sleeve of her prissy off-white suit.

Her tone seemed artificially bright when she said, "I have a cat. His name is Tabby, but I call him Tubby. He thinks he's in charge of my house."

Tom cleared his throat to announce his presence and joined the little conference by squatting beside Angel. "Hello, ladies. Have you picked out a kitten?"

Heather shook her head. "The mama hided them way back there, Daddy." To Abby, she said, "Mama cat hides the babies so the papa won't eat them."

"Oh, gross," Angel exclaimed, shooting to her feet. "I'm outta here."

Tom caught her hand, not wanting her to leave this warm, friendly closeness. "Where're you goin'?"

She flashed him a dark look that made him flinch. "Nowhere. Of course. I just want to be alone. Is that all right?"

Tom felt his cheeks heat up. What did he know about the needs of a girl on the brink of womanhood? He could understand the need for private time, but ever since he'd run across a pamphlet on teen suicide at Donna's office, he'd become very cautious. Maybe overly cautious. He let her small tense fingers slip from his hold. "Sure."

She raced toward the rear of the barn.

As if sensing his worries, Heather held out her arms to him. "Is the daddy cat mean, Daddy?"

Tom scooped his younger daughter into his arms and

settled back against the stack of bales opposite Abby. "Not exactly, honey. Just forgetful. He forgets those are his babies and thinks some other cat planted kittens in his territory. The mama keeps the babies safe until they're big enough to look after themselves."

Abby made a small sound.

He caught a puzzling flash of some dark emotion cross Abby's face before she glanced at her watch. "I should be going."

She stood up quickly, brushing off her skirt. "It's my night to help at the women's shelter. Tell Angel I said goodbye. I'll call as soon as Al's got the plans ready."

Tom looked at Heather, who seemed oblivious to the sudden shift of mood. "Wait a sec," he said, rising to one knee. "We'll walk you to your car."

Abby paused by the gate. "No. Stay. You have a kitten to choose. These are important moments in a girl's life."

Puzzled by both her cryptic words and sudden somberness, he sat back down. She flicked her hand like a wounded butterfly and hurried away.

Heather reached up and laid her small, soft hands on either side of his face and directed his attention to her. "Can we pick the kitty later? My tummy says it's time to eat."

ANGEL SETTLED BACK against the makeshift couch she'd created from hay bales. The soft fleece lining of the old sleeping bag she'd found in the storage room below the loft helped protect her from the scratchy building material.

Just last week she'd remembered the hideaway her father had created for her a couple of summers ago. He'd called it a fort, but she and her friends, Brandi, Laura and Trudy Gills, called it the Hidey Spot. Her dad hadn't been so busy then and had time to cart her friends out to the ranch to play. Angel didn't know if any of the girls still lived around here. Last summer, Angel only spent a few days with her dad because her mother enrolled her in a computer camp, a gymnastics camp and a stupid, three-week leadership camp.

Shortly after the funeral, her father had suggested they try calling some of Angel's old friends, but, so far, she hadn't wanted to. Sometimes it just seemed too hard to explain to people about her mom.

Angel tilted back her head and studied the dust particles floating in the shaft of sunlight coming through a hole in the roof of the barn. It was quiet up here, peaceful. She knew her dad worried about her. He didn't understand why sometimes she wanted the television on as loud as possible and other times she'd want absolute silence, like now. She didn't understand it, either. Maybe she'd ask Dr. Donna. Maybe she'll tell me I'm going crazy.

Sighing, she reached for her new purple clipboard. "Imperial plum," Abby called it. The clipboard, complete with drafting paper and mechanical pencil, was a gift from Abby. Angel ran her finger along the surface of the blue-lined paper. It had a clean, professional feel.

"Measure your furniture," Abby told her. "Your end tables, dressers and beds, and then figure out what that comes to in scale—one foot equals one square. Then cut out the shapes so you can come up with designs."

Abby didn't go into big long explanations. She seemed to know Angel was smart enough to figure things out on her own.

Too bad Dad doesn't understand that, Angel thought bitterly.

Angel knew he was trying, but lately he'd been trying too hard. She felt like one of the colts he was training. He'd play out so much leader, letting the colt think he was free, then snap the line to show him who was boss.

This morning, Angel woke up early and started making

oatmeal. The instant kind. Boil water—add the stupid oatmeal. Any idiot could do it. But she'd gotten sidetracked by Heather, and when she turned back to the pathetic hot plate that was supposed to pass for a stove, the oatmeal was bubbling like one of those volcanic pits she saw on the Discovery Channel. A big old glob spurted out and landed on her arm.

It had burned like hell, and she'd shouted a few swearwords, which made her dad jump off the couch, where he slept, and race to the kitchen. By then, Angel had everything under control and she'd smeared butter on the nickel-size blister the way her mother taught her.

"Oh, no, Angel-babe, that's an old wives' tale. Using butter on a burn can actually lead to infection," he'd said. "Go rinse that off and we'll put some antiseptic ointment on it."

Like he was a mother. How did he know?

Twelve was a sucky age, Angel decided. People expect you to be "responsible" but they don't give you any responsibility.

On the way home from Dr. Donna's that afternoon, she'd asked her dad to drop her off at the mall to do some shopping.

"The mall?" he'd croaked in this froglike voice.

"Yeah, that big place north of town with shops in it. Remember?"

"Alone?" His voice turned dark and serious. Not a good sign.

"Well, it's not like I have a whole lot of friends to hang out with."

He pretended to be too busy driving to look her in the eye. "Dr. Donna told us Abby and her contractor friend are at the house, remember?"

Angel knew an excuse when she heard one. She sulked in the corner, sucking on a hunk of hair.

"Maybe Maria could take you shopping next week," he suggested, a few miles later.

Like Maria wanted to hang out with a twelve-year-old at

the mall. Angel liked Maria a lot, but she had a baby on the way. Angel didn't think she'd be up for any serious shopping in the near future.

"Forget it," she snarled with enough volume to make Heather squirm even closer to their dad. Out of sheer spite, Angel pinched her sister on the meaty part of her thigh. The little twit howled like a puppy caught in barbed wire.

For a second, Angel thought her father might raise his hand to her, something he'd never done before. Her heart pounded so loud she couldn't hear the damn country-western music on the radio. But he didn't. His knuckles were white against the cracked black steering wheel, but they relaxed after a minute. He ruffled Heather's hair and told her, "Grumpy people aren't much fun, are they? Sorry you got caught in the middle of our disagreement, punkin. Your sister will apologize, too, right after she gets done mucking out the foaling stall in the barn."

Remembering, Angel grimaced as she nibbled on the grainy eraser of the mechanical pencil. So far, her dad hadn't mentioned the chore again, but that was probably because Abby was here.

I wish Janey were home, Angel thought. *Dad listens to Janey.* A twinge of guilt made Angel frown. Janey was in the hospital fighting breast cancer. Angel's mother would have scolded her for worrying about her own problems when Janey was fighting for her life. Lesley took breast cancer very seriously. Every October, Angel and her mother ran in the annual Breast Cancer Awareness marathon at Pismo Beach. They did the short run, but still, they made lots of money for a good cause.

Angel thought about this coming October. Who would take her this year? Dad? Not likely. He hated jogging and seemed to get embarrassed if a woman in a bra ad showed up on television. Val? He always told her mother his idea of helping was writing a check. Janey? Angel knew two women from her mother's aerobics class who were breast cancer survivors, but they told her it took them a full year to get back on their feet.

An image of Abby crossed her mind, but Angel brushed it away. Abby was temporary—here for the short term, like Dr. Donna. Once Angel and Heather were better, Abby would move on to the next family in need. That's what Abby herself said when Angel asked about her work.

"I help people get back to the business of living, then I slip into the background so they can get on with their lives," she'd said, frankly.

"You never see them again?"

Abby seemed to read some concern into Angel's question where there was none. Angel was just curious, that was all. "I still get Christmas cards from some of my old clients. I bump into others from time to time and we catch up a little, but it's hard to keep track of all the people I've worked with over the years. It's just the nature of the job."

We're just a job to her, Angel reminded herself as she picked up the sheet of paper with measurements scribbled on it.

Two nights ago, she and Heather and their dad went to Janey and Ed's to measure a set of twin beds. The maple headboards looked boyish, but Dad said he would paint them any color she and Heather wanted.

"I want purple," Heather said.

Angel pretended to gag. "You have absolutely no taste. Nada. Zero. Zip."

The little twit started to cry as if her heart was broken. "I can too taste," she said through her sobs.

Their dad kinda laughed, but he told Angel sternly, "She's only five, Angel-babe. You probably didn't have the greatest taste in the world either when you were five."

"Maybe not, but the only person we can ask about that is dead, isn't she?" Angel had no idea what made her say that.

Her dad looked stunned, but she didn't hang around for him to say anything. She threw down the measuring tape and ran back to the house. Later, when he carried Heather to bed, Angel pretended to be asleep, even though she wanted to crawl into his arms and cry. She stayed rigid, knowing even one movement would be her undoing.

CHAPTER FIVE

"IT'S A FINE LITTLE MACHINE, Tom," Maria said, closing the door of his new microwave oven—that morning's Wal-Mart purchase. She pushed the appropriate buttons and the unit began to hum. A gleaming white mini-iceberg in a sea of rummage-sale castoffs, it was the result of her very gentle nagging. "I'm so glad you bought it. Now the girls can heat up my tamales without so much fuss and bother."

Tom and Miguel were seated at Tom's kitchen table, waiting to sample nachos. The table, with its fake gray-marble top and molded aluminum sides and tubular legs was a long-ago hand-me-down from his parents. Janey told Tom she'd seen one just like it wearing a two-hundred-dollar price tag at an antique store.

"Your tamales are the only reason I bought the machine," Tom said. Maria had promised to keep his freezer stocked if he'd move into the twentieth century.

Tom took a deep satisfying breath. The aroma of chilies, cilantro and tomatillos stewing together with chunks of pork made his mouth water. Chili verde bubbled on the hot plate—the next archaic monster to go, if Maria had her way. When she called Tom that morning, she'd promised him a little "fiesta." Tom was still waiting to hear the reason for the celebration. Although he'd tried several times throughout the day to pry it out of Miguel, the young Hispanic man was the most close-mouthed person he knew.

"Well," Tom said, leaning across the table, "when are you going to tell me?"

Miguel, his dark eyes twinkling, said something to his wife in Spanish—too fast for Tom to catch.

Maria left her preparations and joined them. A petite five foot two inches, she carried what looked like far too much baby. Tom pulled out a chair for her, and she sat down with a sigh.

A moment later, after some silent signal from her husband, she said, "Miguel has a job offer in Modesto. In the city parks department, where his brother, Gonzalvo, works. It's union, Tom. Full benefits and holidays." She delivered the news solemnly, for she knew, as Tom did, this good news for the Fuentes family was sad news for him.

He reached deep to find the enthusiasm they deserved. "That's fantastic, amigo. You won't have to run out in the middle of the night to wade through irrigation ditches and hassle with foolish cows and ornery horses. Is there a place for me, too?"

The young couple laughed, all tension gone. Tom wanted the best for them and this sounded like a terrific opportunity.

"This way I'll be able to go back to junior college sooner and finish my degree," Maria said, wiping her hands on her calico-print apron. "We have tons of family around there to help with the baby.

"Miguel's uncle has a place for us to rent. The tenants are moving to Idaho. It's not as nice as your house, and I'll miss my garden, but you can't have everything."

Tom toasted with his can of Tecate. "To good fortune in Modesto. May you only know success and happiness."

Maria jabbed the hem of her apron to her eyes as she rose and hurried back to the cauldron. Tom discovered his appetite gone.

He rose and walked to the sink where Maria stood staring

out the small square window. A hint of twilight filtered through the walnut trees. He touched her shoulder. "I'm happy for you, Maria. Really. We'll miss you, but..."

"Just my cooking."

He turned her around to face him, moved by the traces of tears on her smooth cheeks. "Your wisdom and patience and girl talk and womanly touches." He pointed to the cheerful rose-print curtains she'd made for the window. "You've helped so much. We'll miss much more than your cooking."

"It's not that far," she said in a rush. "And Miguel will be back to help with the horses."

The horses. Tom and Miguel's breeding program was still in an embryonic stage. Miguel handled the halter breaking and early-stage training—some of which required almost daily attention. "It'll work out. Don't worry. We'll come see you all the time. How else will the girls be able to spoil that little bambino?" He gently patted her very rounded belly.

She shooed him away to finish the preparations. "Angel. Heather," she called. "Are you ready to learn how to make tortillas?"

The two let out whoops of affirmation as they dashed from their spots on the sagging sofa. Tom wandered over to the television where the video, *Chitty Chitty Bang Bang*—another "loaner" from Abby—was playing. He pushed the off button and eyed the room critically. Tiny flip-flops poked out from between the faded burgundy cushions of the sofa. On the end table a mound of books—a combination of schoolbooks, paperbacks and prereaders—clustered around the base of the lamp like a carelessly laid bonfire. Pretty-pink doll paraphernalia, the origin and purpose of which he had not a clue, lay strung out from one end of the coffee table to the other. The room had never looked more lived in, or alive.

Maybe everything in life is a trade-off, he thought. His well-structured life was history, but he had board games and

Barbie dolls to replace it. His friends were moving on, but that was life.

"Daddy," a sweet voice chirped, making his heart catch in his chest. "Come try my tortilla. I made it just for you."

A tear started to form but he blinked it away. This was a celebration.

Later, as Tom leaned back in his chair, stuffed to the gills, Maria said, "You know, Tom, this new job won't start until August, but we could move in with my cousin if you and the girls want to move into your house."

Before Tom could reply, Angel said, "We're building a new bedroom and bathroom and we get to decorate it ourselves, don't we, Dad?"

She didn't wait for his answer, but told Maria, "In our old house, my mom had some lady come in and do the decorating. She picked out everything. Bedspreads, curtains, paint. It was okay and all, but this will be more like our own."

Tom noticed the enthusiasm in her voice. He hadn't realized how important this was to her, and he vowed to make sure the new rooms turned out right. "Go get the sketches, honey, and show them to Maria while Miguel and I clean up."

After washing the few pots and pans and bowls, Tom and Miguel slipped outside. They wandered toward the horse corral that would soon have to be moved. For five years Tom had slept with the sounds of young mares snuffling about outside his window. It had meant more dust and flies than he liked, but the gentle night noises were a comfort, too.

The lack of a moon made the night inky black. The barn's bluish-green vapor light and the yellowish glow of the bug zapper near Ed's patio shone like ancient beacons. After the warmth of the dishwater, the air temperature seemed a shade too cool. Tom rolled down the sleeves of his shirt. It wouldn't be long before summer set in for good. Another change.

"Lots of changes," Miguel said as if reading Tom's mind.

"Too many for an old coot like me."

Miguel made a motion toward Tom's haircut. "You started from the top down, I see."

Tom had fielded his share of razzing the past two days. Johnny Dee nearly swallowed his chaw when he bumped into Tom at the feed store. Maria faked a swoon when she first saw it. Miguel, as usual, had kept his opinions to himself.

"Gotta start someplace, I guess."

With small, economical motions, Miguel rolled a cigarette and lit it. He inhaled deeply, savoring his vice, which he'd promised to give up by the time the baby arrived. "Sometimes I think I'm going to miss this more than...the other. How did you do it?"

Tom didn't answer. His thoughts were elsewhere. *I wonder what Abby is doing.* Maria said she'd invited her to join them tonight, but she was busy. Busy with work? Or busy socially? A woman as attractive as Abby would surely have a long list of suitors.

Miguel punched him on the arm. "How did you do it?" he repeated.

"I...I never smoked."

Miguel's eyebrows rose together. "Not the smoking, the sex. How did you manage when your wife said you had to wait until after the baby is born?"

Tom bit back a smile. Lesley had wanted a massage every night, and Tom was happy to be of service because he loved the feel of her soft, supple skin stretched taut over the new life she carried. He found it extremely erotic, but she didn't. "Thanks," she'd say then roll over and go to sleep, leaving Tom to deal with his problem any way he chose. "Leather helped."

Choking, Miguel nearly swallowed his cigarette.

Tom patted his back with gusto. "Tooling leather. Saddles, bridles, belts. It kept my mind off other things. I made three saddlebags, sixteen belts and a purse for my mother. I've got the tools in the barn if you want them."

Exchanging ribald jests about who was the better leather tooler, the men returned to the porch where Maria was waiting. She scolded Miguel gently in Spanish then leaned over to give Tom a peck on the cheek. "I'm sorry Abby couldn't make it. You need some female companionship."

"I have two female companions who keep me very busy, thank you."

She made a face. "You know what I mean. Abby is the best person I know, next to you, maybe."

Miguel made a huffing sound and she cupped her husband's face lovingly. "Other people, *mio.* No one compares to you. You know that."

Tom's heart felt heavy as he watched them drive away. It was difficult not to envy them their closeness, their love. He missed that part the most, he thought, even more than sex. He missed having another person with whom to share his innermost thoughts.

Maybe someday. Blending a family wasn't easy under any circumstances, but given his daughters' traumatic experience, it would take a truly special woman to handle this challenge.

ABBY HAD NEVER REGARDED herself as a clock-watcher, but this had to be the slowest Thursday on record. Granted, this was the first day of the Butler girls' foray into the Rainbows program, but since that didn't directly involve Abby, she saw no reason why it should keep popping up in her mind.

"Melina," she called out as familiar footsteps trotted past her doorway, "where's the Yang file?"

"In your Out basket, of course. Where is your head today?"

The exasperation in her friend's tone made Abby groan. "In my Out basket, obscuring the Yang file."

As she reached for the file, the phone rang.

"Abby Davis."

"Abby. I'm in trouble."

The breathless voice was Tom's. Her heart punched toward her throat. "Are you okay? Are the girls—"

He cut her off. "Nothing like that. I just ran in from the barn. One of my mares is foaling and there's a problem. The vet's on the way, but I can't leave and the girls are supposed to be in Fresno in an hour, and I kinda hoped you…"

With her heartbeat back to normal, Abby could respond. "I'll drive them."

"Are you sure? I know you're busy, but Maria's in Modesto and—"

"Tom, get off the phone so I can leave." She started to hang up, but his silence made her hesitate.

"I really do appreciate this," he said.

Abby's heart started jumping around again. That voice. That honest, heartfelt, tender appreciation did things to her she couldn't explain.

"Good luck with your mare. I'll be there in fifteen minutes."

She slipped the receiver back in place while shoveling two hours' worth of paperwork into her briefcase. She was half-way out the door when another body tried squeezing past her. "Daniel," Abby exclaimed, drawing her briefcase between them defensively. "Is it important? I have to run. The Butler children need…"

His cologne, probably more expensive than her mother's perfume, filled her nostrils, making her lose her train of thought.

"You mean that cowboy's kids?"

Something about his tone made Abby's hackles rise, but she nodded, not wanting to get into it.

"Abby, I've come to the decision you're too busy for your own good. Every time I call over here you're in family court or at a deposition or in the law library or with clients or meeting with contractors and draftsmen. You need a little downtime."

His concern seemed genuine, but since he was mostly to blame for her frenetic schedule she didn't answer.

"Have dinner with me Friday."

"Tomorrow?" Abby asked, her voice was a squeak.

"Yes. We'll drive up to Bass Lake. Have you ever eaten at Ducie's? It overlooks the lake. Very peaceful."

She'd been there with Landon. The setting was peaceful… and romantic.

"I'll pick you up early so we can take our time driving up. Say, five-thirty? Will that give you enough time to get home and change?"

As he well knew—since he approved her schedule—Abby ate lunch at her desk all week to be able to leave early on Fridays. "I always leave at four on Fridays."

"Great. See you then." He left with a casual touch on her shoulder.

Her equilibrium reeled—whether from the cologne or the railroading, she wasn't sure.

"Not a good idea, kiddo," Melina said, poking her head out of the adjoining office.

"It sure as hell wasn't mine."

Abby didn't wait to hear more. She had something to do. Something important. She and Donna had researched the Tomorrow's Rainbows program when it started up. They both recognized the validity of peer counseling—the kind of empathy adults couldn't give.

She got in her car. As she turned the key, an errant thought crossed her mind. Does Tom wear cologne? The only scents she could associate with him were fresh air, old leather and something utterly masculine she was sure couldn't be found in a bottle. She liked it a great deal more than Daniel's expensive cologne.

"THAT'S BOGUS and you know it," Angel ranted, anger making her voice crack.

Her father hung up the phone and looked at her, obviously trying to be patient. Angel didn't care. She had no intention of putting herself on the line with a bunch of strangers. It was bad enough having to be all perfect and chipper for Dr. Donna, who had an uncanny way of seeing through her mask to make Angel own up to feelings she'd have preferred to ignore.

"You like Abby," her father said. "She gave you that TV and VCR."

"Big whoop," Angel said, kicking off her scruffy mules and drawing her knees to her chest. She hadn't bothered changing out of her sweat pants and nightshirt because she saw how preoccupied her dad was with his horse and she was sure he'd forget about that stupid Rainbows thing.

"I don't want to go without you, either, Daddy," Heather said, showing surprising fortitude in the midst of the shouting match. Usually, the little dork would hide out in the bedroom whenever Angel and their dad got into it.

Angel reached for her soda can, but the couch cushions sank in the middle, throwing off her balance. The can wobbled, spilling soda on her wrist and fingers. "Damn ugly couch," she cursed. "Cheap piece of crap. Everything sucks in this house."

She regretted the words as soon as they left her mouth. Heather's mouth opened and closed like a guppy.

Her dad heaved a sigh, making Angel feel even more guilty—and mad. It wasn't her fault this stupid house was too small and had old furniture and crappy television reception. She didn't want to be here. She didn't want to be in the big house in Riverside with Val, either, but that wasn't the issue at the moment.

"C'mere, punkin," her father said, scooping up Heather in his arms as he headed for the door. "Angel, put down that book and follow me."

Oh, fuck. What now? she thought, laying her vampire novel on the floor so it wouldn't soak up any soda, and sticking her feet back into her slippers.

"I don't have a choice in this matter," he said, hurrying toward the barn. "But you do. Abby is on her way. She'll drive you to the meeting, wait for you and drive you home. I want to take you, but I can't. I have to help Blaze through this birth. I can't make you go, but I want you to."

"Mom wouldn't have made us go to another city with a stranger," Angel said, knowing her words were blatant manipulation, but if it worked…

"Dr. Jessup told you this peer-counseling thing is something that might help you years from now and can really help when you go to school and people ask you questions about what happened to your mom. I know how important this is and I know I should be the one to take you…"

He's gonna cave. Angel couldn't keep a triumphant smirk from her lips.

Her dad chose that minute to look back at her. She immediately wiped the smile off her face but it was too late. She could tell by the narrowing of his eyes. He speeded up, making her have to trot to keep up—not an easy thing to do in bedroom slippers. Little pebbles kept getting caught under her arches, making her cry out. Her dad ignored her plight.

When they reached the stall in the barn, he sat Heather atop a stack of bales not far from the spot where her stupid kittens lived. He pointed at a second bale and gave Angel a squinty-eyed look that made her stomach tighten nervously. He was really upset. The last time he was this upset with her was the summer before last when she and one of the migrant kids dumped half a bag of concrete in a mud puddle to make adobe bricks. The lye flew up in the kid's eyes and he pitched such a fit you'd have thought he was gonna die. Her dad made her clean it all up wearing big rubber gloves. The worst part was that by then the damn stuff was hard as bricks and twice as heavy.

"Sit," he ordered.

In one neat leap, he cleared the stall gate and resumed his examination of the horse. She was breathing hard and looked really tired. Angel liked horses and felt sorry for the struggling animal, but she wasn't above using the situation to keep from going to Fresno.

"She looks bad," Angel said, choosing an empty bucket, which she turned upside down, for her stool.

"Abby will be here in ten minutes," he said. "Blaze may die in that time, but you two are going to sit still and listen to me."

Angel crossed one knee over the other and drew a few strands of hair between her lips. She knew it bugged him, but that was fine with her. The last thing she wanted was to listen to some stupid story of his.

Normally, she loved his stories—he used to tell her a story every night before bed when she came to stay with him in the summer, but lately his stories all sounded more like lectures. Everything had turned so damn serious since her mother died. Nobody laughed anymore—except Abby. She was almost too damn bubbly. Angel wasn't sure if she liked Abby or not, but she knew she didn't want to ride all the way to Fresno with her. Maybe to go to the mall or something, but not to some disgusting group piss 'n' moan session.

"When I was thirteen," her father said, still examining the mare, "I decided I was going to be the next world-champion roper. I had a pair of boots, some old gloves my dad threw out and a rope I found in the garbage dump. My friend, Marty Smith, lived down the road and his dad had a bunch of horses. He let us ride a couple."

He looked over his shoulder. Angel checked her hair for split ends. Her mother always trimmed her hair. Who's going to trim my hair? she wondered, feeling the beginnings of a stomachache. She'd had a lot of those lately.

Her dad went on with his story. "One old chestnut gelding knew a lot more about roping than I did and I worked with him every day after school. I got to be pretty good, and Marty wasn't half-bad, either.

"We entered the junior roping event in Chowchilla. Marty's dad hauled the horses into town. My mom sewed me a fancy shirt with mother-of-pearl snaps. I felt like I could rope anything that moved—my dog, Homer, was afraid to come out from under the porch 'cause I'd rope him."

Heather giggled; Angel hid her smile behind her hair.

"When we got signed up, I discovered Marty was roping off my horse, which wasn't mine at all, of course. I was madder than hops, but what could I do? They called my name, and I hopped up on the strange horse. When they let go of the calf, I kicked that horse and flew out the gate and proceeded to rope myself right out of the saddle. I fell in a heap right in front of the grandstand."

Angel had been to enough ropings to picture it. She couldn't keep from laughing. The mare made a noise that sounded like a person in pain. Her dad massaged the horse's bulging belly with slow, circular motions.

"Poor Daddy. You lost," Heather said sympathetically.

Angel flashed her a look of contempt. Talk about stating the obvious. "That sucks, Dad. I would have died of embarrassment," Angel admitted.

Her dad gave her a look that said she would have won the

prize if there was one. The tightness around her heart lifted some. She really liked it when he looked at her like that.

"I hid out till Monday, then my mom made me go to school. I had to face Marty, who won my trophy on my horse, and all my friends who saw me eat dirt."

Angel wanted to ask but locked her lips together until Heather asked, "What happened?"

"We had a test in English. I got a B, I think."

"With your friends," Angel exclaimed. God, he could be so dense sometimes. "Did they laugh at you?"

He stopped rubbing the mare and looked at her. "Nope. Marty even came up to me and apologized. Said the trophy should have been mine."

The barn grew silent except for the mare's labored breathing.

Finally, giving in to curiosity, Angel asked, "What's that got to do with us going to this Rainbows thing?"

"I think you're afraid to face these other kids. I was afraid, too, but I found out my fears were a lot worse than reality.

"And, believe it or not, that was the day your mama moved to town. She was just a little bitty thing, three grades younger than me, but she was so pretty all the boys were talking about her. And she smiled at me. Not Marty. Me."

In the distance, the dogs began to bark. Angel's heart jumped. Don't let it be Abby. Not yet. I know I should go, but…

"Doc's here, girl, hang on," Tom whispered to the horse.

He stepped to the gate and looked at first Heather, then her. "Much as I want to, I can't take you girls to Fresno. Abby'll be here any minute. Whether you go with her or not is up to you. I can't make that decision for you, but I hope you'll go."

Angel scowled, not saying a word. She hated it when parents did this—made something her decision, as if he knew all along she'd do the right thing. Heather popped up to her knees and said, "Mommy showed me your picture with all your trophies and your pretty horse. I guess you got better, huh?"

Tom winked at her. "Yep, I did."

"I'm getting better, too, aren't I, Daddy? I didn't wet the bed last night." She looked at Angel, as if waiting for some signal, then she jumped to the ground. "I'll go with Abby, Daddy. Dr. Donna says we'll play games and sing songs like at my old preschool. She'd be sad if I didn't go, even sadder than you. Bye, Daddy. Hope your horsey feels better."

Angel watched her skip off.

"Dork," she muttered under her breath. She looked through the sheet of hair hanging in her eyes. Just as she expected, her dad was giving her that look of expectation, as if he'd be real let down if she didn't do the right thing.

"All right," she growled, scrambling to her feet. "I'll go, but if it sucks as bad as I think it's gonna suck—I'm outta there, even if I have to walk back." She stalked off without waiting for his reply. If she was gonna hang out with a bunch of kids, even loser freaks whose families were more screwed up than hers, she had to look good.

NO TEAR TRACKS, but no smiles, either, Abby thought, watching her young charges exit the door of the hospital meeting room.

"Hey, girls," Abby said, rising stiffly. She'd paced for a while but then managed to immerse herself in work until her butt conformed to the molded-plastic chair.

Angel took Heather's hand and tugged her toward Abby. The twelve-year-old moved dully, with none of her usual verve.

"Ice cream," Abby said decisively. "Grammy always said ice cream was the best thing for a girl's troubles. I think she meant boy troubles, but it'll work for this, too. Let's go. I know just the place."

Abby cut across the still-familiar streets of her old hometown and pulled into a busy parking lot. A pink-and-white storefront spilled a welcoming glow into the dim twilight.

After placing their order, Abby led them to an outside table, sheltered from the cool breeze and noisy traffic by five-foot-tall panels of clear Plexiglas. Fresh air. No hospital smell. She passed out plastic spoons and napkins. "Are you sure one banana split is enough for all three of us?"

Angel smiled for the first time. "I'm not too hungry."

"Okay. Hot-fudge sundaes next time." *If there is a next time. If I don't blow it.* Abby felt way out of her league. This was Donna's job. Abby was a rookie.

A tinny voice crackled her name over a loudspeaker, and Abby jumped. *Ice cream! What was I thinking? I should have driven them straight home. They need their dad. So do I.*

Later, as three spoons dipped into the small, plastic boat of whipped cream, nuts and chocolate-swirl ice cream, Abby asked, "Do you miss the city?"

"Well, duh," Angel said with typical adolescent authority. "Who wouldn't? There's all this cool stuff to do and places to go. Like the mall. And all these cool guys."

"Like Jeremy Shmeramy," Heather teased in a singsong manner.

Angel glared at her, but Heather appeared impervious, perhaps feeling safe in the company of strangers.

"I grew up in this city," Abby told them. "It wasn't quite so big then." She looked up, trying to spot a star through the umbrella of urban lights. "I don't think I could ever move back, even if my folks were still living here. The noise, the traffic." She sighed. "Actually, I envy you living in the country."

"My mom hated the ranch," Angel said. "She said the dust and the animals were much worse than smog."

"Real Daddy says my kitty gets to live in the house, but his brothers and sisters have to live in the barn and eat mice," Heather said, apropos of nothing.

Before Abby could comment on her odd name for Tom, Angel reached across the table and shoved her sister's shoulder, sending a glob of mushy ice cream to the floor. "I told you not to call him that anymore," she seethed. "We don't have two dads anymore. Only one. Can't you get that through your thick head?"

Big tears filled Heather's blue eyes and tumbled down her cheeks. In a small voice that broke Abby's heart, she said, "And no mommy, right?"

CHAPTER SIX

ONE LOOK was all Tom needed to send his heart plummeting.

"Bad, huh?" he asked, pulling Angel into a swallowing hug. That she went with no resistance spoke volumes.

She nodded, her long hair getting squeezed in the fold of his arms. "Ouch."

He loosened his hold and eased back, looking into her eyes. "Want to talk about it?"

She grimaced and shook her head. "I just wanna go to bed. Heather slept the whole way, but Mom always said the copilot's job is to keep the pilot awake." She looked over her shoulder at Abby. "I didn't mean that you'd fall asleep. I just…"

Abby brushed aside her apology with an understanding smile. "You're a terrific copilot. Now, go to bed. Sleep well. You deserve it."

Tom watched his daughter shuffle off like a beaten old woman. "Good grief," he whispered. "What did they do to my girls?"

"It's…everything…I guess…just…coming…together."

Tom spun toward her, expecting to find her in a heap on the floor, but she stood rigidly, as if any movement might be her undoing. Without thinking, he took her elbow and guided her to a chair at the kitchen table. "Coffee. I'll heat up a cup right after I put Heather to bed. Sit. Stay." As soon as he was sure his instructions had penetrated the fog that enveloped her, he dashed to the Honda. Heather sat propped upright by the seat belt with Abby's sweater under her head. He eased open the door and unfastened the seat belt, then lifted his sleeping child.

Dead to the world, Heather didn't open an eye when he carried her into the bedroom and stripped off her stretchy pants and Tigger T-shirt. He left her in underpants and undershirt—knowing there'd be a change of sheets to worry about in the morning—and pulled up the spread, making sure her favorite stuffed rabbit was nearby. He kissed her cheek, noting the traces of dried tears.

An arrow of guilt twisted in his heart. "I love you both," he whispered, then withdrew, leaving the door ajar.

Abby apparently didn't know how to follow instructions. He found her standing in front of his new microwave, seemingly mesmerized by the slowly turning carousel inside the brightly lit box.

"New microwave?" she asked, her back to him.

"Maria threatened to cut off our tamale supply if I didn't buy one. And, I hate to admit it, but the darned thing is handy."

The bell's clang made her jump. He reached around her, being careful not to spook her. "Sit down. I'll carry these cups to the table. You look wiped out, too. What happened?"

He watched the effort it took for her to gather together her reserves. "I see victims at all stages of recovery. I deal with pain and heartbreak every day. I'm a professional," she said, emphasizing the word in a tone that made Tom's eyebrows rise. "I don't understand why this hit me so hard."

She pivoted on the heel of her crepe-soled loafers and walked to the table, but Tom sensed she was on the verge of walking out the door. He waited, hot cups steaming in each hand.

She plopped down in the chair like someone awaiting execution.

Tom set the coffee mug in front of her. “Cream? Sugar? Whiskey?”

A flickering smile almost caught on her lips but faded away.

He pulled out a chair and straddled it so he could look at her. Such a complicated lady. A stranger really, but a person he’d trusted with his most precious treasures, his daughters. What did that say about her? About him?

“I really let the girls down today,” he said, taking a sip of the steaming, hours-old liquid. Its acidic bite felt good. “It was one of the hardest things I’ve ever done.”

She looked up, immediately focusing on his pain, as he knew she would. “Being a single parent is the toughest job there is,” she said with feeling.

“But what does it tell kids when their dad chooses a horse over them?” He’d wrestled with his guilt all afternoon and still didn’t have an answer.

She took a sip of coffee after lightly blowing on it. Lesley always did that, too. “You’ll talk about it tomorrow. They’ll talk about it with Donna. They’ll understand. If not right away, then someday…when they’re parents.”

He sighed, feeling years older than he had that morning. “Is it always gonna be this tough?”

A strangled sound, half laugh, half cry, slipped out before she clapped her hand over her mouth. “You’re asking the wrong person. I blew it and I’m the professional here.”

“What do you mean you blew it?”

She took a deep breath and let it out slowly. “I could tell how frazzled the girls were after the session. It can get pretty intense right at first. Donna and I sat in on the inaugural session last year, and that first day I left feeling flogged—and I was just an observer. Everybody’s in pain or denial or acting out—it’s a little overwhelming, but in a good way because there’s also a sense of relief knowing you can say anything and nobody will shut you down or try to minimize what you're feeling.

"Gradually, the individuals in the group begin to bond and form a cohesiveness, but right at first you're alone and people are asking you to put your fears and pain out there for everyone to see. Very scary stuff."

Tom watched, mesmerized, knowing she was revealing truths about herself she might not even realize.

"Would it have made a difference if I'd been there?"

"Yes." Bald, honest. Typical Abby. "Not in group, of course. They're on their own then. But afterward. You would have handled that better than me. I took them for ice cream." Her tone suggested she'd taken them to a porno flick.

"What's wrong with that? It sounds very nice. Thank you."

She shook her head sadly. "They were wiped out. They needed to be home with their dad. They didn't need some lame placebo. Shows you how much I know about mothering."

"Abby, what happened?"

She stared into her cup. "We were sharing a banana split and talking about living in the city versus living in the country. They'd loosened up a little and even smiled once or twice. Then Heather said something Angel took exception to and… things went to hell in a handbasket, as my grammy used to say. Just like that they were both in tears and I…I was mopping up spilt ice cream, for heaven's sake. I didn't know what to say or how to help.

"Angel ran to the car, and I grabbed Heather and charged after her even though I knew she was embarrassed and wanted to be alone, but I couldn't let her be alone outside. Fresno's a big city and I know what happens to kids when…" She shuddered and looked away. "It was a disaster and it was all my fault. I knew they were emotionally spent and I should have driven them straight home and avoided the whole calamity.

I'm sorry, Tom. You trusted me with your children and I blew it."

Tom's heart twisted precariously. He could fall for this woman who cared so deeply. He could fall hard.

"Come here," he said, standing up abruptly. "I want to show you something."

She followed without protest, even when he picked up a flashlight from beside the door and led her outside. She crossed her arms protectively against the mild evening chill. "Cold?" he asked.

She shook her head.

Liar. He took hold of her elbow—for safety's sake, he told himself—and guided her to the barn. She didn't speak, but Tom felt her tension.

"Life is funny," he said quietly, opening the door of the barn. The hinges groaned their usual protest, and nearby a dog gave a muffled bark. "Here I am kicking myself for being the world's worst dad..." He made a *tsk*ing sound when she started to protest. "And you're feeling bad because you couldn't stop two kids from having a spat." He couldn't help chuckling. "We're a heck of a pair."

She pulled away. Maybe she thought he was trivializing her dilemma.

He flicked off the flashlight; a heating lamp glowed softly within the cavern of one stall. He led her to the light.

"Oh," she cried softly. "They both made it. Look at that beautiful baby. Oh, thank God."

"And you."

She shook her head firmly, sending tears tumbling.

"Abby," he said, wishing she'd look at him, but she kept her focus trained on the horses, "if it hadn't been for you, I would have taken the girls—they are my top priority. I'd have left Blaze to fend for herself. Maybe Doc could have saved her alone, maybe not. It's a pretty safe bet the colt would have died. You gave me an option, which I took. Maybe it wasn't the right choice, but it's what I thought I had to do. The girls have to learn about life on a ranch. This is more than just our livelihood, it's our way of life. The animals are important, and an animal in pain hurts just as much as you or me."

He watched her profile in the gentle glow. Her features were relaxed, softer somehow, as she watched the new mother standing guard over her tiny baby. He imagined what effect the light would have on her eyes. They'd probably reflect the golden light like a harvest moon in a bottomless pool. Tom's fingers itched to reach out, brush back the lock of red satin that framed her jaw, and make her look at him.

Get a hold, man. You're not a kid. You're an adult. He gripped the flashlight, willing himself not to draw her into his arms and kiss her. The night had held enough emotional turbulence for both of them.

He cleared his throat. "I did what I had to do. You went above and beyond the call of duty. What more can anybody ask?"

She didn't respond but Tom thought she seemed less distraught. "Besides," he said, smiling, "you mostly see the girls when they're on their best behavior. Those two fight all the time. They're sisters."

She rewarded him with a grateful smile. "Thank you. I probably overreacted. I've been a little stressed lately. Work, my boss…"

"No, thank *you*. For taking them, for caring, for everything." Despite his resolve, he gave her a hug. Knowing he had to cut his losses, he dropped his arms and turned away. "I'll walk you to your car." With that, they left the confines of the barn and moved toward her vehicle.

Tom aimed the beam of the flashlight on the door handle of the Honda, but she opened it before he could reach it. She slipped behind the steering wheel. Looking up at him, she said, "Talk to the girls. If I truly didn't blow this too badly, I'd be happy to drive to Rainbows anytime you need me." She smiled, an honest, Abby smile. "Believe it or not, Thursdays are my slow day, so I'm usually available. Just give me a call."

Her generosity and bravery touched him profoundly. After tonight's experience, Tom couldn't imagine any woman—except possibly Janey—who would have volunteered so freely. "I will."

When she started to close the door, he held it open. "I forgot to ask. What was the fight about?"

Turning away to reach for her keys, she mumbled, "I don't remember."

She tugged the door closed and gave him a quick wave.

"Liar," he said, when Rosie materialized at his knee. Reaching down to scratch the old dog behind the ear, he told her, "She'd be terrible at poker."

"WELL, HELLO THERE, my long-lost love goddess. Long time no see."

Abby grinned at Max Jessup's effusive greeting. She went into his burly open arms and returned his hug with true affection, giggling when he tried nuzzling his bushy salt-and-pepper beard in her neck. "Hi, Max. Good to see you."

"Are you two at it again?" a familiar voice asked from the entrance of the foyer. "Max, it's Sunday. Bring her inside before you scandalize the neighborhood."

Donna's teasing and her husband's warm greeting lifted a load from Abby's shoulders that had been weighing her down for the past two days. "God, it's nice to be here. Sanctuary. No phones. No people." She hurried to give her friend a hug of equal proportion.

"What are we, chopped liver?" Max asked, his latent

New York accent filtering through the laid-back California humor.

"Friends. Much better than people."

"Hmm." He gave his wife an inscrutable look and told Abby, "I'll catch you at dinner, sugarplum. I've got a little project in the garage that needs my attention. You two lovelies will have to try to get along without me for a couple of hours."

His wife of twenty-some years snorted.

"What sort of project this time?" Abby asked. Max was a high-school teacher who always managed to find a kid in jeopardy and an old jalopy in need of repair and somehow fix them both in the restoration process.

"Fifty-six Ford," he said, grabbing a handful of chocolate-covered peanuts from a cut-glass candy dish sitting on an antique sewing-machine cabinet. Donna's house was filled to the brim with an eclectic jumble of antiques, collectibles and junk. Abby's mother called it Decorating's Black Hole, where all the lost and untreasured went to die.

"And a sixteen-year-old habitual truant," Donna added under her breath.

"He just needed the right teacher," her husband replied. "Why, he only missed three days of school this week, not counting Monday, which was an in-service day."

"Which means he was in school one day?" Abby asked, grinning.

"Yep."

Donna slapped his fingers when he tried for another handful of candy. "We're on a diet, remember? Go get greasy. I know you're never quite happy without grease under your fingernails."

"Diet, schmiet," he said, sneaking two little chunks. "You are perfect just as you are, my sweet. Isn't she perfect, Abby?"

He blew them both kisses then hurried down the hallway toward the garage.

Donna watched him; Abby watched her. What would it be like to be that comfortable with another person for so long? She'd give anything to know, and yet a part of her felt as though her chance of ever having that closeness was inching away each day. Or, in Daniel's case, inching too close every day.

"Let's get a beer and go outside," Donna suggested. "Max said he'd grill the fish later, and I already made a salad, so we can just sit back and relax."

Abby smiled. "Just what the doctor ordered."

Donna poured two Coronas into chilled mugs and added a wedge of lime before handing one to Abby. "After your call Thursday night, I was afraid you might have committed hara-kiri before I got to see you."

Abby shrugged sheepishly. "Slight overreaction, I think. You said the girls were fine when you saw them on Friday, right?"

Donna pushed open the sliding glass doors and led the way to a shady spot beneath the veranda. A kidney-shaped pool and a molded fiberglass spa, housed in a redwood gazebo, competed for space in Donna's mini-rain forest backyard. With a big heart and too much work, she couldn't be bothered with pruning and trimming.

She dropped into a large, cushioned Adirondack chair and nodded for Abby to join her in its mate. "Heather and Angel looked great. Very rested and peppy. Their father, on the other hand, looked a lot like you. Gaunt. Bags under his eyes. Tense. Are you two trying to outdo each other for guilt trip of the century?"

Abby sat down, drawing her bare legs under her. After her third sleepless night in a row, she'd tried to resume her usual Sunday-morning ritual: bagels and cappuccino then weeding and watering her garden. For some reason, the peace she usually found in the earthy flora of her small backyard escaped her.

"Angel called me Friday after work," she told Donna. "She apologized for screaming at her sister in public and making me feel bad. I asked her if her dad made her call me and she said, 'No, but he left your card by the phone when he and Heather went to town to buy groceries.' Wasn't that sweet?"

"She respects you for not telling Tom about the cause of the fight."

"I couldn't do that, it would break his heart."

Donna took a big gulp of beer then leaned back with a sigh. Abby did the same. She felt at peace, until Donna asked, "You worry about the state of his heart, don't you?"

Abby groaned. "Today's Sunday. No psychology allowed. I'm just here for food and booze."

"Occupational hazard. Like you trying to help victims. In my case, it's easy to overlook my own psychological needs. In your case, you run the risk of becoming a victim of your own good nature."

"I'm trying to keep my distance."

Donna reached across the wide arms of the chair and squeezed her arm. "I know you are, but there's a lot of need there right now. It's natural to want to help. I don't want you to get hurt."

"Me, too." *Too late,* a small voice said inside her head.

Both women were silent for a few minutes, then Donna said, "I fell for a client once."

Nonplussed, Abby eyed her friend. "You never told me this."

"It was a long time ago. Right out of college. Before I met Max."

"Who was he?"

"Just a man. A young man. A very attractive, very troubled

young man. He had a sort of Joe Montana-Kevin Costner-esque quality about him." She grinned. "And I was forty…all right, fifty, pounds lighter.

"He came to me because he was depressed. Couldn't eat, couldn't sleep, couldn't achieve sexual gratification either alone or with someone." Donna smiled at Abby. "What really got to me was the way he improved when he was talking to me. His blue eyes would begin to sparkle and he'd grin. It was as if I had the power to bring him back to life. Heady stuff for one so young."

"Did you actually…you know, have sex?"

"Clinically speaking? Yes." Donna, her plump cheeks a shade rosier than normal, grimaced. "I'm not proud of myself and I probably would have lost my license if a dear friend hadn't slapped me upside the head and told me I was crazy."

"Clinically speaking?"

"And every other way. She was in the business, too. She suggested I start him on antidepressants and give him a referral."

"Did it work?"

"Like a champ. And you know the kicker? Once he got better, I discovered he wasn't as attractive as I thought. What I was attracted to was the need, which, in turn, fed my ego. Sobering thought, huh? Want another beer?"

Abby finished the last of hers and rose. "Stay put. I'll get them."

When she returned, she asked, "Why'd you tell me that story?"

Donna shrugged. "Guilt. I've been carrying around that awful truth for all these years and…"

"Bullshit."

She chuckled. "You're human, Abby. Not superhuman. Just plain human. Just like me. Just like the rest of us. You beat yourself up over taking the Butler girls out for ice cream and for feeling attracted to their father when you know you shouldn't be, but the fact is, sometimes you don't have any control over these things."

Abby studied her beer, not wanting to meet her friend's eyes.

"In my case," Donna continued, "I came to my senses in time to avoid any huge mess. My client got well and moved away. I switched to child psychology. A few years later, I got a notice from a psychologist in Houston requesting transcripts of my client's files. By then I was happily married, and I sent those puppies off with pure relief."

"What about my case?" Abby asked, almost afraid to say the words out loud. "What about these feelings I have for Tom? Everything between us has been aboveboard, but there are these weird vibrations and I can't tell if I'm sending them or he is or what?"

"Vibrators? I leave you two alone for a minute and the next thing I know you're talking dirty," Max exclaimed from the kitchen. "Wait for me, damn it. I've got to finish hooking up the battery."

Abby laughed. "God, I wish I'd found him first."

Donna grinned. "Oh, pul…lease, as my teenage clients are wont to say, get real. You've already got three guys—make that two and a half, counting Landon—after you. What do you want with a hairy old fart like Max? By the way, what's the scoop on your big date?"

"Well—" Abby started, thinking back to the source of her second sleepless night.

"Wait," Donna interrupted. "Hold that thought. I want to hear all about it on an empty bladder. I'll be right back."

Abby smiled as she watched her friend shuffle into the house, but the smile faded.

Friday night with Daniel, she thought, what can I say? In a way it was perfect, but—

"Have I told you how lovely you look tonight?" Daniel asked once the waitress delivered the bottle of '94 BV merlot. He raised his glass in toast. "To good times and good friends."

Abby lifted her glass to his. How could she not? He'd been the perfect gentleman from the moment he arrived at her house. He'd opened doors for her, chosen Vivaldi for the drive, and, best of all, kept the conversation in the car light and frivolous. Much to her surprise, she discovered they shared an interest in genealogy, although his family lineage was amazingly well documented, while hers was hit-and-miss. His story of his grandparents' and parents' internment in relocation camps in World War II truly touched her.

They'd arrived at Ducie's early enough to stroll around the grounds and watch families frolic in the waves created by speedboats zipping about in the narrow, man-made lake. The forested hillsides encircling the lake glowed in the early-evening twilight. Abby breathed the clean, crisp air and relaxed for the first time since lunch, when Melina had convinced her the evening was going to be a hot date—with Daniel bent on proving his male prowess to make up for his wife's rejection. So far, it was nothing of the kind. Abby tasted her wine. "This is lovely. Thank you."

"No. Thank you for coming. I really needed some friendly female company. No matter how civilized you think things are going to be, a divorce is never amiable. Suddenly that stupid clock somebody you can't even remember gave you for a wedding present becomes a prized possession. It's crazy."

Abby nodded sympathetically, but she had no personal experience with divorce. Billy died to get out of their relationship, and Landon moved in with another woman. The only household items she and Landon had owned jointly were the bar stools, which Abby liked, and a futon, which Abby hated. Since the futon cost twice as much as the stools, Landon was tickled to have it and leave the stools. Unfortunately,

Abby thought as she sipped her wine, once Daniel opened the subject of his divorce, he couldn't get off the subject. She understood how important it was to him, and she tried to be consoling, but by the time she was finishing her salmon, she'd had her fill of the topic.

"What about dessert?" he asked, smiling warmly.

He truly was a handsome man. She liked him. But she knew now, better than before, that like was as much as there was to it. "I'm stuffed, thank you."

"I thought all women loved dessert. Marilyn would take home half her dinner just so she could have chocolate mousse."

Abby smiled mechanically. Maybe her lack of response finally connected in his brain because he dropped his head and sighed. "I've been a complete boor, haven't I?"

"Of course not."

"Yes, I have. I'm sorry. Can I make it up to you? Can I take you dancing?"

Melina's warning sounded in Abby's head. "Thank you, but I'm not all that energetic on Friday nights. I know that sounds like something my old-maid aunt would say, but it's been a long week at work."

He looked at her pointedly. "Is this about that cowboy and his kids?"

A funny buzz skipped through her chest. "I'm handling the Butler case, but it's just one of several. Roy was out two days with bronchitis, and Melina's got cruise fever, so things are hectic." He didn't say anything, but the inscrutable stare continued. "Why'd you ask about the Butlers?"

His finger tapped the leather folder containing their bill. "I don't know. I've had a sense that you're more…involved with this case than usual."

Abby's heartbeat sped up and her face felt warm. "Perhaps I am. Tom Butler's a friend of Maria Fuentes. Remember her from the Adelina Johnston case? I'm a sucker for kids in pain. What can I say?"

He looked up. "Does the same apply to men?"

Abby's pulse arched off the Richter scale. Did he mean Tom or himself? Fortunately, the waitress returned to pick up the check. While Daniel paid the bill, Abby excused herself to use the rest room.

They made small talk on the way home and he gave her a light peck on the cheek when he dropped her off at her front door.

"Well, girlfriend," Donna said, returning. "Tell me all about it."

Abby put the back of her hand to her forehead theatrically. "Oh, pul…lease, let's not go into that."

"I CALLED HER," Angel said, straddling the threshold of the doorway to her father's workroom.

He was seated on a metal stool at his workbench. She wasn't sure whether to go in or not. They hadn't really talked much since Thursday night. He'd offered, but she hadn't quite forgiven him for making her go to Rainbows, although in all honesty it hadn't been as bad as she'd thought it was going to be. In a way, she liked being able to talk to other kids who'd had some of the same kind of sad things in their lives. One boy, four years older than her, lost both his parents to a murder-suicide. He was living with his grandparents. Talk about sucky.

"Called who?" Tom asked, squinting against the bright sun behind her.

She rolled her eyes. "Abby. You're the one who left her card by the phone. Hint. Hint."

"Oh. That was nice of you. What'd she say?"

"That she was sorry if she contributed to our stress. Like it was her fault I yelled at Heather. Why'd she care?" Angel took a step into the room to escape the heat at her back. She'd forgotten how damn hot this valley got in summer. Val and her mom had talked about putting in a pool this year.

"Abby has a big heart, she cares a lot about everything. Remember what Maria told you about how Abby helped her cousin's family?"

Angel remembered. She'd listened avidly when Maria described her cousin's murder and the custody battle. She didn't know why, but lately she felt as if hearing about other people's problems would make her feel better. Donna told her it was a common reaction to traumatic events, but Angel didn't like the feeling. She planned on bringing it up at the next Rainbows meeting. It wouldn't bother her so much if other people felt the same way.

"Yeah, but I still don't get it. Most people are too busy worrying about their own lives to mess with anybody else's."

Her father looked at her sharply. "Are you suggesting Abby doesn't have a life of her own?"

"No," she said, surprised by his tone. "Abby has a life. She was getting ready for a date when I called."

"A date?"

Angel studied her father. He was trying to act indifferent, but Angel could tell he wasn't happy with her news. *Is he interested in Abby? She is pretty, but…* Angel let the thought go. She wasn't sure how she felt about the idea of her father dating. Even someone as nice as Abby. She'd have to think about it.

"Yeah, but she didn't sound too happy about it," Angel finally said. "When I asked her who the guy was, she said, 'An accident waiting to happen.'"

He shrugged his shoulders and made a grumbling sound. Definitely interested.

Angel stepped closer to see what he was doing. His big hands moved quickly, hammering tiny nails into a hunk of suede that was stretched on a wooden board. "Whatcha doing?"

"Stripping."

She giggled. The sound made her feel foolish, but his grin made her relax and smile back. "Eventually," he told her, "I'll braid the strips into reins, and after I tool a headstall and side pieces, I'll have a bridle. Miguel's daddy-to-be present. Do you want to learn how?"

Angel shrugged, determined not to look too interested. "I guess so. Might as well. Heather can't take her eyes off that damn colt and it's getting hot outside. Guess I got nothing better to do."

"Well, pull up a stool." He helped her uncover the only one in sight and draw it right up beside his. "I used to do this with my dad. I wish you could have known your Grandpa Walt. He died the Christmas before you were born. I always felt bad about that. He would have loved you something fierce."

Angel had to squeeze the hunk of leather he handed her real tight so she wouldn't cry. Fortunately, her dad changed the subject by the time he handed her a sharp little blade fitted into a wooden handle that was wrapped with a grubby, slightly sticky gauze. Without tears in her eyes, she'd be a lot less likely to make either of them bleed.

CHAPTER SEVEN

ABBY TURNED OFF the engine but didn't get out of the car right away. No dogs jumped up to scratch her door. The Butler homestead seemed oddly quiet considering she'd been invited specifically to help mitigate the first visit from Val, but it was a welcome sight to her eyes. The previous Thursday's Rainbows meeting after the long holiday weekend had been canceled, so Abby hadn't seen the Butler family in over a week.

Tom had called Abby the Monday after that disastrous first session and said both girls had pleaded with him to ask Abby to be their designated driver every Thursday. She wasn't sure she believed him, but Donna insisted it was natural for young girls to crave adult female companionship. With Maria preparing for both a baby and a move and Janey caught up in a health crisis, Abby was a likely candidate.

Abby had accidentally bumped into Janey the Friday before Memorial Day. She'd driven out to the ranch to drop off a bag of decorating magazines she kept forgetting to leave for the girls. When she parked in the semicircle in front of Tom's house, she saw Angel sitting on the stoop beside a gray-haired woman, their heads bent over a nest of brightly colored plastic lacing.

Abby didn't want to interrupt, but the older woman waved her over. "Hello there," she hailed warmly. Although the temperature was above ninety, the woman, who was about the same size and build as Angel, wore a two-piece jersey jogging suit that made Abby feel even hotter in her wilted linen suit.

The outfit's heather-gray tone almost matched the woman's short-cropped, thinning curls. "You must be the wonderful Abby I've heard so much about."

Abby blushed, but the woman's words seemed sincere. "I can't imagine where you heard that."

"Little birds, I think," she said, making a fluttering motion with her thin, graceful hands. One hand stopped midflutter and thrust toward Abby. "I'm Janey Hastings."

Abby shifted the plastic bag to her other hand and reached out to shake hands. Janey Hastings's touch was cool but her grip forthright. "Abby Davis."

"I've been looking forward to meeting you, Abby Davis, ever since Maria suggested Thomas go see you. She can't say enough nice things about you. Took a judge to make Thomas go, though. For a smart man, he doesn't follow instructions too well, does he?" She looked at Angel for confirmation.

"Nope," Angel said, grinning.

"Most men are reluctant to ask for help," Abby said, rising to Tom's defense before she realized Janey was teasing. A warm blush claimed her cheeks when she noticed Janey eyeing her thoughtfully. "Um, what are you two doing?" Abby asked.

Angel held up a length of colorfully plaited plastic, the individual strands trailing behind like stiff ribbons. "Janey's teaching me how to make lanyards. For key rings and stuff."

The finely webbed lines around Janey's hazel eyes deepened with her smile. She possessed an ageless beauty that seemed only slightly muted by illness. Tom had mentioned Janey's battle with cancer when he explained about the ownership of the ranch. Abby was heartened to see the sparkle in the older woman's eyes at Angel's obvious enthusiasm for the project.

"I learned this back when I was younger than this girl," Janey said, looping a thin arm around Angel's shoulders.

Angel's youth and vitality contrasted with a pallor and frailty that didn't come from age alone.

"Of course, back then the gimp was made out of leather," Janey said.

"Gimp?" Abby repeated, moving close enough to touch the thin, flat strands of purple and orange.

Angel ran her fingers through the rat's nest of plastic. "The string. Janey's friend gave her a bag of crafts to do at the hospital, and she brought some of them home to teach us."

Janey's mouth slanted in a wry grin. "My friend told me the reason I never used plastic when I was young was because it hadn't been invented yet. Some friend, huh?"

Abby laughed. "I have a friend like that, too."

Angel frowned, although Abby didn't understand why. Before she could ask, Angel said, "I'm making a necklace and ankle bracelet for Heather for her birthday in August." She consulted the sporty watch on her wrist then rose gracefully. "I'd better go hide this before Dad and Heather get back from checking the water gates. I'll bring it over to your house tomorrow, Janey, and we can work on it then, okay?"

"Not too early, please. I just can't seem to get going in the mornings anymore," Janey said, looking frustrated.

Abby hefted the bag in Angel's direction. "I've been carting these magazines around for a week. Melina's aunts and cousins keep our waiting room stocked. There are some fashion ones I thought you'd like and a couple of things for Heather."

Angel's smile was quick. "Thanks," she said, clutching the bag to her chest. After giving Janey a quick hug, she dashed off toward the barn.

"What a sweetheart! But she's hurting more than she lets on," Janey said, rising a bit unsteadily. "I wish I could be around more to help them through this."

"Are you okay?" Abby asked.

Janey clasped the single upright post and shook her head.

"As good as can be expected with all the poisons they've poured into this old body. But if it kills the bad cells then I guess I can put up with a little nausea and dizziness." Her face took on a stern look. "Doesn't mean I plan to give up my way of life, though. Ed thinks he can coddle me into staying home instead of helping out with the roundup this weekend, but he's wrong. Haven't missed one in forty-odd years. Don't plan to start now." That was the first Abby heard of the annual roundup that would take place in the foothills. The excitement in Janey's voice had made Abby long to be a part of the festivities, but, naturally, she hadn't been invited. Why would she be?

"Abby's here," a high-pitched voice sang out, jarring Abby out of her reverie and back into the present.

Abby opened the car door and got out just in time for a small, compact body to hurl itself into her arms. Slightly overwhelmed by Heather's unexpected exuberance, Abby hugged her tightly and planted a kiss on top of her sweet-smelling curls.

"We been waiting. Did you bring the 'Tucky Fried?"

"Yep, and potato salad and coleslaw and biscuits. It's all in a cooler in the trunk."

"Come here." Heather tugged on Abby's hand, leading her to a frayed, nylon-webbed chaise longue plunked beneath the front yard's lone mulberry tree.

"We went to a roundup," Heather said, once the two were seated in the small, scratchy space. Her words were delivered with the solemnity of a sermon.

"Really?" Abby said, equally reverent.

"Yep, 'n' me 'n' Daddy sleeped right on the ground," Heather said, more animated than Abby had ever seen her. "Everybody else sleeped in tents, but me 'n' Daddy were real cowboys. With stars and cows for company."

Abby pictured the scene. An ache behind her breastbone

reminded her of the time her family went camping at Lake June and left her home with her grandmother. "You're too little, Abby. The mosquitoes will eat you alive," Abby's mother had explained. Grammy did her best to entertain Abby, but the sense of being left out had stuck with her a long time.

"Weren't you afraid of spiders and snakes and bugs?" Abby asked.

Heather's white-gold curls bounced back and forth. "Nope. Daddy put down a big blue tarp first. He said spiders and snakes were scared of plastic."

"Really?" Abby said. "I didn't know that."

The little girl nodded seriously, squeezing a bit more space out of the lawn chair they shared.

"Did you like sleeping under the stars?"

"Yes, but the frogs were noisy." She croaked theatrically.

Abby's heart swelled; she couldn't believe how good it felt to be snuggled next to this little munchkin. "Where'd Angel sleep?"

"In a tent." Heather wrinkled her nose disdainfully. "With the other girls."

"What other girls?"

"Anna and Rachel. Janey and Ed's granddaughters."

"Oh, right." Tom had mentioned Ed's son and his family were coming from Colorado to help with the roundup. "How old are they?"

"Old." Heather fingered a tiny embroidered rose on the lapel of Abby's sleeveless, denim blouse. "They go to college. But they were real nice. They want me 'n' Angel to come visit them sometime. They live near some mountains and..."

Peripherally, Abby saw Tom round the corner of the house; he came to an abrupt halt when he spotted them. She didn't have a chance to read his look since Heather's reaction to seeing him was a high-pitched squeal of joy. "Daddy."

"There you are, my little baked clam," Tom growled in his

best Big Bad Wolf imitation. "I've been looking for a sweet neck to nibble on." He charged forward, arms outstretched.

Heather clasped her arms around Abby's neck, nearly strangling her, but Heather's daddy was quicker. He scooped her up and tossed her in the air. "Gimme a bite," he cried, eliciting peals of laughter.

"No, Daddy, no. Let me down. I'm gonna wet my pants."

He set her down contritely. "Sorry, punkin."

She wiggled away, then stuck out her little pink tongue. "Just kidding. Ha. Ha. Fooled you." She dashed away toward the construction zone to the left of the house—the renovations were progressing well—ducking under the yellow Caution tape flapping in the midmorning breeze.

"Go clean out the litter box," he called after her.

Shaking his head in hopelessness, he dropped into the second, ancient chaise longue. It creaked in protest. "Hi," he said, closing his eyes and heaving a big sigh. "I didn't hear you drive up. The dogs must have recognized your car."

Abby had a hard time forming a reply. He looked good—way too good. More relaxed than the last time she saw him, which had been when he'd shown her the new foal. Since then the sun had done nice things to his hair, which was growing out to a less military style, and the pale strip above his upper lip matched the rest of his face's healthy tan.

He'd swapped his usual cotton shirt for a black jersey T-shirt that sported an image of Garth Brooks on it. Evidence, no doubt, that Angel had carried through with her threat to perk up his wardrobe. Abby liked how it emphasized his muscular torso.

"I'm here." Well, duh, as Angel says.

He turned to face her and seemed mesmerized by something on her lips. She licked them to make sure her lipstick wasn't messed up from Heather's exuberant buss.

He sat up suddenly, swinging his legs over the side of the

chaise to face her. "I really appreciate your coming. It's not a big deal, really—Val and I have always gotten along reasonably well, but it's his first time up here since—"

Abby understood, perhaps better than she should. She could almost feel his ambivalence about welcoming this man, this "other" daddy, into the world he was trying to create for his daughters.

"I wouldn't have bothered you if Ed and Janey were around, but Ed had to take Janey back to Stanford for another treatment."

No hat to shade his eyes. Abby couldn't help noticing how the cloudless sky intensified the blue of his eyes. Way better than Paul Newman. She made herself look down. Sneakers instead of boots. Why does that make him more approachable?

"By the way, Janey said to tell you thanks for the flowers."

Abby shrugged, trying to keep her mind on the conversation. "My roses seem to thrive on neglect and cat poop." His chuckle twanged some errant chord inside her rib cage. "I really enjoyed meeting Janey. She reminds me of my grandmother. How's she doing?"

"Pretty good, but she tires easily and it really ticks her off. They had to come back early from the roundup, but Ed told Janey her body needed pampering, not sleeping in a camper." His rueful smile made certain body parts hum. "Lord, she hates it when Ed's right."

Abby looked away, blinking at the faintly visible outline of mountains. "Nice day, isn't it?" she asked inanely.

"We didn't pull you away from anything important, did we?" Tom asked, watching her face.

"No. Not really. I finally broke down and hired a gardener, so my weekends are a bit more relaxed."

A serious look pushed down on his flaxen eyebrows. "Can I ask you something personal?"

The gentleman, again. "Sure."

His Adam's apple rose and fell. "Are you seeing someone?" An endearing blush colored the hollows of his cheeks. "Angel told me that's the proper way to put it these days."

Am I? Do two dinner dates and one closed-mouth kiss qualify? Daniel had invited her to accompany him and his daughter and new son-in-law to Reno over the Memorial Day weekend, but she'd declined because of her traditional family get-together—one she'd have dumped in a heartbeat if someone had invited her to a roundup.

"You don't have to answer."

She brushed aside his disclaimer with a backhanded motion. "I'm still thinking. My boss is going through a divorce and he's asked me out a couple of times, but…"

Tom frowned. "People going through a divorce are dangerous," he said with feeling. "I know. I was hell on wheels."

Abby sat up, too. Their knees, hers bare, his in faded denim, almost touched. "You? You're too much of a gentleman."

"No such animal when your wife up and leaves you. I partied hardy for the better part of a year. Stomped on a couple of hearts along the way, too." He looked sad, and more than a little sheepish.

"I'm sure you didn't mean to hurt anyone."

"'Course not, but that doesn't help when it's your heart that's been stomped on."

Abby felt privileged to be the recipient of such heartfelt truths and replied in kind. "After Landon moved out, I went just the opposite way—I didn't even want to think about dating."

"He hurt you bad."

She looked at Tom's hands, loosely clasped between his knees. Powerful hands, toughened by life, yet gentle. "No. Landon's a great guy—fun-loving, gregarious, but after a while it was like being involved with the social director of a cruise ship. He'd come home at 3:00 a.m. singing Eagles songs, and I'd drag in at the same time after counseling a family whose child had been killed by a drunk driver. It just didn't work."

"What's the new guy like?"

"Daniel?" Abby thought a moment. "Suave, articulate, intense. He takes his job as seriously as I do mine, but I always feel as though he has another agenda. It's the politician in him."

Tom's face soured. "Never had much use for those types, 'specially after what happened with Heather."

Abby knew all too well the frustration of plowing through the red tape of most criminal courts—a system even more convoluted when a child was involved.

Before she could stop herself, she reached out and clasped his forearm. His skin radiated warmth; bundled muscles bespoke strength and power. "At least they're here now, and safe."

"Dad," Angel called from inside the house, her tone oddly flat, "Val just called on his cell phone. He's turning off 99. He says he'll be here in ten minutes."

Abby jumped to her feet as if doused by a bucket of cold water. She moved back, giving Tom space to stand. He looked at her curiously before walking toward the house. Abby followed, wiping her sweaty palms on the backs of her khaki walking shorts.

"So," she said, bending down to pet Rosie before hurrying to catch up with Tom, "you had a big roundup last weekend."

They skirted the bright, unblemished concrete slab, which looked too small to possibly match the dimensions on the plan. She'd never ceased to marvel at this optical illusion.

Tom moved without haste, surveying the work. Tilting his head, he eyed it as if imagining the finished product...or, perhaps, picturing it through the eyes of the man who'd married his ex-wife.

"A few weeks behind schedule, but between Ed and Janey's troubles and mine..." His broad shoulders rose and fell. "It worked out."

"What do you do at a roundup—other than the obvious, rounding up animals?" She sensed his tension and wished there were some way to soften the impact of this upcoming meeting.

"Brand, inoculate, castrate."

"Sounds charming."

"And tasty." He grinned at the face she made.

God, she liked his smile.

She made herself look away and saw Heather clamber to the top rail of the horse corral to scout for Val's vehicle. Abby returned the little girl's exuberant wave.

"Heather's sure excited," she said neutrally, knowing there was no easy way to get through this meeting. "The girls haven't seen their stepfather since the funeral, right?"

Tom squatted near a stand of copper pipes thrust through the concrete like amputated fingers. "He calls about once a week."

"Do you get the feeling Angel isn't quite as enthusiastic about this visit?"

Tom lifted one shoulder. "Sometimes I don't know what's going on in her head. She keeps everything inside. Has she said anything to Donna?"

Abby shook her head. "I don't know. The only thing she ever said to me was that her mother should never have left home that night in the first place." Abby sighed, remembering the months after Billy died. "It's natural to want someone to blame for what's happened. Maybe she blames Val."

He made a soft sound that made her ask, "Do you blame him?"

He looked away. When he answered, his voice was low and troubled. "No more than I blame myself."

She knew that feeling, and she also knew better than to cover it up with empty platitudes. "Do you know anything more about the guy they arrested?"

Tom hunched over slightly, as if warding off a blow. "The girls are always around when Val calls, and I don't know how much to tell them. What do you think?"

She wasn't prepared for such a direct question. "Donna tells parents that as long as they're open, children will ask what they need to know when they need to know it."

"I just wish it was all behind us," he said tersely. Rising abruptly, he turned and walked away.

Abby didn't follow. She leaned against the wall of the house, letting the heat penetrate to the knot of tension between her shoulder blades. With her eyes closed she could almost picture the completed addition. The girls would begin painting and decorating, Tom would pretend to be overwhelmed. And where would Abby be? Back at college? Stuck in her same old rut at work? With Daniel? Alone?

"What about Val?"

Abby's eyes flew open; her heart jolted. Tom stood opposite her, barely a foot away, intently studying her face. She couldn't imagine how so large a man could move so quietly. "What?"

"What do we do about Val? Where does he fit in?"

Abby understood what he was asking. This wasn't about territory or custody. Tom would do what was best for his daughters even if it meant welcoming his ex-wife's second husband into his life. "I'd say play it by ear. Let the girls decide. Maybe he'll be a kind of uncle, an old friend of the family who made them happy once upon a time, a fatherlike figure they can rely on when their real father doesn't understand them."

His frown segued into a scowl. "Believe me, Tom, no father understands his daughters all the time."

His scowl looked both fierce and endearing. She smiled to lighten the mood. "I speak from thirty years of experience, Tom." She pushed off from her resting place and paced, her leather sandals making sandpaper sounds on the smooth concrete. "My folks were at my brother's house for Memorial Day. Do you know what my dad said to me at the table in front of my teenage niece and nephew?"

Tom, who paced beside her, shook his head.

"He told me, 'You know, Abby, women over thirty have a better chance of getting hit by a car than getting married.' My poor sister-in-law nearly choked to death on a bite of blueberry pie."

She detected a smile trying to worm its way onto his lips. "He loves you."

"I know, but it was humiliating." She fought her own smile, but it overpowered her self-righteous indignation. Laughing together, Tom looped his arm, companionably, across her shoulders. Where that friendly gesture might have led, she'd never know, because at that moment the dogs began barking. Val had arrived.

ANGEL PLOPPED BACK DOWN on the lumpy sofa. She covered her face with a corduroy throw pillow that smelled faintly of her father, faintly of dust. Could a person smother oneself to death? she wondered. Probably not, some sort of self-protective system would kick in at the last minute, she decided. Too bad.

Her deep sigh warmed the space around her lips. She knew she couldn't stay hidden forever. She wasn't a silly kid like Heather who still couldn't play hide-and-seek worth beans. Heather always hid in the last place Angel did. Talk about unoriginal.

Unfortunately, there were no good hiding places on the ranch that her father couldn't find. Besides, Angel knew she was expected to help welcome Val to their home. Her dad had even invited Abby over to make it one big happy family.

Angel didn't understand that move. Not that she had anything against Abby. Abby was a nice person who tried very hard not to make waves, kinda like Heather. It had been Angel's idea to make Abby the driver to the Rainbows thing each week. It beat the hell out of listening to country music in her dad's crappy old truck. Abby let them choose the music, although last time she brought a cool book on tape, *Julie of the Wolves,* that really made the trip fly.

Nope. Angel didn't mind Abby's presence, even today when Val was coming. She figured her dad needed a little extra reinforcement in case something ugly happened, like if Angel found the keys to Ed's gun rack and shot Val.

"Damn," Angel swore, scrunching her face to keep the tears back. She liked Val, maybe even loved him once, but if he hadn't had a fight with her mother that night, Lesley would still be alive.

"SINCE WHEN does Santa Claus drive a sport utility vehicle?" Tom muttered, reaching into the cavernous opening for yet another box. Abby, who seemed to have affixed herself to his side since Val's arrival, let out a small laugh.

"He is sort of a one-man Toys for Tots," she said, her voice low, even though Val and Heather were thoroughly occupied on the lawn unpacking yet another crateful of goodies. Angel sat in a lawn chair, a small box of personal trinkets between her knees. She'd been unusually subdued today, and Tom was worried about her.

He was worried about a lot of things. "Where am I going to put all this cra…stuff?"

Dropping the box in place, Tom reversed positions and

plopped his butt down on the threshold, inhaling a whiff of "new car" smell. Thirty grand. Minimum. Where did Val…? He put the thought aside, catching the speculative look on Abby's face.

She saw too much, and cared too much, and, damn, he liked her.

"The barn?" she suggested, tacking on a smile that made him tuck his hands under his butt. "It's the size of a small castle."

Using the respite to stretch muscles taxed by all the lifting and carrying, she arched her back, massaging her neck with one hand. Nothing about her conservative shorts and neatly pressed blouse cried "sexy," but the whole package—tousled hair, sun-kissed cheeks and radiant glow from pitching in where needed—made him ache to touch her.

The moment he'd seen her sitting with Heather, Tom realized how much he'd missed her—not that it came as any big surprise. Despite his best efforts to the contrary, he'd found himself thinking about her throughout the holiday weekend, alternately kicking himself for lacking the guts to invite her and congratulating himself on dodging a bullet.

He knew any kind of emotional involvement was out of the question at this point in his life, but the temptation to see her had overridden common sense when he asked her to join them for Val's visit.

A cursed weakness, his father would have called it. "We Butlers are accursed with two weaknesses, son," his father once told him. "Pride and fancy. We pride ourselves on always fancying the wrong women." Tom hadn't believed him, even after Lesley, but now he was beginning to wonder.

"Lose the scowl," she advised, turning back to the yawning mouth of the shiny black vehicle. "Here they come."

"I'm not scowling."

She peeked at him. "No, actually, that's more of a 'Meet

me outside with your six-shooter' look, isn't it?" Her grin was too infectious to resist.

"What's so funny?" Angel asked, squeezing between them.

"Your dad's concerned about space since the addition won't be done for a few more weeks. I volunteered to store the video games and computer at my house."

"No way!" Angel started to pout until she caught Abby's wink. "If anything, you can store Heather's Barbies. She's got like six million."

Heather, hand firmly tucked in her stepfather's, was close enough to hear that comment and let out a cry. "That's not fair."

Tom rolled his eyes. "Time out. Abby was kidding. Since Val was nice enough to bring all this stuff, we'll find a place for it. But, some of it will have to stay in boxes until the addition is finished. Otherwise, there won't be room for us. So, pick out a few things that can fit in your room and we'll put the rest in a safe place in the barn, temporarily." He stressed the last word to short-circuit any tantrums.

To his surprise, both girls looked at Abby, then meekly sighed, "Okay."

After the last box was unloaded, Tom offered Val a beer.

"Great," Val said. "How 'bout you, Abby? Will you join us?"

Kneeling in the midst of what looked like a giant yard sale, she looked up, a fistful of Barbie-doll clothes in one hand, three of the long-tressed dolls in the other. So far, Heather hadn't been able to narrow down her selection to less than ten dolls. "Sure. Thanks. It's getting pretty warm," she said with a smile.

Always the ladies' man, Tom thought petulantly, before turning toward the house for the beers. What is it about that guy that pisses me off?

His designer clothes, for one thing, Tom thought. Angel, who seemed to be having a hard time giving her stepfather the time of day, practically gushed about Val's navy knee-length shorts and yellow, white and navy blue polo shirt. Tom didn't get it, but that didn't surprise him. What did surprise him was his reaction to the abundance of boxes Val had brought. Tom knew ahead of time Val planned to bring the remainder of the girls' clothes and possessions, but it shook him to the core to realize how much stuff his daughters owned—more than he'd ever thought of possessing. The rift between their two worlds seemed wider than the Grand Canyon. How can I possibly make this work?

Tom took three beers and two sodas from the refrigerator shelf and headed back outside, letting the screen door bounce closed behind him. Val sat at the weathered redwood picnic table, his back to Tom. His arms moved expressively, highlighting some story to Abby, who watched, rapt, directly across from him. Tom couldn't quite stifle a surge of jealousy.

He handed each girl a soda then plunked two cans on the table before his guests. Abby eyed him, puzzled. He took a long swig of beer before sitting down beside Val—not his first choice, but the smart one.

"I was just telling Abby about the drive up. A maniac in a little red RX7 zipped in and out of traffic about ninety miles an hour. An accident waiting to happen. I expected to see it upside in the ditch, but a few miles down the road, the car was pulled over with two highway patrol units behind it and they had the driver in handcuffs." He paused dramatically. "It was a kid. He couldn't have been much older than Angel, sixteen max. Scary, isn't it?"

"What scares me is the fact that the kid's parents probably bought him that car," Abby said, popping open the tab on her beer can. "A lot of parents think they can buy a kid's love with things. But all the stuff in the world can't replace a parent's attention and discipline and love."

Val sat back as though she'd hit him, and Abby suddenly looked stricken, apparently realizing how her words might be taken in light of all the toys and gifts strewn across the lawn.

"I…I didn't mean you, Val. This is entirely different. These girls have been through something extraordinary, and what you've done is very generous and kind. I meant parents who abdicate the role of parenting and try to make up for it with…"

He waved off her explanation. "I know what you're saying and I agree. I know a lot of people like that. Lesley used to give me a hard time about my gift giving, but the truth is I'm just a compulsive shopper." He shrugged. "When I see something I think the girls would like, I buy it for them. I did the same with Lesley.

"After she passed away, I ran across three or four things I'd bought for her but hadn't had a chance to give her. A sapphire ring in a platinum setting. She would have loved it." His dark eyes misted and he looked away.

In the beginning, Tom had been prepared to hate the man Lesley married, but he could never quite manage it in light of Val's earnest need to please. The man positively bent over backward to be nice to Tom.

"How have you been getting along?" Tom asked, surprised to find he actually cared. "Business okay?"

Val shrugged. Physically, he was Tom's match, but something about Val's weight-lifter build seemed contrived, as if the muscles were for show only. He wore his thinning black hair slicked back from his high forehead and gathered in a ponytail at the nape of his neck. For the first time, Tom noticed a few strands of silver threading through it.

"It was touch-and-go for a while," Val said soberly. "I

honestly didn't know if I'd be able to swing it. Les ran the daily show while I focused on marketing and promotions. She handled the books, contracts, employees, all that.

"Fortunately, Les's assistant, Bridget, kept a lid on things until I could take over. I just promoted her to assistant manager." Tom couldn't interpret his smile, but something made him wonder if Val had a personal interest in the woman. It wouldn't surprise him. Val didn't strike Tom as the kind of man who could stand to be alone for long.

Abby leaned forward, resting her elbows on the table. A modest pose, but from Tom's angle a gap between buttons exposed a tantalizing wisp of lace. The view, combined with an occasional hint of floral perfume, made him miss her question.

"What did you say?" he asked.

Her well-defined eyebrows arched.

"She asked the name of my business," Val answered, oblivious to Tom's muddle. "Fitness West, One and Two. We carved a pretty nice little niche for ourselves, but I have to admit, most of it was Lesley. She had this ability to read what people wanted before they knew what they wanted." He beamed with pride. "She introduced step aerobics before anyone else—even designed and marketed her own steps."

Tom frowned. It always surprised him, and hurt a little, to find out things about Lesley he wouldn't have dreamed possible. When she was his wife, she barely managed to balance the checkbook. How could he have been so blind to her capabilities and needs? No wonder he lost her.

"Dad?" Angel called from beneath the tree. "Can we keep the boom box?"

"It's yours from last Christmas, remember?" Val answered before Tom could say anything.

A spear of pain twisted in Tom's gut. He tried to keep it

from showing, but the look of sympathy in Abby's eyes told him he wasn't successful.

"Oops," Val said. "Sorry. Old habit, I guess."

Tom shrugged. "No problem."

He twisted on the redwood bench seat to see what Angel was talking about. The molded plastic box in her hands looked ominous, like something gang members would hoist around in the mall. "We'll give it a try. But let's put a limit on the number of records you bring in."

"Records?" she exclaimed. "Nobody listens to records anymore."

"Tapes, then."

She rolled her eyes dramatically.

Tom looked to Abby for help.

"CDs," she mouthed softly.

"Ten CDs apiece. And nothing with bad language." He made his voice as stern as possible. He couldn't save much face, but he'd try for a little.

With the girls bickering over CD titles, Tom asked Val, "Any news about the suspect in Lesley's murder? What's the district attorney doing?"

Val's features hardened. "That bozo. I talked to my lawyer on Friday to see if we could sue for incompetence."

Abby sat forward. "It's a long frustrating process, Val, but it has to be done right or the defendant could walk."

Tom wondered if her defense came from feelings for her boss.

"Well, believe me, if the slimeball walks, he won't get far," Val said, tersely.

Abby reached out with both hands and covered Val's clenched fists. "Val, a terrible person took someone very special from you, but don't give him anything else. If you let your need for revenge consume you, he'll have taken your life, too."

All of a sudden Val's composure crumpled, tears welled up in his eyes and he dropped his head in his hands. "It's my fault. He killed her but it's my fault she was out there in the first place." Tom looked toward his daughters. Heather had disappeared but Angel sat frozen, staring at her stepfather, a look of anguish on her face.

"Val—" Tom started, but Abby shook her head.

"It's natural for survivors to blame themselves," she said softly.

"No," the anguished man cried. "You don't understand. We had a fight. Les thought I was having an affair. She took the girls and left because she was too upset to be around me. She said she couldn't bear to look at me."

Tom felt his gut twist. A part of him wanted to grab Val on Lesley's behalf and shake the truth out of him. A more rational part understood all too well the daily makeup of a marriage, its highs and lows. He and Lesley had had their share of fights.

"Val, I won't ask you if you deserved it," Tom said, but before he could finish, Angel sprang at her stepfather, hitting him with her fists.

"Well, I will. Did you do it, Dad? Did you? Were you sleeping around? Is that why my mom is dead?" she cried, pounding her fists against his hunched shoulders.

Tom caught her hands in his and pulled Angel to him, soothing her struggles just as he did Heather's troubled nightmares. "Calm down, Angel-babe, it's okay. Let it go."

Val turned to them, one hand hovering inches from Angel's shuddering back. "No, Ang, I didn't do it, but I was thinking about it, and that makes me sick to my stomach." His face twisted. "There was a girl at the club, a new member. I—your mom knew me like a book, and she knew I was looking and she wasn't about to let me get away with it."

He gave a rough, hurtful laugh. "At first, I was mad at your mom, but as soon as she left, I realized what a fool I was. I was married to the greatest woman in the world. I had the perfect family and I put it all in jeopardy because of a cute body." Tom glanced at Abby; her eyes were filled with sadness.

"I was writing out my apology—you know how much your mom loved seeing things in writing—" a ghost of a smile touched his lips "—when the police knocked on the door."

Tom felt Angel's breath catch and hold. He loosened his grip. She wiped her tear-soaked face with her hands—a little-girl gesture that made his heart twist. "Can I see it?"

Val looked at his hands. "I burnt it. Along with my hair cream and—some other things. I was stupid, Angel. I don't deserve your forgiveness because I'll never forgive myself, but I hope you won't hate me forever."

Angel looked at Tom with a softening he remembered seeing in her mother's eyes. Lesley's nature thrived on drama—they'd had their shouting matches, too, but the making up was always worth it because Lesley had too big a heart to hold a grudge for long.

Then Angel looked at Abby. "They told me at Rainbows that blame kills people from the inside out," she said.

Abby smiled softly and nodded encouragingly. "When there's no changing something, you have to let go so it doesn't eat you up."

Angel put her hand on Val's shoulder. "One guy in the group is only seventeen but he's got an ulcer. His brother died in a car wreck. They'd been drinking and smoking pot. The other brother was driving, but my friend still blames himself for not dying, instead." She shook her head, the long tresses dancing like a sheet of fine silk. "Mom wouldn't want you to blame yourself forever." Her lips turned up a fraction. "Maybe a couple of years, but not forever."

Val blinked back tears and pulled her into a hug.

For once, Tom felt no competition, no angst. Angel had enough love to share with both her fathers. He should have known that all along.

CHAPTER EIGHT

"WAL-MART."

"Toys 'R' Us."

Why did I think I could handle this? Abby silently groaned, listening to the argument between Heather and Angela escalate. Taking the girls shopping for a baby gift had been her bright idea, but suddenly Abby felt way out of her league.

"The mall," Abby stated assertively. "Most of the stores there are in Modesto, too, and Maria can exchange anything she doesn't need."

Angel huffed moodily. "Wal-Mart's cheaper."

"Toys 'R' Us has more stuff," Heather grumbled.

"But I'm driving, and you're giving me a headache."

That quieted them down. For their ages, both Butler girls showed remarkable empathy. Abby attributed that to their dad. She'd never met a man as sensitive to her thought patterns and emotions. When she'd called to invite the girls shopping, he suggested they wait until she'd had time to recuperate from Friday's court date. That he even recalled her casual mention of the victim statement she was scheduled to deliver for a non-English-speaking family blew her away.

"Sorry, Abby," Angel said sheepishly. "Are you all right?"

Abby waved off her concern. "Fine. Just a little tired. It was a crazy week at work."

Friction at work—an undercurrent generated by Daniel's attention—added to her tension, but Abby was honest enough to admit that the birth of Maria and Miguel's new son, Aurelio Miguel, on Wednesday, had triggered old angst, and a new, disturbing reaction—envy. Dueling conflicts battled in her mind. "Why not me?" one side cried. "You had your chance and blew it," the other side taunted.

"So," Abby said, hoping to rekindle some spark of enthusiasm in her young charges, "did you talk to Maria? Is he the most beautiful baby ever born?"

"We saw him," Heather said from the back seat. "Daddy took us to the hosp'tal. He's red and really ugly, but Maria likes him."

Abby glanced in the rearview mirror. Heather's outfit consisted of an eye-straining combination of hot-pink shorts with a violet-and-orange-striped tank top. At least she'll be easy to spot in a crowd, Abby thought.

Summer vacations traditionally meant swimming parties, slumber parties, family vacations. What would it mean to Tom and his daughters? she wondered, recalling the way Angela had showed off her independent study report card as if it were a "get-out-of-jail-free" card. Abby had recognized Tom's look of worry, too.

"Any ideas for a gift?" Abby asked, cracking open her window. A succession of big rigs roared past, but the midmorning air felt invigorating.

Both girls simultaneously shouted suggestions above the highway din.

"Wait." Abby hastily rolled up her window. "We need a list. I'm not too experienced in these matters. My mom and sister-in-law picked out a crib and layette for my new niece. All I had to do was write a check. I don't even know what kinds of things a baby needs."

When both girls started speaking, Abby held up a hand. "One at a time. Angela first."

Angel, in frayed cutoff shorts and a belly-exposing top right out of the sixties, twisted to face her. "Well, I know Maria's mom and sisters gave her a shower and she got tons of practical stuff—two or three baby monitors, a stroller, a backpack, a bunch of diapers and a couple of diaper bags. And Miguel's brother gave them a crib and all that stuff."

"Zikes. We're in trouble."

Heather piped up. "Babies like toys."

"You like toys," her sister growled. "Babies can't even see toys right away. Their eyes aren't focused all the way."

Abby recognized the tone of authority. "How do you know so much about babies, Angel?"

"I used to help out on Saturday mornings at my mom's step aerobics class. I worked in the child-care room. She'd pay me, plus I got tips. Two of the moms traded off, too, and I listened to them talk." She settled back in the seat and her voice became more wistful. "Afterward, Mom would take me out to lunch and sometimes we'd go shopping. Mom was a great shopper."

It was the first time Abby had heard Angel open up about her mother. "Well, I'm a terrible shopper and we could use all the help we can get, so…how 'bout we take your mom along with us today?"

"What?" Angel gawked as if Abby had lost her mind. "She's dead."

Abby nodded, tightening her grip on the steering wheel. This was more Donna's department, but she plunged ahead, anyway. "True, but your memories of her are very much alive, so we can use those to help us pick out the right gift. In a way, she'll be guiding us."

Abby let the idea sink in a minute then asked, "What kinds of things would your mom be looking for if she were shopping for a baby gift?"

"Toys," Heather piped up.

Angel shot her a quelling look. "Shut up, dufus. This is serious. Mom took shopping seriously but she had a good time doing it. Sometimes, she bought silly stuff. Things that made you laugh but made you feel special, too."

"Like what?" Abby prompted.

"Well…at Christmas, Mom bought Val a juggling set." She grinned at her sister. "Remember? One of the balls broke the lamp and she wanted to get mad at him but couldn't and we all laughed."

Abby relaxed a little. "Let's start with that. Item number one—something silly. What else?"

Heather leaned as far forward as her seat belt allowed. "She picked out nice stuff, too. Like Angel's doctor boots."

Angel, who'd exchanged her standard black combat boots for a pair of sandals, explained. "Doc Martens. Mom said where shoes were concerned you should buy quality over quantity."

Abby wiggled her toes against the cork sole of her Birkenstocks. "I agree. Let's make that number two—something nice."

She caught Heather's beaming smile in the mirror.

"Mom had a way of always finding something special," Angel said softly. "Like this necklace she gave me for my birthday." She fingered the fine filigreed chain at her neck. A small pendant encircled a golden-hued stone. "It's my birthstone. I told her I liked opals better, but she said this was her favorite because it stood for the day I was born, which was one of the two best days of her life."

Tears clustered behind Abby's eyelids. She brushed aside the moisture beneath her sunglasses. "Your mom would want us to make this a happy day because babies are happy things, right?"

Angel shifted, visibly shaking off the sad memories. "Right."

"Three gifts—silly, nice and special. Three of us—four, counting your mom. How hard can it be?" she asked, pulling into the parking lot. "Let's go."

AN HOUR and forty-five minutes later, Abby's feet hurt and her shoulder ached from carrying her purse. They found the first two items on their list easily—perhaps nudged with a little heavenly help—but the third eluded them, and all three earthly shoppers were getting cranky.

"This is heavy," Heather complained, toting a Goofy gift bag sprouting yellow and blue tissue paper. Inside nested a ridiculously overpriced two-piece outfit that would be outgrown in six months tops, but its giraffes playing catch were too cute to pass up.

"Shut up," Angel grumbled. "That's nothing compared to this." In her arms rested a two-foot by three-foot gaily wrapped box containing a little red wagon—every boy's first wheels. Heather spotted it right off the bat and couldn't be dissuaded, even though baby Aurelio wouldn't be able to use it for a couple of years.

"I'll pull him in it when he gets older," she vowed.

Abby and Angel had acquiesced, deeming it a truly silly gift for a baby.

Abby looked at her watch. She'd told Tom they'd meet him at Miguel and Maria's at one o'clock. "Let's get a frozen yogurt," she suggested. "I always knew shopping was hard work. Maybe that's why I don't do it."

"How do you buy things? Presents and stuff?" Heather asked, holding the bag in one hand, Abby's hand in the other.

Abby squeezed it lightly. She couldn't believe how warm and anchoring that little hand felt. "Catalogs. I order books and CDs off the Internet. At Christmas, I give my niece and nephew savings bonds. Not glamorous, but they get so much stuff from their parents and grandparents, it's almost obscene."

"You can never be too obscene at Christmas," Angel quipped.

Abby smiled. To her surprise, she'd enjoyed the morning. Both girls were bright and intelligent and fun. They helped ward off a peculiar emptiness she'd felt growing in recent weeks. Melina, naturally, attributed Abby's mood to Daniel's low-key but persistent pursuit.

"Tell him the truth, Abby," Melina suggested at dinner the previous night—Abby's excuse for avoiding Daniel's invitation to a gala fund-raiser. "Tell him you could never fall for a guy who doesn't wear cowboy boots."

Abby didn't bother protesting. As Melina put it, if Tom and Daniel were Web sites, Tom's "hits" would have outnumbered Daniel's five to one. Unfortunately, Abby couldn't dabble with that site without doing real damage to her entire operating system.

"Oh, look," Angel said breathlessly, bringing Abby back to the present.

Abby followed the girl's outstretched finger to a kiosk in the center of the mall's rotunda. Against a lattice background hung a small, perfectly executed quilt. Its puffy sky of pale blue material with fuzzy white clouds hosted a heavenly collection of ruddy-faced cherubs.

"It's b*eeuu*tiful," Heather gushed, letting go of Abby's hand to rush forward.

Abby agreed. The craftsperson had bestowed upon each angel a different personality: peaceful, mischievous, serene and joyous.

Abby dug in her purse for her credit card.

"Don't you want to know how much it is?" Angel eyed her questioningly.

"Nope. It's perfect. That angel up in the corner has eyes the color of your birthstone. And that little guy on the cloud has your hair, Heather. I'd say your mom is one terrific shopper, wouldn't you?"

Both girls looked at each other before nodding—at first tentatively, then with glee.

TOM LEANED his head back against the nappy fabric of the Fuenteses' couch and closed his eyes. The tiny child sleeping in the crook of his arm brought back memories that made tears form beneath his eyelids. He would never forget the joy and knee-bending fear that walloped him the instant he held Angel—a squalling bundle with black hair and red, furious cheeks—in his arms. A bolt of love, possessiveness, responsibility—he wasn't sure he could name it—hit him like a fist to the gut. He knew his life would never be the same.

"You're tired, Tom," a soft voice said. "Let me take him."

Tom opened one eye. Maria, looking both exhilarated and exhausted, stood before him in a shapeless dress, a diaper hooked over one shoulder. "Oh no you don't," he whispered back. "As long as I've got him, I can take a break."

In all honesty, this week had been hell. The backhoe driver installing underground power lines uprooted some mangled telephone cable. News from Stanford wasn't good: Janey's adverse reaction to some drug had scared the bejesus out of Ed. With Miguel freaking out over false labor, then the real thing, Tom found his workload doubled. Plus, he wasn't prepared for summer vacation, or, more to the point, his daughters' expectations of a fun-filled, action-packed summer.

If it hadn't been for Abby ferrying the girls to Fresno and taking them shopping this morning, he wouldn't have known a minute's peace, although, in a way, she compounded his problems, too.

Tom shifted against the cushions. There was no excuse for

such juvenile dreams in a man his age. Just when Heather's bad dreams seemed to be slacking off so he could get a decent night's sleep, erotic images of Abby plagued his dreams, leaving him drained, edgy and damn horny.

"Daddy's got the baby!" a voice exclaimed, jolting Tom back to reality.

The cushions to his right sank as Heather jumped to his side. "Can I hold him?"

Angel sank down beside him on his left. "Shh, he's sleeping," she whispered. "Hey, he looks better, doesn't he? Abby, come see him."

Tom's heart jumped skittishly, forcing a lump into his windpipe. Juggling her purse, car keys and the packages his daughters dumped in her arms, Abby looked harried but beautiful. He couldn't read the look in her eyes but sensed her hesitation.

"Come," he beckoned.

She set the gifts on the floor beside a spanking-new baby stroller and took two tentative steps toward the couch. Not fast enough to suit Heather, who bounced to her knees and stretched to grab Abby's hand. "He won't bite. He doesn't have any teeth yet."

Abby's smile made his pulse jerk.

She looped her hair behind her ears and leaned over. Her fair skin looked as soft and touchable as baby Rey's; Tom could have spent hours tracing the scattered freckles across her shoulders.

"He's beautiful," she said, blinking rapidly.

Tom detected her scent—a subtle, fresh floral, above the nose-prickling samples his daughters had obviously doused on every available spot. He started to offer her the baby, but she backed away, a blush claiming her cheeks.

"No, thanks. I'm not good with babies. But you look right at home."

Without thinking, he lifted Rey in his arms, kissing his petal-soft skin, inhaling that remarkable baby scent. "I love babies," he said. "Horse babies, pig babies, girl babies." He winked at Heather, making her giggle.

"Hi, Abby," Maria said, hurrying in through the doorway that led to the dining room and kitchen. "Thanks so much for coming. And for the flowers. They're so pretty."

Tom watched with interest the way Abby deflected any praise that came her way. When Miguel joined them to open the gifts, Tom noticed she stayed out of the hoopla, letting the girls bask in the praise. While she seemed pleased by Maria and Miguel's exclamations of pleasure over the presents, she remained detached, as if visiting with clients, not involved with friends.

"You must stay for dinner," Miguel told her, giving Abby a friendly squeeze around the shoulders. "We have enough food to feed an army. Tell her, Tom, she has to stay."

Tom grinned. "Maria's mother would be insulted if you didn't. And, believe me, you don't want to insult Señora Garza. She may be tiny, but she's powerful. Miguel calls her Mighty Mouse."

"Shh…" Miguel put a finger to his lips, mischievously.

Abby smiled back. "Okay. I'll stay. Thank you."

"No. Thank you for all these great gifts. This wagon is terrific." He snatched up the box. "I'm going to the barn. Coming, Tom?"

"No way, amigo. You've worked me hard enough this week."

Once Miguel left the room, Abby shifted on the straight-back chair nestled in the small bay window. The afternoon sunlight, spilling in through the windows, imbued an aura of gold around her shoulders and head. She crossed one long, sleek leg over her knee, unconsciously displaying her nervousness.

"I must owe you a small fortune," Tom said.

She brushed back a lock of hair. "Forget it. The money you sent with Angel was fine. Everything was on sale, except for the quilt, and that was my gift."

He watched her inspect the house, not surprised by the small knot in the pit of his stomach. Despite Maria's cheerful wallpaper and lace curtains, there was no disguising the basic simplicity of the house. To the left of the front door was the living room, to the right a nook Tom had intended to use as an office. Maria's sewing machine and various baby paraphernalia made it look cluttered.

A sudden cry from the bundle in his arms brought three females out of the woodwork. Abby, he noticed, instinctively started forward but stopped herself.

"He's probably hungry," Maria said, plucking him from Tom's arms. "I'll go feed him. Do you girls want to come?"

Tom started to intervene, remembering how Lesley liked to nurse Angel in private—he didn't know if she'd nursed Heather—but Maria and his daughters were up the stairs and out of sight before Tom could open his mouth.

"You're good with babies," Abby said.

Tom heard a stiltedness in her tone he didn't understand.

He reached for his long-ignored beer and took a drink. "Ugh," he said, making a face. "Warm. I know where Miguel keeps his stash. Wanna come?"

She didn't answer but followed him through the sunny, south-facing kitchen to the back porch where a red plastic ice chest sat beside a wooden swing suspended from the rafters. When Tom bought the place, the ratty appendage had housed two broken washing machines and a dysfunctional freezer. He'd immediately replaced the screens and installed the swing, picturing a romantic spot where he and Lesley could smooch and grow old.

He plucked two dripping cans from the icy water and sat down on the swing, leaving plenty of room for Abby to join him. The heat of the previous week had eased off when a Delta breeze swept southward, bringing blue skies and moderate temperatures. The view was as picturesque as a postcard.

"How charming! I love porches. This is a great place," she said, sitting stiffly against the upright back.

Her praise relaxed a knot in his stomach and opened a door to feelings he'd been trying valiantly to ignore. "Thanks. It was a labor of love."

At her puzzled look, he said, "Didn't you know? This house is mine. I bought it ten—no, eleven, years ago. It was pretty run-down and I fixed it up."

A dark look crossed her face and he saw her fingers tighten around the can. He didn't understand her reaction.

"Is there something wrong with that?"

"No," she said firmly.

"You seem upset."

"Just surprised." She took a small sip of beer. "You never mentioned it before. It's a wonderful house. You could have moved in here and saved the headache of building the addition."

"And kick these guys out? Not my style."

Her gaze dropped to her hands as if embarrassed. "Of course not."

Tom fought the urge to lift her chin and kiss her.

After choking down a big gulp of beer, he pointed toward the fenced pasture spread out behind the small barn and detached garage. Half a dozen horses grazed on the irrigated land. "The house came with fifteen acres. I could have put in almonds or pistachios, but Miguel and I decided to go together on a little breeding operation. Quarter horses."

"Really? Land baron and breeder?" She shook her head, obviously bemused by something. "You play your cards pretty tight to the vest, as they say."

Puzzled by her tone, Tom cocked his head and waited for an explanation.

"My grandfather died before I was born. Everyone says he was kind and generous to a fault..." Like his granddaughter, Tom would have added, if she hadn't plowed ahead. "But he never discussed finances with his wife and, when he died, he left my grandmother penniless. Worse, actually, since he was hospitalized for several months with no insurance. Grammy had to move in with my folks and basically start from scratch."

"Are you saying I'm like your grandfather because I didn't tell you about this house?"

She held up a hand. "It's your business, and I know you're not comfortable talking about finances."

He bit down on a smile. She was so damn pretty, especially when she got a burr under her saddle.

"I admit I'm a little closemouthed about money—mainly 'cause I don't have much, but we can talk about it if you want." A sudden thought struck him, something his father used to tell him: "Marry a woman you like to talk to. When you get older you'll be doing a lot of it."

She shrugged one shoulder regally. "The point is..."

Tom decided to cut to the chase. "The point is, something's going on between us that's got you nervous, so it's easier to make up reasons not to like me."

A flash of color swept across her features; her eyes changed to a stormy gold-green that would haunt his dreams tonight.

"I...I like you." Chin up, defiant, her protest lost impact

when her gaze slipped to his chin. "You're a very nice man. A gentleman." She almost didn't get out the last word because Tom leaned over and pressed his lips to hers. Still moving, butterfly-like beneath his own, their sweetness, even flavored with beer, sent a shaft of desire burning through him.

Undoubtedly startled, she put up a hand to push him back, but as he deepened the kiss, tasting her, she left the hand resting against his shirtfront. Her response pushed him further than he meant to go.

When he looped his arm around her shoulders, she jumped back as though electrocuted.

"This is terribly unprofessional and I apologize," she said, rising and moving away a step on what looked like wobbly legs.

Tom wasn't too steady himself. "I kiss you, and you apologize? How come?"

She peeked through the square of glass in the kitchen door before turning back to face him. The glow in her cheeks made him long to pull her into his arms and finish what he'd started—it would be sweet and hot and... He shook his head, making himself focus on her words, not her lips.

"...your daughters' advocate. I have a job to do and it's unprofessional to—you know what I mean, Tom. This is the real world."

He didn't like her cool, professional tone. Or the truth behind her words.

"Angel and Heather are the only ones that matter here," she said.

He couldn't fault her commitment to his children, but he sensed something else in her reaction and the way she couldn't quite bring herself to meet his gaze. He'd never met anyone like her, so complex, so caring and so damn sexy in the most understated way.

She sighed. She eyed the seat beside him but opted to sit

on the cooler instead. "Tom, we haven't spoken about this, but I'm thinking of quitting my job either this fall or next spring so I can go back to school."

One part of him yipped in glee—if she wasn't his daughters' advocate, she could be his…something else. Another part realized she was talking about leaving.

"Why?"

She tucked a swath of hair behind her ear. He hadn't paid close attention to her ears before, but they were perfect. Not pierced, he noticed.

She cleared her throat, drawing his attention back to her eyes. A man could never grow tired of looking at those eyes. "A lot of reasons. All personal."

Her tone slammed the door on his speculation and fantasy.

"This shouldn't have happened, but since it did we need to put it behind us for your daughters' sake. They've made a lot of headway, but they're not through the woods yet. There are four seasons of grief. And they're just starting summer."

Her words were more effective than his midnight cold shower.

"You're right. The girls need you, and I don't want to do anything that messes that up." He hunched forward, careful not to touch her. "I like you, Abby. A lot. And we both put something in that kiss, but…I know my duty. It won't happen again."

"HIS DUTY," Abby muttered, snatching a container of Ben and Jerry's out of Donna's freezer.

Abby slammed the door of the bottom freezer compartment, kicking it for good measure.

"Why am I letting this get to me?" she asked, ignoring Donna's bemused look. "It was just a little kiss, and he backed off when I told him to."

Donna's sandy eyebrows shot up. "Because you're disappointed? You didn't really want him to stop."

"No. Yes. Was that a question?" Abby shoveled a spoon into the frozen block of calories. "You know I wouldn't get involved with a client. We've already had this talk."

Donna fenced her spoon against Abby's. "Talk is cheap. Unless you're on the phone with a lawyer. Speaking of lawyers, I saw Daniel at the arts council fund-raiser last night. The man looks fabulous in a tux."

Abby shrugged. "I don't want to talk about Daniel. I've got to have a talk with him—he's just not my cup of tea, although I promise to be more diplomatic than that." She swallowed a bite of frozen nectar. "Did I tell you I think I made a real breakthrough with the girls?"

"And their father."

Abby stuck out her tongue. "It was so neat this morning. They opened up to me about their mom. They might be moving into another stage of grief."

"What stage is Tom in?"

Abby looked for cynicism in her friend's tone but couldn't find it. "I don't know. You know it must have been very hard for him not to share in Heather's birth. He loves babies. You should have seen him holding baby Rey. His hands are so big, you'd think he'd be clumsy, but he was gentle as a surgeon. I've never seen a man as comfortable with a baby."

Abby read Donna's speculative look. "What?"

"You're in love with the man."

Abby's mouth dropped open but the words of denial wouldn't come. She couldn't move past the image of Tom, after dinner, tenderly rocking the restless baby until Rey's whimpers diminished. Watching the scene, an old pain surfaced, reminding her of a heartache she'd buried years before. A yearning so poignant and sharp, all breath left her lungs, making her turn away before she humiliated herself by falling to her knees crying.

"I don't want to talk about it," she said wistfully.

"Yes, you do. But I'm not the person you need to talk to."

Abby looked away from the truth in her friend's eyes. "What's wrong with me, Donna? I thought all this was behind me."

Donna squeezed her arm supportively. "Old wounds that aren't quite healed can lie dormant for years, slowly festering. It only takes a pinprick to make them open up, gushing all that toxic waste."

Abby groaned. "What a disgusting metaphor!"

"It's late. Come back tomorrow and I'll have a better one, but I'll have to charge you full price." She eyed Abby with a look Abby knew all too well. "Why are you so sure Tom would be scandalized by something that happened almost ten years ago? Something you had no control over?"

Abby swallowed. "Tom epitomizes old-world sensibilities, Donna. He wouldn't condemn me, but he wouldn't understand. Women in his world don't have abortions." She said the words in a rush, inwardly sickened by the memories they provoked. "He'd be kind and sympathetic but secretly horrified."

Donna shook her head. "We could go into the history of this if you need to, but I'm more curious why you're so convinced Tom's response would be negative. Maybe you're more afraid he would understand. What would you do then?"

The truth of her friend's words brought already raw emotions even closer to the surface.

Donna walked to Abby's side and looped her arm around Abby's shoulders. "I don't know Tom well enough to say what he'd think, but, honey, if you can't be open with him, you can't go forward in the relationship. And if you can't go forward, you can't get involved. He's not another Landon."

Abby almost smiled at the ludicrous comparison. "I know that."

In a tone Abby remembered from her time as a patient, Donna told her, "Then you need to begin distancing yourself from that family, Abby. For all of your sakes."

Abby closed her eyes. "I know."

CHAPTER NINE

MUD MADE gulping sounds around his boots as Tom finished unearthing the recently soaked dirt covering the lid of the new septic tank. Once the plumbing was hooked up, this larger tank would serve the bunkhouse and addition as well as a new shower and toilet added to the barn. Late Friday afternoon the construction crew backfilled the gaping hole to avoid any accidents, and thoughtfully soaked the dirt to assure compacting.

Unfortunately, someone forgot to cover the open flange, a three-inch-wide black plastic hole in the floor of what would soon be Heather and Angel's new bathroom. How—*why* a kitten would crawl into such a small, uninviting opening was beyond him, but Heather's kitten somehow managed to do just that and now it was his job to rescue the little thing.

"Gad, it's hotter than Hades and not even noon," Tom said, swiping at a grimy rivulet coursing down his cheek.

He dropped to his knees in the mud, leaning forward to gain purchase for his lever. A muscle in his lower back sputtered, warning him not to go there.

They'd already spent a futile hour at the other end of the pipe, dangling bits of salami on a string like a fishing lure, listening to mournful meows.

"I can hear her, Daddy," Heather said, one ear flat to the ground. "She knows you're coming."

And she's probably backing up even farther in the pipe,

he groused silently, trying to figure out how he was going to coax the frightened creature into the tank.

"You've gotta save her, Daddy," Heather pleaded, dirt highlighting streaks of tears. "It's dark in there, and she's scared. I know she is. Oh, please, Daddy, please get her out."

Heather's wail multiplied Tom's frustration factor. The kitten wasn't the only one fearing the outcome of this rescue—Tom didn't know how he'd live with himself if he failed to save his little girl's pet.

Using the flattened end of a crowbar, he pried open the lid. Grimacing, he upended the heavy cover, letting it topple to the mound of odoriferous, baking mud. He stretched out perpendicular to the inky crater, pebbles and twigs poking his chest.

Craning into the pit, he eyeballed the black hole at the top of the concrete tank.

"Here, kitty, kitty," he called.

The hollow chamber echoed like a tomb.

"Do you see her, Daddy?" Heather asked, flopping down beside him. "Is she okay? Is she safe? Why doesn't she come out, Daddy? What if she's stuck?"

An image of his little girl crashing headfirst into the empty cavern made him elbow her back. Rising to his knees, he drew Heather to her feet and gave her a gentle shake to stop the panic he could feel building inside her. "Run get Angel, honey. She's helping Janey with paperwork. I'll have to drop this ladder in here. She can fit down there easier than me." He maneuvered the fiberglass ladder into the hole, propping its protruding rungs against the far side of the opening.

"Abby's coming, Daddy," Heather said, watching him. "She could do it."

"Abby? Who called her?" He regretted his angry tone and flinched at Heather's puzzled look, but the last thing he needed today was Abby. She seldom left his thoughts as it was, but, at least, he'd managed to avoid any face-to-face meetings throughout the past two weeks.

"I did, Daddy. She helped me name Esmy, remember? She has to be here." Esmeralda the kitten was named for a character in *The Hunchback of Notre Dame* video—Abby's halfway-through-Rainbows gift to the girls. Despite the awkwardness stemming from Tom's impromptu kiss, Abby continued to work on his daughters' behalf, as well as running interference on the remodeling job by keeping tempers cool and optimism high. He'd have had an ulcer by now if it weren't for Abby, but that didn't mean he was ready to see her.

"I know, honey, but you shouldn't have bothered her. Saturday is her day off."

Heather tilted her head, eyeing him as if he were suddenly spouting Greek. "Daddy, we're not her work. We're her family."

Something hot and painful burned in his throat, and Tom had to look away. Fortunately, the dogs alerted him to Abby's approach and he had several seconds to get control of his emotions before a cloud of dust preceded a screeching Honda into the yard.

Abby flew out of the car and raced to the mud pit.

Tom squinted against the white glare of the noon sun reflecting off gravel, trying to see more than a willowy shadow. When she squatted to hug Heather, his mouth turned to sandpaper; his knees would have buckled if he hadn't been flat on his belly. Tank top, no bra and skimpy shorts that barely covered her fanny. Even his fantasies hadn't come up with that one.

"Hi," she said breathlessly. "I came as fast as I could. Is Esmy okay?"

"Still meowing," he replied, when he found his voice. "Heather, go get your sister."

"Okay, Daddy."

In the yawning silence Tom swore he could hear his sweat forming. A rivulet inched past his ear. His T-shirt felt like a soggy body cast and smelled like ripe horse manure.

Something white dangled in front of his salt-blurred vision. He blinked. A pristine tissue extended from Abby's long, graceful fingers—half moons of dirt beneath each nail. "You're going to evaporate in this sun," she said. "Isn't there some other way of getting the kitten out?"

Her concern didn't lessen his frustration. "We're going to try Angel in here on the ladder."

"I could—"

"No," he snapped. He already owed her too much without adding to the debt. He grabbed the first thought that came into his head. "Liability. Couldn't risk it."

The tissue slipped from her grasp, fluttering like a dead dove to the bottom of the tank.

A clatter of metal and a chorus of voices interceded on his behalf. He twisted around to see Ed and Angel lugging a white net bag between them. Janey and Heather brought up the rear, moving at a slower pace. Janey, at home for a two-week hiatus between cancer protocols, looked wan but determined to get on with her project of researching her family tree. She'd proven a real lifesaver by hiring his bored and belligerent elder daughter as a secretary and assistant.

"We brought a sunshade," Angel said, helping Ed to dump the various aluminum tubes and canvas awning on the ground. "Hi, Abby."

"Hello, Abby. Why didn't you call us sooner, Tom?" Ed asked, surveying the situation with a grin. Not waiting for an answer or a greeting, he said, "'Course, that's not the way to handle a cat stuck in a sewer pipe, you know."

Tom climbed to his feet, brushing off globs of mud. "Really?"

"Yep, just leave it be..."

"Now, Ed, just hold your mouth," Janey scolded. "'Morning, Abby, you look nice and cool, despite the heat."

Abby looked down as if just then realizing what she was wearing. Her face flushed red. "I was gardening when Heather called," she said, plucking at the fabric that clung so provocatively to her breasts. "I didn't stop to change, just jumped in the car." As if to divert attention from herself, she asked, "Should you be out in the sun? It's hotter than blazes."

"Damn right," Ed said, scowling, "but the darn woman won't take it easy. Tom, give me a hand here."

The last thing Tom needed was an audience.

"I'll do that," Abby said. "My brother's got a sunshade just like this."

A glimpse of white bottom beneath a fringe of shorts when she bent over to pick up the aluminum poles made Tom's knees buckle. "We don't have to turn this into a sideshow," he muttered. "Angel, shimmy down the ladder and call the cat. When she pokes her head out, grab her," Tom said, pointing to the hole.

Angel looked at him as though he'd just sprouted a second head. "Me? No way. Uh-uh. I'm not going down some smelly hole." She backed away from him, eyes flashing.

Normally, Tom might have paid more attention to Angel's pallor and odd reaction. After all, she'd always been part tomboy ready to jump into any kind of foolish danger. But today, heat and hormones blurred his observation skills. "It's not smelly. It's brand-new. Besides, you're not going all the way in it. Just a few steps down the ladder."

She eyed the muddy, boxlike gap like a young colt ready to bolt. "No. I won't do it. You can't make me." Her tone was shrill with a tremor of hysteria.

Abby, who was anchoring one slim post upright while Heather and Janey held two other corner posts, abandoned her post and rushed to Angel's side. "It's okay, sweetheart," she said, stepping between Angel and the hole. "Lot's of people are afraid of small spaces. It's called claustrophobia."

Angel's back stiffened. "I'm not afraid of anything, but I'm not going down that hole." Her bottom lip trembled.

Abby looked at Tom. "Let me do it."

Tom's frustration level rose a notch. Not only should Abby not be here, she had no business interfering with him and his daughters. "No. Angel can do it. It's not dangerous."

Abby put her hands on her hips and gave him an exasperated look. "Tom, you're being unreasonable."

Janey suddenly appeared at Tom's elbow. "This sun is getting to be too much for me, after all, Thomas. Heather, dear, let's go inside and try to sweet-talk your kitty out on that end. She's a girl, right?" Heather, who hovered near Janey's leg, showing her usual signs of unease when tempers started to flare, nodded vigorously. "Well, sometimes girls need a little wooing. Let's go try."

Tom wondered if that last hint was for his benefit. An image of Lesley flashed into his head. "You can be so damn stubborn, Tom Butler," Lesley used to say. "When you get something stuck in your head, I need dynamite to change your mind."

"All right, be my guest," he said to Abby. "But if you fall—"

Abby gave Angel a quick squeeze then moved to his side. Together they walked to the edge of the hole. Tom looked at Abby and realized in a flash of insight she was as terrified of the prospect of going into that small, dark space as Angel was. She squared her shoulders and flashed him a brave smile. "Okay then. Let's do it."

Tom's heart melted, and he knew in that instant he loved her. He opened his mouth to speak, but a sudden shout stopped him. "Daddy. Daddy," Heather's high-pitched voice called. Tom looked over his shoulder and saw her running toward them, a tiny glob of fur squeezed against her chest. "She came right out of the toilet, Daddy. Esmy's safe."

Tom's head pounded and his heart hurt. It could have been heatstroke, but he was afraid it was more permanent than that. He turned to Ed, who was leaning against the half-assembled sunshade. The older man seemed highly amused about something.

"I think you're right about checking on the herd, Ed. I'll take off as soon as we have this situation under control," he said. Ed's suggestion last night to take a couple of days in the mountains had fallen on deaf ears, but that had been then. Now he needed some time alone to get his thoughts together. "I hate to ask, but could you and Janey watch the girls overnight?"

"They could come home with me," Abby said before Ed could answer. "Donna's visiting her son and Melina's on a cruise. I don't have any plans and I'd love the company. Really."

Tom hesitated—not on behalf of his children.

"I have to stop by and feed Donna's cat, but she has a pool. Do you guys swim?" she asked the girls.

Their whoops of joy made Tom flinch.

"And we could pick up pizza and some movies," Abby went on. "It'll be kind of like a slumber party."

"Sounds cool. Can we, Dad?" Angel asked, not quite meeting Tom's gaze.

Tom knew she was embarrassed about her earlier scene. He pulled her into his arms and gave her a hug.

"Looks like you're outvoted, boy," Ed said, guffawing. "As we say in the fishing business, it's time to cut bait 'n' go home."

Tom recognized the truth in the older man's words. Unfortunately, this time he was the fish, and he was hooked good.

BY SATURDAY EVENING Abby's family-room carpet resembled a war zone between the Popcorn Fanatics and the Jelly-Belly Coalition. The glass-and-cherrywood coffee table had been pushed aside to accommodate two young bodies and Abby's cat, Tubby, wooed against his better judgment by bits of lime candy and eager affection.

"I like the Mulan bedspread best," Heather said, using elbow jabs to secure a better position over the pile of magazine clippings.

A manila envelope filled with decorating ideas gleaned from glossy magazines and a scaled-down floor plan of the girls' new room had arrived in the mail while Abby was at the ranch.

"Too red," Angel argued, nudging Heather's paper bed out of the way. "I like this one—pink and green. Pretty, without being geeky. What do you think, Abby?"

From her perch on the couch, Abby eyed the arrangement. "Very feminine. You have a good eye for color, Angel. The Mulan print is pretty, too, Heather, but it'll be out of style as soon as the next Disney movie comes out. I doubt if your dad will want to fork out the cost for a new one every year. And, remember, girls, my mother never sent a price list with these cutouts. Knowing her, I bet they were clipped from the ritziest magazines on the market."

Angel sighed. "You sound just like my dad."

"Do I?" The comparison made Abby smile. Abby regretted the awkward stiffness between her and Tom that hadn't been there before their fateful kiss, but she could hardly blame him, since she'd gone out of her way to maintain a professional detachment. Then, something had happened during their tussle over who was going into the septic tank. His attitude changed. He seemed resigned about something. What it was, she hadn't a clue.

Abby glanced at her watch. "Six bells. I'd better start the pizza. You guys ready for our appetizers?"

Too absorbed in their planning to answer, both girls nodded.

Abby headed for the kitchen. Not unscathed in the youthful occupation, the usually pristine countertops displayed a collection of juice bottles, popcorn bowls, an unopened box of sugarcoated cereal that made Abby's teeth ache just looking at it, and three plastic video boxes. So far, they'd only watched one movie about twins who try to get their divorced parents back together. Heather liked the funny parts; Angel seemed intrigued by the romance between the father and mother.

Abby and Angel had carried on a rather in-depth discussion about divorce while sharing a bowl of popcorn. "People who have children shouldn't get divorced," Angel maintained. Heather and the cat were stretched out a few feet away on the floor in front of the entertainment center.

"I'm sure they all wish things had worked out differently," Abby said. "A big part of my job is counseling victims of domestic abuse. I tell them no one should stay in a relationship where one person bullies the other, children or no children."

"That didn't happen with my mom and dad."

"No, of course not. Your dad is kind and gentle and very big-hearted. Whatever happened between him and your mom stemmed from something else that made them unhappy. Believe me, there are as many reasons for divorce as there are people."

Angel fiddled with the remote and in a low voice said, "Maybe if they'd stayed together, she'd still be alive."

Impulsively, Abby put her arm around the young girl's shoulders and squeezed. "Hasn't Donna told you about the troublemaker words?"

Angel sniffed and shook her head.

"Woulda, coulda, shoulda and if. She has a story about each of them. Let's take 'if.' Haven't you heard the old saying 'If the dog hadn't stopped to pee, he'd have caught the rabbit'?"

"Yeah," Angel said, grinning. "Dad says it all the time."

"Well, if you're the dog, that's a bad thing—you go hungry, but if you're the rabbit, you get home safely and everybody's happy. Either way, what happened happened and there's no going back, so *if* isn't a very useful word, is it?"

Angel smiled and nestled comfortably against Abby's shoulder until the movie ended, then she plopped belly-first on the floor to help her sister spread out the clippings. Abby didn't know if her words had helped in any way, but she felt a bond between them that hadn't been there before.

The phone rang as Abby pulled the take-'n-bake pizza out of the refrigerator. She set it on the counter, picked up the portable and walked back to the oven to adjust the setting. "Abby Davis."

"How spontaneous are you?"

Abby's heart plummeted. Tom was miles from a phone, but one part of her had hoped it might be him.

"Hi, Daniel. What's up?"

"You. Me. A little waterskiing?"

Abby glanced out the window. Long shadows were creeping across the lawn. Sunset may have been a couple of hours off, but the nearest lake was forty minutes away.

"Tonight?"

"Not exactly. I thought we'd drive to my cabin at Big Bear, spend the night, then go skiing right after breakfast…unless something better comes up." The message couldn't have been clearer.

"I have houseguests this weekend, Daniel. Angela and Heather Butler."

"That cowboy's kids?" His tone sounded petulant, little-boyish.

"Yes. We're having a slumber party."

He grumbled something about "juvenile escapism" before hanging up. I've got to clear the air about this next week, Abby told herself. How could she date Daniel when his kisses left her cold, while Tom's one kiss haunted her dreams and played havoc with her mind?

Abby replaced the phone and popped the pizza—half plain cheese and half mushroom, red peppers, olives and salami, into the oven. When she turned around, Angel was standing in the doorway.

"I DIDN'T MEAN to eavesdrop, but...did you just blow off a date because of us?" Angel asked. So far, she'd had a pretty decent time at Abby's, and she sensed Abby liked having them there, but she'd understand if Abby wanted to dump them off on Janey and Ed so she could be with her boyfriend.

Abby poured cranberry-kiwi juice into one wineglass and white wine into another and motioned to a stool. Angel slipped into it and reached for the juice.

"The man who called is my boss, and, although we've gone out to dinner a couple of times, I don't think it's a good idea to date someone you work with. I plan to make that clear to him on Monday."

Angel took a sip of juice, then asked, "Would that let my dad out?"

The three plates in Abby's hand clattered against the tile countertop. "I beg your pardon?"

"You and Dad don't exactly work together but you kinda got together because of your work and I just wondered if you'd go out with him...if he asked you." Before Abby could answer, Angel went on, "I think he's lonely. He says he's too busy to be lonely and we're all the company he needs, but Janey says men need women more than women need men."

"She does?" Abby transferred her chopping board and a

bunch of parsley to the island, keeping her focus on Angel. It was one of the things Angel liked best about Abby—she paid attention. Adults rarely did.

"Dad told you Janey hired me to help research her family tree, right?"

Abby nodded. "Tom said you were helping out, but he didn't say how," she said, taking a sip of wine. "That's awesome. Can I hire you next? My family tree's a mess. There's this whole limb that's lost somewhere in Romania."

Angel smiled. One thing she knew about Abby was she didn't say things she didn't mean. "Beats doing nothing," Angel said.

"What about friends? Surely there are kids your age around?"

"I hang out with a couple of girls at Rainbows, but that's… different." Angel didn't try to explain, but she could tell by Abby's nod that she understood.

"Two summers ago, I met some girls at Bible camp, and Dad's been bugging me to call them, but…" Angel couldn't explain why she didn't want to renew her old friendships. Maybe she was too weird to fit in now. After all, she didn't have a mother.

Abby seemed to hear what wasn't said. "I know what you mean. It's hard to pick up relationships after a period of time has passed. It'll be even more awkward for your friends, too, because people are always afraid of saying something wrong. But it sure beats being bored to tears." She took a sip of wine. "I used to live for summer vacation, then when it got here, I'd drive my grandmother up the wall moaning and groaning about not having anything to do." Abby smiled and seemed to drift back in time a minute. "Do you know what she did one day? She carted me off to the library and told me, 'Read all these books. That'll give you plenty to do.'"

Angel made a face. "Don't tell that one to my dad. He already nags me about watching too much boob tube."

"I won't. I promise."

Angel took a drink of juice. Lately, it felt as though she couldn't do anything to please her dad. He praised her for working with Janey but seemed disappointed when he came home and found the house a mess. He never complained, but Angel could tell he was disappointed.

Janey said Tom was just overly tired from handling so much responsibility, but Angel thought it was something else. In the six months she'd been living at the ranch, he'd gone from his laid-back self to a grumpy old father. If her theory was right, Abby might be the one to help get her dad back to normal, and maybe even help salvage Angel's summer vacation.

"Janey said men aren't emotionally equipped to raise a family alone." Angel didn't know if she believed that, but it got her thinking about how her dad felt about being stuck with her and Heather. Maybe he'd get desperate and marry the first woman who came along. Would she and Heather have any say in the matter?

Abby handed Angel a paring knife and two lemons. "Would you please cut them into wedges for our shrimp?" She nibbled on a piece of parsley, then said thoughtfully, "I'm not sure I agree with Janey. I think that some people just make better parents. Period. Your dad is miles beyond me in that respect."

Angel heard something sad in her tone. "How do you know? You don't have any kids."

Abby's face changed. Angel swore she could see a sad, haunted look in her eyes, like how her dad looked when he talked about her mother. The look disappeared in a flash and Abby said brightly, "I've observed a lot of families over the years, and as far as I can see, your dad's doing a great job of parenting."

"I know," Angel said grudgingly. She cut into the first lemon, breathing deeply of the clean citrus smell. She liked the smell of Abby's house, in general. Little bowls of potpourri and scented candles added a feminine touch missing from her dad's house. It made Angel homesick in a way she couldn't explain, because Val had allergies so her mother had never bought fragrant things. But there were still the smells of the cleaning person and her mother's perfume and something intangible Angel couldn't name but missed just the same. "I'm not complaining. But I know Dad had to change his whole life because of us. I don't know how much he dated before, but having two kids can't make it any easier getting a date."

Abby laughed in that way that always made Angel want to laugh, too. "Are you kidding? Two kids as neat as you and your sister are pure gravy. He'll be beating women off with a stick once he's ready to start dating."

Angel lined up the lemon halves and cleanly quartered them. She glanced up to find Abby looking at her. Abby was beautiful, not like a model but in a real way. She was a good person and she seemed to like them. Angel had been thinking about it for a couple of weeks, and she'd decided if her dad had to have a woman in his life, he could do worse than Abby. Then, this septic-tank thing today clinched it. Angel almost cried with gratitude when Abby took her side. It was almost as if Abby knew that looking at that black hole made Angel think of her mother's grave.

"You never answered my question. Would you date Dad if he asked?"

Abby's cheeks colored and she stuttered, "I…um, it would be very unprofessional of me to…that is…"

The oven timer clanged, making Abby knock a pile of minced parsley to the floor. "The pizza's half done," she said, rushing to the pantry for a broom. "We need to serve our shrimp appetizers. Why don't you call Heather to wash up?"

Angel knew avoidance when she saw it. Adults were masters of it. She shrugged. "Okay."

EVEN THOUGH he knew he was late, Tom took his time driving to Abby's house. He followed the directions she'd given him, studying the neighborhood. Abby's house, situated at an angle on a corner lot, appeared older than its neighbors—stucco siding, shake roof, forest-green shutters and mature trees lent a charm the newer, bigger houses lacked.

He left his hat on the seat and ran his fingers through his unruly locks, wishing he'd had time for more than a quick dip in the chilly lake with a bar of soap.

"Hi, Daddy," Heather called from the doorway. "We stayed up till midnight 'n' watched three movies and I slept with Tabby—he really likes me, but Abby calls him Tubby 'cause he's kinda fat." Heather whispered the last word before sprinting barefoot across the hot sidewalk and launching herself into Tom's open arms.

She wore a bright orange, two-piece swimsuit he hadn't seen before. He squeezed her until she protested. "Not so tight, Daddy. Tubby doesn't like it when I squeeze him either. See?" She thrust out her hand. A Day-Glo orange adhesive strip bisected her hand. "Abby wanted to call the doctor 'cause it bleeded, but Angel told her it was nothing. We went to the store and I got to pick out the ban'age. It matches my new swimming suit."

"New…?"

She backhanded him, muffling his words. "Kiss it to make it feel better. Mommy always did."

He obliged with a gallant flourish. "Does it still hurt?"

"No, silly. It was just a scratch. Angel says Abby worries too much. She worried about you, too."

"Why me?"

"You said noon and it's nearly four," Abby said softly from

the shadow of the doorway. The arched portal lent a European flavor to the entry; a twiggy wreath thick with dried flowers hung on the planked door.

"Sorry about that. I got a late start. Couldn't find a couple of cows." He wished he hadn't accidentally sat on his sunglasses; they'd have given him something to hide behind. Although he'd spent the better part of two days trying to talk some sense into himself, the truth couldn't be denied: he was in love with Abby Davis.

"Were they okay?" Abby asked, holding open the door to admit him. Her khaki shorts were fashionably sloppy; the rust-colored top was cropped, exposing bare midriff. A plastic clip of some kind held her hair back, but errant strands framed her face. Tom's fingers itched to brush them back behind her ears.

He interpreted her tone as polite and caring, but still cool, as it had been since their kiss. Obviously, this gut-wrenching desire was all one-sided.

"Yep. One had a new calf."

He ducked going through the doorway and shifted Heather to his left hip. The tiled foyer was cool and welcoming. "Sounds like you guys had a good time."

Abby closed the door and smiled at Heather, who planted a big, sloppy kiss on Tom's cheek. The worried look left Abby's eyes and he heard her soft, wistful sigh. "We had fun, didn't we, Heather?"

Heather's bright curls danced across his line of vision and she used her small hands to turn his face to look into her eyes. "We ate pizza 'n' nachos 'n' jelly beans 'n' popcorn..."

"Don't give away all our secrets," Abby scolded teasingly. "He'll never let you come back."

To Tom, she said, "We pigged out on junk food yesterday, but we ate real food today. There's pasta and shrimp salad left, if you want some."

He started to decline, planning to pick up a fast-food sandwich on the way home, but Heather wiggled free and pulled his hand, leading the way through the hallway toward the back of the house. "Come on, Daddy. Try it. Abby's a good cook. Real good."

Tom would have liked more than a quick glimpse of the dozen or so family photos grouped together on the wall, but Abby ushered him into a light-filled kitchen with a counter bar. An adjoining dining room seemed to share duty as a greenhouse, by the look of the lush, ceiling-high tropical plants.

Sitting on a soft stool, elbow up to the bar in the snug, aromatic kitchen with three females to wait on him, almost made up for his lonely night, Tom decided. The mountains had offered quiet, but the peace he craved eluded him. Too many thoughts raced through his head, and heart. They followed him down the hill, but he put them aside to watch in fascination the interplay between Abby and his daughters.

"Didn't you say your dad would like that new salad dressing?" Abby asked Heather, who was hanging on the open refrigerator door.

"The Parmesan cheese is on the counter, Angel," she said, giving the girl room to toss, quite messily, the reheated fettuccine. "You added just the right amount at lunch."

Angel served him a heaping mound of noodles adorned with pretty touches of red and green. "Wow," he said after the first bite, his taste buds exploding. "This is great. What is it?"

Abby's cheeks colored like a schoolgirl's. "Just pasta with sun-dried tomatoes, fresh parsley and roasted garlic. Your daughters helped every step of the process."

Heather climbed into the chair beside him. "We picked the green stuff from Abby's garden. You can eat it if you have bad breath." In a lower voice, she added, "But it doesn't taste as good as gum."

Abby's eyes twinkled as she looked up from putting a plate in the dishwasher. He'd have given anything to be able to take her in his arms and kiss her. Fortunately, he had his daughters close by to keep him sane.

When Abby and Heather disappeared into what Tom guessed to be the living room, he asked Angel, "Did you guys get along okay? Heather didn't have a nightmare? Or wet the bed?"

She reached across the counter to put a hand on his arm in such an adult gesture of reassurance it almost took his breath away. My little Angel-babe is growing up. "No more wet beds, Dad. Wait till you see the great underpants Abby bought for Heather. They work like nighttime diapers only they look like real pants. Abby's sister-in-law told her about them."

"Great. I'll buy a box. What about the nightmares?"

Angel shrugged. "She didn't wake up once."

"Really? Wow."

"I think we wore poor Heather out, didn't we, Angel?" Abby said, walking in during Tom's exclamation. "We went swimming at Donna's, grocery shopping, watched two and a half movies and ate nonstop." She puffed out her cheeks.

If she'd put on an extra ounce of weight it sure didn't show, Tom thought. He noted a bit of color on her legs and arms, though. "Did you put sunscreen on Heather? She swims like a fish but burns easily."

Abby poked her upper arm and frowned. "I kept Heather lathered up but forgot about myself. I'd have fried if Angel hadn't warned me."

Tom scowled. He didn't like the idea of Abby neglecting her own safety.

"Dad," Angel said, distracting him, "we need a couple of minutes to get ready." She leaned into him and whispered,

"Keep Abby busy, okay? We're making her something, and it's not quite done."

He nodded just before she disappeared.

"What was that all about?" Abby asked, refilling his glass of water.

He pushed back his plate and rose, stretching to relieve the cranky muscles that hadn't been in a saddle for several weeks. "They need a couple of minutes to get their things together."

"I'll help..." She started to turn toward the doorway, but Tom caught her arm, stopping her in her tracks. She looked at him, her eyes big and surprisingly brown today.

"They need privacy. Something for you, I believe."

Her lips formed an O but no sound came out.

Tom knew the smart thing would be to let go of her, but his fingers thought otherwise. They tightened, just enough to absorb the energy and warmth from her rosy skin. "I thought about you," he admitted, immediately wishing he could take back the words.

"You shouldn't."

"Lots of things I should and shouldn't do, but some things I don't seem to have control over. You're one of 'em. I head out to my special place where the wild grass stays green all summer and the frogs sing and the crickets talk and I lie down at night and look at the billion or so stars and I tell myself, 'Don't think about her.' But wham. There you are."

Instead of pulling back as he expected, she stepped closer to him. Close enough to smell. "What kind of perfume is that?"

Her forehead knit. "I'm not wearing perfume."

He closed his eyes and breathed deeply. "I like it."

His free hand went to the base of her spine and reeled her in. His fingertips connected with bare skin, warm and velvety. Her hips met his at a good spot. Her breasts touched his chest.

"Are you dancing, Daddy?" Heather asked, poking her head through the doorway. "Where's the music?"

Abby jumped back guiltily. "Good point. I'll go put some on."

"Coward," he softly murmured, then looked at his daughter, who was far too young to have such a mischievous look on her angelic face.

The soft strains of something classical filtered into the room.

"So," Abby said, joining Tom and the girls a moment later. This time she left an arm's length between them. "What's up?"

Angel surreptitiously handed her sister a piece of paper the size of a greeting card. Heather stepped forward and handed it to Abby. "We made this last night while you were in the shower."

Abby accepted it with great formality and held it out so Tom could see it, too. The cover displayed brightly colored explosions above a patch of green. The red, white and blue flags scattered around made Tom's stomach tighten.

"It's beautiful," Abby said. "I'm so glad we ran across that old box of color crayons."

"Open it up," Angel said, a look of mischief on her face.

Abby opened the folded piece of paper. "Please join us for our Fourth of July party," she read aloud.

Tom's stomach turned all the way over. He had no trouble picturing Abby with his friends and family, but what would she think of a small-town festival complete with rinky-dink parade, barbecue and dance? Would a city girl have fun or be bored to tears?

Abby glanced at him, as if waiting for some encouragement. "I'd love to come, but maybe you should work this out with your dad first. He may have already invited other people."

Angel snorted. "Yeah, his friends and their stupid kids. But there won't be anybody I know there except you and Ed and Janey. Please say you'll come."

Tom wondered if this had something to do with Angel's moodiness. Was she afraid to meet other kids? Maybe having Abby around would make it easier for her, another safety net or something.

"Yeah, Abby. I need you there, too," Heather said. "What if I have to go potty and can't find Angel? Daddy can't take me 'cause he's a boy, 'n' I don't wanna go alone. Mommy always told me I had to take a buddy with me. She was my buddy before but now she's not." Her bottom lip popped out.

Abby sank to one knee and opened her arms. "Okay, sweetie. I'll go. You can be my buddy and I'll be yours." Heather surged into her arms and hugged her fiercely. Abby looked up as if begging for approval.

Tom smiled. It was either that, or cry.

CHAPTER TEN

ANGEL CHOSE one of the few remaining picnic tables in the park and heaved the wicker hamper onto the graffiti-grooved planks. She hopped up beside it to wait for the others.

What a geek fest, she thought, eyeing the small community park. People were already starting to stake out spots on the curb for the Fourth of July parade. Big whoop. The high-school band, some National Guard guys with flags, a few fat men on horses and politicians in convertibles. Big deal. When Heather first brought it up at Abby's house, Angel saw this as a way to get Abby and her dad together, but now she didn't care. She wasn't speaking to him anymore.

Mom would have understood, Angel thought, drawing a strand of hair between her lips. At least she wouldn't have had a cow if I asked to go home for a week.

A week in Riverside. See Caitlin and everybody. Shop in some real stores. Hang out. Big deal.

But when she asked her dad, he went all closed up and squinty-eyed.

"Did you talk to Val about this?" he demanded.

"No. I'd rather stay with Caitlin. Paige—Caitlin's mother—said I was welcome anytime."

He never really answered her, but Angel knew he didn't want her to go. Janey said he was just being overprotective and told her to be patient. Donna wouldn't back her up, either.

"It's a bigger step than you think," Donna told Angel. "Maybe your father is wise to want to hold off."

Sweeping her hair over one shoulder, Angel saw her father wrestle a cooler out of the back of the truck. Even being mad at him, she couldn't help being proud of how he looked.

He exchanged greetings with a dozen different people—while organizing their picnic supplies. Angel's heart flip-flopped in her chest. He worked so hard, doing all the things it took to run a ranch, plus caring for them, but there were things he just didn't understand.

Peeking through a curtain of hair, Angel scanned the park. Old people and families. Her dad had invited some of his friends, who had kids her age, but the last thing Angel needed was to be foisted on some poor kid who had enough friends of her own.

"Hey, aren't you Angel Butler?" a voice asked.

Angel spun around, drawing up her knees so her feet were flat on the table.

She recognized the chubby blonde who rushed up to greet her but before Angel could answer, the girl asked, "Remember me? I'm Trudy Gills." She pushed her palms against her cheeks and opened and closed her lips, fishlike.

"Yeah, sure, I remember."

The girl hopped up on the table beside her. The legs of her madras-plaid shorts rode up, pinching her plump thighs, and her white eyelet blouse tied just below fledgling bosoms exposed folded layers of baby fat. Suddenly, Angel didn't feel so bad about her choice of outfit: black denim shorts and rust-red tank top with spaghetti straps.

"I'm going to 4-H horse camp this year," Trudy told her. "Second week of August. They still got openings if you wanna come."

"I might be going back ho…down to Riverside to see friends."

Trudy lowered her voice. "All of the J-hotties are going to be there."

"Really. What's a J-hotty?"

"Jared Thomas. Jorges de Mano. Joey Dimenico."

"Oh." Boys.

"Move your butt, Angel, this is heavy," her father said, lugging the oversize cooler toward the table.

She and Trudy scrambled down. Suddenly unsure of herself, she stood mute, feeling stupid.

"Hi, Mr. Butler. Remember me?"

After dumping his load, Tom plopped down on the seat so he was eye level with the smiling girl. "Larry Gills's daughter, right? Tanya?"

Her bubbly laugh eased something tight in Angel's chest. "Trudy," both girls said at once.

"Oh, right. Sorry."

"That's okay. I kinda like Tanya better." She turned to Angel. "Wanna go get a snow cone? The line gets like a mile long after the parade."

Angel looked at her father. They hadn't spoken since last night when she'd stormed off to the barn, cussing as loudly and colorfully as possible.

His eyes were shaded by his cowboy hat, but his lips curled up at the corners. He fished a couple of bucks out of his pocket. "Have fun. Come back when you're hungry. Bring anybody you can round up. Between Abby and Maria, we've got enough food to feed an army."

Angel took a step, but for some reason turned back and hugged her dad. Tears threatened to ruin the makeup she'd put on just to spite him, but she forced them back. Fortunately, Trudy was busy tying the laces of her thick-soled patent-leather sneakers.

"Nice shoes."

"Thanks. You can borrow them sometime."

"Cool."

"Did you ever meet Jenna Macabbee? Her brother's band's playing this afternoon. He's the coolest. Wait till you see his tattoo."

TOM WATCHED Angel and her friend walk away. His heart hurt. If his arm were tingling, he'd have thought he was having a heart attack. Did this kind of thing happen to dads who grew up with their kids instead of jumping into their lives midstream?

"She's made a friend. How wonderful!" a familiar voice said behind him.

"They knew each other from when Angel was here before." He couldn't turn around until he was sure there weren't any tears in his eyes. "I've been trying to get Angel to call Trudy, but Angel wasn't interested."

"The timing wasn't right. She wasn't ready and now she is. I think it's great."

Tom glanced behind him. Abby's arms were heaped to eye level. A bag of marshmallows teetered on top. He spun around in time to field the puffy bag.

"My mother would have called that a lazy man's load," he said, his voice too stern. He relieved her of three quilts and a rattan mat, revealing the top half of her sleeveless, V-neck denim sundress. Pebble-sized red, white and blue beads nestled against her lightly tanned throat.

She cocked her head at him and smiled, her glossy honey-colored lipstick inviting a kiss. "Tell that to your other daughter. She's the one who loaded me up."

She turned away to spread out the remaining quilt. Despite

her effort to bend demurely, her dress, a loosely tailored affair with buttons from top to bottom, rose above midthigh, giving Tom a great view of her legs and a glimpse of red lace.

Suddenly sweating, Tom opened the second button of his shirt and rolled up his sleeves one more turn. He made himself turn away. "Where's Heather?"

"Helping Janey and Ed. I hope Ed remembered his dolly." After spreading out the other blankets, she straightened up and wiped a bead of sweat from her upper lip. "Is it too early for a beer?"

Tom laughed. For the first time in weeks he felt relaxed. He couldn't explain it. Last night's confrontation with Angel, a week of dreading how he'd handle his attraction toward Abby in public all just sloughed off like old skin.

THREE HOURS LATER, amidst a triangle of aluminum tables, portable grills and folding lawn chairs, Tom stretched out on a musty-smelling sleeping bag and cocked his hat over his face to block the sun filtering through the canopy of trees. The noisy horde of friends and family had disappeared, spreading out in all directions. Closing his eyes, Tom listened to the hum of voices and laughter.

What a great day! They'd lucked out, weatherwise. Unseasonably mild with rare high clouds leading the way for some misguided Pacific front, the valley sky was true blue, the temperature well below ninety.

"Looky there," Janey exclaimed, her voice laced with humor. "Just proves my mama was right. There's no fool like an old fool."

Tom rose up on one elbow. Regally sitting in a rattan peacock chair, her baldness disguised by a Middle Eastern print turban, Janey looked exotic, not recuperative. Tom followed her outstretched finger.

Ed—dead center in a cluster of men, each pushing seventy—elbowed his way to the throw line of the horseshoe pit, posturing for the sake of the decades-younger women at the opposing pit.

"When you got it, flaunt it," Tom said dryly.

"He can tell that to his chiropractor tomorrow."

Tom chuckled and eased back down.

"How come you're not over there with them?" She made a snuffling noise. "Oh, I know. You're above all that foolishness. You don't need a woman in your life."

Tom readjusted his hat. He heard a lecture in the offing.

Janey threw something that managed to knock his hat askew.

Groaning, he sat up, crossing his legs. "Okay. Let's hear it."

"You're wound tighter than a pig's tail in January. It's plain as day you care about Abby and, for a smart woman, she's positively goofy when you're anywhere in sight. Why don't you do something about it?"

"Not that simple."

"Hmmph," she snorted. "Truth is, dear heart, you're wrong. Nothing like a brush with death to get your priorities straight.

"Did Ed tell you Peter and Maureen are flying out next week? They're thinking about selling their empty nest and moving out here to be closer to us. I begged Pete to do that years ago—before you came to live here—but he had to do his own thing. One thing cancer's shown me is life doesn't wait for us to make time for it."

Tom traced the groove of his inseam with his thumbnail. "I know what you mean, but there's not just me to consider. I don't want to upset the girls."

"Pooh." She fanned the air with a folded fan Heather had made for her. "You don't think the girls were upset all week watching you mope around? They love you, Tom. They want to see you happy."

"I am happy. Most of the time. The girls have only been here six months. It's not like I was a big dater before they came. I can get by. Besides, a ready-made family with two kids in therapy isn't exactly the kind of thing you spring on somebody."

"Don't blow that smoke around me, Tom Butler. We're not talking about somebody. We're talking about Abby. Cancer gives a person twenty-twenty where bullshit is concerned. You love that gal."

He reached for his hat, any kind of protection from this blunt honesty.

"You're afraid, aren't you? You think Abby might do the same thing Lesley did—love you and leave you."

He crammed the hat down tight. "It's crossed my mind."

"Lesley Pimental was looking for a ticket outta this one-horse town and you were it. Her mama was the same way. Ruby thought a man was the answer to her problems. Five husbands later and she still hasn't got a clue." She shook her head in disgust. "I learned a long time ago that answers come from inside, not outside. Abby already knows that. She has the answer, she just hasn't asked the right question yet. But she will."

Janey reached out and took his hand. He thumbed the yellowish bruise left by the IV needle. "I went to a counseling group at the hospital, Tom. Know what one gal with colon cancer told me? She said, 'When I was first diagnosed, I was afraid of dying. Now, I'm only afraid of not truly living.'"

Tom thought about her words a moment then squeezed her hand. "You're one smart lady, Janey Hastings. I don't know what I'd do without you."

She squeezed back. "Well, I'm licking this damn disease,

so you're not going to have to worry about that for a long, long time. Now go find your girls. All three of 'em."

"BETH, LET ME GET a picture of you and Johnny Dee," Abby said, motioning the Moores together in front of the bandstand. The music, such as it was, had attracted a large group of young people, including Angel and Trudy and a substantial following of teenage boys and girls. Johnny seemed convinced something sexual would take place if he wasn't on patrol. Beth ribbed him about old guilt coming back to haunt him. Nearby, Heather stood with a group of youngsters watching a clown juggle bright scarves.

Abby focused the wide-angle lens. A nice couple. Fourteen years of marriage, Beth told her. Thirteen good, this past one not so hot. But they were working at it.

"Smile."

As soon as the shutter snapped, Johnny swooped Beth into a backward dip and lip lock.

Grinning, Abby turned away, casually scanning the crowd. She was enjoying the day, after all. Her weeklong trepidation about meeting Tom's friends had eased once Maria and Miguel arrived with baby Rey. The Fuenteses and the Hastingses went out of their way to make Abby feel welcome. Chad "Chubs" Raines and his wife, Annette, had eyed her curiously but were distracted by the arrival of the Moores, who'd brought their two kids plus a niece and nephew the same age.

After a huge lunch of hot dogs and barbecued steaks and more side dishes than she could count, Abby found herself chatting with the other women about children, families and the economy. Every once in a while she'd feel Tom's gaze on her, but she was too replete to worry about it.

Johnny broke her mellow reverie when he stepped toward her, hand out. "Your turn. Let me get one of you and Tom."

Abby's heart lurched. "Tom?" She looked toward the blankets where she'd left him napping. From nowhere, a lanky form in faded denims, crisp white shirt with sleeves rolled back to the elbows and gray leather "pointy-toe spider killers," as Ed described Tom's dress boots, materialized at her side. She took a step back.

Johnny snatched the camera from her numb fingers and shoved her to the right. "Closer, not farther apart."

Tom's solid shoulder kept her from stumbling. Abby glanced at Beth, who grinned knowingly. "Smile, Abby."

Lowering the camera, Johnny made a face. "Take off the damn hat, Tom. Why don't you learn to wear a ball cap like everybody else?"

Abby felt him shrug. To her extrasensitive skin, even that slight motion felt full of portent. It set other feelings in motion, making her jiggly inside. "Just take the darned picture, Dee," Tom told him.

"Put your arm around her."

"Take the darned picture," Tom and Abby said together.

Fighting a grin, she looked at him; his lips turned upward, too. Even shaded by the brim of his hat, his eyes reflected the cloudless blue of the sky. Damn, she missed being able to look into his eyes.

"Now, that was more like it," Johnny said, walking up to them. He passed the camera to Abby, who accepted it, unable to make herself break the connection with Tom. "Listen, buddy, we have to do something before it's too late."

"About what?" Tom's eyes held a question that didn't seem to have anything to do with Johnny Dee.

"Them."

Tom also seemed reluctant to move away from Abby, but Johnny stiff-armed him, sending him back a step. "Boys. Walking, talking pillars of raging hormones."

While the two men discussed youthful lust, Beth drew Abby's attention to a group of women Beth called the "town scions, such as they are." Abby only partially listened.

"If that was my guy, I'd have my claws out about now," Beth said in a low voice.

Confused, Abby looked around, finally spotting Tom and Johnny a few feet away. Tom seemed to have acquired a new appendage—a twenty-something redhead in extremely short shorts and halter top plastered to his front, her belly button pressed tight to the big silver bucklc at his waist.

A rush of adrenaline fueled by jealously surged through Abby's system before she could stop it. Fighting a slight wave of nausea, she asked in a stiff voice, "Who is she?"

"Laurie Pimental. His ex-wife's ex-sister-in-law."

"I beg your pardon?"

"Laurie used to be married to Lesley's brother, Raymond. He's in jail, she probably ought to be."

Abby looked away, hating thc way thc young woman's fawning made her gut churn. "Tom can handle it, if he wants to. Some men like that."

Beth shot her a look. "Not Tom Butler. You're obviously the person he's interested in, and Tom wouldn't dream of two-timing somebody. He's the most honorable man I have ever met."

Beth took Abby's arm and led her a few steps away. "Let me tell you about Tom. Johnny and I started dating in eighth grade. We broke up once right before senior prom, and I sort of threw myself at Tom. He was so kind and sweet I ended up crying my eyes out and telling him my whole life story. There was a lot of alcohol abuse in my family, and Johnny was partying pretty heavy back then. The idea of reliving my mom's life terrified me. Tom is the one who made Johnny go to counseling with me."

Beth stepped closer and lowered her voice. "You probably don't know this, but Johnny and I are the reason Tom wasn't home when the cops first called about Lesley. We were fighting, and I'd packed up the kids and moved to my folks' place in Fresno. Johnny and Chubs went out drinking and bumped into Tom. He'd been up in the mountains for a week. He's not much of a drinker, and he hadn't eaten all day. Anyway, the booze did a real number on him. Johnny hid his keys and left him sleeping it off in his truck. That's where the highway patrol found him the next morning."

She frowned. "He blamed himself, not Johnny or me."

Abby could picture it. Honorable. Noble. She knew that about him, respected him for it, possibly even loved him for it, but that didn't change things between them.

To keep from looking at Tom and the human leach, Abby scanned the crowd for Heather, who had been ten feet away not three minutes earlier. Squinting, she pivoted in each direction. No mop of white-blond curls in sight.

"Heather," Abby called, instinctively heading in the direction where she'd last seen her. "Beth, do you see Heather anywhere?"

"She was here a second ago."

Abby's heart sped up. She spotted Angel and waved her over. "Have you seen Heather?"

Angel shook her head, as did her pudgy shadow.

"Run to the picnic spot, see if she's with Janey."

Obviously alert to the fear in Abby's voice, Angel didn't hesitate.

Abby sent Beth back to enlist Tom and Johnny in the search while she headed toward the 4-H and FFA exhibits. Heather loved animals.

Fighting back all the dire images of faces on milk cartons, Abby picked her way through the crowd, trying to look in all directions at once. A throng of people blocked her way. As she eased around them, she realized she'd reached the line for the portable bathrooms, which were at the outskirts of the festivities.

She turned back, recalling a wire-fenced enclosure beneath a stay of elms. The 4-H petting zoo. As she neared a fence of straw bales, a flash of white caught her eye. In the far corner of the pen sat Heather, a huge duck on her lap.

Abby flew past the startled young attendant. "Heather," she cried breathlessly, tears brimming. She dropped to her knees, the scratchy straw poking her bare skin. "Why didn't you tell me where you were going? I thought I lost you."

Clearly puzzled by Abby's tone, Heather shook her head. "I only just walked here. This is Ferdinand. Like in the movie."

Abby shooed the duck away then pulled Heather into her arms. Rocking back and forth, she squeezed her tight. Relief opened the floodgate. She closed her eyes but couldn't stop the tears. "Oh, baby, don't ever scare me like that again."

When she opened her eyes, she found Tom watching from just outside the fence. His smile thanked her for finding his daughter; the look in his eyes made her heart dance.

ABBY CLOSED HER EYES and inhaled. No smell on earth could be sweeter than a man's scent mingled with spray starch. Tom's shoulder beneath his neatly pressed shirt made the kind of pillow she could lean her head against for the rest of her life, if she let herself—which, of course, she couldn't. But, Abby told herself, one night can't hurt.

With tiny, white lights twinkling in the trees surrounding the grass dance floor, Abby felt like Cinderella at the ball. The magic would disappear at midnight and she would go back to being responsible, but for the moment she was free to drink it all in, every splendid moment.

The band, a fifty-something ensemble complete with an accordion player, set the mood with old standards like "Stardust" and "Fly Me to the Moon." Tom danced with simple grace. He held her close but with respect and dignity. His strong arms made her feel safe. His heart seemed to beat in time with hers.

"Look," he said, directing Abby's attention to the row of kids perched on the split-rail fence that flanked the band shell. Angel, laughing and pointing with the others, looked happy—quite a change from the petulant youngster Abby had escorted to Fresno on Thursday. "They think because we're old we can't have fun. I'm having fun. What about you?"

"I don't think *fun* quite covers it," she said, looking into his eyes, wishing she could memorize the twinkling humor she saw reflected. So often lately, he'd been as serious and somber as his elder daughter, but tonight both seemed transformed. Angel because she'd reconnected with her friends; Tom because…Abby wasn't brave enough to explore that one.

His oh-so-masculine lips narrowed slightly and his forehead creased. "No?"

"No. A *fun* day earns a paragraph or two in my journal. This one's more like four or five pages," she told him honestly. He rewarded her candor with a sweet kiss at each corner of her lips. It would have been so easy to turn her head to meet his lips, but a swell in the level of heckling made her bury her face against his shoulder.

"My brother always said I'd pay for sneaking up on him when he was making out with his girlfriend," she muttered.

Tom's chuckle rumbled through his chest.

"Daddy," Heather cried, wedging between their legs. "It's time for the fireworks. Look, Abby, look."

Tom hoisted Heather to one hip and took Abby's hand, leading the way to the curb, where the rest of their group had gathered. Abby glanced over her shoulder and saw Angel and her friends racing to find a good vantage point. A sudden sense of fullness, of perfection within a moment, brought tears to her eyes. She squeezed Tom's hand. Her handsome prince with two wonderful daughters. Cinderella never had it so good.

CHAPTER ELEVEN

TOM HUNG UP the receiver of the phone with exquisite care to keep from hurling it across the room.

"Something wrong?" Ed asked, poking his head in the doorway of the box-filled room that would soon be the ranch's new office. Janey had commandeered the old office for her genealogy research, telling Ed, "Thirty-five years of having an office in my house is long enough."

Ed used the move as an excuse to buy a new computer, which he planned to coerce Tom into using. First, Tom had to find time to get it out of its box.

Tom sighed and ran a hand through his hair. "I think it's called the brush-off, but it's been so long since I've dated, I'm not real sure," he said honestly.

On the Fourth of July, Tom was certain things were heating up between him and Abby. They'd danced, laughed, even squeezed in a furtive kiss before Angel and her friends found them. By the time he fell asleep that night, he could picture their wedding and the birth of their child. But that was Sunday. Now it was Friday afternoon and he had yet to talk to Abby, let alone do anything that could result in propagation.

She'd even bailed on driving the girls to Rainbows yesterday, telling Angel her boss had scheduled a meeting, which she couldn't avoid. When Tom tried calling her at home after their return at ten, there'd been no answer. He figured this was the same boss who was trying to date her.

Tom rolled his shoulders trying to ease some of the tension.

"I finally made a decision about allowing Angel to go to Riverside and wanted to run it past Abby," he told Ed. Tom trusted Abby's judgment; he needed her input. He missed her, damn it.

"Did you try her office?" Ed asked, lowering his body to the used but serviceable leather couch.

Tom nodded. "I just talked to her friend, Melina. She sounded apologetic as hell, but she said Abby has been in meetings all week—something about their boss finding some money to hire two new employees, and Abby handling all the interviews."

"She's a busy lady."

Tom sighed. "I know. But—"

"You thought things had changed between you."

Tom eyed his friend, the man who in many ways knew him better than his father. "Yep."

Ed steepled his callused fingers. "Could be Abby's just plain busy. Could be she's developed a case of what's commonly called cold feet. You've seen it happen when you're breaking a colt," Ed told him. "You get 'em to a spot you think they're comfortable with you, then—*wham*—somethin' spooks 'em. Just takes time and patience."

Tom sighed. "A part of me knows that. The girls need time. I need time. Abby needs time." He looked at the freshly painted walls of what had once been the tack room. "But then there's the seventeen-year-old inside me who wants it all right now."

Ed hooted. "At least you're honest." He rose, using the arm of the sofa for leverage. "Son," he said, "do yourself a favor. Go drown that kid in a cold shower, then load up your girls and take 'em down south. Janey don't have to go back till Thursday so I can keep an eye on things. Angel needs to make peace with her old life, and I'm thinkin' it might not hurt to put a little space between you and Abby for a time. Might be her feet'll warm up by the time you get back."

ABBY COULDN'T CONTAIN the excitement bubbling in her chest as she pulled into the Hastingses' driveway. She hadn't seen Tom in a week. Last Sunday, the Fourth of July, something had changed between them, something that both thrilled and terrified Abby. She hadn't been deliberately avoiding Tom all week—well, maybe she had, a little, but work had provided the perfect excuse not to see him until she could get things straightened out in her own mind.

As Melina told Tom, Daniel had appointed Abby moderator of the hiring committee. Her days were packed with résumés and interviews; her nights were filled with dreams of dancing in Tom's arms.

She could have called or made a better effort to return his calls, but she didn't want to do that until she knew what she was going to say. Indecisiveness was not a trait she liked in herself or others, but Abby found herself flip-flopping on this issue like a politician before election day.

And my decision is? she thought, slowly extricating herself from the car. She looked toward the newly painted addition visible through the leafy walnuts. *To go for it, of course.*

Janey's invitation to Sunday dinner gave Abby a much-welcomed chance to see the family she missed. With any luck she and Tom could slip away to discuss the possibility of seeing each other socially. It was a big step, one that meant she would have to reassign his case to another advocate, but she thought he'd agree.

"Hi, Abby," Ed said, opening the door for her. "Come in. We're tickled pink you could come."

Abby walked into the flagstone foyer. Straight ahead, in the step-down living room, a wall of glass provided a panoramic view of fields and orchards beyond the knoll. "What a view!" Abby exclaimed, handing Ed the bottle of wine in her hands.

He ushered her into the room. "We like it. Makes me feel like a king some days."

Janey, entering through a swinging door to the right, hurried to Abby's side and took her hands in a warm greeting. "Hello, dear," she said, smiling. "We're so glad you could come. I'd hoped Tom and the girls would be here, but they won't be back from down south until Wednesday. Heather absolutely refused to miss the Rainbows picnic."

Abby knew all about the picnic. She couldn't go because of Daniel's first-ever VOCAP four-day staff retreat that she was coordinating. Melina said it was retribution for dumping him. Abby argued the dumping was mutual, since Daniel was the one who'd called her into his office two weeks earlier and demanded to know whether they had a relationship or not. Abby couldn't lie. She felt bad for letting him think he'd ever had a chance to win her heart. Her only solace was that rumor had it Daniel was already involved with a woman from the mayor's office.

Abby's disappointment must have shown, although she did her best to hide it. Ed handed her a glass of wine. "Here. This'll help."

"I didn't know he'd made up his mind to let Angel go," Abby said, sipping the red wine.

Janey glanced at her husband. "I think Ed helped point Tom in that direction. Ed told him Angel needed to put a few ghosts to rest. I sure hope it was the right decision."

Ed shrugged his burly shoulders. "You can't go forward with your life if you're always looking back," he said sagely. "Now that Angel's got some friends around here, she's got something to compare to her old life. She has a good head on her shoulders and she's always liked the ranch. I think it'll work out the way it should."

Abby hoped he was right. She hadn't had a chance to talk to Angel about her new friends, but Heather told Donna that Tom was thinking about getting Call Waiting because Angel was constantly on the phone.

During dinner Janey explained about Tom's compromise: he agreed to drive Angel back to Riverside if she agreed to four days, not a week. That way he could take Heather to a few amusement parks, and even visit a guy who was interested in purchasing one of Tom's colts.

Abby was impressed, but not surprised. Tom's flexibility was one of the things she admired most about him. She only hoped that it extended to his social life, because as much as she wanted to be included in that life, she knew she wasn't going to be able to give him what he'd want—marriage, babies, the whole nine yards. She hoped he'd settle for a love affair.

"THANK YOU, dear," Grace Davis said, practically patting Abby on the head like a child. "Come back for me around four."

"Come back?" Abby exclaimed. "Mother, you can't be serious. You can't just...I need...the girls don't even..."

Abby knew Heather and Angel were staring at her as if she'd lost her mind. Maybe she had. Her mother, the woman who'd unloaded her infant daughter on her mother-in-law to raise, had just volunteered to hang wallpaper with two children—children she'd never even met until ten minutes earlier. Granted, Grace had talked with them on the phone before deciding on which decorating scheme to follow, but still.

"You...you want me to leave?"

"Yes, dear," Grace said, relieving Abby of the two oversize shopping bags she'd just hauled in from the car.

"But I can help." Abby detested the pleading sound in her voice.

Grace looked at Abby through the fashionable, gold-rimmed reading glasses perched on the end of her nose. "Don't you remember what happened when we tried wallpapering your guest room?"

Abby shuddered. A near brush with matricide. If Melina hadn't intervened, Abby would have dumped a pan of wall-paper paste over her mother's head.

While Abby watched, Grace rolled back the sleeves of her paint-splattered smock and handed a wide roll of wallpaper to Angel and two smaller rolls—the border—to Heather. "Clear off the kitchen table, girls. We need room to spread out." She looked toward the dining nook. "My, what a nice fifties dinette!"

Grace briefly surveyed the room before turning her attention back to the collection of shopping bags at her feet. She tapped a tastefully lacquered nail against her still-smooth cheek and hummed, thinking.

She never really ages, Abby thought, admiring her mother's punkish haircut, an avant-garde blend of silver and red. Grace would be seventy next year, but she still worked four days a week and played golf the other three. Abby both envied her and resented her.

"I believe I have everything I need, dear," she said, smiling warmly. "This will give you a couple of free hours to yourself. You work much too hard."

That theme had been discussed at length last night; Abby wasn't about to get into it again. "But, Mom, I want to help."

Grace's lips pursed—a look Abby remembered well from childhood. It meant her mind was made up. "You and I don't work well together, dear. We're too much alike, I guess."

Abby blanched at the thought.

"But the girls—"

"Look eager and intelligent," she said, cutting Abby off.

Grace beamed at her two helpers as if genuinely pleased to spend time with them. "And we've already determined they have exquisite taste. Don't worry, dear, we'll get along fine."

Heather and Angel, avidly watching the interplay, smiled back. *But I want to spend time with them.* She'd missed them, having barely managed twenty minutes with them in the past three weeks, thanks to Daniel. He'd scheduled an employee orientation meeting so Abby wasn't able to drive the girls to their final Rainbows meeting. She'd shared the pain but been cheated out of the triumph.

"Come see our room," Heather said, taking Grace's hand. Abby's heart constricted jealously.

"Oh, Abby," Grace said. "Let's not forget a before-and-after picture. Where's my camera? I know your father packed it somewhere." Abby's father had remained in Palm Desert.

Abby fished a small silver Nikon out of Grace's tote bag and followed them to the addition. She hadn't seen it since the carpet went in.

"Light and airy," Grace said. "Very good choice of carpet, Abby."

It wasn't much, but compliments from Grace Davis were rare. "Thanks."

After a dozen shots, Grace hustled Abby off.

"Wait," Heather said, dashing to Abby's side. With a conciliatory smile, she deposited a marble-size piece of blue bubble gum in Abby's hand.

Abby popped the rock-hard treat in her mouth and left with a smile on her face. Masticating with conviction, she plopped down on the front step. Heat, that ghastly, pizza-oven heat of summer, immediately tried to melt her. A sprinkler methodically arched back and forth over the ragged little patch of lawn, dousing Heather's bike with staccato bursts. "Now what?" Abby asked Rosie, who hogged the only available patch of shade. The old dog thumped her thick tail twice—whether in greeting or to annoy the flies, Abby wasn't sure.

She held her hand to her forehead and squinted through desertlike heat waves toward the ranch house. Abby knew Janey and Ed were back in Stanford for Janey's final series of treatments.

Abby had meant to call to wish them good luck, but the time flew by in a haze of tension generated by the new staff and Daniel's autocratic attitude. Abby would have postponed her mother's visit except she didn't want to disappoint the girls, who couldn't wait to add the finishing touches to their new bedroom. Last night, after her mother went to bed, Abby worked up the nerve to call Tom, but Angel, who, along with Trudy Gills, was baby-sitting Heather, told her Tom was at a fish fry at the Elks Club with Johnny. It seemed everyone had a life but her.

"So," Abby said, stroking Rosie's sun-heated coat, "do I drive all the way home and come back in two hours or what?"

Rosie's ears perked up. Abby tilted her head and strained to listen, too. A clanking sound echoed from the direction of the new horse corral. Curious, she rose and headed in that direction.

If a picture was worth a thousand words, the image of Tom, shirtless, sweating, looking like a model for some sexy calendar, was worth a million. Abby's fingers tingled as if she'd just touched metal after walking over carpet. A smile sprang to her lips even when she tried to banish it. This feast for the eyes nourished something puny and starved in her soul. Suddenly, whatever was lacking in her life—that essence that made daylight brighter, jokes funnier and oranges sweeter—hit her full force. A little dizzy, she grabbed for the closest fence post.

With legs spread a shoulder-width apart on either side of

the steel fence post he was in the process of driving into the ground, Tom lifted a heavy-looking tool in place above the post and slammed it down with brute force. His gloved hands curled tighter on the handles of the pounding tool. He raised it a few inches and repeated the process. With each upward stroke, his shoulder muscles bunched from the strain, giving Abby a heart-stopping display of muscle power. His pectorals were molded like a young Arnold Schwarzenegger's. Although she'd long admired Tom's solid build, Abby hadn't realized the strength that went along with those muscles.

Each clanging sound made Abby's blood pulse in her ears.

A miniature dust devil sent the powdery soil at his feet billowing upward. Coughing, he reached for a water bottle sitting in the skinny strip of shade at the base of a previously positioned post. Without a belt, his jeans rode low, giving Abby a glimpse of shorts and white skin. The upper three inches of denim around his waist was dark with sweat.

His thumb popped the cap. He took a gulp then tilted his head back, squirting water across his face. Under his frayed, misshapen straw cowboy hat, a blue bandanna was knotted to absorb moisture. His skin looked flushed from the heat and sun. Grimy rivulets of perspiration and water coursed down his neck, leaving trails meandering over dust-coated muscles, fanning out in the diamond-shaped patch of chest hair.

He swished a mouthful of water from cheek to cheek then turned and spat. The stream landed two feet in front of her. A few drops sprinkled her bare toes, making her jump.

His eyes narrowed. "Sorry. Didn't see you there."

"Hi," she said, her gum getting tangled with her tongue. Blushing, she moved the nasty wad to one side.

He lifted one hand to push back his hat a notch. A lukewarm greeting, at best.

Suddenly, a bolt of lust swept through her. Why in the hell

was she being so damn noble? She had needs, too. She was trying to be adult about this, trying to be circumspect, to do the right thing for his sake and the sake of his children. Did he appreciate her restraint? Apparently not. He was looking at her as if he thought she'd been avoiding him on purpose, as if she didn't want him. What woman in her right mind wouldn't want him?

The force of the blood moving through her veins made her chest ache. Her palms were sweaty while her feet felt cold. Wavy lines across her vision made her blink. This is either lust or heatstroke. Either way, there was only one cure.

TOM'S HEART SLAMMED against his chest.

"Hello, Abby." He kept his tone neutral, studying her face and eyes with a trainer's intuitiveness. What had Ed said about giving her time to recognize her feelings? Was that desire he saw? Wasn't this too soon to try again?

One part of his brain shouted out the obvious: cutoff shorts and flip-flops. Too much leg and ten toes with lilac polish. Little blue tank top and white lace underthings. Shit. She didn't play fair.

He dropped the sport bottle, giving it a kick for good measure. When he reached for the heavy-gauge steel post driver, the top-heavy post wobbled drunkenly. He'd have kicked it, too, but probably would have broken a toe.

He looked again. The raw desire in her eyes nearly sent him over the edge. Where the hell were her sunglasses when he needed them?

Goddamn it, how much am I expected to take? Tearing his gaze from her, he stalked to the newly installed water trough. Yanking off his gloves, he let them drop then pitched his hat toward the barn and plunged his upper torso into the tepid water. Blindly, he reached for the shirt that should have been hanging on the post.

"Here," she said.

Squeezing out his soaked bandanna, he used it to wipe his eyes. She stood an arm's-length away, offering him the shirt like an invitation—one she knew damn well that he couldn't resist.

With a groan, he pulled her against his bare, dripping chest and crushed her lips beneath his. Her arms flew around his neck. He felt his shirt drop from her grasp and slide down his bare back. She pressed her body against him as if trying to crawl under his skin.

Her tongue met his with a passion he didn't expect. Part defense, part offense. He couldn't really tell where one started and the other left off. She tasted of bubble gum; the silliness of it made a laugh catch in his throat.

Choking, he pulled back. "Why are you here?" he asked with his first good breath.

"You know I can't stay away."

She reached up and pulled his head down to finish what he'd started. Her fingers moved in his wet hair. Her scent, as fresh and intoxicating as a field of wildflowers filled his nostrils. He followed the flowery trail lower, spreading kisses along her jaw, stopping to nuzzle the tender depression at the top of her breastbone.

Her sweet moan tantalized him, spurring him lower. He placed his hand over her breast, and felt her tremble. Her nipple solidified through both shirt and bra. He pulled the shirt free from the waistband of her shorts and worked his hand upward, lifting the jersey material over her quivering ribs. His focus centered on the rounded white breast and rose-tipped nipple straining against translucent material.

Forcing his impatient brain to slow down, he dipped a finger beneath the lace.

"Small..." she started to say.

He stopped her words with a kiss. Kneading the breast that

fit his hand perfectly, he deepened the kiss. A groan deep in her throat almost sent him over the edge. Whatever illusion of control he thought he possessed disappeared like a sinner's good intentions.

Her hips wiggled provocatively against his. His body ached to do what it was designed to do. Tom reached behind her with both hands cupping her buttocks and lifted her that inch or so to fit against him.

She moaned against his lips. "Tom, I've missed you. I need you."

His heart quickened its already frantic beat. His chest sizzled from the sensation of her rigid nipples pressing against him. In his mind, he could almost taste her. Honey. She'd taste like honey. His mouth watered, but when he tried to swallow, nothing happened.

Like a freight train braking at full speed, it took a minute for the message to reach all the way down the line.

With a groan of pure agony, he pulled back. "No."

Her hand slid around from his buttocks to the hard length between them. She cupped him; her thumb flicked across the straining zipper. "Your body says yes."

Her simmering, husky tone beckoned like a siren in a Greek tragedy. Months of longing pushed toward the point of no return. Do it. This is what he wanted. Why wait? Take what she's offering. Where? The barn. He knew where to find an old sleeping bag. Or they could use the couch in his office. No lock, but…

The images imploded.

"No." He shook his head, trying to move the blood back from his extremities. "Not here. Not like this."

He put both hands on her shoulders and moved her back a step. "My body says, 'Yes, please, God, yes.' My heart says, 'Yes.' But my head says, 'Get a grip, man. We're not seventeen and Abby deserves better than a roll in the hay.'"

The glimmer of passion, which had turned her eyes copper, was extinguished like a flame in a storm. She dropped her chin. Tom pulled her back into his arms. The heat still surged between them, but he could control it now. He had to. This was too important.

"We need to talk."

She wouldn't meet his eyes but nodded. "I know."

"Wait here." He glanced around for a spot of shade, but the glare of direct sunlight had turned the whole south side of the barn into a convection oven. Funny, he thought, I didn't notice that a minute ago. "No. It's hotter than hell here. Come to my office."

He stooped to pick up his shirt then took her hand, which felt as small and compliant as Heather's, and led her into the barn. The interior passage was shadowy, but Tom could have found his way blindfolded.

He opened the door, letting her go in first. The small room was crowded to the point of claustrophobia. Two five-foot file cabinets in one corner, a fax machine under the window, his grandfather's old oak desk heaped with papers, and in the far corner a stack of unopened boxes—his new computer.

"This used to be the tack room." Tom sniffed. "Still smells like one, but what do you expect? This is a ranch."

She stood unmoving. His heart sped up. This wasn't going to be easy. He tried to inject a bit of levity. "Maybe I could hire your mother to decorate it."

He gave her credit for trying, but the wished-for smile dissolved before it registered on her lips.

"Is it cool enough in here?" he asked, slipping his arms into his shirt. A tiny air conditioner hummed in the lower half of the window. "Why don't you turn it up?"

Robotlike, she took a step in that direction, but stopped in front of the fax machine.

"You got a fax," she said, not turning around. "It's from Daniel. I recognize the letterhead."

He walked to his desk and eyed the sheet of paper. "What's it about?" he asked before he picked it up.

"A formality. Informing you that you've been assigned a new caseworker."

He snatched it out of the tray. "Why? What's wrong with my old one?"

She turned to face him. "She's either promoted or fired. She's not sure which, and frankly, she doesn't care."

Tom hated this lethargy. It was such a far cry from the passion he'd witnessed just minutes before. He reached out and took her hand. "Come and sit down. Do you want a soda or anything?"

She shook her head.

They sat side-by-side, hunched forward, hands resting on their knees.

Tom wasn't sure how to begin.

"I'm sorry," Abby started.

He put a finger to her lips and shook his head. Water drops sprinkled his arm. He finger-combed his wet hair with an impatient swipe.

"Abby, what happened outside was…great. Incredible." He grimaced, wishing he were a cowboy poet instead of just a cowboy. "I'm pretty sure it would have been the best sex of my life. But I want more than that."

She looked sideways. Finally, a spark of curiosity kindled in her eyes.

"Abby, I love you."

Her eyes opened wider.

He didn't wait to see if she'd tell him she loved him back. He knew she cared; he was pretty sure she loved him, or at least loved his daughters and liked him a lot. He could work with that, but first they had to get past the obstacles she kept erecting to keep him at a distance.

"Abby, I need to know why you always kiss and run."

Her mouth opened and closed like a guppy.

"Whenever something starts happening between us, you head for the hills. I don't know what the problem is, but I know it's not because of your job."

"True." She took a deep breath then went on in a rush, "I knew about Daniel's decision before I came out here today, but it wouldn't have mattered. I'd already made up my mind that you and I…that we…it was going to happen." She made a futile attempt at a smile. "I just didn't think it would happen like that." Her cheeks blossomed with color.

He loved her blush and had to make a fist to keep from touching her.

"I feel like I got sideswiped by a truck." She pretended to peek over her shoulder. "Are there skid marks?"

He waited, letting her lead the way. After yesterday's session, Tom asked Donna about his daughters' progress and asked whether or not it would be wise to date Abby. Donna, in her mystic, patient-client tone, told him, "Abby has ghosts. We all do. You show her yours, and maybe she'll show you hers."

Not totally convinced psychology wasn't just a bunch of hooey, he was willing to give it a try. "Is it because of the girls and Lesley? That 'year-of-grieving' thing you told me about?"

Her left eyebrow rose. "The four seasons of grief?"

"Right. I asked Donna about that, and she said the girls will always miss Les and in some ways they'll always grieve for her, but they've come a long way toward getting past the worst of it. Heather only has nightmares once or twice a week now. But if you think they need a year, then we'll wait. I don't need a year, Abby. I did my grieving a long time ago." His jaw tightened, and he made himself flex his fingers to relax. He didn't like talking about that time in his life. "I took it pretty hard when Lesley left me. Drank too much. It was ugly." He shook his head. "Got even worse when I found out she was pregnant with Heather. I parked my truck with a camper shell on the back in front of her apartment building. Les told the manager I was a stalker. He called the police.

"I came home to lick my wounds, but I still thought—hoped—she'd come back to me. I don't suppose I really gave up hoping till she married Val. But that was four years ago."

He looked at her. Sympathy and understanding showed in her expressive eyes. She always had empathy for others but so little for herself.

"Tell me about Billy," he said gently.

She sat back as though he'd slapped her. "Did Donna tell you…?"

"No. She said that's up to you."

BILLY.

Abby took a deep breath. "I fell in love with him when I was seventeen—without really knowing him. I loved an image, a product of his mother's hopes and my imagination."

Abby told him about the report she did for school, the story of a heroic soldier who lost his leg in the war. She told him about meeting Billy years later at his mother's funeral, his tragic aura, a lost soul in need of succor. "I thought I could heal him. I thought my love could make him whole."

Tom settled back, positioning himself with enough room to watch her face. She couldn't bring herself to meet his eyes. Her humiliation over throwing herself at him was bad enough, but dredging up these old memories was worse.

"I more or less threw myself at him, but Billy was looking for something, too. Maybe he thought I was the answer. He invited me to move in with him but refused to make love with me until he was tested for AIDS because he'd been with a lot of women in Hawaii." Abby sighed. "I found that incredibly noble." Saying the words made her throat constrict. She'd kept these memories locked away for a reason—they hurt.

"When my folks found out about us, there was a big uproar because of the difference in our ages, but I ignored it." Abby had expected her parents to be upset, but it crushed her that her brothers couldn't support her choice. The worst part was learning they were right.

"Billy tried. It wasn't all his fault, but I built that pedestal awfully high. Gradually he fell back into his old habits, blocking his pain with drugs and alcohol."

Tom took her hand. The room was far from chilly, but her extremities were frigid.

"I switched my major from prelaw to psychology. I thought I could cure him. Unfortunately, I couldn't even help myself or..." She pinched off the thought. She couldn't open that door. Not yet.

"Donna and I've talked a lot about this. She thinks Billy was suffering from clinical depression, but it could have been manic depression because sometimes he'd stay up for four or five days at a time." Abby sighed. "Of course, that could have been from the drugs. I was so damn naive, but I learned a lot in a hurry. One thing I learned is, you can't save someone who doesn't want to be saved."

She rubbed her neck. Tom brushed her fingers away and gently prodded the tense muscle. She closed her eyes. "One day I came home from school and found him passed out. The place was a mess. I hadn't been feeling too great myself, and I said some things I shouldn't have said."

Her heart raced, remembering the look on Billy's face. "'So much for hero worship,' he said. Then he told me what really happened in Nam. How he lost his leg. Not because of bravery but because of a drunken mistake.

"I felt so sorry for him. But when I tried to comfort him, he freaked out. He—" She flashed back to that moment when her world went haywire. Billy lashing out. Those powerful arms that could be so tender and loving, suddenly turning to weapons, squeezing her, punching her. Abby didn't know if it was memory or imagination, but she swore she could tell the exact blow that ended their child's life, even though she hadn't known she was pregnant at the time.

She didn't realize she was shaking until Tom put his arms around her.

"It's all in the past, Abby," he told her softly.

She relaxed her fingers and made herself breathe. "I…I left and didn't come back for three days. Maybe he thought I wasn't coming back. I'll never know. He didn't leave a note."

Tom made a harsh sound; Abby couldn't look at him. "Death by hot tub," she said, trying to be flip. "The coroner ruled it an accidental overdose of drugs and alcohol combined with the hot water."

Tom squeezed her shoulders supportively.

"In his will, he left me the house. My dad and brothers cleaned it out, sold the hot tub and gave Billy's stuff to some veterans' group. They found me an apartment close to school and listed the house with a rental agency."

She smiled, picturing a happier memory. "Four years later, Donna and I went to the house together. It wasn't so bad. There were crayon marks on the wall. The ghosts were gone."

He stroked the side of her face with the back of his finger. "Are they?"

She nodded, wishing it were that simple.

"I love you, Abby. I know the timing stinks, but there's not much I can do about that. We have a shot at something good, if you're ready to try."

He waited, ever so patiently. Kindness and love warmed his blue eyes to the color of a robin's egg. His love was that fragile, too. She could hurt him. Badly.

"I love you, too. I think."

His forehead knotted, creating deep furrows. "You're not sure."

"I'm not exactly an expert. This isn't anything like what I felt for Billy."

"Thank God." He frowned. "And Landon?"

"That wasn't love. We were just good friends who slept together."

He made a primitive growling sound.

She grimaced. "I'm sorry. But it happened."

"I know. I had a couple of flings after Lesley." He moved closer. "I'm not an expert on love, Abby, but I know how I feel about you. I want to make love with you. I want to wake up in the morning and see your face on the pillow beside me. I want the rocker next to yours in the old folks' home."

She closed her eyes, hating herself for what was coming, powerless to change it. Why do we have to make life so complicated? Why do we have to get hung up on lifelong commitments and families?

When she opened them, she found him sitting back, a wounded look on his face. "You're not going to marry me, are you?" he asked. "You'll have sex with me. You'd have done that in the hayloft if I'd pointed the way, but you won't marry me."

His insight frightened her more than she wanted to admit. "I...I can't marry you."

"Why not?"

Abby knew she'd had her chance to be a mother, and she'd failed to protect her child. How could she trust herself to be responsible for the lives of Heather and Angel—the only two children Tom would ever have if he married her since she was no longer able to conceive? "The girls."

His mouth dropped open and his eyes filled with hurt and confusion. "You love the girls, and they love you."

It took every ounce of strength she possessed to stand up. She put her hand on his shoulder—felt him flinch as though struck. "I know. That's why I can't marry you. Trust me, Tom. I'm not the person you want to be their mother. I wish I were, but I'm not."

She was one heartbeat away from tears. "This isn't easy for me, Tom, and it may not make sense, but I know my limitations. I suck at relationships. I loved Billy, but, basically, when it comes right down to it, I killed him."

"Abby," he cried, "that's not true."

She put her finger to his lips, touched by his impassioned support.

She moved away, putting some distance between them. "I thought I could do this, Tom—get involved with you without really getting involved, but I can't. It wouldn't be fair to you or the girls.

"It may look cowardly but I'm trying to do the brave thing. The right thing for you and your family. I never meant for it to come to this. I'm sorry."

"What did you think would happen between us, Abby?" His voice was keen with hurt and disappointment.

She closed her eyes. "Sex. Friendship. I don't know. Maybe if we could take it slow, I could—"

When she looked at him she saw the truth, a truth she'd always known. Tom was an all-or-nothing kind of guy. He loved with all his heart and expected the same from the person he loved. Abby wanted to be that person, but it wasn't possible. She wasn't whole; a part of her was missing.

"I'm sorry, Tom," she said, not daring to look at him one last time. She left the office and hurried through the barn.

THE SUN AND HEAT stopped her halfway to the house; a pain in her gut doubled her over. Deep breaths helped, just as Donna taught her so many years before. By the time she got to the porch, her hands had almost quit shaking. She knocked politely and called out in a voice that almost sounded normal.

"We're not done yet," Angel said, opening the door for her. "But it looks great. Come see."

Abby did her best to act enthused—the job was spectacular. The border—a looping trail of hyacinth and delicate ivy—encircled the room. The west wall and desk area was papered with a complementary print. Lacy curtains created a Victorian flavor. Her mother's expert touches were subtle but dramatic.

"Mom, I'm not feeling well," Abby said lamely. "The heat's done a number on me."

Her mother eyed her shrewdly. The girls looked at her with concern.

"You look pale. Why don't you go home, dear? Lie down. I'm sure Mr. Butler will give me a ride when I'm done here."

As much as she hated to burden Tom with her mother, Abby welcomed the chance to be alone to come to grips with her decision. Her loss. Even if it was the right thing to do, it hurt like hell.

"Bye, baby love," Abby said, giving Heather a squeeze. "Be good."

Heather's bottom lip popped out, perhaps she was sensing Abby's tribulation.

Angel followed Abby to the car. "What's going on? Did you and Dad have a fight?"

Her intuitiveness unnerved Abby. She went for a halftruth. "I got fired from your case today. Your dad has the fax in his office."

"So?" Angel asked, hands on hips. "You don't come here to be with us because it's your job. Do you?"

A quick hurt now would save a bigger hurt later, but Abby couldn't bring herself to lie. "Of course not, but it gave me a good excuse to be here. Now I won't have one because they gave your case to one of the new field officers, whom I will be training. Which is why I won't have a lot of time to socialize."

Angel frowned, a dark scowl Abby hadn't seen for a while. "But I'll still take you guys shopping for school clothes if you want me to," she said, trying to sound upbeat. "Remember? The Modesto Mall. The Friday after horse camp."

"What about Dad?" Angel asked. "When we were driving back from Riverside, we talked about you and him maybe getting together."

"You did?"

"Yeah. He asked me how I'd feel about you two going out."

Abby's hand tightened on the Honda's door handle. The heat seared her palm, but it was so much less painful than the hurt in her chest, she ignored it. "What did you say?" Abby asked in a small voice.

Angel shrugged, her long air bouncing as a single sheath. "I told him to go for it." She gave Abby a serious look. "Mom always hoped he'd remarry. She said he was the kind of man who needed a family."

Abby flinched, holding back her tears by sheer willpower alone. "I agree. But—" She couldn't say more.

Angel's face screwed up in confusion. "You turned him down?"

Abby opened the car door, turning her back to Angel. "It's not the right time for either of us, Angel. Your dad's busy with the ranch and you guys, and I'm going back to college—"

"That's bogus," Angel interrupted. Her eyes got all squinty

like Tom's. "Totally fucking bogus and you know it! Adults make me sick." She turned around and stalked to the house. The screen door slammed behind her. Its reverberation hummed in Abby's chest all the way home.

CHAPTER TWELVE

THE HUM OF ENERGY in the VOCAP office drowned out the therapeutic sound of Abby's tiny waterfall. Marta, the most recent hire, was a large, bilingual woman whose voice penetrated the walls like gamma rays. She'd spent twelve years in the Sacramento City Attorney's Office before going back to school to get her degree in counseling. What she lacked in experience, she made up for in opinions.

Abby told herself the new energy was a good thing, but one part of her longed for the low-key craziness of years past.

Kicking off her open-toe pumps, Abby pulled out her bottom drawer and withdrew a pair of sneakers. She'd arranged for Friday afternoon off so she could take Angel and Heather shopping. A staff meeting that morning with Daniel and the others had required her presence in business dress—silk, lime-colored walking shorts with tangerine shell and matching jacket that she hoped lent her an air of confidence, but she wasn't about to crucify her calves for fashion.

Melina sidled into the room like a spy. She closed the door. "Are you ever going to tell me what happened between you and that cowboy?"

"I already did."

"The whole story," Melina persisted.

I found him then I let him go. End of story.

After her steamy confrontation with Tom, Abby did something her grandmother called "mustering your chickens." She sealed up those painful aspects of her life and focused entirely on the one thing that had given her so much joy over the years—her work. She'd bustled into the office the following Monday morning with a box of jelly doughnuts and a big smile and set about mending fences and building new relationships with the crew that she'd pretty much overlooked for three weeks.

By the end of the day, Abby feared her effort was too little, too late. Melina, naturally, supported her without hesitation, but the other original advocates seemed dazzled by Daniel's promises to streamline operations. The new people were loyal to Daniel, whose restructuring plan seemed intent on downsizing Abby's role in VOCAP.

When she approached Daniel about her concerns, he'd ripped into her. "You used to be the best. Dedicated. Focused. But you lost it, Abby. I don't know if it had to do with that cowboy and his kids or if it's just plain burnout, but you're not the same person anymore, Abby. I don't know where that person is."

Abby had tried to muster a defense, but her heart wasn't in it. Maybe her heart had vacated the premises along with the person Daniel thought he knew.

"I'll get it out of you someday," Melina said, brushing back a lock of thick, ebony bangs. "Anyway, Tom Butler's the least of your problems. Daniel may have a new girlfriend, but his feelings were hurt when you brushed him off. Forget women scorned. He's as dangerous as a wounded moose."

Abby couldn't help but smile.

"This isn't funny," Melina scolded. "He can't take your head but he'd probably settle for your job."

After Melina left, Abby rocked back in the chair she'd occupied for almost seven years. Melina's perceptions were sound. Things were changing. Did she care? Not as much as she should, she thought with a sigh. Maybe it was burnout.

Maybe it was something deeper, a dissatisfaction with her choices in general. She knew what Donna called it.

Abby's midweek inquiry about sleeping pills had prompted a three-hour session over pizza and beer. "You're losing it here, pal," Donna had said. "Zonk-city."

"Show me that term in a psychology textbook."

"That's my word. The preferred terminology is fucked-up. Now, stop playing the martyr and tell me what's going on."

Abby swallowed her pride and admitted her feelings for Tom. She even went into some detail about their encounter outside the barn. To her surprise, Donna grinned and said, "Max would be so jealous. He's always had this fantasy about doing it in a hayloft."

Abby slugged her. "We didn't do anything. Well, we kissed, and he told me he loved me, but that was it."

"That sounds like a pretty big it, girlfriend. I know people who lived together for several years and never used the *L*-word." Abby caught the reference to her relationship to Landon and stuck out her tongue. Donna laughed. "Abby, decide. Do you love him? Yes or no."

"It's not that simple."

"Why not?"

"The girls…"

"Crapola," Donna said with such force a piece of pepperoni flew off her pizza. "It's not about Heather and Angel. It's about you forgiving yourself. It's always been about that."

Abby recognized the truth in her friend's words, but knowing with your head and knowing with your gut were two different things.

"Angel came to session alone yesterday," Donna told her. "Heather had a sore throat, and—"

"Anything serious?" Abby interrupted.

"Not your concern. You opted out of that role, remember?"

A pain shot through Abby's chest. "Go on."

"She spent the whole time talking about you and her father. She said you called her the next day, after she cussed you out."

"She didn't cuss me out. She was upset. I didn't realize how upset until Tom called—"

Donna interrupted. "He called you? The woman who turned him down? Brave man."

"He is brave and kind and a wonderful caring father who has so much to share, and I'm a sniveling coward."

Donna nodded. "Agreed."

"I can't do it, Donna. I can't tell him what I did."

Donna sighed. She wiped her greasy fingers on a paper napkin then laid a plump hand on Abby's arm. "We talked this out years ago, Abby. You didn't have a choice."

"We always have choices, Donna. That's what life is—one big choice. I blew it, and I don't deserve anyone as wonderful as Tom."

Donna gave Abby a hug. "You're pretty wonderful yourself, my friend, and I think seven years with VOCAP constitutes penance. Why don't you give yourself time to let all this soak in then reevaluate? You've only known the man for four months. You can both use the time. If he asks my opinion I'll tell him not to give up, just give you time."

Abby glanced at the clock on her a desk: eleven-fifty. She didn't have time to stew about her problems today—she was going shopping for school clothes with her two favorite girls.

"WHAT ABOUT this sweater, Abby? Do you think it makes me look fat?"

Abby eyed the model—willowy as a young sapling with fledgling breasts giving definition to the hideous, olive-green turtleneck. They'd already filled a shopping bag with underclothes, including two new training bras. Abby hoped Tom didn't have a coronary when he saw them.

"I like the striped one better. That color clashes with the pants." The drab brown polyester hip huggers reminded Abby of a cross between something she would have worn as a teen and something the old men at the rest home wore. "What do you think, Heather?"

"It's ugly."

Angel stuck out her tongue. All three of her reflections in the mirror did the same, making Heather laugh.

"Maybe I'll try the orange top. Mom always said orange was my color."

Abby smiled. "Honey, with those cheekbones and skin tone, any color is your color."

She was rewarded by a happy smile. Their conversation on the way to Modesto seemed to have eased any remaining ambivalence Angel had about what had happened between Abby and her father. Abby had started by admitting she hadn't been honest with Angel. "I didn't treat you fairly, Angel. You're a very perceptive person, and I wasn't prepared to answer questions about my relationship with your father. I didn't mean to hurt your feelings."

"I'm not five, you know," she said softly, although Heather, in the back seat, seemed engrossed with a talking book Val had sent her. "I knew something was going on between you two."

"We have feelings for each other, but we're trying to do the right thing. The adult thing."

"Why can't you two just be together? I don't get it."

Abby struggled with her answer, finally telling her, "It's a matter of timing. Mine sucks."

Angel snickered at Abby's colloquialism.

"You and your sister are your dad's first priority. It has to be that way. It isn't fair to any of you to have me in the picture right now. I care about him, Angel. I care a great deal, and I think he feels the same about me, but our relationship is secondary to making sure you and Heather get back on track."

"If it weren't for us—"

Abby didn't let her finish the thought. "If it weren't for you, I'd never even have met your dad. Sweetie, think about it. Next week you start at a new school. That's a big deal. New teachers. New friends. You're going to need your dad's help, and he wants to be there for you. Being a single parent is a tough job. He'll need to stay focused. Doesn't that make sense?"

"I guess," she conceded. "But you could still date."

Abby's heart squeezed at the hopeful sound in her voice. "We'll still see each other because I'll still see you guys. It's just that relationships take time and energy. Didn't you tell me things had changed between you and your friend in Riverside when you went down to visit?"

"Yeah, Caitlin was totally weird. She acted like I'd been living on another planet."

"Well, this is the Valley," Abby said, drawing a chuckle. "I don't know what will happen between your dad and me," she added honestly. "But I hope you and I can be friends, no matter what, okay?"

"Okay."

Now, waiting for Angel to change, Abby shifted the shopping bag to her left hand and reached out to stroke the satiny curls of the blond head at her side. "Do you like your new outfits, Heather?"

Heather nodded and yawned simultaneously. When they'd arrived at the mall, their first stop had been McDonald's for lunch then they'd headed right to the largest department store because its children's section carried variations of all elementary-school uniforms. Today's choices were less strict than Abby remembered from her parochial-school days.

According to the list Heather's school had provided, children could choose from a mix-and-match selection of slacks and skirts in several colors.

"All these clothes aren't my birthday presents, are they?" she asked, apprehensively eyeing the bulging bag.

"Of course not. These are school things. What do you want for your birthday?" Abby knew Heather was turning six in eight days. She wondered if Tom had a birthday party planned.

"A pony. Like Blaze's baby. Only he's a boy, and Daddy says boy ponies aren't as nice as girl ponies. Like, duh."

Abby laughed. This vibrant little person had come a long way since that first day when Tom carried her into VOCAP. Grace was thoroughly charmed by Heather, and apparently the feeling was mutual since the first thing Heather asked when she saw Abby was, "Did you bring my fairy grandmother with you?"

"What else do you want?" Abby asked.

"A potty Barbie."

Abby's mouth dropped open. "Excuse me?"

"She comes with a little toilet and real toilet paper."

Abby couldn't believe such a thing existed, but Heather seemed certain of it. Abby's gift, a set of Kipling stories, included *Riki Tiki Tavi*—one of her favorites from childhood. Probably a geeky gift, Abby thought, but she could picture herself reading it to her. Then, like an arrow in the heart, reality struck.

Tom hadn't even stuck around to see her today. He'd left an envelope with twelve twenty-dollar bills on the table and a scribbled note that read, "Abby, Thanks for doing this, Tom." How could she blame him for not wanting to see her? He'd offered her his love and she'd turned him down cold. She didn't deserve any better.

"This is way cooler, huh?" Angel asked, spinning in a little circle. The bright color made her olive skin tone glow. Such a beauty on the verge of womanhood. Abby remembered what a painful, awkward time that was in her life without having a woman in whom she could confide. Could she help Angel through these years or had she blown that, too?

Abby blinked away unwanted tears. "Very nice."

"What about it, Squirt? Do you like it? Heather? Where's Heather?"

Abby glanced around. "She was right here a second ago." Dropping to one knee, she peered under the clothing racks. "Heather? Come out, come out, wherever you are." No small feet in brand-new burgundy Mary Janes.

Straightening up, she put her hands on her hips and let out a sigh of frustration. "Not again," she said, remembering the petting-zoo incident. Fear and panic bubbled on a back burner, but she ignored them. "She can't have gone far."

Angel looked furious. "Why does she do this? Dad gave her a huge lecture about scaring you when she ran off at the picnic."

"Well, let's not panic. You change, and I'll start looking. You don't suppose they have any ducks around here, do they?"

Abby spotted her first, just moments later. A tiny towhead at the perfume counter is not easy to miss. Abby slowed her pace and walked toward Heather, framing in her mind the appropriate scolding. It wasn't easy disciplining someone who looked so adorable standing on her tiptoes looking at little winged sculptures masquerading as perfume bottles. Abby was no more than two steps away from Heather when Angel flew into her line of sight, a scowl the size of Milwaukee on her face.

Abby reached out for Heather the same instant Heather reached out to touch the fragile-looking bottle closest to her.

"You little twit," Angel barked. "It's my turn to try on clothes. You already had your turn."

Heather, who seemed almost transfixed by the perfume bottle, jumped, her hand accidentally knocking over one of the little glass vials. The fragile glass orb did a roly-poly dance then toppled over the edge of the table, shattering on the black-and-white marble floor.

Before anyone could react, Heather opened her mouth and let out a cry of such anguish Abby and Angel both froze in their tracks. Abby saw two attendants in pink smocks rushing toward them. Other shoppers turned in horror.

Abby dashed forward, dropping to one knee. "Heather, honey, are you cut?" she cried, pulling the shrieking child into her arms. "Heather, it's okay. I'm here. I've got you."

Heather didn't answer. The small container seemed to have disintegrated on impact, leaving behind only a cloying aroma and a hysterical child.

Abby rose. Heather's little legs automatically locked around Abby's waist. Using her free hand to dig in her purse, Abby tossed two twenties on the counter. "Sorry," she said to the clerks, then shouldered her way through the assembling crowd.

Lugging their many bags of clothing, Angel raced ahead to hold the door open.

Abby looked at her over the sobbing child's head. Angel's bottom lip quivered, too. "That was our mother's perfume. It was the only kind she wore."

TOM LEANED OVER and placed a gentle kiss on Heather's forehead. Asleep at last. He'd been sitting beside her for the past twenty minutes, holding her hand, waiting for the sedative Donna gave her to take effect.

"You'd better get to sleep, too, Angel-babe," he whispered toward the other twin bed where Angel was reading.

Angel snapped off her bedside lamp. The ever-present glow from the night-light in their adjoining bathroom cast a comforting glow in the room. Tom never ceased to marvel at how lovely their bedroom addition had turned out. The pale green bedspreads and subtle purple touches were both warm and whimsical.

"I love you, Dad. Tell Abby we're sorry."

She'd told him the whole story of their afternoon shopping adventure and Heather's calamity. Poor Abby. This experience would have been ten times worse than the one at the picnic.

Tom kissed Angel on the cheek. "I will. Sleep well."

He closed the bedroom door and walked down the hall, drawn to the low murmur of voices. The new hall runner, an "addition-warming" gift from Al Carroll, absorbed the sound of his boot steps.

Two women sat at the kitchen table. One he'd come to respect and admire; the other he loved more than he thought possible. Donna's back was to him. Abby was talking in low, hoarse tones. The telltale red around her nose and puffiness beneath her eyes told him how much she cared.

"Heather's asleep," he told them. "And Angel soon will be."

Donna turned in her seat to look at him. Abby dropped her head to her hands as if her neck was too weak to support the weight.

"I need a drink. How 'bout you two?"

"I'll pass," Donna said. "But make Abby's a double."

Abby shook her head. "I need to drive home."

Donna took her hand and said in a slow, deliberate cadence, as if giving instructions to a child, "No, you don't. You need to stay here in case Heather wakes up. She'll need to see you and be sure you're all right. That was an extremely turbulent event and you two need to comfort each other to get past it."

Tom poured two juice glasses a quarter full of brandy. Where the bottle came from he hadn't a clue.

"I could come back first thing..." Abby started.

Donna shook her head. "No. I've given Heather a light sedative to help calm her, but Angel was just as traumatized—she just hides it better. Like you."

Tom set the glass in front of Abby and took the chair to her right. "Drink. You need this."

She wouldn't look at him. He knew she blamed herself, even though Angel's version of the event proved no one was to blame. He breathed a little easier when she lifted the liquor to her lips and swallowed, grimacing at the harsh flavor.

Donna signaled him with her eyes. Tom looked toward the door. Abby's purse was on the floor, along with four department-store bags. Apparently they'd accomplished quite a bit of shopping before Heather's mishap. Tom rose and collected the whole assortment and carried it to the far corner of his bedroom. She couldn't leave without her keys and her keys were in her purse, he'd stake his life on it.

When he came out, Donna was talking in a low, serious voice. "I want you to stay here, Abby. I don't want you to be alone. Tom will make sure you're okay."

The look of anguish in her green eyes nearly broke his heart. "Don't make him do that, Donna. He must hate me."

Tom strode to her side in two giant steps. He squatted beside her and waited until she looked at him. "Don't ever say that again. No matter what happens between us, I know how much you love those kids, and I know you want what's best for them."

Donna gently scolded her friend. "You know how I feel about fault and blame, Abby. The bottom line is—both girls are safe.

"In a way, this might even have been the key we needed to reach deeper into Heather's subconscious. Abby said Heather cried herself to sleep in the car, sobbing for her mother," Donna told Tom. "Do you realize she hasn't once brought up the subject of her mother in session? The Rainbows counselors said the same thing. Outwardly, she's adjusting well, but she ignores any effort to bring out her feelings about her mother's death."

Tom pictured an incident that had confounded him last week, then said, "I gave her a picture I had of Lesley. In a frame. Put it on her dresser. The next day it was gone. She'd put it in the drawer. When I asked her how come, she just shrugged and said, 'I don't know.'"

Abby withdrew a limp tissue from the pocket of her wrinkled silk jacket. "Angel and I kept talking to her, trying to get through. Finally, she just played out. She fell asleep sobbing, 'Mommy, Mommy, Mommy.' It broke my heart. There wasn't anything I could do."

Donna pushed the brandy closer and made her take another sip. "You were with her—that's all anyone can do. This is something she needed to face."

"What do you suppose set her off?" Tom asked.

"The perfume," Donna and Abby said together.

"How? Why?"

"Angel said that brand is the kind their mother wore," Donna said. "So Heather associates it with Lesley. Maybe the shattered bottle signifies death in a way a five-year-old can understand." She rose, and put a hand on Tom's shoulder. "Call me if she wakes up before morning, but I think she'll make it through the night. I'd like to see them both tomorrow. Any time."

"Tomorrow is Saturday."

She shrugged. "Healing happens when it happens—days, months, years later." The last she seemed to direct toward Abby, who looked away. "I'd like to follow through while it's still fresh and a little scary."

She pointed a finger at Abby. "Stay here. This is where you belong. Okay?"

When Abby hesitated, Tom stepped in. "She'll stay. I promise."

After Donna was gone, Tom wedged an old Zane Grey novel, one of his father's favorite authors, under the door to keep it open and turned off the air conditioner. The little window unit did its best, but the two-week heat wave taxed it to the max. He walked to the window above the kitchen sink. "More brandy?" he asked, slamming the heels of both hands against the frame of the window above the kitchen sink. The sticky sash inched upward.

"No thanks. My stomach's on fire the way it is."

"Are you hungry? Maybe you should eat—"

"I couldn't. Thanks." She let out a little sigh. "You're being awfully nice about this."

He propped open the back door and turned off the porch light so the bugs wouldn't congregate. "Abby, this wasn't your fault," he said, walking toward the table.

She rose and stretched, one hand massaging her lower back. Tom remembered her saying she'd carried Heather all the way to the car. He sped up. "Let me."

She jumped, as if poked with a stick. "No. I'm fine."

"You're not fine. You just went through hell and back. Heck, shopping itself is my idea of hell. Notice I wasn't brave enough to go with you." His humor seemed to loosen her up a little. She let him guide her to the couch. "Sit sideways. I'll just give your neck and shoulders a quick rub. I learned a lot about muscle pain when I was on the circuit."

She sat stiffly at first, but gradually he felt her muscles unwind. Being able to touch her, even through layers of silk jacket and blouse, was a gift. The soft material offered little barrier, and the warmth of her skin radiated to his fingers. Her scent, not the cloying expensive perfume he pictured Lesley wearing, teased his nose. Her hair brushed the tops of his hands like gossamer threads.

"Angel said you rode in the rodeo."

"I was a team roper. Different breed of cat."

"Really? Don't they have steer roping in rodeos?"

"Rodeos have a bunch of events. Bronco busting, bull riding, steer wrestling and roping. Team roping has its own circuit. Sometimes ropers'll do rodeos, but if you're roping professionally, you don't have a lot of time to earn the points you need to qualify for the finals. Part of the trick is picking the right events.

"Some ropings, like the BFI—the Bob Feist Invitational up in Reno—take place right after or just before a big rodeo so cowboys can do both and earn a few extra bucks."

She rolled her neck, making her hair whisper across his fingers. "What do you mean by team? A whole bunch of you…"

He chuckled at the image. Few people outside the sport understood it, even though roping had been around for years. "There's two on a team. A header and a heeler. The header tries to get a rope around the steer's horns then turn him so the heeler can catch his back legs. All in about six seconds."

"Wow. Sounds difficult."

"Takes practice. And teamwork and a good horse. The circuit wasn't as big when I was roping, but now it runs from the East Coast to Hawaii. You ante up your entrance fee, and if you're lucky you can win enough prize money to pay your way to the next one."

"Angel said you were one of the best."

He shrugged. "I had a good horse."

She snorted at his humility.

"No, I mean it. Goldy—Hall's Golden Boy—was one of the best. He took the American Quarter Horse Association's Horse of the Year award twice."

She rolled her shoulders at his deepening touch. A little sigh escaped her lips. "Which were you? Head or heels?"

"Heeler. I made it to the Nationals the year before I quit." The year Lesley found out she was pregnant with Angel.

"Did you win?"

He ran his thumb alongside the ridge of her spine; her shiver made his heart skip a beat. "We had it nailed then my steer slipped a hoof—that's a five-second penalty. It wound up being about a fourteen-thousand-dollar mistake."

She made a choking sound.

"It's a tough business. Ask the losing quarterback the day after Super Bowl and he'll tell you the same thing."

"Why'd you quit?"

"I got hurt."

She turned. His hand accidentally grazed her breast. "Badly?"

A sudden surge of longing made him rise and walk a few steps away. "I broke my arm. Nothing big. I could still work, I just couldn't throw worth beans. I missed the rest of the season, and when it came time to start training for the next year…it just wasn't there."

"What wasn't there?"

How could he explain the depth of energy, drive and determination it took to propel a person into the competitive world of professional sports? His disillusionment had been a long time coming; the injury just sealed it. "I don't know. The drive, I guess. Lesley said it's like getting back on a horse after he tosses you, but it wasn't like that. I still rope for fun, but back then I was—"

She had a thoughtful look on her face. "Burned out?"

"Yeah, I guess. I knew I wanted something else. Put down roots. Stop living out of a horse trailer. I sold Goldy to buy the little house where Miguel and Maria used to live."

"Used to? They've moved already?"

Tom sighed. Fatigue was catching up with him, and it hadn't been easy saying goodbye to the friends he'd grown so close to over the past couple of years. "That's where I was today. I helped them load everything up in Ed's horse trailer. They didn't want the girls to see them leave. They're planning a big housewarming party in a couple of weeks, and I'll take the girls up then."

Abby sat back on the couch and closed her eyes. "So many changes."

He snapped off the overhead light. The new exterior floodlights added a soft shadowy quality to the room. A night-light in the bathroom illuminated the way to the hall. He walked to the couch and held out his hand. "Come on. You're exhausted."

She shrunk back. "I can sleep right here."

He shook his head. "Not if you want to be able to straighten up in the morning. Trust me, it's a lousy bed."

When she opened her mouth to protest, he dropped to one knee in front of her. Her eyes were shadowed, but he didn't need to see them to know her fear. "Abby, it's been a lousy day for all of us. I could really use the company. We won't do anything. We don't even need to get undressed. Come on."

He held out his hand. Two heartbeats later, she put her hand in his.

CHAPTER THIRTEEN

ABBY'S FIRST WAKING thought was: home.

She came to full consciousness by tracking the individual elements of her languor. Tom's arm heavy and secure around her body, his hand tucked innocently below her breast. His warm, even breath tickled the back of her neck in a soothing way. Her buttocks nested against the curve of his pelvis—spoon-fashion, somcthing she couldn't have pictured herself enjoying. She and Landon were individual sleepers who jealously guarded their territory on the bed. Cover thievery and bed hogging were grounds for reprisal in the morning.

Keeping her eyes closed, she savored his scent, picturing it as a magic shell protecting her from the encroaching day. She could drift back to sleep, or turn ever so slightly and start something she was pretty sure Tom wouldn't be anxious to stop. But that wouldn't be fair to him. He deserved more. The truth, at the very least.

Carefully, she shifted to her back. Traces of pink peeked through the curtainless window. She recalled her mother's anguish over not having time to do something about Tom's bedroom. "He doesn't even have curtains," Grace had wailed, as if the idea violated some canon of design law.

Tom awakened. Abby felt a slight tensing of his arm. She turned her head and was rewarded with a smile. Her heart swelled painfully.

It would be so easy to stay here forever.

"Are you okay?"

His first concern was for her. "I'm fine. I didn't expect to sleep, but I was dead to the world. Did Heather wake up?"

He shook his head slightly. "I checked on her a couple of times, but she was fine." A lock of hair fell across his forehead. She brushed it back. She loved the springy texture.

"What time it is?" Out of habit, she'd removed her jewelry before washing her face and brushing her teeth with the cellophane-wrapped toothbrush he'd given her last night. "I buy 'em by the gross."

"O-dark-thirty," he said, his voice husky and full of portent. "Too early to get up, but not too early to be up."

He kissed her, igniting feelings too close to the surface. Her body cried out to respond, but she gently pushed her hand against his chest. His heart pulsed beneath her fingers. She stifled a cry of regret.

He broke off the kiss, cradling her jaw in his work-roughened hand. "Wishful thinking on my part. The girls will be up soon. Go back to sleep."

"No. I have to tell you something."

He stiffened. "Can it wait?"

She shook her head. Now, before she lost her nerve.

He moved away and sat up. He glanced toward the window then back to her. "I'll put on some coffee. I don't know about you, but my brain needs a little kick-start in the morning."

Abby made a quick trip to the bathroom. Her shorts and shell were a mass of wrinkles; she smoothed them as best she could. Fortunately, she'd hung her jacket over the back of a chair and it covered a multitude of flaws. She patted a cold washcloth to the puffy bags beneath her eyes and brushed her teeth. By the time she walked into the kitchen, she could smell the aroma of coffee.

Tom was waiting for her with a red plaid stadium blanket and two steaming cups. "Follow me," he said, leading the way to the back door.

Puzzled, she wedged her feet into her deck shoes and followed. Dew tempered the morning, making it cooler than seemed possible since the afternoon would undoubtedly repeat yesterday's century mark. She smiled as she passed the neatly enclosed washer and dryer room that Al Carroll had salvaged from the former lean-to.

"You haven't seen this, have you?" Tom asked, drawing her attention to a small, redwood arbor. A simple nook, just four posts with two-by-four joists and one-inch-square redwood crosspieces, housed a sturdy redwood glider.

"Wow. Where'd this come from?"

"Ed and Janey bought the glider. Al helped me build the rest."

"It's fabulous. I bet you see the most wonderful sunsets."

"Sunrises, too."

He used a towel to wipe the dew from the glider then spread out the blanket. As soon as she sat down, holding the two mugs he'd handed her, Tom joined her and pulled the edges of the blanket around them. "Snug as two bugs in a rug," he said, taking his mug.

They drank in silence, watching the pink glow on the horizon intensify. Meadowlarks trilled their happy greeting. The air smelled of earth, animals and butterscotch, from the coffee. If not for her nervousness, Abby would have enjoyed the peaceful moment.

Finally, she said, "Tom, when I told you about Billy, I left out some parts."

He waited, his gaze on her now. In a way, his silence felt like a safety net. He would listen. He wouldn't be able to understand, but she knew he'd try.

"Billy was in a lot of pain. Some mental, some physical. While he was in the hospital, he became addicted to painkillers. When he got out, he bought a bar in Hawaii with some friends and basically stayed stoned or drunk the whole time he lived there.

"When we got together, he wanted to change his life around. I truly believe that, but…" She sighed, remembering the handsome young man with so much potential. "It just didn't work out. Emotionally, he had good days and bad. The worst involved alcohol and drugs."

She rolled her shoulders to loosen up the tension and took another sip of the now-cold coffee. "Remember I told you I left for three days?"

She felt him nod.

"I left because that night he beat me up so badly I barely made it to the hospital before I passed out."

Tom let out a harsh groan. "Oh, Abby."

She gnawed at her bottom lip. "He was a proud man, but he felt so diminished. Not just his leg, but the circumstances of his accident. He told me he felt his whole life was a lie." She pictured herself at that moment—straight home from her psychology class, full of "fix-it" tips, ready to make him all better. "I tried to mother him, I guess. I only made things worse. He grabbed me and threw me against the coffee table. He was very strong. I didn't know how to fight back." She flinched when Tom moved closer. "I think I blacked out from pain."

She forced herself not to double over. "The X rays showed four cracked ribs and a concussion."

"Abby," Tom said, looping his arm round her shoulder. "Oh, sweetheart."

She held up her hand, but its jittery shaking made her curl her fingers into a fist and bury her hand in her lap. They'd stopped gliding. "Somehow, I got to my car. I don't remember driving, but somehow I made it to the hospital.

"When I woke up, my parents and brothers were there.

Everybody looked so serious, they told me the police were looking for Billy, but he'd disappeared."

She took a deep breath. "My brothers left when the doctor came in. He told me about my ribs and said I had a concussion and some kidney damage. Then he told me that the baby I was carrying was dead."

She felt a shudder pass through him. "I didn't even know I was pregnant."

He tightened his grip, for which she was grateful. It helped her say the rest. "They told me it would probably self-abort, but they recommended—given my physical and emotional trauma—a therapeutic procedure, they called it. Basically it boils down to an abortion."

She fought to keep her coffee in her stomach.

"None of it was your fault, Abby." His eyes were full of sorrow and sympathy.

"I could have left Billy. I knew how he got. He'd slapped me once before and squeezed my arm so hard he left bruises, but I chose to stay."

"You're a caring person. You were trying to help him."

She made a snorting sound. "That's right. Abby the Magnificent to the rescue." At his look of confusion, she said, "That's what my grandmother used to call me. She told me I could do anything I set my heart on. And I believed her. I wanted Billy—the hero I'd created—to be real. To be well." Sorrowfully, she turned to Tom. "It was ego. Pure ego. I was positive I knew best."

"You were young."

"But I wasn't dumb. I was in college. Spousal abuse wasn't kept behind closed doors anymore. I knew my relationship with Billy wasn't healthy. I did everything in my power to make him happy. Sometimes it worked, sometimes it didn't. When it didn't, he blamed me. I was too loud, too young, too dumb, a bitch, a nag." She smiled ruefully. "It wasn't until

I started working at VOCAP that I learned how powerful a weapon words can be. They can slice to the bone and shred every ounce of self-confidence a person possesses."

"Even knowing that doesn't keep you from blaming yourself. Right?" he asked, his voice low and hard.

"I *knew* Billy was sick. He needed help. If I'd called the police the first time it happened…"

"If, Abby. If. Isn't that one of Donna's trouble words? I read those pamphlets you sent about victims' rights. The one on spousal abuse said, in the past the police stayed out of domestic issues, unless the woman got killed."

"I should have tried."

"Why do you do that?"

"Do what?"

"Beat yourself up about something that happened ten years ago." His eyes narrowed shrewdly. "Is this why you think we can't be together? You think I'd somehow think less of you for this?"

Abby's stomach turned over. "It's part of the reason."

He waited.

Unconsciously, she moved her hands to her abdomen. No visible scars, but…the wounds were still affecting her life. "The abor…procedure was quick and fairly painless. I had some bleeding for a few days but nothing serious. I didn't start having problems—female problems—until two years later. Heavy bleeding. Bad pain. My doctor did a laparoscopy. He said there was some scarring and my fallopian tubes were damaged. He couldn't say for sure why, but he said there was a seventy percent chance I'd never have children."

Tom's arm pulled her close, supportively. He pressed her head to his chest and lowered his chin to the top of her head. "I'm so sorry, Abby. I know how much you love kids."

A fist squeezed her heart; she scooted back, trying to catch her breath. "It's not about me, Tom. When you remarry, you'll want more kids. I've seen how you are with babies. You love babies."

He frowned. "I have two great kids. If you and I had a baby I'd be tickled pink because it was part of you and me together, but that's the least of my worries. I love you, woman, not your tubes."

She smiled, it was impossible to resist his heartfelt pledge. She caressed his jaw, rubbing her palm against the sandpaper bristles. She would treasure this moment forever. "You're the most incredible man I've ever met."

"But?" he said, his blue eyes darkening.

"You say it doesn't matter, but I think it will. Someday. I don't want you to settle for less than you deserve."

He opened his mouth, but whatever he intended to say was lost when a very faint cry interrupted the morning's quiet. "Daddy?"

Tom gave her a long, serious look. "This isn't over, Abby. We can work this out."

Abby wanted to believe him, but she knew in her heart she didn't deserve the life he was offering. He'd come to realize it, too, in time.

TOM AND ED STOOD companionably, elbow-to-elbow, at the gate of the new corral. Tom had unloaded the mares and their offspring in their new quarters earlier that morning. The final heat wave of summer had broken finally, giving a much-needed respite. Animals and humans alike seemed to mellow when the temperature stayed in the eighties. Fall wasn't far off, Tom could sense it. His daughters were halfway through their first week of school. So far, so good. Ed and Janey had returned from Janey's checkup, along with Peter and Maureen. This was the first chance Tom and Ed had managed to find a moment to talk. He sensed something changed in the older man's attitude. Tom was pretty sure he knew what it was.

"Ed, let's cut the pussyfooting. We're ranchers not lawyers. You want Pete back here."

The older man let out a sigh. "Janey wants him home. He's my son. But you know I've come to think of you as a son, too, Tom."

Tom smiled. "My mama might not have objected to that, but I think my daddy would have had some concerns." At Ed's chuckle, he went on. "You know how I feel about you and Janey. We don't have to get into that. I don't want you thinking my feelings are gonna be hurt if you bring Pete into the business. In fact, it's a great idea. Without Miguel around, I practically have to piss on the run. Gets kinda messy."

Ed spit into the dust. "Maybe we need to hire another hand. Peter's an advertising executive, not a rancher. He turned his back on this a long time ago."

"He was a boy. Now he's a man. A smart man. He knows about computers, right?"

Ed nodded slowly.

"Well, I got one in my office that isn't even out of the box yet. Maybe you can get him out here and start him doing some of that on-line stuff you were talking about. Why not let Pete handle all the paperwork end of things?"

"And you and me'd handle the real work?"

"You don't think I'd abandon you to a greenhorn, do you?"

Ed's relief showed in his smile. "That's the best news I've had since Janey's doctor told me we don't have to come back for six months."

"She's looking good."

"She's feeling good. The tests look clear and she's started on a drug that they're studying to see if it can prevent the cancer from spreading or coming back. She feels good to be involved in that. Helping other women."

Tom sighed. “I’m glad to hear it. Makes what I gotta tell you a little easier.”

Ed’s big, freckled hands gripped the barbless wire. “Oh, Lord.”

“This is gonna look darned ungrateful after you just got done putting a pile of money into that addition, but the girls ’n’ me are moving out.”

Ed’s jaw dropped open. “What?”

“My house is sitting empty. An empty house is an easy target. Yesterday, I found some beer bottles out behind the barn. Kids partying. Vandalism comes next. Plus, my mares need someone looking after them.”

“Couldn’t you rent it out again?”

“I could, but I figure Pete and Maureen are gonna need a place to live when they move back. That new addition would make a real fine master bedroom.”

Ed’s eyes lit up. “And Pete can keep an eye on things when you’re not here.”

“And he’ll be nice and close to that darned computer you’ve been trying to cram down my throat.”

Ed clapped a hand to Tom’s back. “We’re gonna get you outta the saddle and belly up to a computer one of these days, son, mark my words.”

“I guess so,” Tom’s voice was less than enthusiastic. Val had given his old computer to the girls. So far, Tom had managed to avoid hooking it up, but once they moved into the three-bedroom house, that might change. In fact, he planned to use the computer to get back into their good graces.

ABBY STARED at a gangly Joshua tree a few feet beyond the low stucco fence separating her parents’ Palm Desert home from the desert. How anyone could consider that greenish-gray, bristly, misshapen thing a tree was beyond her.

“Juice, dear?”

Abby spun around. She hadn't heard her mother rise. Grace liked to awaken at her own pace. She called it her reward after so many years of marching to other people's drums. She still worked in the design studio of a local furniture store, but her employers accepted Grace Davis's hours as her own.

"Sure. Thanks. I was going to make coffee, but I got sidetracked."

Grace glided gracefully to the whitewashed cupboards in the compact, artfully spare kitchen—no fussy decorator's clutter for her. A huge ceramic bowl filled with bananas, oranges and apples provided the only color accents.

The house was one of a thousand replicas—pseudo-adobe with red tile roofs and minicourtyards. Two bedrooms, two-car garages. Emergency panic buttons in each of the two bathrooms made Abby think the builders believed those were the only places old people ever got sick.

"Just as well," Grace was saying. "Your father only drinks decaf. I drink hot molasses water in the morning. You should try it. Much better for you than coffee. But I bought these individual coffee bags right after you called." She plopped a square bag on a string into a soup bowl-size mug and added boiling water. "Black, right?"

"Yes, please." While her mother fussed around the kitchen, Abby dunked her coffee bag. The mindless motion gave her time to reflect on the odd turn of events that had propelled her to the desert.

Daniel had shown up at her office door the Monday after her long, emotionally charged weekend with Tom and the girls. She'd spent the better part of Sunday playing board games with Heather and Angel, and even joined the family for a brief horseback ride around the property, but in the end, she left with nothing settled between her and Tom.

Daniel's sudden proclamation shocked her. "Abby, you're outta here."

At first, Abby thought he was firing her, but then he explained an audit of VOCAP's accrued vacation-time records showed Abby was ninety-seven hours over the limit. "Take it or lose it, Abby. New policy."

Since she didn't have a choice in the matter, she'd called her parents to see if they were between cruises. "Come tonight," her mother told her. "No, on second thought, that's a long drive. Start fresh tomorrow. Your father will be ecstatic."

"Is fruit and toast all right? We only have eggs once a week in omelets," Grace said pleasantly, bringing her back to the present.

"Toast is fine. Thank you."

Grace's hand stopped in midair above the toaster. The smile on her lips seemed wistful. "Your grandmother taught you such fine manners."

Abby let the observation pass. At the same instant she realized Grace was only setting two places at the table. "Where's Dad?"

"Golfing. You have to get out early. This is a desert, you know."

Their first evening together after her eight-hour drive was fairly brief. They shared a light meal, took a stroll around the neighborhood—bringing Abby up to speed on all the gossip—then went to bed. Abby was asleep the minute her head hit the pillow.

"It's Wednesday, Mom. How come you're not getting ready for work?"

"I told them my daughter was coming for a visit, and I wouldn't be in this week or next."

Abby was surprised, and touched. "Really? You didn't need to do that."

"Yes, I did." Grace looked across the distance separating them. "Abby, do you realize this is the first time you've come to us for solace?"

Abby hadn't realized her mother read the reason for her trip so clearly. All Abby had said on the phone was that she had an unexpected vacation.

Grace went on. "Even after what happened with Billy, you chose to stay in Welton instead of coming home."

"I had school." A lame excuse considering the depth of her anguish.

Grace carried a plate with four slices of toast on it to the table. She went back for a bowl of pink-grapefruit slices, chunks of banana and juicy-looking slivers of mango. "Let's eat. More water for your coffee?"

Abby refilled her cup from the spotless stainless-steel tea-kettle. "How did you know I…that I might need…?"

Grace pursed her lips. Without lipstick, they were less youthful. Tiny lines made them look withered. For the first time, Abby had a sense of her mother's age. A peculiar pang knotted in her chest. "Abby, dear, you're my daughter. We haven't been close, but I still feel as connected to you as I did the moment you were born."

The words surprised Abby as much as they moved her.

Grace took a sip of black liquid that looked just like coffee. She selected a triangle of toast and set it on her plate but didn't take a bite. She looked reflective when she said, "I don't want this to sound ungrateful. Your grandmother was a wonderful woman who did an absolutely fabulous job of raising you, but she also had an uncanny way of making it an either-or proposition for me. We never really spoke about it out loud, but I knew if I turned you over to her to care for, I was—in a way—giving you up."

She shook her head and hurried into an explanation to cut off Abby's question. "Maybe it was my own sense of guilt. You have to remember, Abby, back then women had very well-defined roles. Some women were working and raising families, but that was usually because of death or divorce. I was blessed with an understanding husband who wanted me to be happy and fulfilled."

Abby chewed a bite of toast. It tasted like sawdust. She examined it more closely—crusty, dense and fibrous, perhaps it *was* made of sawdust.

"When I found out I was pregnant for the third time, I wasn't terribly pleased. I truly regret feeling that way, but it's the truth. Then your grandfather died, and although I loved Quincy dearly, I saw his death as a way of being able to have my cake and eat it, too. Agnes needed help, I needed help. We'd help each other."

Abby shrugged. "I have no complaints."

Grace looked at her seriously. "Perhaps not, but I do. Agnes was from a different generation, and, as much as she loved you, she resented me for not doing my God-given duty.

"I looked at it as a win-win situation. Agnes had meaningful employment. I kept the job I loved. You were cared for in your own home." Her eyes looked sad, and she frowned. "I just didn't figure it would cost me my daughter's love."

Abby started to protest. "Mother—"

"Think about it, dear. You were Grandma's girl. When you were sick, she cared for you. When you fell down and skinned your knee, you ran to her. When she died, you grieved so much I was worried sick, but in the back of my mind—God forgive me—I thought, now we'll have a chance to be close. But it was too late."

Abby's heart squeezed painfully against her rib cage. She hadn't guessed any of this.

An image came to her. She was sixteen. Her first date. "I remember one time when you came in my room and starting talking to me—girl talk, you called it. I thought you were going to try to tell me about the birds and the bees. In a way I wanted to hear it—that wasn't something Grammy would have talked about, but I didn't want to be disloyal to her."

Grace nodded. "I know. At least, I figured as much. I was prepared to be patient. I always figured there'd be time, but then you fell in love with Billy."

Chagrined, Abby said, "I really put you guys through hell, didn't I?"

"We were worried about you. I was afraid Billy might turn violent. His father was like that."

"He was?"

Grace nodded. "Don't you remember me telling you the reason Billy's mother divorced his father was because he beat her? You didn't believe me."

"His mother was abused?" Abby asked, shocked. "I don't remember that."

Grace related the story as she knew it. Abby had heard a thousand like it over the years. A pattern of abuse that became generational. "Such a sad, sad time," Grace said. "We were so happy when you met Landon. I thought he was just the ticket, but your dad said Landon was too 'insubstantial' for your tastes."

Abby smiled.

"What about Tom?" Grace asked, causing Abby's bite of toast to lodge sideways in her throat. "He seemed pretty substantial to me that afternoon I helped the girls with the wallpaper. I was quite impressed that a man who'd just received the brush-off could be that cordial when he drove me to your house."

"He told you?" Abby croaked.

"Of course not. Angel said you 'dissed him.' I put my own interpretation on that. Was I right?"

Abby swallowed a mouthful of lukewarm coffee. The bitterness made her shudder. Suddenly, to her surprise, Abby blurted out, "I love him, Mom. He wants to marry me."

Grace's smile slowly segued to a frown of concern. "I hear a big but dangling."

Abby smiled. Her mother's silly aphorisms were legendary.

"Are you afraid to tell him about Billy?"

"I told him everything," Abby said with a sigh. "He said it didn't matter. Even my tubes—none of it mattered to him. The only part he didn't understand was how I could be so forgiving toward everybody else and not forgive myself."

Grace rose suddenly. "I know the answer to that one. Come with me."

Curious, Abby followed her to the master bedroom. The spacious suite with ivory walls and cathedral ceiling could have graced the cover of *House Beautiful.* Abby took a seat on the bed, sinking into several inches of down. Her heart began beating erratically the second her mother withdrew an old jewelry box from the closet. "Is that Grammy's...?"

"Hopeless chest," Grace finished.

"I'd forgotten all about it." As a child, Abby had been permitted to carefully examine each of the cherished, often whimsical, mementos her grandmother had saved over the years. A single glittery earring. A campaign ribbon supporting Woodrow Wilson. A silver bracelet adorned with tiny charms, including one from Saint Louis.

"Do you remember this?" Grace asked, passing her a small, store-bought valentine card, brittle with age.

Abby studied the precious card. It looked in almost-perfect condition except that it had been ripped in two and was held together with invisible tape—the kind used in modern times, not when it was first given. She traced the slightly raised heart in the middle where a boy and girl sat holding hands. She knew the trite verse by heart, and she knew what she'd see when she opened it up. The elegant inscription read: "To my Aggie. With love and admiration, Quincy E. Davis. Your husband."

She turned it over. The scar looked ugly and mean. "I don't remember it being ripped," she said, puzzled.

"You did it."

The card fluttered to the carpet. "Me?"

Grace picked it up. "The day after Grandma died. It happened so fast. Agnes went into the hospital for exploratory surgery. They removed a tumor in her stomach. They didn't know if it had spread, but they told us she'd probably live another few years, maybe longer. But Agnes went to sleep that night and didn't wake up."

"She gave up. She didn't even try," Abby said in a small voice.

"You always were hardest on the ones you loved the most. You were so mad at Agnes you tore the card in half. You couldn't forgive her for dying."

Abby walked to the window and looked at the distant mountain peaks without really seeing. "I hated her for a while. She left me all alone." Cringing, she realized too late how that must have sounded to her mother.

"I think she was being noble," Grace said, her voice gentle. "Agnes lived through the hell of watching her husband die. She kept him at home for as long as possible then spent every single day with him in the hospital, watching him waste away. Besides the emotional toll, it cost her every penny of Quincy's insurance and all their savings."

Grace shook her head sadly. "She once told me she wouldn't dream of putting us through that. 'I'll go when I'm called,' she said. 'I won't fight it the way Quincy did.'"

Abby blinked back tears that clustered in her eyes. She had no trouble picturing her grandmother saying that. Looking over her shoulder, she told her mother, "I'm glad she didn't suffer. She would have hated the indignity."

Grace put the valentine card away and closed the lid of the box. "This is yours, you know. She wanted you to have it."

"How come you never brought it out before?"

She shrugged. "I guess I was waiting for a sign from above."

Abby, who'd attended parochial school at her grandmother's behest, didn't consider her mother a terribly religious person. "I beg your pardon?"

Grinning impishly, Grace said, "A little angel called me and said you were sad. She was afraid you might need a little help finding your way home. And since guidance was more your grandmother's specialty than mine, I thought this might be the right time to bring out the hopeless chest."

Abby walked to the bed where her mother was sitting.

"An angel, huh? The kind with long brown hair?" When Grace smiled, Abby leaned down and put her arms around her mother—a gesture she couldn't recall doing voluntarily beyond hello and goodbye. "Am I?" Abby asked. "Hopeless?"

"Hopeless?" Grace asked, her voice thick with emotion. "My daughter? Not on your life."

CHAPTER FOURTEEN

"HOW WILL Abby know where to find us, Daddy, now that she's back from her trip?" Heather asked, looking up from her coloring. She was stretched out on Tom's bed, using a hunk of cardboard as a base upon which to complete her art project. Homework, Tom assumed.

"Huh, Daddy? What if she thinks we're lost?"

"I'll call her later—after she gets home from work. This is her first day back in the office. I left a message on her machine yesterday but I couldn't remember my damn…I mean, darned, cell-phone number and the telephone company's not coming here until tomorrow."

He decided to upgrade his service with a separate line for the computer, since, with a daughter hitting puberty, he'd never get to use the phone otherwise.

Heather looked up. "You said a bad word."

"I know. I'm sorry."

She frowned, her face suddenly pensive. "Mommy said bad words, too. Sometimes."

Tom lifted a wooden box the size of a large briefcase from the cardboard box he was unpacking. He kicked the empty packing box aside and lowered the weighty burden to his bed. Made of unvarnished pine, the rustic box with poorly mitered corners showed the wear and tear of years of use. His eighth-grade wood-shop project—a gun case for the antique pistol collection he intended to have one day. He raised the lid.

The scent of cleaning oil billowed out like embalming

fluid. The royal-blue velvet lining his mother had sewn looked moth-eaten in spots. His father had helped him arrange the layout to accommodate four long-barrel pistols. Three spots were filled. The fourth—his 1847 Walker—had been sold to pay off Heather's hospital bill. Best deal I ever made, Tom thought, smiling at the little girl coloring so industriously.

Tom wasn't sure what to do with his collection. The guns were one of the few interests he had shared with his father. He remembered his father telling him, "The history of weapons makes a fascinating study in human nature. Man's inhumanity to man, always looking for a faster, more deadly weapon, pretty much sums up the future, I fear."

A born pessimist who often sought solace in a bottle, Walt Butler also possessed a gift for storytelling and a voice that charmed his listeners. Tom liked to remember the times the two of them shared at Walt's workbench, assembling the pieces of a black-powder reproduction he'd ordered from some catalog.

Walt's pride and joy was an 1851 Navy Model Yanks. "Wild Bill Hickok carried a pair of 'em with ivory grips when he was a lawman in Abilene," he'd say, then burst into song about "the prettiest town he ever seen."

After Tom's mother died, Walt didn't sing much. He told Tom, "Genevieve was my voice. My hope." Walt soon developed a bad cough that resisted all cures.

"Mommy said a bad word at me," Heather said in a small voice. "That night."

Tom looked at his daughter, catching the sadness in her tone. Donna had warned him that as Heather's memory of her mother returned, she'd become more comfortable talking about it. "Honey, sometimes people say things they don't mean," Tom said, closing the case and sliding it beneath his bed.

"But, Daddy, Mommy was mad at me. She said I was bad."

A fist closed around Tom's heart. "Baby, you're not bad. Mommy loved you very much. Maybe she was upset about—"

Heather interrupted. "She was mad because I told her I didn't want to go with her. I wanted to stay at Caitlin's with Angel. I cried and kicked the door. Mommy said good little girls do what they're told, bad little girls had to sit in the back seat until they could be nice." Her bottom lip quivered.

Tom pulled her into his arms. "Oh, sweetness, you're the nicest little girl in the whole wide world. Mommy was angry, she didn't mean it like that."

Tom brushed aside her crayons and sat down, scooting her into his lap. "Did I ever tell you about the time Mommy saved my life?"

Her mop of white-blond curls danced against his chest.

"Well…I'd been at a roping out of town and won the big prize—eight hundred dollars, cash. This was before Angel was born, and your mommy and me were renting a little place over near Chowchilla. Mommy was a waitress at a truck stop, and somebody who came through there told her about my big win.

"On the way home, my truck broke down. A buddy took my horse with him, so I just locked up the truck and started walking. It was real late by the time I got home. I tried to be quiet, but Rosie was tied up by the back door, barking like crazy." Heather's eyes grew wide with anticipation. "All of a sudden, there was this loud boom and something went flying over my head.

"I hit the ground, belly first. That's when I heard your mom laughing. Seems she'd been waiting up with a shotgun full of buckshot because she figured I was out drinking up my winnings and she was gonna teach me a lesson."

Heather frowned. "Mommy tried to shoot you?"

"She wasn't trying to hurt me, only scare me. But you know what? She scared somebody else, too.

"Suddenly, there was this commotion by the garage. Somebody'd been hiding out, waiting to ambush me. That's what Rosie was barking about. Mommy's shotgun blast scared him away and probably saved my life."

Heather's smile lightened the weight on his chest. "Mommy was brave."

"Very brave. Do you know what else she did that was very brave?" Heather shook her head. "Just to make sure her most special little girl was safe, she parked her car under a big light in the middle of the parking lot, even though it meant she had to walk farther to get to the bank. She made sure you were safe because she loved you very much."

Heather tilted her head. "Really?"

He squeezed her tight. "Really."

She wiggled back and looked up at him. "Daddy, when you call Abby, would you tell her I have a present for her?" she asked, leap-frogging to a new subject with the agility of a six-year-old. She reached behind him and picked up the drawing she'd been working on.

As Tom studied the picture his heart swelled in his chest.

"Did I get Abby's hair the right color?"

Tom couldn't say for sure, the tears in his eyes were making it hard to focus. Before he could regain his composure, Angel appeared in the doorway of the bedroom.

"Goddamn it," Angel said, her voice heavy with disgust. "If it's not one thing, it's another. Where's the cell phone?"

Tom pulled his attention from the paper in his hand to his daughter standing so belligerently, hands on her hips—a pose he'd seen many times in the past two weeks. She hadn't been any more thrilled about the move than Heather, until he promised Angel her own room. She'd agreed with the stipulation Abby's mother would be called upon to help decorate it.

"The phone?" he asked blankly. He wasn't used to keeping track of dental floss-size telephones. "In my jacket pocket, I think. The denim one hanging on the back of the chair." He nodded toward the small desk and chair in the far corner.

Janey had insisted on sending over nearly every spare piece of furniture in her house. The desk, a blond, square thing, reminded Tom of a kid's desk, although the computer sitting atop it looked anything but childlike. In this matter there was no negotiating: the computer was a useful tool, but he wanted it where he could keep an eye on it.

Angel stalked to the desk. He could tell by the set of her shoulders that she was upset. "What's wrong, kiddo? Tough homework assignment?" So far, their teachers had only glowing reports of the girls' transition. He credited a great deal of that to their participation in Tomorrow's Rainbows and the counseling Donna continued to give, although they now only saw her for one hour every other Saturday.

Angel scowled at him. "I'm starting my period."

Tom's heart missed a beat. "Already? Aren't you too young?"

She gave him a dry look. "Gee, thanks, Dad. Make me feel even better."

He flinched. "Sorry. This is a little out of my league. Do you need to see a doctor?"

She rolled her eyes. "I need Abby."

"SAY IT ISN'T SO, Joe," Melina said, her eyes awash in tears. She plopped theatrically into Abby's spare chair—the same chair Tom had used the first day he came to her for help. He'd looked so out of place, and yet he fit. Even from the first, he fit in her life.

"Did Daniel really fire you? The nerve. After all these

years. After all you've done for VOCAP. The bastard. We can sue. He's just doing this because you wouldn't date him. We can prove—"

"I quit, Mel," Abby said.

Short and simple. She repeated the speech she'd given Daniel this morning. "I'm burned out. Everybody saw it coming except me. I was in denial, but I realized the truth when I was on vacation. I'm ready for a change and so is VOCAP."

Daniel then broke the news that he'd hired her replacement—a Ph.D. candidate who was looking for a position where she could really make a difference. According to Daniel, she was qualified, eager and married. Why the last made a difference, Abby didn't know, but she wasn't surprised to learn Daniel had already hired someone else. All in all, they parted amiably, her two-week notice a mere formality.

Rocking back in her chair, Abby pushed aside the box into which she'd been sorting the keepsakes and memorabilia that had accumulated over the years. A plaque from the County Community Action Association, a tea caddy from a family whose son had been killed by gang members, a beaded necklace Heather Butler made in Rainbows.

Melina took a tissue from the box on the desk and dabbed at her eyes. "Are you sure? What are you going to do now?"

"I'm going to finish my degree and start grad school. As soon as I have my master's, I'll probably hang out a shingle with Donna."

She and Donna had had a long talk last night when Abby returned from her trip. "I'll take the kids, you can handle their parents," Donna had told her, not the least surprised by Abby's decision.

"What about the Butlers?" Melina asked.

Abby fingered Heather's tiny beads. Her grandmother wasn't overly religious but she did put stock in the symbols of her faith. She'd always kept a strand of rosary beads hanging beside her bed. Abby never knew what kind of sign Agnes expected them to reveal, but now she could appreciate the soothing quality of the motion. She manipulated one bead and noticed for the first time an image on the opposite side of the small, smooth bead. She turned each bead over until she read the message it spelled out: I Luv You, Heather.

Abby missed them so much. She'd sent three postcards from the San Diego Zoo, but she hadn't seen or talked to any member of the Butler family in more than two weeks. Tom's message on her machine last night welcomed her home, but when she tried his number there was no answer. No one answered at the Hastingses', either. Abby had already made up her mind to drive out to the ranch as soon as she finished cleaning out her desk. She had bridges to mend; she only hoped it wasn't too late.

When the phone rang, she answered formally, "Abby Davis."

Melina rose to leave, but Abby stopped her.

"Really?" she said, grinning. "That's great. I'm happy for you. Truly, I am." She had to stifle a giggle working its way up her throat. Finally, the person on the other end of the line said goodbye, and she could release the pent-up laughter.

"That was Landon," she said, hurrying to explain. "He called to tell me he and Deirdre just got back from Tahoe. They got married."

"What?" Melina sputtered. "I thought he was a confirmed free spirit, and she was some kind of psychotic nag."

Abby lifted her shoulders and let them fall. "Who can predict the course of true love?"

Melina sat forward. "Speaking of which, what about Tom Butler?"

Abby thought a moment. How could she put into words all the feelings churning through her head and heart?

Before she could formulate an answer, the phone rang again. "Abby Davis."

She sat up abruptly, causing the bead necklace to fall to the floor. "Angel? Slow down. What's the matter? You what? I'll be right there." She started to hang up but caught Angel's cry and put the receiver back to her ear. "You moved? When? Okay. I got it. I'll stop at Wal-Mart and be there as soon as possible."

Abby hung up. Her heart was beating double time. "She called me, Mel. Me. Angel started her period and she called me." Suddenly, Abby gulped. "What if I blow it?"

"How can you blow it?"

Abby grimaced. "Do you know what my mother did when I called her at work and told her I'd started? She told everybody in the store—even complete strangers. I was so embarrassed I never went there again."

Melina looked sympathetic. "My mother just told me to go talk to my older sister."

"What do I buy?" Abby asked, grabbing her purse.

Melina waved off the question. "They make a zillion products for younger girls. It's really big business. Don't worry, you'll do fine." She stood up when Abby did and opened the door. "Did you say they moved?"

"Angel said they moved into Miguel and Maria's old house. It makes sense, I guess, but I got the impression Tom had some bad memories associated with it. Who knows? We all have ghosts, right?"

Melina looked at her curiously. "I don't know about that. I think yours are gone, girl. What'd you do? See an exorcist while you were on vacation?"

Abby thought about her friend's question as she drove to the house on Plainsborough Road. For the first time in her life, Abby had enjoyed every moment spent with her parents. She golfed with her father. She hiked to the top of a canyon one morning with her mother and a group of senior hikers. The three of them piled into Grace's urban assault vehicle and drove to San Diego to visit Jarrod and his family.

The two weeks flew by and, despite missing Tom and the girls, Abby left the desert feeling rested and healed. Grace insisted she take Agnes's hopeless chest, and Abby planned to go through it at her own pace, no longer afraid of the memories.

Who could say if Agnes had made a conscious choice to die or if the fear of being ravaged by illness was more than her heart could handle? Either way, while she was alive, she'd given Abby a precious gift: unconditional love. Only after Agnes's death did Abby begin to put restrictions on the love she shared with others.

She'd withheld love from her mother because she was afraid of diminishing the love she'd felt for her grandmother. She'd dived blindly into a relationship with Billy, sure she could turn hero-worship into love. Poor Landon never had a chance because, by then, Abby was so fearful of losing she didn't even ante up when the game started.

But Tom had demanded her complete participation, and, finally, she was ready to play. As the roofline of the little house came into view, Abby's heart beat faster in anticipation. Such an exciting game, but the stakes had never been higher.

TOM WATCHED the Honda approach. His heart felt lighter knowing she was near, but at the same time weighty. Just because he'd made some changes didn't mean Abby would welcome them. From his perch on the top step of the porch, he watched her get out of the car. She moved with such grace, her carriage proud but not haughty. Her black, double-breasted business suit with crisp white blouse looked too formal for her surroundings, but she corrected that by kicking off her high-heel shoes and tossing them into the car.

"Hi, cowboy," she said, her voice light and welcoming. Heedless of her nylons, she hopped from grassy patch to grassy patch until she reached the concrete approach at the bottom of the steps. The image reminded Tom of the first day they met.

"Hi, stranger. Long time no see. You've been missed."

"Have I? That's nice to know." Her green eyes lit up. Lingering rays from the setting sun cast her hair in bronze. Her lips, shimmering with a recent application of lipstick, looked inviting.

"Where's the rest of the greeting party?" She held out a plastic bag like a peace offering. "I brought stuff—female stuff."

He'd been dreading this part. He didn't want Abby to think Angel's plea was a ruse to get her out here. This wasn't the way he'd planned it, but he wasn't one to pass up an opportunity when it fell in his lap.

"Janey dropped by right after Angel called you. Ed took Peter and Maureen up to the city to catch a plane and isn't due back till nine or so."

"Are they still thinking about moving out here?"

He nodded. "Yep. They're putting their house on the market as soon as they can."

"I bet Janey's ecstatic."

"She's happy. Ed was a little nervous—he thought my nose would be out of joint about having to work with Peter. I told him it was about time I had some help around there." He paused, not anxious to break the news that he'd abandoned the building in which she'd invested so much time. "Since they'd need a place to live and the bunkhouse was looking so good thanks to you and your mother, I decided I should be the one to move out. This house was sitting empty…so we moved."

Abby eyed the building with a thoughtful look, then said, "I'm so glad. It needs a family."

Pivoting on one heel, she pointed toward the ancient oak tree a hundred yards to the right. "I had a dream about that tree while I was gone. Isn't that crazy? Of course, it's understandable—there are no real trees in the desert," she told him with mock seriousness. Her features took on a dreamy quality when she went on. "One night, I saw that tree with a rope swing, and I was swinging higher and higher until my toes touched the lower branches. I felt so free and happy."

With a girlish look, she added, "You were pushing me."

Tom's heart missed a beat or two. Was there a message in her dream? Did he dare to hope? The planking beneath his butt seemed harder than it had a few minutes earlier. He scooted forward, his elbows resting on his knees..

"Anyway, you were saying…?" she prompted, pulling him back from his fantasies.

"Janey came by and invited us for pizza. Ed hates pizza—it's been their one ongoing argument for the past fifty-three years. I told her you were coming. I didn't say why you were coming—I didn't want to embarrass Angel, but Heather blurted it out and Janey was so matter-of-fact about it, Angel seemed to shrug it off, too." He frowned. "Janey said they'd stop at the store on the way to the pizza place."

Abby burst out laughing. "Do I feel silly!" She gave the plastic bag a shake. "You should have seen me at Wal-Mart, agonizing over which product was perfect. That's what took me so long."

"You're not offended? Angel was pretty upset when she called you."

Abby tossed the bag on the top step. "A girl's first period can be a big deal, but it doesn't have to be. I'll be around if she wants to talk."

Tom dropped the twig he'd rubbed smooth. "Heather was afraid you might want to move back with your folks or…"

Abby's hoot made Rosie, who seldom left her spot under

the rear porch, bark. Blushing, she covered her lips. "I had a great time and I love my parents, but good grief! They eat wooden bread and drink molasses, and they're on the go all the time. I had to come home to rest, they wore me out."

Tom studied her. This was a new Abby. She seemed at peace in a way he hadn't seen before. "You're healed," he said, recognizing the truth of his words.

"Almost," she said softly. She closed the distance between them, moving to the bottom step. Tom caught the scent he could have identified blindfolded.

Tom made room for her between his knees and she took it. Eye-to-eye, he met her look, afraid to blink. His heart stalled, waiting to see if his dreams were about to come true or if his imagination had conjured up a wraith that would disappear before his eyes.

"I missed you," she said.

He missed her, too. He wanted her more than he could put into words, but he knew he had to be smart this time. There was too much at stake to blow it.

"Abby, I've been thinking—even cowboys do it, from time to time," he said, afraid of appearing too serious since that hadn't worked the last time. "I..." He hesitated then leaned to one side to extract a piece of paper from his rear pocket. "I did some research while you were gone."

He handed her the paper and waited while she unfolded it. He watched her expression turn from curiosity to amazement. "Tom, these are Web sites."

Her shock seemed profound. "Peter gave me a few lessons on the computer and I went on-line. Angel told me I could find anything on the Internet, so I went looking."

"You did this for me?" she said in a small voice.

"I'd do anything for you, Abby."

She turned, holding the crumpled paper to the light spilling from the living-room window. As she read, he told her about his many hits and misses on the information superhighway. "It's not a complete list, of course, but, Abby, it's amazing how much information there is about new fertility treatments, including fixing up damaged fallopian tubes."

He saw her surreptitiously bat away a tear. "The last one on the list is an adoption hot-line," she said in a small voice.

He put his hands on her waist and pulled her closer. The wool was stiff and formal but she wasn't. "I want whatever makes you happy. If you want a baby, then we'll do whatever it takes to make that happen." He grinned at her. "We haven't even tried the old-fashioned way yet. Who knows? We might get lucky."

Her laugh lifted a load from his heart. "Who could be luckier than me? I love you, Tom Butler."

Instinct told him to kiss her, but he had a whole speech planned about agendas and patience. He wanted her to know he could wait as long as she wanted. "I love you, too, and I'd like for us to get married, but I won't push you, Abby. I know your job is important—"

"I got fired today," she said, interrupting him. "Or, I quit. Depends on whose story you believe."

"Oh, babe," he said, pulling her close, offering comfort. "Are you okay?"

He stroked her back, wishing she wouldn't melt against him quite so provocatively when he was trying to set the record straight about his intentions. Marshaling his restraint, he moved her back far enough to make eye contact. "I know how much of yourself you put into VOCAP, but you said you were interested in going back to school. Maybe this will work out for the best."

"Maybe," she said, worrying her bottom lip in the most provocative way. His groin tightened, and he had to stifle a groan.

"Whatever you decide, the girls and I will be here waiting

until you're ready for an instant family." He swallowed against the knot in his throat. "As long as I know you want us."

The softening in her eyes was his first clue, the sweet, joyful smile on her lips the second. "Tom, you already are my family."

Momentarily stunned, he sat there with his mouth open, until she laughed and threw her arms around him. He had no choice but to hold her tight. And kiss her.

ABBY'S HEART never felt fuller. Tom's arms were warmer, stronger than she remembered. His scent enveloped her, and she couldn't imagine ever not wanting to feel him beside her.

There were things to resolve. Her college plans. Her idea of setting up a practice with Donna. And, most important, the girls.

"What will we tell Angel and Heather?" she asked, nuzzling the open V afforded by his worn denim shirt. "We can't let our feelings for each other rush them into something they're not ready for."

He pulled back, giving himself room to rise. With a tender smile, he reached for her hand. "Come. I want to show you something."

A little unnerved by the seriousness of his tone, Abby hesitated just a second then put her hand in his. No limits, no restrictions. She was betting on unconditional love.

At the threshold, he paused, a boyish grin on his face. "This may be rushing things, but..." He bent over and scooped her into his arms.

"Tom. Put me down. You'll ruin your back." Despite her protest, Abby's heart swelled at the romantic gesture. In a way it sealed things more finally than a signature on a marriage license. "I'm not a bride."

"You're my bride, and you will be until the day I die."

Abby blinked back tears, tightening the hold around his neck. "I love you, cowboy."

He opened the door and marched through the portal. Once inside, he kissed her soundly then lowered her feet to the floor. "Wait here," he said, dashing toward the staircase. "If I take you upstairs I'll never let you back down, and the girls will be home any minute."

Suddenly alone and feeling a bit overwhelmed, Abby looked around. Boxes mingled with familiar furnishings. The house was once Lesley's, but Abby couldn't feel any ghosts. Maybe Lesley's spirit sensed Abby had no desire to diminish her daughters' memories of their mother; she only hoped to add her own.

She looked up when she heard Tom's boot steps hurrying down the stairs. In his hand was a piece of paper, which he handed to her like a little boy bringing home a blue ribbon. Abby's first impression was of crayon markings, bright and crude, obviously the work of a young child. She turned it horizontally and studied the drawing.

Tears filled her eyes, blurring the images. "Oh, Tom."

"She made it for you," Tom said, his melodic voice husky with emotion. "It almost made me cry."

Abby blinked rapidly, relishing each image: a square house with a porch, four windows and a big tree in the corner. Standing in front of the house were four figures, two big, two small. She'd labeled each person, printing with obvious care: Daddy, Angel, me, Abby. Abby's name, however, had been crossed out and above it, written in green, was the word *Mom*.

"She was most concerned about getting your hair color right."

Abby cupped his jaw with her free hand. How could one so masculine, a hero right out of a country-western song, be so sensitive? "Are you sure they're ready to let another woman into their lives?" Abby asked, afraid to believe her great good fortune. "It hasn't been a year."

He kissed her sweetly. "Christmas is coming," he said, nibbling a path along her neckline. "They wouldn't have time to feel sad if they were getting ready for a wedding."

Dizzy with desire, she clung to him. "Thanksgiving is sooner."

His warm breath tickled her ear while his teeth playfully nipped. "Too close to Angel's birthday. I already promised her a big slumber party for all her friends. Not my idea of a honeymoon."

She had some honeymoon ideas of her own and didn't necessarily need a wedding to put them into practice.

He pulled back suddenly, leaving her bereft.

"Columbus Day is coming up."

"Columbus Day," she whispered, threading her fingers into his wavy hair, fluffing out the impression of his hat line above his ears. "If it's okay with the girls, you've got a date. Now, kiss me, cowboy."

And, gentleman that he was, Tom obliged his true love's request.

"HAVE WE GIVEN them enough time?" Angel asked tensely, squinting toward the little, white house a quarter mile off the road. She and Heather had put a lot of thought into this plan and she didn't want to blow it.

"Relax, honey," Janey advised. Janey had helped coordinate the tactical aspect of getting the two girls out of the house once Angel got Abby to come there. For an old person, Janey had proven to be downright romantic. "You're too young to get an ulcer. Adults have to work themselves into lifelong commitments. They don't see things so black and white like young people do."

Angel sighed, hating the truth but recognizing it. "But it's so obvious, Janey. Dad and Abby are meant for each other. You know what Dad's been like since she left, and when I called Grace, she told me Abby was positively blue, missing us."

"Yeah," Heather said. "Abby's gotta be my new mom because her mom is my fairy grandmother."

Angel rolled her eyes. She'd given up trying to break her sister of the habit of labeling people. Angel liked Grace, too—a whole lot better than her real mom's mother, although she did feel better after taking Donna's advice and writing Ruby a letter of forgiveness. She could understand how upset Ruby was and how she wanted someone to blame for what happened. But Angel knew from being at Rainbows that sometimes bad things happened for no reason, and you had to go forward with your life. You couldn't let it hang over you forever. Angel knew her mother would want her to be happy and have a full life. She'd want the same for her father.

A memory came to her. She and her mother were sharing a plate of Thai food at an outdoor bazaar, and Angel asked Lesley why she'd divorced their dad. "You know, honey," Lesley told her, "your dad is a great guy. One of the best. But he's an old world kind of guy, and I'm a new world kind of woman. It just wasn't meant to be. But someday he'll meet a woman who's looking for that kind of man and they'll live happily ever after."

"Mom would have wanted Dad to be happy," Angel said, her voice sounding kind of funny.

Janey slowed the car to make the turn. "I know, dear. Let's just hope Abby feels the same way."

Nervous, Angel threaded a hunk of hair between her lips and chomped down, but she hastily spit it out, recalling the promise she'd made to her father. He had enough on his mind without worrying about her nervous habits.

Angel glanced at her sister in the back seat. For a little

punk, she wasn't too bad. She'd been a good sport about drawing the picture, even though she thought it was a bit obvious.

"Oh, look," Janey said.

As the car slowed, Angel heard Heather's seat belt snap open; her sister plopped over the seat for a better view.

"They're kissing," Heather screeched. "Look, Angel, they're kissing."

"Right on," Angel said, trying to keep tears from coming. She wasn't about to do something as childish as cry.

"They look nice," Heather said.

Angel looked again. They did. The two people framed in the doorway of the little house looked perfect.

"We're home, kiddo," Angel said. And for the first time since she arrived in the valley, she meant it.

EPILOGUE

ABBY'S HEAD was spinning. She couldn't decide if it was from the excitement or the delicious realization she was now and forevermore Mrs. Tom Butler.

"I'd say this shindig turned out pretty darned fine, Mrs. Butler," her husband of two hours said as they danced beneath the pink and white streamers suspended from the rafters of the hayloft. An ocean of organdy, miles of pink ribbon and a small tropical island of potted palms had transformed the Standing Arrow H barn into Cinderella's castle.

"Perfect. Absolutely perfect," Abby said, savoring the sight of her father waltzing with Angel. No father could have looked more distinguished; no grandfather could have been prouder to welcome two new granddaughters to the clan. "If you'd told me back in September that I'd be dancing in a barn on February fourteenth, I'd have said you were crazy."

Tom grinned. "Who could have reckoned on the Dynamic Duo?"

That was the code name she and Tom bestowed on Grace and Heather. From the minute Abby and Tom announced their intention to marry, those two joined forces to collaborate on all wedding plans—right down to setting the date. "It has to be Valentine's Day, Daddy. It has to be," Heather announced. Until that moment Abby hadn't realized how intractable the six-year-old could be—a trait shared with her grandmother-to-be.

"Of course it has to be Valentine's Day," Grace said when

they called her that evening. "You don't for one minute believe I could plan your wedding by, say, Christmas or Thanksgiving, do you?" Abby and Tom both were too embarrassed to suggest their original plan.

"I really can't get over this," Abby said, her heart so full of joy she felt certain she'd either weep or have a heart attack before the party was over. "I swear they made a pact with the devil to get this finished on time."

Tom brushed his nose against her cheek. "Never doubt the power of friendship," he said. "Or Janey Hastings. Since the doctors gave her an all-clear, she's back to being a force to be reckoned with." Abby looked across the dance floor to the buffet where Janey and Ed were heaping great mounds of barbecued beef and Portuguese beans on guests' plates.

She sensed his happiness. The madhouse anxiety of the past few weeks would have killed a lesser man. In addition to wedding plans, he had to deal with Angel's volleyball schedule and hectic social agenda, Abby's college classes and volunteer work at the Battered Women's Shelter, as well as the sale of her house and subsequent move. But the outcome was worth it, especially seeing the triumph on the faces of Grace and Heather.

"You know," Abby said, studying the two who seemed to have forged an unbreakable bond, "I wouldn't be surprised if they went into business."

Tom groaned. "That's all we need—a six-year-old wedding consultant."

As if to banish the thought, Tom whirled Abby in a circle, making the billowy skirt of her pale pink gown twirl like a princess's. Grace, Angel and Heather had purchased the gown on a shopping trip to the Bay area. Abby had been horrified by their audacity. "Pink? I'll look like an upside-down ice-cream cone." All three found that image hilarious.

"It's called champagne-pink. It's the hot new color, Abby.

You'll be rave," said Angel, who was Abby's maid of honor. "Besides, it'll look really neat with our bridesmaid dresses."

Her mother delivered the most convincing argument. "It was on sale, dear. We saved your father a thousand dollars." If that didn't win her over, the dress's beaded pearl bodice and soft organdy skirt did.

"Have I told you that you are the most beautiful bride in the world?" Tom whispered. His voice still had the power to make her toes curl, and she couldn't wait to start their honeymoon. Since they both felt strongly about maintaining a certain decorum in their relationship in front of the girls, she'd never spent the night at the house, and he'd only stayed with her a half-dozen times when the girls were at slumber parties or with Janey.

"Are you going to tell me now?" Tom asked, kissing her long and suggestively.

Abby blushed. How this matter of a wedding gift had become such a hot topic, she wasn't sure. Probably her mother's doing. But she did know positively, her gift to him wouldn't be revealed until they were alone. "Not yet."

"Not even a hint?"

Abby pictured the elegantly wrapped box tucked in her suitcase. More symbolic than functional since she'd already used up three just like it, her gift was a home pregnancy testing kit.

"Let's just say it's something you'd never guess in a million years," she said, smiling.

When some odd changes in her body began showing up in late January, Abby attributed them to stress, but her mother had suggested otherwise. "You're pregnant," Grace said, hugging her to the point of asphyxiation. Even three litmus tests couldn't convince Abby, but her doctor confirmed it last week.

Although her first impulse was to call Tom from the doctor's office, she decided to wait for a private moment. There would be time when they returned from their honeymoon to share the news with the rest of the world.

Abby called it a miracle, but her mother was more pragmatic. "You're healed, Abby. From the inside out." That, Abby didn't doubt. Angel and Heather had helped remove any fear Abby had about being a mother. This baby wasn't a replacement for the one she lost so many years before. She'd been given a second chance but it came about through the love of one man, and their child was a gift they would treasure together.

"Are you ready, my fairy princess?" Tom asked, breaking into her reverie.

Abby looked into his twinkling blue eyes and smiled. "I'm ready, my cowboy prince. Don't we need to tell the girls goodbye?"

"Oh, don't worry. They're waiting for us." He took her elbow to guide her toward the double doors, which had been closed to keep out the chilly evening. The sun, which had shone so brightly and warmly during their outdoor wedding ceremony, was long gone.

As if by magic, the doors opened outward and Abby spied her carriage—Tom's brand-new pickup truck, the one she'd insisted they purchase from the proceeds of the sale of her house. Today, the top-of-the-line dually was adorned with a hundred pink and white bows. If trucks could look embarrassed, this one positively blushed.

Her father opened the passenger-side door and helped her up to the running board, where she stood and waved while Tom went around to the driver's side. Being certain to make eye contact with those who mattered most, she smiled and mouthed, "I love you."

Melina, standing beside a handsome young man in a western suit, waved the bridal bouquet she'd triumphantly snagged.

Val hoisted Heather up high enough to wave exuberantly. Miguel and Maria stood beside Abby's brothers, holding little Rey. Beside them, Grace and Angel, distributing cups of birdseed, chorused back, "We love you, too." Donna blew her a kiss then wiped the tears from her eyes.

"You done good, sweetheart," her father whispered gruffly, his eyes moist. "Your grandma would have been proud of you."

Abby had to dab at her own tears as the truck pulled away, but she couldn't stay sad for long on the happiest day of her life. She turned in the seat, pushing her voluminous wedding gown out of the way. "So, cowboy, where are you taking me?"

He pulled her into the crook of his arm. "To the sun and stars…just you and me and a couple hundred curious cows. Think you're up for it?"

"Just try and stop me." Abby snuggled close, content beyond imagination yet alive with anticipation.

As they turned on the main road, Tom had to wait for a tractor to pass. He flashed a glance toward the ranch. "The kids are going home with your folks, right?"

Abby smiled and said softly, "Two of them are. We're keeping the new one with us."

"The new one…?" Tom's confusion turned to disbelief. "A baby? Really?"

When she nodded, his eyes filled with tears and he pulled her into a tight embrace. "Oh, Abby, that's the best wedding present in the world. I can't believe it. How…?"

She chuckled softly and whispered, "The old-fashioned way—love."

* * * * *

In Tina Leonard's new miniseries, CALLAHAN COWBOYS, six bachelor brothers compete for ownership of the family ranch. The winning cowboy must get married—and have as many babies as possible!

Here's an excerpt from THE COWBOY'S BONUS BABY, available July 2011, only from Harlequin® American Romance®!

Aberdeen stared at the sleeping cowboy's handsome face. *Trouble with a capital* T. "Did he tell you his name? Maybe he's got family around here who could come get him."

"No," Johnny said. "He babbles a lot about horses. Talks a great deal about spirit horses and other nonsense. Native American lore. Throws in an occasional Irish tale. Told a pretty funny joke, too. The man has a sense of humor for being out of his mind."

"Great." Aberdeen had a funny feeling about the cowboy who had come to Johnny's Bar and Grill. "I'm going to see who he is," she said, reaching into his front pocket for his wallet.

A hand shot out, grabbing her wrist. Aberdeen gasped and tried to draw away, but the cowboy held on, staring up at her with those navy eyes. She couldn't look away.

"Stealing's wrong," he said.

She slapped his hand and he released her. "I know that, you ape. What's your name?"

He crossed his arms and gave her a roguish grin. "What's *your* name?"

"I already told you my name is Aberdeen." He'd said it not five minutes ago, so possibly he did have a concussion. "Cowboy, I'm going to look at your license, and if you grab me again like you did a second ago, you'll wish you hadn't.

HSCEXPHAR0611

So either you give me your wallet, or I take it. Those are your choices."

He stared at her, unmoving.

She reached into his pocket and pulled out his wallet, keeping her gaze on him, trying to ignore the expanse of wide chest and other parts of him she definitely shouldn't notice. Flipping the wallet open, she took out his driver's license. "Creed Callahan. New Mexico."

He grabbed her, pulling her to him for a fast kiss. His lips molded to hers, and Aberdeen felt a spark—more than a spark, *real* heat—and then he released her.

She stared at him. He shrugged. "I figured you'd get around to slapping me eventually. Might as well pay hell is what I always say."

Find out what happens next
in THE COWBOY'S BONUS BABY,
available July 2011,
only from Harlequin® American Romance®!

And be sure to watch for more CALLAHAN COWBOYS, *including a bonus Christmas novella, throughout 2011.*

Copyright © 2011 by Tina Leonard

HSCEXPHAR0611

REQUEST YOUR FREE BOOKS!

2 FREE NOVELS PLUS 2 FREE GIFTS!

Harlequin® SuperRomance®

Exciting, emotional, unexpected!

YES! Please send me 2 FREE Harlequin® Superromance® novels and my 2 FREE gifts (gifts are worth about $10). After receiving them, if I don't wish to receive any more books, I can return the shipping statement marked "cancel." If I don't cancel, I will receive 6 brand-new novels every month and be billed just $4.69 per book in the U.S. or $5.24 per book in Canada. That's a saving of at least 15% off the cover price! It's quite a bargain! Shipping and handling is just 50¢ per book in the U.S. and 75¢ per book in Canada.* I understand that accepting the 2 free books and gifts places me under no obligation to buy anything. I can always return a shipment and cancel at any time. Even if I never buy another book, the two free books and gifts are mine to keep forever.

135/336 HDN FC6T

Name (PLEASE PRINT)

Address Apt. #

City State/Prov. Zip/Postal Code

Signature (if under 18, a parent or guardian must sign)

Mail to the **Reader Service:**

IN U.S.A.: P.O. Box 1867, Buffalo, NY 14240-1867
IN CANADA: P.O. Box 609, Fort Erie, Ontario L2A 5X3

Not valid for current subscribers to Harlequin Superromance books.

Are you a current subscriber to Harlequin Superromance books and want to receive the larger-print edition?
Call 1-800-873-8635 or visit www.ReaderService.com.

* Terms and prices subject to change without notice. Prices do not include applicable taxes. Sales tax applicable in N.Y. Canadian residents will be charged applicable taxes. Offer not valid in Quebec. This offer is limited to one order per household. All orders subject to credit approval. Credit or debit balances in a customer's account(s) may be offset by any other outstanding balance owed by or to the customer. Please allow 4 to 6 weeks for delivery. Offer available while quantities last.

Your Privacy—The Reader Service is committed to protecting your privacy. Our Privacy Policy is available online at www.ReaderService.com or upon request from the Reader Service.

We make a portion of our mailing list available to reputable third parties that offer products we believe may interest you. If you prefer that we not exchange your name with third parties, or if you wish to clarify or modify your communication preferences, please visit us at www.ReaderService.com/consumerschoice or write to us at Reader Service Preference Service, P.O. Box 9062, Buffalo, NY 14269. Include your complete name and address.

HSR11

SPECIAL EDITION

Life, Love and Family

THE TEXANS ARE COMING!

Reader-favorite miniseries Montana Mavericks is back in Special Edition with new loves, adventures and more.

July 2011 features *USA TODAY* bestselling author

CHRISTINE RIMMER

with

RESISTING MR. TALL, DARK & TEXAN.

A Texas oil mogul arrives in Thunder Canyon on business and soon falls for his personal assistant. Only one problem–she's just resigned to open a bakery! Can he convince her to stay on–as his bride?

Find out in July!

Look for a new
Montana Mavericks: The Texans Are Coming **title**
in each of these months

August | September | October
November | December

Available wherever books are sold.

www.Harlequin.com

SEMM0711

Love Inspired®

After her fiancé calls off their wedding, Brooke Clayton has nowhere to go but home. Turns out the wealthy businessman next door, handsome single father Gabe Wesson, needs a nanny for his toddler—and Brooke needs a job. But Gabe sees Brooke as a reminder of the young wife he lost. Given their pasts, do they dare hope to fit together as a family…forever?

The Nanny's Homecoming
by Linda Goodnight

ROCKY MOUNTAIN HEIRS

Available July wherever books are sold.

www.LoveInspiredBooks.com

LI87680

ROMANTIC
SUSPENSE

Secrets and scandal ignite in a danger-filled, passion-fuelled new miniseries.

When scandal erupts, threatening California Senator Hank Kelley's career and his life, there's only one place he can turn—the family ranch in Maple Cove, Montana. But he'll need the help of his estranged sons and their friends to pull the family together despite attempts on his life and pressure from a sinister secret society, and to prevent an unthinkable tragedy that would shake the country to its core.

Collect all 6 heart-racing tales starting July 2011 with

Private Justice

by *USA TODAY* bestselling author

MARIE FERRARELLA

Special Ops Bodyguard by **BETH CORNELISON** (August 2011)
Cowboy Under Siege by **GAIL BARRETT** (September 2011)
Rancher Under Cover by **CARLA CASSIDY** (October 2011)
Missing Mother-To-Be by **ELLE KENNEDY** (November 2011)
Captain's Call of Duty by **CINDY DEES** (December 2011)

www.Harlequin.com

HRS27734

THE NOTORIOUS WOLFES

A powerful dynasty, where secrets and scandal never sleep!

Eight siblings, blessed with wealth, but denied the one thing they wanted—a father's love. Haunted by their past and driven to succeed, the Wolfes scattered to the far corners of the globe. It's said that even the blackest of souls can be healed by the purest of love....

But can the dynasty rise again?

Beginning July 2011

A NIGHT OF SCANDAL—*Sarah Morgan*
THE DISGRACED PLAYBOY—*Caitlin Crews*
THE STOLEN BRIDE—*Abby Green*
THE FEARLESS MAVERICK—*Robyn Grady*
THE MAN WITH THE MONEY—*Lynn Raye Harris*
THE TROPHY WIFE—*Janette Kenny*
THE GIRL THAT LOVE FORGOT—*Jennie Lucas*
THE LONE WOLFE—*Kate Hewitt*

8 volumes to collect and treasure!

www.Harlequin.com

HP13000

Looking for a great Western read?

We have just the thing!

A Cowboy for Every Mood

Visit

www.HarlequinInsideRomance.com

for a sneak peek and exciting exclusives on your favorite cowboy heroes.

Pick up next month's cowboy books by some of your favorite authors:

Vicki Lewis Thompson
Carla Cassidy
B.J. Daniels
Rachel Lee
Christine Rimmer
Donna Alward
Cheryl St.John

And many more...

Available wherever books are sold.

ACFEM0611R